The Royal Academy of Magical Baking

THE ROYAL ACADEMY OF MAGICAL BAKING

BOOK ONE

ANNE CREWS

Podium

Podium

The Royal Academy of Magical Baking

CHAPTER ONE

Cakes, Magic, and You

Lyra Treble's parents had always told her to "keep on singing." They firmly believed that every problem could be solved and every good moment improved by breaking out into song. This meant the Treble household was never completely silent, even at night. *"Music is powerful"* was their family motto, and they lived by it.

They were bards, after all.

And it was good advice, generally. "Keep on singing" had helped Lyra quite a bit over the years. When her mind was muddled or her emotions tangled, even humming a tune could clear the air and lift her spirits.

But for the first time in her life, Lyra was beginning to wonder if her parents' advice applied to *all* occasions. Maybe there were some moments in life when a little music-making might actually hurt more than it helped.

For example, the final entrance exam for the Royal Academy of Magical Baking.

Most of the day hadn't been so bad. Just being at the academy was a thrill. The classroom they were using for this important event was airy and spacious, with a vaulted ceiling and big windows that let in lots of natural light. The mahogany paneling gleamed warmly in the morning sun. Each of the twelve candidates had their own mini kitchen station, fully equipped with everything they would need to prepare their cake. Families and spectators had to wait outside. For hours, Lyra and the other eleven hopefuls had been lost in their own private baking worlds, the room filled with only the bustle of creation-in-progress.

But now the baking part was over. All that remained was the judging. That meant waiting while the academy's three top chefs moved slowly from station to station, examining each cake in minute detail and making notes.

It also, apparently, meant absolute silence.

Lyra perched on the edge of her stool, resisting the urge to drum her toes against the rungs. The room was starting to feel far too big with far too few people in it. Minute after agonizing minute crawled by, but still, no one spoke. Even the chefs did not confer as they looked, smelled, and tasted each candidate's offering. The only sound was the scratching of their quill pens on their parchment notebooks.

Definitely not a time to keep on singing.

Lyra clamped her mouth tightly shut. She had a bad habit of humming without realizing it, especially when stressed or anxious. To distract herself, and hopefully keep any renegade notes firmly inside her soul, she studied her fellow candidates. The room was too large for her to see the far end, where the judges had started, but she had a good view of the half-dozen stations closest to her.

Directly across from her was a girl so covered in flour that Lyra wondered if any had gotten into the actual cake. If Lyra was remembering correctly, the girl had introduced herself as Ginger Crumble. Ginger looked even more anxious than Lyra. She was gripping the edge of her stool and craning her neck to watch the judges' slow progress, oblivious to the fact that she resembled nothing more than a somewhat dusty ghost.

Beyond Ginger, at the end of the room, was a girl named Caramelle Meringue. Lyra wasn't likely to forget that name quickly. Not that Caramelle would ever give her the chance, of course.

The sight of the other girl sitting primly on her stool, hands folded serenely, her workstation as neat and perfect as the coils of auburn hair pinned atop her head, took Lyra back to earlier that morning . . .

Lyra had not slept at all the night before. She had made a noble attempt, mostly to appease her concerned mother, but gave up after a few hours and spent the rest of the night poring over her recipe, humming quietly. At an hour before dawn, she had dressed, slipped out the door of their small brownstone, and practically sprinted the few blocks to the Royal Academy of Magical Baking.

She had been so sure she would be the first to arrive that she even chided herself the whole way that her eagerness was overkill. But when Lyra skidded to a stop outside the main gates, this girl had already been sitting at the extreme end of one of the benches, hands folded, auburn curls carefully arranged.

"Flavor, Texture, or Presentation?" the auburn-haired girl had asked, before Lyra could even catch her breath.

Lyra had collapsed onto the other end of the bench. "What?"

"Flavor, Texture, or Presentation?" the other girl repeated slowly, pronouncing each word with elegant precision. "The three tracks for the academy. Which are you going for?"

"I . . . um . . ." Lyra took a deep breath, trying to calm her racing heart. "I thought we didn't have to choose until the end of the first year. Right?"

"Texture is my specialty," the other girl said. "The Meringue family has always gone for Texture. I'm Caramelle Meringue." She extended one hand formally for a brief shake. "My tutor, Master Chiffon, said I'm already more consistent than Praline Puff was at my age."

Lyra looked at her blankly.

Caramelle's eyebrows rose slightly. "Praline Puff? Professor Puff?"

"Oh, *Professor* Puff!" Lyra's head was swimming with details she had been trying to absorb about the Royal Academy mixed in with all the recipes and spells she'd been cramming for the past few months. "She's the headmistress for, um—"

"Texture," Caramelle said coolly. "And my tutor would know. He taught Professor Puff when she was a student here."

"Right. Your tutor . . . What was his name again?"

The eyebrows rose higher. "Master Chiffon? Former headmaster of Texture? Current royal chef for Texture in the palace kitchens?"

Lyra tried to appear enthusiastic. The name was only ringing the vaguest of bells, lost amidst the deluge of extracts and enchantments swirling in her memory. But she didn't want to appear rude or ignorant. "Of course," Lyra said with what she hoped was appropriate awe. "The royal chef for Texture. I'm amazed he has time to tutor anyone with such an important job."

"He doesn't, really, but he insisted. Old friend of the Meringue family." Caramelle tossed her head. The auburn coils did not budge. "He said I show such great promise, it was an honor to assist my rise."

"That's . . . great," Lyra said when a long pause indicated Caramelle was waiting for a response.

Caramelle nodded graciously. "I told him the honor was entirely mine. It is *so* important to find the right tutor. That's what can really set you apart." She swept an appraising glance over Lyra, studying her in the flickering light provided by the gas streetlamps framing the academy's gates. "Who was your tutor?"

"Oh. Um—"

The arrival of a young man on a bicycle saved Lyra from admitting her tutor had been a tattered copy of *Cakes, Magic, and You* that her dad had found in a secondhand bookshop.

"Top of the morning!" the young man said as he swung off his bicycle and onto the bench between the two girls in one smooth motion. "Or maybe it's too early for that. What comes before the top of the morning? What's higher than the top?"

"The crown?" Lyra suggested.

A grin lit up the young man's whole face. Standing, he bowed formally to both the girls. "Crown of the morning to you, fair baking hopefuls. Boysen at your service, of the Berry household."

"Ah, you're one of the Berry brothers." Caramelle's mouth smiled, but her eyes did not. "Going in for Flavor, I suppose?"

"Couldn't really do otherwise and hope to show my face at home." Boysen flopped back down onto the bench between the girls. "You're the Meringue kid, right? Carrot-Bell?"

"Caramelle."

Caramelle's smile had gone rigid, but Boysen didn't seem to notice.

"That's it. I knew it was Cara-something. Nice to meet you, Caramelle of Meringue." Boysen turned to Lyra. "And what's your story? What silly name did your parents foist upon you in the hopes of inspiring you towards culinary greatness?"

"I'm . . ." Lyra swallowed. "My name is Lyra. Lyra Treble."

"Treble?" Caramelle's eyes narrowed in undisguised suspicion. "I don't recognize that name. Is it some experimental new pastry?"

"Not exactly." Lyra swallowed again. Her mouth felt dry, like it wasn't used to this much talking without breaking into song. "It's a musical term. You know, treble clef, bass clef."

Caramelle stared at her. "Your family . . . aren't . . . bakers?"

"No," Lyra confessed. "They're bards."

"All of them?" Even Caramelle's perfect auburn coils seemed to vibrate in her astonishment, like they might spontaneously combust at any moment. "Not a single baker in your whole family tree?"

"Afraid not."

"Nothing wrong with that," Boysen said, taking advantage of Caramelle's shocked silence to reinsert himself into the conversation. "Just because magical professions tend to run along family lines doesn't mean they always have to. There was a girl in my brother Razz's class from a family of carpenters. No one could touch her in Presentation."

Caramelle recovered enough to shoot Boysen a venomous glare. Then she turned back to Lyra. "So, are you going in for Presentation, then? Think your performance skills will transfer?"

"I-I'm not sure." Lyra had a sudden urge to hide under the bench. Instead, she tried to fold her hands as primly as Caramelle's and forced her spine to stand a teensy bit straighter. "I do like to perform, but I like baking more. All of baking—Flavor, Texture, Presentation, everything. I love it all. And I want to get better. So I decided to enter the Royal Academy of Magical Baking trials, and now I'm here."

"Lyra Treble . . ." Boysen's eyes lit up even brighter. "Hey, I know you. You're part of the Any Weather Bards! Salts, you guys are grand. It's your whole family, right?"

"Yes. My parents and my brothers and me." Lyra's face flushed in a bewildering blend of embarrassment and delight. "You've been to a show?"

"Dozens," Boysen replied. "Used to go every week, but then prep for the academy got too intense."

Lyra glanced at Caramelle, but she was gazing at the gates, as if willing them to open and let her escape this imposter.

"Did you have a tutor?" Lyra asked, deciding to focus on Boysen.

Boysen groaned. "Try five. Each of my brothers took it upon himself to ensure I was fully prepped for these trials."

Lyra couldn't help but grin. The air around Boysen radiated warmth, like a batch of cookies fresh from the oven. She could feel her exhausted nerves slowly starting to settle. "You have five brothers?"

"Three older, two younger. All absolutely determined to help me 'reach my potential.' Even the two youngest, who barely know a sweet spell from a savory, turned into little taskmaster terrors."

"And your parents let them?"

Boysen gave a good-natured shrug. "The family that gets stressed together, stays together. Plus, we have a good record so far."

"Good?" Caramelle echoed, suddenly returning her attention to her two benchmates. "Perfect, rather." She leaned forward, speaking to Lyra around Boysen. "Every single Berry brother so far has gotten into the Royal Academy. Both parents too."

"That's where they met," Boysen explained to Lyra. "Dad didn't make it past the first year, but Mom got all the way through to graduation."

"They wrote a cookbook together," Caramelle said, still directing her words to Lyra. "*The Berry Basics*. It's part of Professor Honeycomb's Flavor curriculum. Didn't you know? Master Chiffon had me read it two years ago."

"Wow." Lyra's frayed nerves flared up again, buzzing in agitation. She looked from one to the other of her two companions. "You both have a lot of . . . preparation."

"A lot to live up to, you mean." Boysen was still grinning, but a small sigh escaped him as he leaned back against the stone wall. "I honestly don't know what I'll do if things go south today."

"You've got a fifty-fifty chance," Lyra said encouragingly, employing the same mantra she'd been using to bolster herself during the past few weeks. "You've made it all the way to the final twelve, and they pick six of us to get in. Those are pretty good odds."

"But it's not just about today." Caramelle's voice dripped with false sweetness, like an overdose of some sugar substitute. "They pick six to start, of course, but only three will be left by the end of the first year. Three terms, with an exam at the end of each, remember? And the student with the lowest result gets dropped."

"Asked to leave," Boysen corrected.

Caramelle ignored him, giving Lyra a fake-sugar smile. "Of course, they also give an award each of the three terms to the student with the top result. The—"

"Stellar Enchantment Pin," Lyra rushed to say, relieved to find something she did know. "To wear on your chef's hat."

Caramelle smoothed her hair, as if already imagining a pin-laden hat atop the sleek curls. "Master Chiffon told me that today is very important. They choose six, but they're also already getting a feel for the top three. He could usually predict who would be left at the end of the year based on the results of this exam. He was rarely wrong."

"But he *was* wrong sometimes," Boysen countered. Then he turned to Lyra with a grin. "My dad says that's the great thing about baking. Even after years, you can still be surprised. Always."

That was when Ginger, the soon-to-be flour ghost, arrived and was followed shortly by a boy who honestly looked like he might lose his breakfast at any moment, along with everything else he'd ever eaten. Boysen and Lyra moved as one to comfort him. By the time they had learned his name was Mac, short for Macaron, and gotten him at least relatively stable, the rest of the candidates had trickled in. The gates opened just a few minutes after . . .

Back in the silent tension of the present, a movement in the corner of Lyra's eye broke her reverie. She blinked, realizing she'd been staring unfocusedly in Caramelle's direction for a while. If Caramelle had noticed, she gave no sign. She simply kept sitting on her stool, motionless and utterly poised, waiting for the judges to come and examine her truly gorgeous culinary creation.

She picked that workstation on purpose, Lyra realized. *She knew they'd come to it last. Guess she wants to make sure they end on a high point.*

The movement in the corner of her eye continued. Lyra turned to the workstation behind hers and then had to stifle a laugh. Boysen was trying to get her attention. He was waving one of his towels discreetly below the level of the counter so that only a bit of white flashed occasionally in view of the rest of the room. As soon as he caught Lyra's eye, he grinned. He then proceeded to wrap the towel around his own neck and pretend to strangle himself.

Lyra was so fully occupied trying not to laugh that she didn't notice the three figures approaching her workstation. A gentle cough from behind made her turn around.

She froze.

There, standing by the end of her counter, were the three most famous magical bakers in the country. She had plenty of time during her long wait to remember their names and positions.

Professor Praline Puff, headmistress of Texture.

Professor Lavender Honeycomb, headmistress of Flavor.

Professor Basil Genoise, headmaster of Presentation.

They each gave her a kind smile and cordial bow, which she numbly returned. Then they all bent over her recipe scroll to learn what to expect when they sampled her cake.

Lyra's judging had begun.

CHAPTER TWO

JUDGMENT DAY

The challenge set for this final entrance exam was surprisingly simple. Lyra reread the instructions at the top of the scroll, upside down, as the judges examined the recipes and spells she had written underneath:

Bake your favorite layer cake with exactly THREE layers (no more and no fewer than three). The layers must be stacked. You can include more than one flavor of cake, filling, and frosting, but it is not required. Choose ONE spell each for Flavor, Texture, and Presentation. Include these spells and your recipe below.

That was it. Her favorite three-layer cake, with flavor and decoration left entirely up to her preference. Only one spell each for the three judging categories. Lyra wasn't complaining, but still . . . For the Royal Academy of Magical Baking, and after a year of trials that had progressed from difficult to fiendishly complex, the task felt shockingly basic.

But as the judges pored over her scroll, Lyra began to wonder if she had missed something. Was there some secret baking code hidden in those seemingly meager instructions? Had her eleven fellow bakers all picked up on this code, thanks to their tutors and their years of immersion in the magical baking world?

She seemed to be the only final candidate from a non-baking family. The judges didn't know that, of course. They didn't ask for the students' names or identify them in any way. The Royal Academy was brutally intense, but fair. They wanted everyone to have an equal chance. It was ability that mattered, not background or connections.

But I bet the judges still recognize a lot of these students, Lyra thought in a sudden panic. *If they're related to alumni or just move in the right circles . . .*

Lyra glanced back at Caramelle. The auburn-haired girl wasn't paying any attention to Lyra's judging. She was staring out the window with an air of determined unconcern.

Then Lyra's gaze flicked over to Boysen, sitting at the workstation behind her. He was leaning forward over the counter, watching the judges almost as intently as Lyra had been. Catching her eye, he grinned and silently mouthed a single word.

Breathe.

She took a deep, shaky breath and made her best attempt at a smile. Then she turned back around, giving her full attention to the three professors, whose taste buds were about to decide her fate.

Lyra watched anxiously as the judges finished reading through her scroll of recipes and spells. She watched anxiously as they nodded thoughtfully at the paper, then at each other. And she watched anxiously as each professor took turns examining the cake itself, turning it this way and that and sniffing delicately.

Then Professor Puff cut three slices of cake, all exactly the same size, and deposited them on three plates. Moving almost in unison, the professors lifted the plates to their noses and inhaled deeply. They poked at the cake with a fork, scraping to analyze the crumb. Finally, they each cut a small bite and placed it in their mouths, closing their eyes and chewing with reverent dignity.

As one, they opened their eyes. They looked at the cake. They looked at the scroll.

Then they looked up at Lyra. And, for the first time since entering the room, one of them *spoke.*

"You chose a deepening charm for your Flavor spell?" Professor Honeycomb asked, her voice golden and layered.

"Y-yes," Lyra stammered. "Since it's a vanilla cake, I thought that charm would help bring out the dark richness of the vanilla without being too sweet."

Professor Honeycomb nodded. Professor Puff spoke next, each word smooth and even.

"For Texture, you used Master Pavlova's Spell of Fluffening?"

"Yes." Lyra didn't dare say she had chosen that spell mostly because the name made her giggle. "I—that's how I like my cakes. Light and fluffy."

Professor Puff's mouth turned up in what might have been the ghost of a smile. "Me too."

Then she bowed slightly, giving the floor to Professor Genoise.

"When only allowed one spell for Presentation, most students aim for the complex or virtuosic." His voice was so soft that Lyra had to lean in to hear, but it was also thrilling, like a strain of ethereal music. "You have chosen Madame Temper's Chant of Precision. A cleanliness spell, focusing on the neat and orderly."

The professor raised his eyebrows, and Lyra realized he was waiting for her explanation.

Again, she dared not give the full truth. She couldn't exactly tell the academy judges that most Presentation spells were way too complicated for her meager baking-magic skills. Lyra would be capable of those spells one day, she was sure. She just needed training and time.

And the only way for her to get both those things was to make it into the academy.

Lyra took another deep breath.

"I'm a messy baker," she said. "Neatness doesn't come naturally. So I thought, for a cake as important as this, I wanted it to be neat more than anything."

All of that was absolutely true. What's more, all three professors nodded in apparent agreement.

"It is important to recognize one's own weaknesses," Professor Genoise said kindly, "as well as one's strengths. It allows one to prioritize appropriately for every different occasion."

Lyra dropped a quick half curtsy. "Thank you."

She expected the judges to move on, but they still stood there, looking at her thoughtfully.

"You are sure you used only those three spells?" Professor Honeycomb asked. "Nothing extra?"

"Just those three," Lyra replied. "One for each category, right?" Then panic struck, and she gasped. "Oh, sharps. Were we supposed to do more? Was it three spells for each category? I thought—"

"No, you were correct," Professor Puff assured her. "The limit was three spells total. One each for Flavor, Texture, and Presentation. It is just . . ." She looked at Professor Genoise.

"It is surprising," he said, continuing the thought, "when working with spells so basic as these you have selected, to achieve this level of . . ." He looked at Professor Honeycomb.

"Enjoyment," she supplied. "A truly delightful eating experience. The most 'fun' bite of cake I've had in years."

Lyra could have sworn there was a choir singing somewhere nearby. Several, in fact.

"Thank you," she said again. Her voice came out in a whisper, but the judges heard anyway.

"Thank *you*," Professor Puff said with a smile.

The other two professors echoed their thanks, and then they moved over to judge Ginger Crumble's cake.

Lyra swiveled weakly on her stool, clinging to the counter to keep from falling off. Boysen was beaming, bouncing on his stool with barely contained glee. He gave her two subtle thumbs-ups, mouthing the word *fun*.

She nodded, too dazed to respond. Then she turned back around to conduct her own examination of her cake.

They had asked for her favorite, so she had given it to them. A vanilla cake with vanilla cream cheese frosting and a sprinkling of chocolate chips in between the layers. She sniffed, poked, and got a tiny taste. Sure enough, it was light and fluffy and delicious, just like the other dozen versions of this cake she had made in preparation for this day.

It certainly tasted "fun" to her. But it would, of course. This was her favorite cake. She wasn't sure why the professors had been so excited.

As Professor Genoise had pointed out, Lyra's decoration was simple. She had piped a ribbon of dark red frosting around the top and bottom and then dotted the ribbon with pale pink rosettes. A larger clump of rosettes, dark red and pink, graced the center of the cake. Thanks to Madame Temper's Chant of Precision, the frosting was smooth and the piping as neat as a pin. But again, she didn't see much cause for the judges' glowing praise, especially once she started looking around at some of the other students' offerings.

Lyra had been so consumed with her own creation and her own fears that she hadn't been paying much attention to what the other students were producing. Even during the long wait for the judges to reach her counter, she had been mostly zoned out in anticipation.

And a good thing too. If she had really seen the cakes produced by her fellow candidates, she might have left the classroom in tears before the judging even began.

Lyra had thought herself pretty daring for using two colors in her decoration. One glance at Ginger Crumble's creation, though, revealed that Lyra had a lot to learn about "daring." Ginger had somehow shaped and frosted her cake to make it resemble a honeycomb. It was a perfect dome, like a beehive, and covered in a network of perfect interlocking hexagons. Lyra had no idea how the girl had found time for so much detail or what level of spell would produce that precision. It did, perhaps, explain why both Ginger and her workspace were still covered in flour.

The judges seemed just as appreciative as Lyra. Now that they were closer, Lyra could see that the judges were having some form of exchange with each student, though hers had been the only interaction that included words. Professor Puff nodded at Ginger, and Professor Honeycomb shook the girl's hand warmly. Professor Genoise was the best: he actually took off his chef's hat, laden with pins, and gave Ginger a small bow.

Flour-strewn ghost that she was, Ginger had put her Presentation potential beyond doubt.

The judges then crossed the aisle to Boysen's workstation. Lyra had just enough time to give him an encouraging smile before the three professors demanded his full attention. While they began their examination, Lyra got her first good look at Boysen's cake.

She bit back a gasp.

Boysen had said he was a Flavor guy. Lyra was sure this was true, but he clearly had a flair for Presentation also. His cake was a perfect sphere. His Presentation spell must have gone into keeping it balanced, which meant the decoration was all manual. And it was *exquisite*. The frosting was a warm cerulean, like the sky at midday. Swirls of whipped cream dotted the smooth blue surface, looking so real that Lyra could have sworn they were actually clouds moving in some gentle breeze. Billows of more whipped cream piled around the base of the cake, like it was nestled in a bank of those clouds.

Professor Genoise took one look at the cake and clapped Boysen on the shoulder immediately. Professor Puff gave him an approving nod after her knife cut cleanly through the sphere. And the first bite was barely in Professor Honeycomb's mouth before she was scurrying around the counter to give Boysen a hug.

Boysen's face flushed almost to the bright red of his berry namesake, but he was still grinning. He nodded his thanks to the judges and shook each of their offered hands. As they walked away, he looked at Lyra and drew his hand across his forehead in a "*whew!*" gesture.

She gave him a round of silent applause, and he bowed with mock formality. Then they both turned to watch the last student's encounter with the judges.

It was finally Caramelle Meringue's turn.

Lyra felt her heart sinking into her shoes with each step the judges took towards the auburn-haired girl's spotless workstation. The first sight of Ginger's cake had impressed Lyra. Boysen's cake had left her gobsmacked.

Caramelle's cake made her want to slink off her stool and hide behind the counter.

It looked like a wedding cake for royalty. The three tiers seemed to float on top of each other, decreasing in size from bottom to top. The frosting was a blinding white, smooth as a field of newly fallen snow. Intricate piping formed a river of gold roses, winding around and around the cake to culminate in a mass of the same golden flowers on the top tier.

But it wasn't just the neatness and the precision that sent Lyra's spirits plummeting. Caramelle's cake seemed to shimmer, like it was radiating a tangible glow of excellence. Some incredibly high-level Presentation spell was at work here.

And this from a girl who had identified *Texture* as her true specialty.

Boysen caught Lyra's eye. He gestured towards Caramelle's counter with raised eyebrows.

Wow, he mouthed.

Lyra just nodded, then turned her full attention to the judging in progress. She thought she felt Boysen's eyes on her, but she couldn't look away from the Meringue show.

If that's the standard, she thought glumly, *then I'm sunk. This whole year was a waste of time.*

Caramelle smiled graciously throughout her judging, as elegant and poised as her culinary creation. Each of the professors made their appreciation clear. Professor Honeycomb limited herself to a slight bow, but Professor Puff surprised Lyra by performing a little jig of delight. Professor Genoise kissed Caramelle's hand. Her Flavor might not be hug-worthy, but her Texture and Presentation were obviously as wonderful up close as they seemed from Lyra's seat.

Then it was done. All twelve students had been judged. Lyra expected the professors to withdraw for some deliberation, but apparently, there was no need. They proceeded immediately to the platform that stretched across the back of the room, arranging themselves in a neat triangle around the teaching podium.

"We wish to thank all of you for your efforts," Professor Puff began. "Not just today, but over the past year of trials. Each of you has worked with laudable diligence to reach this point, and we honor you."

She and her fellow judges began a brief round of applause, and the twelve students all joined in politely.

Professor Honeycomb's smile beamed across the room. "Every year, I think I know what to expect from these trials. And every year, the young magical bakers in this country exceed those expectations. Each of you has surprised me today, and for that, I thank you."

"Indeed, you are all to be commended," Professor Genoise said smoothly. "But I am afraid we can invite only six of you to join us at the academy. The rest of you will, I am sure, find other ways to continue your magical baking journey. We wish you the very best of the sweet and savory in your endeavors."

He unrolled a scroll that had been left on the podium. The three professors all pored over it briefly, glancing up occasionally at the room and checking it against their own notes. Lyra guessed it was a seating chart, revealing the names of each of the candidates.

She was proven right a moment later when Professor Genoise proclaimed, "Here are the six students who have gained admittance into the academy: Aniseed Mint, Macaron Fondant."

Professor Puff took the scroll. "Ginger Crumble," she announced in her smooth, even voice. "Lyra Treble."

"Boysen Berry," Professor Honeycomb trilled. "And Caramelle Meringue."

Lyra's heart lifted slowly from her shoes, rising faster and faster through her chest until it got stuck in her throat. Either that invisible choir was singing again or her ears were ringing.

Was that me? she thought dizzily. *Did they say my name?*

Boysen's smile blazed in the corner of her eye, so bright she had to look. His whole face was alight with joy. That was confirmation enough for Lyra, even before she caught an unmistakable wink from Professor Honeycomb.

Professor Genoise rolled up the scroll and spread his arms wide.

"Welcome," he said, his soft voice somehow carrying through the whole vast space. "Welcome, you worthy six, to the Royal Academy of Magical Baking."

CHAPTER THREE

Spatula, Whisk, Pestle, Zester

I'm not sure about this, Lyra." Melody Treble's normally pleasant voice was sharp with anxiety. "I thought this baking thing was just a phase."

"Or a hobby," her husband suggested. "Everyone needs a hobby to blow off steam."

They had been unusually silent all afternoon while helping Lyra pack. Now, as they stood with their daughter in front of the Royal Academy of Magical Baking's magnificent gates, the reality of the moment seemed to hit home for Harmon and Melody Treble, forcing them to speak.

"Look at your brother Canto," Lyra's mother suggested. "He loves painting, and he's quite good at it. But he didn't go rushing off to the Royal Academy of Visual Arts."

"He knows painting is a hobby." Harmon Treble scowled up at the gates. "It helps him relax, and that makes him a better musician overall. But it's not his profession."

Melody nodded, pursing her lips. "It's a hobby, Lyra. Like my embroidery, or your father's potted plants. Why can't baking just be your hobby?"

"I don't know," Lyra said quietly. "But it can't. Baking is not my hobby. It's more than that."

Lyra's right hand was fused around the packet of welcome scrolls Professor Honeycomb had handed out at the end of the exam that morning. The parchment was nearly worn through from her tight grip, but she couldn't let go. It was the only thing convincing her that this was actually happening.

"I'm just not sure about this, Lyra," her mother said again.

Her father nodded. "You've been a bard your whole life. And now, all of a sudden, that's not enough?"

"I started these trials a year ago," Lyra reminded them. "It's not 'all of a sudden.' And you've both been supportive. You let me skip Any Weather rehearsals to practice my recipes. You bought me that book, Dad. I thought you loved my baking."

"We do." Harmon's voice was grim. "Just like we love Canto's painting."

Lyra clutched the scrolls tighter. "Why'd you let me keep going? I mean, if you felt this strongly about it?"

"We never expected you to get this far," Melody said bluntly. "You're very talented, Lyra, but you haven't had training like these other kids. The basic spells alone—"

Harmon held up a hand to his wife and put his other arm around Lyra. "It's not that we don't believe in you, Treblette. Quite the opposite. We just don't want to see you get hurt or set yourself up for disappointment."

"And we'll miss you," her mother put in plaintively. "Especially during shows. Your brothers are a splendid trio, but your rhythm guitar and vocals . . ."

Harmon squeezed Lyra's shoulder. "You'll be leaving a big gap, Treblette."

"Maybe not for very long." Lyra gazed up at the gates, which suddenly seemed very much like a mouth waiting to gobble her up. "They took six of us, but only three will be left at the end of the year. They cut the lowest performer at the end of every term. So, if I crash and burn over the next few months, you might just get your wish."

"We don't want you to crash and burn," Melody assured her, rushing to wrap her own arm around Lyra from the other side. "It's just . . . Oh, flats. Words are such tricky things. I can't get the right ones out unless I'm singing."

"Please don't," Lyra said hastily with a quick glance at the pedestrians passing behind them in a steady stream. "I get it. I do."

And she meant it. Standing there between her parents, their affection flooding her from both sides, she understood.

Her father sighed. "We love you, Lyra."

"Love you too." Then, under her breath, Lyra sang the first line of their family favorite, the closing song for all the Any Weather Bards shows. "*I know it's never certain / when we'll meet again . . .*"

Pressing their heads close together, her parents finished the line, singing so quietly that only the three of them could possibly hear. "*So I'll watch through the curtain / and think of you till then.*"

They each planted a kiss on top of her head. Then they stood back and let her shoulder her own two bags and make her way through the gates.

Considering its national importance, the Royal Academy of Magical Baking was a relatively small campus. Its rigorously exclusive program meant there were never more than twelve students in residence at any given time. Other than the exam hall, which had hosted that morning's final entrance event, there were only six other buildings within the stone walls. The largest and most central was the main hall, which housed the academy kitchens, dining commons, student practice kitchens, and one classroom each for Flavor, Texture, and Presentation studies. Behind the main hall was a greenhouse, surrounded by the academy orchard and gardens. The southern end of campus was the residential area, with a dormitory for the students and three small cottages for the professors.

The welcome scrolls included a map, but even without it, Lyra would have had no trouble finding the dormitories. She turned right as soon as she passed through the gate and tried to move a bit faster. The welcome feast was starting in less than an hour, and she wanted to get settled into her room first.

As she walked along the broad pathway, paved with wide gray stones, she wondered who her roommate would be. The dormitory had three floors, one for each year of the academy's program. The four rooms on each floor were like large apartments. The top two floors had only three residents each, of course, with one extra room for overflow studying or academy guests. But the first years would each be starting with a roommate.

I hope it's Ginger, Lyra thought as she approached the tall dormitory building. She hadn't gotten a good look at Aniseed Mint that morning, but at first glance, the raven-haired girl seemed even haughtier than Caramelle.

And as for Caramelle herself . . .

Lyra really, *really* hoped she'd be rooming with Ginger.

She trudged up the three shallow stone steps and paused for a moment, looking at her new home. Every academy building was constructed of the same gray stone. It gave the whole place a solid feeling, like a visible testament to the institution's enduring legacy. The carefully groomed ivy was also a nice touch. Lyra thought it gave each building the appearance of a neatly decorated cake.

Taken all together, the Royal Academy of Magical Baking was an impressive place. The buildings stood proudly, as if daring time to do its worst. Yet, though Lyra definitely felt all the weight of the school's imposing presence, it wasn't overwhelming. She decided it was the cheerful red color of all the doors that saved the whole place from drowning in its own importance. The red paint added just the right dash of cozy to the academy's recipe.

Lyra took a deep breath, trying to inhale enough of that cozy cheer to calm her rising tide of nerves. Then, with determined confidence, she pulled open one of the dormitory's red doors and strode inside.

The foyer had a staircase on either side, leading up to the second and third floors. Lyra passed through the foyer and pulled open another door to find herself in the first-floor central living area. Each floor was built around its own communal space, for times when that year's students wanted to gather for group meals or study. Directly inside the door were two couches facing each other across a magical indoor fire pit. Beyond them was a dining table with six chairs. A kitchen took up the rest of the room, large enough for six Aspiring Bakers to make a glorious mess simultaneously.

The walls on the left and right each had two doors, all currently closed. Lyra knew from the welcome packet that they were all named after various pieces of baking equipment. She recited their names quietly to herself, starting with the room on her immediate left and moving clockwise.

"Spatula, Whisk, Pestle, Zester." Her gaze landed on each door in turn before settling on the back right corner. "And I'm in Pestle."

Moving around the common area, she navigated to the correct door. It was painted the same cozy red as all the other doors and had a hand-drawn picture of a pestle hanging in the center. Suddenly unsure of the etiquette, Lyra knocked.

A rustle of movement sounded on the other side of the door, then it was pulled open.

Lyra's heart took a nosedive.

"Caramelle," she said.

The auburn-haired girl stared at her for a moment. Then, to Lyra's complete astonishment, Caramelle's face broke into a wide smile.

"Lyra!" Caramelle threw her arms around the stunned former bard. After a brief hug, she stepped back and threw the door open wide. "Come in! Oh, I'm so glad we'll be roommates. I was hoping to get to know you better!"

Lyra stood in the doorway, frozen in shock. "You-you were?"

"Of course!" Caramelle's eyes shone with delight. Genuine delight, as far as Lyra could tell. "I think we can learn so much from each other. I've got loads to pass along from Master Chiffon, and you . . . Well, you must be doing something right. I've never heard of the professors *speaking* to a student during the judging."

"You haven't?" Lyra still seemed unable to move, but Caramelle ushered her in and closed the door behind her.

"Never. You caused quite a stir, Miss Treble." Caramelle laughed. "Treble! I do hope you won't make *trouble*, Miss Treble."

This was by no means Lyra's first encounter with that tired old joke, but Caramelle was so clearly tickled by it that Lyra tried to play along.

"I don't plan to," she said, forcing a smile and a laugh. "I just want to learn about baking."

"As do we all." Caramelle was suddenly serious. She took both Lyra's hands in her own, looking her straight in the eye. "This place is hard, you know. That's why we've got to stick together."

Lyra couldn't stop her eyebrows from rising. "Really? I thought it was super competitive. Especially this first year."

Caramelle waved one hand dismissively. "Oh, sure. We're all hoping to move into our own room on the second floor next year. But each of us is really just trying to become the best baker we can be, right?"

"Of course," Lyra said.

"Of course! And the only way to become the best baker you can be is to make use of every available resource." Caramelle gave Lyra a dazzling smile. "Including our fellow bakers."

Lyra hesitated.

Maybe I judged her too quickly, she thought. She was probably just nervous this morning, and it made her come across all . . . Meringue-y.

Lyra looked around the room. On the right was a small living nook with one couch and one overstuffed armchair nestled around another magical fire pit. Two twin beds stood against the left wall, each with an accompanying desk and small bookcase. As with the common area, a large kitchen took up the rest of the room. A door on the right-hand wall led to an adjoining bathroom with the Zester apartment.

Each room has a huge kitchen, but two rooms have to share one bathroom, Lyra mused. At least the Royal Academy of Magical Baking made its priorities clear.

"What do you say?" Caramelle coaxed. "Can we decide, right here and now, to have each other's back this year?"

Lyra took another look around the apartment. The room was reasonably spacious, but it was still far too small a space to share with an enemy, especially considering the intense weeks ahead.

She took a deep breath, then returned Caramelle's smile. "Absolutely," she said. "That sounds really nice."

"Sweet and savory!" Caramelle gave her another, even quicker hug. "Now, let's get you unpacked. The welcome feast starts in just a bit, you know. We can get there early and choose our seats!"

CHAPTER FOUR

Things for People to Eat

Friendly Caramelle was a nonstop flurry of pleasant conversation.

"I hope you don't mind I took this bed," she said anxiously. "It's close to the door, and I'll probably be staying out late in the practice kitchens most nights, so I thought it would help me not disturb you."

"I don't mind at all," Lyra assured her. "That's really kind."

Caramelle beamed. "And feel free to borrow any of my books." She indicated the bottom row of her bookcase, which was already packed tight with recipe tomes and baking spell scrolls. "I know they'll be giving us our textbooks, but Master Chiffon curated a list of supplemental materials for me to bring. Just let me know when you need one. Oh, you brought your guitar!"

She pointed at the instrument case slung across Lyra's back. Lyra flushed.

"My mom made me," she admitted. "But I guess it's a good idea. Music helps me relax."

"Hobbies are very important," Caramelle said solemnly. "Master Chiffon was insistent that I keep a hobby. I took dancing lessons twice a week."

Lyra's eyes brightened. "I love dancing! Maybe I could join you sometime? Do they let guests sit in?"

"Oh, I doubt I'll be going much this term." Caramelle laughed. "This term is all about preparing for the first exam. I'm afraid I'll be a very boring roommate. But we can be boring together, right? Hold each other accountable, share study tips . . ."

"Late-night practice sessions in the kitchen," Lyra offered.

Caramelle clapped her hands. "That's the spirit!"

Once Lyra's few belongings were unpacked, she ducked into the bathroom to freshen up. She had been standing at the sink only a few moments when a tentative knock sounded from the adjoining room.

"Come in," Lyra called.

The door opened, and Ginger's copper-colored face peeked inside. When she saw Lyra, her eyes widened in relief.

"I am so glad to see you!" Quickly, she stepped into the bathroom, closing the door behind her. "I wish I could have roomed with you, Lyra."

Lyra glanced at her own door, making sure it was closed. "Me too," she confessed. "What's Aniseed like?"

Ginger grimaced. "Aniseed Mint, of the royal Mints," she chanted. "I've been in school with her for years. Just because her great-great-great-granduncle or something was the first royal chef of Flavor, she thinks we're all just flour beneath her fingernails." Ginger rolled her eyes. "Of course, I shouldn't be complaining to *you*. You got stuck with The Meringue."

"Caramelle doesn't seem so bad, actually," Lyra said.

Ginger's eyebrows rose.

"No, really," Lyra went on. "I mean, she was pretty awful this morning, but just now . . . she's been nice. Really nice. Wants us to stick together and help each other."

Ginger's eyebrows rose even higher, disappearing into her dark wavy hair.

"The Meringue doesn't mix with mere mortals," she said. "The Meringue must always be first and best."

"Why do you keep calling her 'The Meringue'?"

"The Meringue is not a person," Ginger explained. "The Meringue is a force of nature, and as such, ought to be treated with the same reasonable fear."

"Fear?"

"Healthy sense of self-preservation." Ginger put a hand on Lyra's shoulder. "Tangle with The Meringue, and you end up with egg on your face," she said gravely. "And all over your clothes, and in your hair, most likely."

Lyra laughed. It was impossible not to like Ginger, but she also didn't want to discount her new roommate so quickly.

"Caramelle doesn't seem so bad," she repeated. "I want to give her a chance, anyway."

Ginger pondered a moment. "It's true, I've never heard of The Meringue using phrases like 'stick together and help each other.' Perhaps she got hit by a runaway rolling pin and was transformed into a decent human being. If you're game to try, may salt season your path." She linked her arm through Lyra's. "But if The Meringue explodes on you . . . I'm right across the bathroom."

She gave Lyra's arm a quick squeeze, then released her and turned to the mirror. She ran a brush through her hair and splashed some water on her face. Then, with a cheery wave, she was gone, leaving Lyra alone with her reflection.

Lyra stared into the mirror. Her brown hair was tied into a loose bun, held out of her face by a red headband. She was still wearing her traditional bardic clothes, a warm yellow tunic over black leggings. Her brown eyes looked wide and, suddenly, very scared.

She could practically hear her mother's voice, echoing like a discordant jangle of notes: *I'm not sure about this, Lyra.*

"Neither am I, Mom," she whispered. "But, by all the sharps and flats, I'm surely going to try."

She smoothed a few stray hairs under the headband, then turned to go.

Whether she was dealing with "Caramelle" or "The Meringue," she didn't want to make her late to the welcome feast.

"Lyra! Caramelle!"

Boysen's jubilant voice greeted the two of them as soon as they opened the door to the main hall. He bounded across the foyer, lifting both hands for a high five with each girl.

"First to arrive at the exam this morning, first to arrive at the welcome feast. How're you settling in? Which rooms are you?"

"Pestle," Lyra and Caramelle said at once.

Boysen looked from Lyra to Caramelle, then back again. His quick eyes seemed to be making some sort of assessment. Then he broke into his own broad grin.

"Good for you, say I. Good for you both." He waved to a young man with dark brown skin hovering by a set of double doors to the right. "Mac and I haven't quite reached your level yet, but I'm sure we'll get there. Mac! Macaron Fondant! Come and say hello to the girls!"

Mac crossed the floor timidly. Lyra recognized him as the terrified student she and Boysen had talked down from a figurative ledge of nervous puking that morning.

"Hello to the girls," he said, his voice barely audible.

Boysen laughed. "That's the spirit, Mac." He leaned in, speaking to Lyra in a loud conspiratorial whisper. "Macaron's got an excellent sense of humor. Regular wit, this one. Just needs a bit of encouragement."

Lyra took Mac's hand, shaking it warmly. "Pleased to see you again, Macaron Fondant. I didn't get a proper look at your cake this morning. What did you do?"

"C-coffee," Mac stammered. He cleared his throat and tried again with a bit more confidence. "Coffee genoise sponge, with marzipan filling."

"And fondant on top?" Lyra guessed.

Mac groaned but gave her a tiny smile. "Only because my parents would have killed me otherwise. I actually don't like fondant all that much. I prefer buttercream." His eyes, wide behind a pair of glasses, drifted to Caramelle and settled there. "There's a special kind of buttercream, made with meringue . . . That's my favorite."

Caramelle didn't appear to be listening. She hadn't even glanced at Mac. Her gaze was fixed on the double doors to the right.

"Aren't they letting us in yet?"

She didn't seem to be asking anyone in particular, but Boysen supplied the answer.

"Afraid not. Apparently, there's some great formal to-do." He winked at Lyra. "Wouldn't be the Royal Academy of Magical Baking without a bit of ceremony, right?"

Before she could answer, the front door opened behind them to let in Ginger.

"Made it!" she sang out gaily. "My dad made me promise I'd be on time to the welcome feast. It's his favorite memory from this place."

"Your dad went to the academy?" Lyra asked.

"For one year," Caramelle said sweetly.

Ginger ignored her. "He came so close," she said to Lyra. "Made it all the way through the third term. He was the last one cut that year."

"My dad didn't even make it that far," Boysen said. "Second term final was his downfall."

Lyra hummed a low note. "That must've been hard."

"Sure, but it wasn't devastating. Baking never is. At the end of the day, we're just making things for people to eat, right?" Boysen smiled. "Besides, he'd already met my mom by then. He says that was better than any Stellar Enchantment Pin or baking certification."

"How precious." Caramelle was also smiling, but her gaze was fixed on the front door, where the sixth new student had just entered. "I see Aniseed has finally decided to grace us with her presence."

Aniseed's emerald eyes swept the foyer. Apparently dissatisfied with what she saw, she tossed her sheet of raven-black hair and strode to the double doors on the right. She pulled one open without hesitation and entered the dining commons.

"Can-can she do that?" Mac asked.

Boysen whistled. "Looks like she just did."

Seconds later, the door opened again, and Aniseed was escorted back into the foyer by a rather irate-looking Professor Puff.

"Half a moment, all of you," the professor called across the foyer. Then she disappeared into the dining hall, closing the door firmly behind her.

Awkward silence reigned in the foyer. Resisting the habitual urge to fill that silence with song, Lyra tried to focus on the room itself. Just like the exam hall and the dormitory, the foyer to the main hall was paneled in rich mahogany, shining warmly in the evening sun streaming through large windows. Staircases on the left and right led up to the three upper levels, where the classrooms and practice kitchens were. Directly across the foyer was another set of particularly magnificent double doors, leading to a fancy reception hall reserved for special events like graduation.

"Ever been inside?" Boysen asked.

Lyra jumped, realizing she had been staring at the reception hall doors.

"No," she said longingly. "But I imagine it's pretty grand. The welcome scroll told me the royal family always attends the graduation ceremony."

Boysen nodded. "They do indeed. They're a pretty grand sight themselves, but the room is even better."

"You've been?" she squeaked.

"Twice," Boysen replied. "For Cran and Straw, my older brothers."

"Sharps and flats," Lyra breathed. She gazed longingly at the doors. "I wonder if I'll get to see inside?"

Boysen nudged her shoulder with his. "I'm sure you will. Anyone who can get the professors to break their famous 'silent judging' rule is bound for greatness, I'd say."

Lyra was saved from having to come up with a response by the opening of the dining hall doors.

"New students of the Royal Academy of Magical Baking," Professor Puff announced, "you may enter."

Caramelle linked her arm firmly through Lyra's. "Ready, roomie?"

Lyra took a deep breath. "Guess I'll have to be."

Aniseed had already flounced inside as soon as Professor Puff cleared the doorway. The rest of the first-year students crossed the foyer in a tight group, huddled together as if for safety. But as soon as they crossed the threshold, Lyra felt her muscles relaxing. The dining commons had the same high ceiling, mahogany panels, and large windows as every other academy building she'd seen thus far, but it just felt so . . . normal.

There was a small round table in the center of the room for the professors and any visiting dignitaries. Three of the room's corners contained a similar round table, one for each year of students. The back right corner was filled with a small platform and another set of double doors that led into the academy kitchens.

Looking around, Lyra felt the knot of anxiety begin to loosen in her stomach. What was it Boysen had said? *At the end of the day, we're just making things for people to eat.*

Despite the prestige and pressure of the academy, this was just a room where people gathered around the table and ate. She needed to keep remembering that.

CHAPTER FIVE

Disaster Cake

Welcome!" Professor Honeycomb smiled warmly at the first years from her place at the center table. "We are truly delighted to have you join us. When we say your name, please step forward and give a wave so the other students know who is who."

They went down the line, introducing each new student to the second and third years. Once everyone's name had been called, Professor Genoise indicated the table in the front left corner, directly inside the doors.

"You may take your places," he said. "Then we will get on with the evening's festivities."

Caramelle pulled Lyra with her, securing the two seats facing the center of the room. Boysen slid into the chair on Lyra's other side, with Ginger next to him. Looking almost as nervous as he had that morning, Mac perched on the seat beside Caramelle.

That left Aniseed with the chair facing away from the rest of the room. She glared at the table frostily, then turned to the professors.

"That table is rather crowded," she said, her voice ringing shrilly across the relatively small room. "I wonder if I might sit with the second years instead."

Lyra was stunned. Beside her, Caramelle inhaled sharply.

The professors, however, seemed unfazed.

"Please take your seat, Miss Mint," Professor Genoise said mildly. "With your first-year colleagues."

Aniseed waited three beats, as if expecting someone to intervene. Then she turned on her heel, deliberately pulled the chair out from the table, and sat on the very edge of it. Her ramrod posture radiated so much icy disdain that Lyra shivered.

"Well, then. Welcome, all!" Professor Genoise stepped back, spreading his arms to indicate the whole room. "If this morning's final entrance exam was any indication, this will be a year of special excellence in the exalted history of the Royal Academy of Magical Baking."

Professor Puff stood, joining him. "Indeed, Professor. And what better way to begin such a year than with an excellent feast?"

"I couldn't agree more," chorused the second and third years. Apparently, this bit of the speech was an academy tradition.

Professor Honeycomb smiled as she stood with her fellow professors. "Well said, Aspiring and Apprentice Bakers. Of course, we cannot begin the feast without introducing the visionary responsible for its creation. Students new and returning, I give you Chef Peppercorn Flax!"

The second- and third-year tables broke into wild applause as the doors to the kitchen burst open, revealing the largest man Lyra had ever seen. The grand chef's hat atop his graying black curls added half a foot to his already significant height. He was nearly as broad as he was tall and clothed entirely in white. Smock, pants, hat, even his shoes were snowy white and sparkling clean. His apron had been white at some point, but it was now covered in flour and a multitude of stains in various hues.

The older students continued applauding, all rising from their chairs. A few even whistled. Chef Peppercorn Flax's face, already red from the heat of the kitchens, flushed even redder as he beamed at the whole room from the podium.

"I don't know what they're so excited about," Caramelle whispered to Lyra. "His story is so sad."

"Sad?" Lyra echoed.

"He was the top student of his class at the academy," Caramelle explained. "He could have been the royal chef of Flavor. The queen actually offered him the job, but for some reason, he wound up here instead."

"Because he wanted to." Boysen leaned across Lyra, joining the girls' whispered conversation. "He's an old friend of my parents. This was always his dream job."

Caramelle's voice was incredulous. "Cooking for students? When he could have been cooking for royalty?"

Boysen shrugged. "Seems like a much more fun job to me."

"Me too," Lyra said softly, watching the chef as he waved at the older students.

"Thank you," Chef Flax called. He gave one more deep bow, then achieved order with a sharp whistle. "Thank you, one and all, but that is quite enough. I left choux pastry in the oven, which is far more important to me than your adoration." He winked broadly at the third-year table. "Though, adoration is always welcome. Preferably after the meal."

A ripple of laughter ran around the room.

"I look forward to spending more time with all of you," Chef Flax continued. "And most especially, I look forward to getting to know our new students.

Having sampled the fruits of your labor this morning, I must echo your esteemed professors: this is sure to be a year of particular excellence at our beloved Royal Academy of Magical Baking."

He bowed towards the first-year table, then gave the room a cheerful wave.

"See you all later, and remember—"

"Save room for dessert!" shouted the second and third years. Chef Flax laughed merrily and disappeared into the kitchens to another round of applause.

The three professors took his place on the podium, wheeling a tray cart to the front. Lyra blinked. On the tray cart was a cake stand displaying the messiest looking cake she had ever seen. It was the color of mud, like someone had tried to mix far too many different hues in the frosting. Its sagging middle hinted at some fundamental miscalculation within as well as without.

"We like to start off every year with a demonstration," Professor Puff began. "First years, gather round."

Lyra and her classmates obeyed, clustering around the podium. Professor Honeycomb cut a piece out of the cake and passed it around.

"Take a small bite," she instructed. "Each of you."

Again, they obeyed, though more reluctantly. Not only did the cake look like a mess, but it smelled faintly of beet. *Rotten* beet.

"Revolting, isn't it?" Professor Honeycomb's voice rang out cheerfully as the first years tried not to gag. "This is a disaster cake. My two colleagues and I made it together."

"We have been baking long enough to know all the possible mistakes," Professor Genoise went on smoothly. "So we made them deliberately. The Presentation is a disgrace."

Professor Honeycomb nodded. "The flavor is abysmal."

"The texture has collapsed." Professor Puff raised a delicate silver spoon, the handle as long as a wand. "But all is not lost, so long as you know the right spells."

She let the spoon hover over the cake. Her gray eyes were calm but intensely focused. Lyra could almost feel the air vibrating.

Then the Texture headmistress delivered a series of light, rapid taps on the cake, rotating around it expertly with the silver spoon-wand. Though the instrument barely touched the surface, a burst of blue light exploded with each tap, vanishing instantly into the cake. After twelve taps, delivered expertly in a pattern too intricate to follow, Professor Puff stood back.

Lyra gasped. The cake was *growing* before her eyes. She caught another faint shimmer of blue as each layer lifted and became light and fluffy and everything you would want a cake to be.

Before anyone could recover, Professor Honeycomb stepped forward. She had no long delicate silver spoon. Instead, she held her empty hand out over the cake, palm down. The headmistress of Flavor closed her eyes for several seconds, then opened them as she twisted her wrist with a sharp *flick*.

A sphere of green light burst out of the cake. It lingered, glowing, then began to shrink, as if the cake was drawing the light back into itself. When the last bit of green disappeared into the cake, Lyra inhaled with a smile. Rather than beet, the cake was now emanating a faint, perfectly balanced aroma of lemon and lavender.

Professor Genoise stepped forward. He held two long silver spoon-wands, one in each hand. Unlike Professor Puff's, the Presentation headmaster's instruments were exquisitely carved. He raised them both and began waving them over the cake.

To Lyra, he looked like a conductor leading an orchestra. But instead of filling the air with music, the two spoon-wands left streaks of purple light behind them. The streaks wove together like ribbons, faster and thicker, until the cake was covered with a delicate purple glow. Then, with a final elegant flourish, Professor Genoise brought his tools together and tapped the top of the cake lightly.

The purple ribbons vanished in a cloud of sparkling smoke to reveal a cake now decorated within an inch of its life. Every color of the rainbow was represented in precise and equal measure, swirled delicately into a perfect depiction of a sunset sky.

Wordlessly, Professor Honeycomb cut another slice from the cake and passed it around.

"Behold," Professor Genoise said as the first years reveled in the delicious treat. "The Presentation is now perfect."

Professor Puff nodded solemnly. "The texture is flawless."

"And the flavor is rich." Professor Honeycomb beamed at the first years. "This is what the Royal Academy of Magical Baking is about, Aspiring Bakers."

Professor Genoise gestured grandly at the now magnificent cake. "Our aim is to equip you sufficiently in all three disciplines so you can produce creations as exquisite as this, even after everything goes wrong."

"But you have a long way to go," Professor Puff warned. "These spells my colleagues and I have performed today are as risky as they are complex. Not even our third years have attempted them yet. We share them now merely as a demonstration of the baking accomplishments that await you if you continue on this noble path."

"Hear, hear!" Professor Honeycomb took the empty plate from Mac. "Now, return to your table, Aspiring Bakers, but don't sit! Let's all stand and raise our glasses for the academy toast."

Lyra and her fellow first years scrambled back across the room as the second and third years rose to their feet. The professors moved sedately as they returned to their table and lifted glasses of sparkling cordial.

"We expect you to make your own pledge to these principles we have demonstrated here today," Professor Genoise said. "To Flavor, Texture, and Presentation!"

The dozen students in the room echoed as one: "Flavor, Texture, and Presentation!"

Everyone drank, then resumed their seats.

"What'd I tell you?" Boysen whispered to Lyra. "Wouldn't be the academy without a bit of ceremony."

Professor Genoise lifted his hand. "One last order of business before Chef Flax sends in the first course. Second years, would you rise and introduce yourselves to our new students? Just so they can give a friendly greeting when you pass each other in the halls."

The three students sitting at the table in the front right corner of the room all stood, but Lyra couldn't concentrate. She was suddenly realizing how hungry she was. Breakfast had been out of the question that stress-filled morning, and lunch had gotten lost in a flurry of packing. Now her stomach was beginning to growl so loudly that she feared Chef Flax might hear it all the way from the kitchens.

Professor Puff's voice cut across her thoughts. "Thank you, Aspiring Bakers. Now, would our third years please stand?"

The table in the back left corner stood.

Professor Puff went on, "Pay attention, new students. You will be getting to know our third years quite well. As you may know, the academy curriculum culminates in an apprenticeship of sorts. Each of our senior students has focused their studies on a different principle of baking. This year, they will be assisting us as we strive to teach you those principles."

Professor Honeycomb pointed at a tall, lanky young man with messy brown hair. "For Flavor, I am thrilled to have Razz Berry as my assistant."

Razz waved, shooting a particularly broad wink at the first-year table.

Lyra nudged Boysen. "You didn't tell me your brother is still a student here!"

"Sadly, yes." Boysen rolled his eyes. "There are six Berry boys. You'd think my parents would have spaced us far enough apart to avoid situations like this, but . . . oh well. My younger brothers, Mull and Whortle, are twins. Who knows what they'll do."

"For Texture," Professor Puff said, "I have the honor of being assisted by Hyacinth Roulade."

Hyacinth waved at the first years. Her light brown skin was so smooth and perfect, Lyra wondered if she actually had been carved out of marble. But her smile was warm and friendly, and her whole being shone with cheerful ease.

Texture classes might actually be fun, Lyra thought.

Then Professor Genoise announced, "And for Presentation, it is my distinct privilege to introduce to you my assistant, Cardamom Coulis the Third."

Suddenly, Lyra forgot everything else.

She forgot her growling stomach. She forgot her apprehension about classes starting the day after tomorrow. She even, for a moment, forgot her own name.

Lyra's father had once told her, *The first time I saw your mother, it was like I'd seen a song made visible. She was music itself, in physical form.*

Lyra had never really been sure what her father meant . . . until now.

Cardamom Coulis III was perfect. His dark hair was swept smoothly to one side, revealing an elegant nose and delicately sharp cheekbones. Dark eyes sparkled against flawless olive-toned skin. His smile was somehow simultaneously both open and mysterious.

But there was something else at work that made him more than the sum of his exquisite parts. Like Caramelle's cake that morning, he seemed to radiate appeal, as if he were constantly casting a virtuosic Presentation spell over himself.

He was a song made visible. He was music itself, in physical form.

"On behalf of my fellow seniors, I'd like to welcome our first years." Even Cardamom's voice was musical. "We look forward to working with you."

Lyra heard her roommate sigh beside her.

"Sweet and savory," Caramelle whispered dreamily.

Lyra couldn't speak. The invisible choir was back, singing so loudly that she could barely hear herself think. She just nodded in agreement as Cardamom led his table in a brief round of applause for the new students.

"Thank you, Cardamom," Professor Genoise said. "I believe that concludes the welcome ceremony."

Professor Puff nodded at Professor Honeycomb, who crossed to the kitchen doors and knocked three times.

"Chef Flax!" Professor Honeycomb called. "We're ready for you!"

The doors opened, and several dishes appeared suspended in the air as if held by invisible hands. Lyra gasped. The next moment, the dishes began floating across the room towards the center table, then landed elegantly and precisely in front of the professors. The smells wafted around to the other tables and wrapped Lyra in a heavenly cocoon of aromatic anticipation as another round of dishes emerged and headed for the third-year table.

The invisible choir got louder. Once again, Lyra remembered her mother's words from that morning, echoing like a half-remembered nightmare. *I'm just not sure about this, Lyra.*

I am, Lyra thought as the first steaming dish landed in front of her. She breathed in deeply, the heady scent of basil mixing with the intoxicating reality of Cardamom Coulis III, sitting only a few dozen feet away.

No more doubt. No more anxiety.

Lyra Treble was exactly where she was meant to be.

CHAPTER SIX

Chef Peppercorn Flax

"Lyra! Wake up!"

Lyra rolled over with a groan, squinting at the window. "It's still dark outside. What time is it?"

Caramelle gave her another cheerful shake. "Nearly dawn, sleepyhead! C'mon. Rise and shine!"

"*Nearly* dawn?"

"I know." Caramelle sighed. "It's shameful. I overslept after all the excitement of yesterday."

"Overslept?" Lyra repeated, but most of the word was lost in a giant yawn. "Shouldn't we wait to 'rise and shine' with the sun?"

Caramelle's eyebrows rose in shock. "Sunrise is like midmorning for a baker. I would usually have a loaf of bread proofed and in the oven by now. Don't bards get up early?"

"Nope," Lyra replied, sitting up groggily. "We're usually out late with shows or rehearsal. Mornings are very . . . slow in the Treble household."

"Then it's a good thing you're rooming with me." Caramelle pulled Lyra to her feet. "Got to get you out of those performer habits and into a true baking schedule."

The next fifteen minutes were a blur to Lyra, but at the end of them, she found herself sitting with Caramelle at the first-year table in the dining hall.

"No one else is here," Lyra whispered, looking around at the otherwise empty room. "Are we really that late?"

At that moment, the doors swung open once again to admit Professor Puff.

"We're right on time," Caramelle said with satisfaction. Then, her smile brightened, "Good morning, Professor!"

"Good morning, Aspiring Bakers." The Texture headmistress gave them each a cordial nod before taking her place at the central table. She was followed closely by Professor Genoise and finally a yawning Professor Honeycomb.

"Of course, today is a bit more relaxed, since there are no classes," Caramelle whispered to Lyra, after exchanging friendly greetings with both professors as they entered. "The other students are probably still sleeping. But we want to make a good impression. The professors see us already here, they know we're diligent, right?"

Lyra caught the look of approval in Professor Genoise's eyes as he glanced over at their table. She nodded fervently. "Makes sense. And thanks. For, y'know, getting me here . . . on time."

Caramelle squeezed her hand. "That's what roomies are for."

The kitchen doors opened, and a set of dishes came floating through the air. Lyra expected them to serve the professors first, but to her surprise, they soared straight to the first-year table.

"I guess they serve guests in the order of arrival?" Lyra guessed, gazing with admiration at the steaming plate of eggs and bacon in front of her. "How do they know from inside the kitchen? And how does the floating spell work?"

Caramelle waved a dismissive hand. "Probably some menial kitchen staff magic. Bakers don't concern themselves with the service side of the industry."

The doors opened again, but this time the dish that appeared was not floating. Chef Peppercorn Flax himself stood there holding two plates heaped with cinnamon rolls.

"Good morning, early risers!" he called, his voice booming genially around the room. "Happy Cinnamon Roll Sunday!"

"Cinnamon rolls!" Professor Honeycomb clapped her hands. "Oh, how I've missed these."

"You can make them yourself while the students are on break, Lavender," Professor Puff observed calmly.

The Flavor headmistress grinned up at Chef Flax as he deposited one plate at the professors' table. "Not like Peppercorn's. Believe me, I've tried."

"That's because our head chef guards his secrets closely. Especially regarding these beauties." Professor Genoise picked up a cinnamon roll, sniffing delicately. "One of these days, Flax, I'm going to get it out of you."

Chef Flax merely winked in response, then strode across to the first-year table, presenting the other plate of cinnamon rolls to Lyra and Caramelle with a deep bow. "Special treat for the first to arrive!"

His smile warmed Lyra right through, delighting her almost as much as the delectable aroma emanating from the plate. She tried to match it as she replied, "Thank you, Chef Flax."

"Oh, call me Flax. Or Peppercorn. Or just Chef, if you like. One name is enough for me." Chef Flax gestured to the plate of cinnamon rolls. "Go on, try one. The heating spell lasts a while, but it's still best to eat them when they're fresh."

Cinnamon rolls were Lyra's favorite breakfast treat, and these were the most perfect specimens she had ever seen. Each was a generous portion but still small enough that one wouldn't feel bad about having a second, or even a third. They were perfectly round with shiny sides that denoted an egg glaze. The tops were slathered in just the right amount of cream cheese frosting. An extra dusting of spices over the frosting hinted at the rich flavors waiting within.

Reverently, Lyra chose a particularly plump, especially sticky roll and took a large bite. Her eyes closed. For the next several seconds, she was lost in a blissful haze as all other senses gave way to taste.

"Sharps and flats." Lyra sighed once the exquisite bite was finally swallowed. "That is . . . priceless. I can see why you deliver them by hand."

"I don't, usually." Chef Flax chuckled. "But I wanted the chance to meet the creator of that incredible cake we all enjoyed last night. How *did* you do it?"

Lyra nodded in agreement as she turned to Caramelle. "I've been waiting to ask you the same thing. Especially about the gold roses. How did you manage to make them so shiny?"

"I think the head chef was talking to you, Lyra," Caramelle replied coolly.

"Me?" Lyra looked back at Chef Flax. "You mean my cake?"

"That's right. Miss Treble, is it?" Chef Flax extended a hand. "Allow me to congratulate you on a truly exceptional creation."

"Oh, thanks," Lyra said faintly, reaching her hand out instinctively as she tried to process what she was hearing. "You can call me Lyra. Or Treble. Whatever you prefer."

"Pleasure to make your acquaintance, Lyra." Chef Flax turned to Caramelle, extending the same hand. "And congratulations are, of course, due to Miss Meringue here also. A dazzling display of skill, especially for one so young."

Lyra felt the air around Caramelle soften at the praise.

"Thank you, Chef Flax." The auburn-haired girl took the offered hand graciously. "And thank you for the feast last night. I look forward to the next three years of meals from your kitchens."

Chef Flax clapped his hands. "Three years! That's what I like to hear. You two will go far, I can tell." Turning back to Lyra, he leaned conspiratorially across the table. "I would like to discuss that cake with you soon, Lyra. I saw your recipe, and I just can't wrap my head around how those spells produced that delicious dream."

"I'm not sure myself," Lyra confessed. "But I'm happy to tell you anything."

Chef beamed. "I'd be most obliged. Confidentially, of course. Baker to baker."

A sudden thought struck Lyra, and she grinned mischievously. "If, in return, you share some of your cinnamon roll secrets with me."

Chef Flax threw back his head and laughed heartily. "You'll definitely go far,

Lyra," he said eventually, his red face creased with merriment. "I'm afraid those particular secrets are far too valuable. But, if you like, you can help me make the next batch."

"R-really?" Lyra stammered. "I can—you'll let me come back to the kitchens? I can watch?"

"Not just watch. Assist!" Chef Flax said. "A bright baker like you will definitely pick up on a trick or two by observing, but even more by participating. Bring your plate."

"Oh, thank you!" Lyra stood, scrambling to gather her plate and utensils. "Thank y—"

Caramelle placed a firm hand on her arm. "I don't know that we have time, Lyra. Maybe we should just finish eating, and—"

"There's plenty of time!" Lyra exclaimed. "Classes don't start until tomorrow. There's nothing going on this morning."

"That's not true," Caramelle replied smoothly. "The third years are giving a tour of campus, remember?"

Lyra shook off her roommate's hand. "That doesn't start until ten o'clock. We'll be finished by then. Right, Chef?"

"Right indeed, Lyra." He offered an arm, which she took, then turned to Caramelle. "The invitation includes your colleague also, of course. What do you say, Miss Meringue? Care for a peek behind the curtain?"

"That's all right." Caramelle smiled sweetly. "When one has been baking as long as I have, there is so little mystery left to enjoy. I prefer to preserve it whenever I can. But thank you."

Chef Flax nodded solemnly. "As you wish, Miss Meringue. Shall we, Lyra?"

"Yes, please!" Lyra grabbed one more cinnamon roll for her already full plate, then matched Chef Flax's stride back towards the kitchen doors.

"Found a friend, Flax?" Professor Genoise called as they passed.

"I believe so, Professor," Chef Flax said gaily. "With any luck, I'll have her making better cinnamon rolls than you within the hour."

Professor Genoise smiled, as did Professor Puff, but Professor Honeycomb laughed merrily. "Back into the inner sanctum, Aspiring Baker Treble! That's a great honor. Keep your eyes open and enjoy it!"

"I will," Lyra assured her, casting one more glance back at the first-year table as she arrived at the kitchen doors. Caramelle was studiously eating, her auburn head bent fully over her plate. Then one of the dining hall doors opened, and Lyra's eyes were drawn irresistibly to the shimmering, practically incandescent figure of Cardamom Coulis III.

Through the corner of her eye, Lyra saw Caramelle's head snap up and flash a radiant smile at the newcomer. Then the kitchen doors swung shut behind Lyra, blocking her view.

"This is where the magic happens," Chef Flax's voice boomed beside her. "Quite literally, in fact."

Feeling a pang of regret at the loss of an opportunity to speak to Cardamom, Lyra forced her head around to take in the Royal Academy kitchen.

She gasped.

This could be nothing else but the kitchen of a magical baking school. The room was smaller than she had expected, roughly the same size as the dining hall, but it still felt spacious. Stoves and ovens alternated with countertops and drawers around all four walls, the pattern broken only by the doors she had just walked through and another set of doors in the opposite wall. A massive island stood in the center of the room. Its polished marble top was covered with bowls, a rolling pin, and various cinnamon roll ingredients.

Lyra was struck by the differences from the exam hall in which she had spent the previous morning. Instead of rich mahogany paneling, the kitchen walls, floor, and ceiling were all bare gray stone. While the exam hall contained a line of giant windows, the kitchen boasted only three small circular panes of glass, each barely two feet across and set in the center of the three outer walls. Peering at the window in the east wall, Lyra could just glimpse the faint pink that heralded the oncoming sunrise.

Yet, the room was brightly and cheerfully lit. Torches burned in sconces along the walls, and a hanging iron chandelier graced each of the room's four corners. All the fires burned so steadily, Lyra was sure it must be magical.

There was also magic at work in the room's temperature. Despite all the sizzling of bacon and the delicious aromas that spoke of ovens at work with breads and pastries, the air in the kitchen was pleasantly cool. Hesitantly, Lyra reached out and touched one of the walls. The stone was not only cold to the touch, but it radiated an icy aura. She pulled her hand back quickly.

"Those walls are something else, aren't they?" Chef Flax asked, noting the movement. "Powerful cooling spell. Adjusts automatically to counteract the various heat levels without and within to keep this space an even temperature constantly. Has to be renewed once a week. Otherwise, I'd be the main thing getting cooked in this room." He pulled out a handkerchief and mopped his face. "I carry my own heating around with me, you see."

Lyra nodded, but the magically regulated temperature was not the most compelling aspect of the Royal Academy kitchen. Far more impressive, in light of the extensive culinary efforts underway wherever she looked, was the absence of any other people.

"You . . . you're in here by yourself?" she asked, staring around in wonder. "You do all this work alone?"

"Salts, no." Chef Flax chuckled. "Bumble here is my sous chef."

A flurry of movement to the left made Lyra turn her head. There, whizzing back and forth between two pans of bacon, was the largest flying squirrel she had ever seen. It was at least a foot across when it spread out its arms and legs to soar from one pan to the other. A small white chef's hat sat securely atop the creature's head, standing out sharply against its bright red fur.

As Lyra watched, the flying squirrel turned over four pieces of bacon with one expert flick of a spatula. Then it darted over to another pan and sprinkled in a handful of pepper with one paw while its abnormally long tail nimbly adjusted the heat.

"Bumble!" Chef Flax called. "Come and meet Lyra!"

Bumble held up one paw in a "*just a moment*" gesture. Twisting, it launched itself across to the island in one mighty leap.

Chef Flax waved a hand. "Don't worry about the dough. Lyra here is going to help us with the next batch."

Bumble held up the "wait" paw again. Scooping flour out of a bag with the other paw, it began dusting the counter with rapid flicks, chattering amiably in squirrel language.

"Can you understand it?" Lyra whispered.

"Bits and pieces." Chef Flax sighed. "That's all I've been able to pick up over the years. Shame too. He's already a great companion, and he understands me just fine, but it would be nice to have a real conversation. I keep meaning to take lessons. One of the former students here turned out to be a bit of a dud, baking-wise, but is an absolute whiz at animal dialects. He's offered to teach me, but I never seem to have enough time."

Having dusted the counter to his satisfaction, Bumble leaped over to Chef Flax and Lyra, landing lightly on the large man's shoulder.

"Bumble, this is Lyra Treble, one of our new first years. Someday soon, she's going to explain to me how she used three of the simplest baking spells on record to create the most enjoyable cake I have ever had the pleasure of encountering."

Bumble bowed low, then leaped over to Lyra's shoulder, chattering excitedly.

"He's honored to meet you," Chef Flax translated, smiling. "I can tell you that much. He got a tiny taste of that vanilla cake too."

"The honor is entirely mine . . . Bumble," Lyra said, blushing and trying hard not to giggle as the flying squirrel's whiskers tickled her ear. "Did you give him that name, Chef?"

"Certainly not. That's his right name. First word I learned in his language. Right, Bumble?"

Chef Flax made a strange chattering noise, and Bumble made a sound in return that sounded suspiciously like a giggle.

"It's a . . . lovely name," Lyra assured the bright-eyed sous chef.

"Bit odd, of course, but don't let the name fool you," Chef Flax warned. "He's much less messy than I am. More efficient too."

Bumble chattered what Lyra guessed was confirmation of this claim.

"So, just you and Bumble." She looked around again at the multiple cook stations all going at once to produce a variety of pleasing aromas. "That's still a lot of work, isn't it?"

Bumble chattered indignantly.

"Remember that there are rarely more than fifteen people to serve at a time." Chef Flax chuckled. "The occasional banquet with invited guests, sure. But otherwise, we're a cozy family here. Just enough work to keep me and Bumble pleasantly busy." He rubbed his hands together. "Speaking of, we'd best get a move on with these cinnamon rolls. The second years are a ravenous bunch."

Bumble chattered a mournful affirmative.

"And afterwards," Chef Flax continued, "if you'd like, I could show you the greenhouse? I know the third years are giving the grand tour later, but they tend to zip through these parts of campus. Not nearly enough time to see all the good stuff."

Bumble leaped from Lyra's shoulder to a cupboard and returned a second later with a clean apron for her.

She smiled. "Let's get baking!"

CHAPTER SEVEN

Hum, Sing, Scream

By the time Lyra had her apron tied and her hair tucked under her headband, Chef Flax was already mixing ingredients for a new round of cinnamon rolls.

"Watch carefully," he said, cracking eggs into the huge bowl. "Every baker has to find their own method, but we can still learn from each other."

Bumble darted around the island countertop, collecting spices from various containers and tossing them into the bowl by tiny handfuls. He chattered to get Lyra's attention and nudged a jar of salt in her direction.

"Really?" she asked, eyeing the jar nervously. "Me?"

Bumble made a chattering noise that resembled an indignant snort. He pointed meaningfully at Lyra's apron.

"He says if you want to be a baker, you'd best do some baking," Chef Flax explained. "Wise creature."

"But . . ." Lyra hesitated, looking at the giant bowl of dough. "How much should I put in? One teaspoon? One and a half?"

Chef Flax chuckled. "I've got it taken care of. Start with a pinch, and then keep going until it's right. You'll know."

Bumble chattered encouragingly and gave Lyra's hand a *go-get-'em* pat. Summoning all her courage, she took the smallest possible pinch of salt and transferred it carefully into the mixing bowl.

A burst of pale yellowish-green light erupted from the bowl, making her jump back. Chef Flax laughed merrily while Bumble thumped his tail on the counter in appreciation.

"Great start!" Chef Flax clapped a floury hand on Lyra's shoulder. "I told you I had it covered. Just keep going until the light is a deep green, about the shade of kale. Then you'll know it's ready."

Mystified, Lyra added another pinch of salt to the bowl. The burst of light was more truly green this time, but closer to snow peas than kale. She gathered another small pinch, voicing her questions as she went.

"You're doing a spell, right? Flavor identification?"

"Something like that," Chef Flax replied. "You probably won't learn it for a while, as it's not very useful for new bakers. It requires an in-depth grasp of the specific flavor profile you're going for."

"So, you cast the spell based on that flavor profile, and then the colors show when you've reached it?" Lyra asked.

Chef beamed at her. "Exactly. Works best on a recipe you've done hundreds of times. Very helpful if you have a cold or just aren't in the mood for taste tests. Or if you don't want to measure and weigh out everything."

Bumble clambered up onto Lyra's shoulder, chattering. Chef Flax listened for a moment and nodded.

"Exactly. Also very useful for *training* new bakers. I've already cast the spell, so as long as you follow the colors, you'll be fine."

Lyra added several more pinches before the light reached the desired shade.

"That reminds me, Chef." She looked at his apron, white underneath its stains. "Why isn't your apron green? Aren't you a Flavor specialist?"

Bumble snort-chattered again, and Chef Flax chuckled. "What gave you that idea, Lyra?"

"Well . . ." Lyra concentrated on wiping the salt from her fingers onto her own white apron, internally hoping she hadn't stumbled into some baking culture faux pas. "Weren't you offered that job at the palace? Royal chef of Flavor?"

Chef Flax's eyes twinkled as he added a chunk of butter into the mixing bowl. "Only because that particular post was open at the time."

Bumble chattered a comment from his spot on Lyra's shoulder.

"Yes, yes," Chef Flax agreed. "And I apprenticed under the Flavor headmaster as a third year here at the academy. But I would have been just as happy in the other two disciplines. It just so happened that one of my fellow students loved Texture more than life, and the other was brilliant at Presentation. So I went with Flavor. Quite happily, I might add. And then, right before I graduated, the royal chef of Flavor retired."

"But you didn't take that job," Lyra said. "And you don't wear a green apron now."

Chef Flax shook his head. "I've always been impatient with these rigid divisions. Using the three disciplines to organize the curriculum is all well and good, but every baker worth their sugar knows you need all three to make anything worthwhile."

The Meringue family has always gone in for Texture.

Caramelle's words at their first meeting echoed in Lyra's thoughts. Lyra looked down at her own white apron, thinking hard. "What if you happen to be really, really good at one particular thing?" Another image crossed her mind: the chapter of complicated Texture equations at the very back of *Cakes, Magic, and You.* Lyra shuddered. "Or really, *really* bad at another?"

"Then you find a style of baking that showcases your strengths and shores up your weaknesses," Chef Flax said cheerfully. "And always spend more time with your weakest discipline. It's not fun, but it's the only way to grow."

"What's your weakest discipline, Chef?" Lyra asked, realizing too late that the question was probably rude.

He shrugged, apparently unconcerned. "Not sure, to be honest. Probably Presentation. Haven't thought about it in a while."

Lyra blinked. "Really?"

"No time." He spread his hands, indicating the many active stoves and ovens around the room. "Far more important things at hand! Not that growth isn't important," he added hastily. "I just think too many bakers waste too much time pondering those three rigid boxes, trying to make themselves fit in one. What about working hard to *combine* all three, somehow?"

Bumble leaped across to Chef Flax's shoulder, chattering emphatically.

"Bumble agrees with me." Chef Flax poked a finger affectionately at the squirrel's stomach. "We've had some good talks about the need for more inter-disciplinary baking."

Bumble chattered again, tweaking Chef Flax's ear for good measure.

"Ah. Misinterpretation on my part." He chuckled, rolling up his sleeves. "I mean, he does agree with me. I know from the past. But that's not what he's saying now. At the moment, he's more focused on the task at hand. As should we be! Time to get kneading."

Chef Flax dug his hands into the bowl, and Lyra gasped. Not just green, but blue and purple light burst from the dough in streams, interweaving around Chef's arms before traveling back down into the bowl. The tricolored light show surrounded the dough like an expertly woven living basket, pulsing as the magic brought about the desired Flavor, Texture, and Presentation elements for this stage of the recipe.

"That's—you're—" Lyra stared at the luminous dough, which was rising and proofing before her eyes. "That's all three! At the same time! How are you doing three spells at once?"

"Decades of practice," Chef Flax assured her, keeping his eyes on the bowl. "Not to be attempted by anyone with fewer gray hairs than I."

Bumble chattered indignantly.

"Any *human* with fewer gray hairs than I," Chef Flax corrected himself. "Though, my flying friend knows very well that he's as old as I am. Squirrels don't turn gray with age, you see."

"I see," Lyra said faintly. "It's just . . . I've never heard of anyone doing two spells at once. Even two from the same discipline."

"I won't say it's common. As we were just saying, the baking world is a bit fixated on keeping the disciplines separate. One at a time. Find your spot and excel in it." The motion of the chef's hands began to slow down as the colors deepened and sank into the nearly completed dough. "But most accomplished bakers *could* run a few different kinds of spells at once if they wanted to. All three of your professors are more than capable. They're just not so inclined."

Bumble leaped down onto the flour-dusted countertop and sprinkled a layer of cinnamon over a large rectangular section. Chef Flax removed his hands from the bowl, giving Lyra a smile.

"That's our cue. Time to turn this out and roll it flat! Care to do the honors?"

Trying not to shake too much with excitement, Lyra turned the magically proofed lump of dough out onto the cinnamon-floury countertop. Bumble handed her a well-floured rolling pin, and she went to work, rolling the dough into an even rectangle.

"Excellent," Chef Flax said approvingly. Bumble also gave what sounded like an affirmative in squirrel language. "Now, while you're rolling, why don't you perform that Presentation spell you used in your entrance exam? Madame Temper's Chant of Precision, correct?"

Lyra froze. "Now?"

"When else?" Chef Flax winked at her. "Not much use later, especially once the second years get their greedy paws on these rolls."

"But . . . I thought Presentation spells come at the end," Lyra said desperately. "If you're not doing them all at once, I mean. Texture first, then Flavor, then Presentation. It's the finishing touch, right?"

Bumble chatter-laughed.

"Hush, you culinary rodent," Chef Flax chided his animal companion. "Lyra's right, as far as the textbooks go. Texture, Flavor, Presentation is a practical, well-established sequence of events."

Bumble bowed apologetically, then nudged Lyra's hand, reminding her to continue rolling.

"But it's not the *only* correct method," the chef continued. "With neatness spells in particular, I've found it's very helpful to perform them throughout the process. Keeps things tidy from start to finish so you're not left trying to fix a sloppy mess at the end."

Lyra took a deep breath. "I'll try."

Taking great care to keep the rolling pin moving steadily, Lyra began mentally reciting Madame Temper's Chant of Precision. To her bewildered delight, purple sparkles immediately began appearing around her hands and swirling over the rolling pin before sinking into the dough.

Her fingers tingled. Magic was surging through the enriched dough, smoothing over any rough spots leftover after kneading, binding the ingredients together while still maintaining the light, proofed texture. Within minutes, the Chant of

Precision aligned the lump of dough into a perfectly smooth flat rectangle on the counter.

Lyra couldn't hold back a shout of joy. "It worked! I could *feel* the molecules snapping into place. You were right: it'll be so much easier to work the dough like this and keep everything neat!"

Bumble leaped straight up to Lyra's head and performed a gleeful jig that, somehow, did not put even one of her hairs out of place.

Chef Flax joined in the happy laughter, but he was also watching Lyra closely. "Do you always hum while you bake?"

Again, she froze. "Was I humming?"

"Very quietly, under your breath. Impossible to hear without standing right next to you."

"Good." Lyra sighed in relief. "I mean, I'm glad it's not noticeable. It's a bad habit of mine. I'm trying to break it, I swear. I know it's not allowed."

Chef's eyebrows rose. "Allowed? Of course it's allowed! Did you think all baking must occur in total silence?"

"It certainly felt that way yesterday at the exam, so—"

"Stop right there." Chef Flax waved his hands for emphasis. "Don't judge the baking world by the Royal Academy trials. Everyone there is wound tighter than under-proofed bread, professors included."

Lyra felt hope rising in her chest. "So . . . it's okay to hum?"

"Hum, sing, scream if you need to," Chef Flax said with a grin. "Bumble and I have full concerts sometimes. He's got a beautiful baritone that goes just right with my tenor range."

Bumble somersaulted off Lyra's head and landed neatly on one knee. Placing a paw against his heart, he sang a short line of wordless melody in a surprisingly deep voice.

Lyra wiped her flour-stained hands and applauded. "Let me know when your next show is. I'll bring my guitar!"

"That would be quite an honor," Chef Flax said solemnly. "One of the Any Weather Bards, performing in *our* kitchen!"

"You-you know the Any Weather Bards?" Lyra stammered.

"Of course! Rarely miss a show. I often go with the Berrys. Old friends, you know." He smiled. "We all think you and your family are splendid."

Lyra was too full of embarrassment and pleasure to form any coherent response other than, "Thank you. I-I'm glad I brought my guitar to school now."

Bumble twirled to express his excitement for future music-making, then scampered over to one of the spice containers. Pointing at it with one paw, he chattered animatedly.

"All right, all right." Chef Flax groaned good-naturedly. "Bumble here claims we need more cinnamon."

"Claims?" Lyra echoed.

With great effort, the flying squirrel lifted the container and staggered over to Chef Flax, displaying its near emptiness.

"Yes, yes. I'm sure it's true." Chef Flax offered a hand, which Bumble used to jump from the countertop all the way to the doors on the kitchen's opposite wall. "But it's also just an excuse to visit the greenhouse. It's his favorite spot on campus."

Lyra smiled at the small sous chef currently clinging to the door handle and waving his tail to urge them on. "Really? Why?"

Chef Flax winked. "Come and see. I told you I'd give you a tour of the greenhouse anyway." He strode to the doors, holding one of them open for Lyra to pass through.

CHAPTER EIGHT

Bumble and Sprinkle

At first glance, the Royal Academy greenhouse was a standard indoor growing space for plants. It was the same size as the kitchen, though the fully glass walls made it a completely different sort of experience. But despite the chill of the dawn light streaming through the windows, Lyra felt pleasantly warm. She didn't have to touch the glass to know that this room, like the kitchen, was under the influence of a temperature-regulating spell.

A second look at the actual plants growing in neat rows revealed that this was no ordinary greenhouse. One corner was occupied by a single massive basil plant, full and round and reaching up to the ceiling. Lyra counted four rosemary bushes, three glass cases of ginger, and two large clumps of star anise. Seven pots on a table right by the door held miniature trees, each one two feet high and bare of any leaves or fruit. They all appeared to be made entirely of cinnamon bark.

If the size and richness of the plants were not clue enough, the room's magical nature was evident in the behavior of these plants. They were in a continual state of self-harvesting. As Lyra watched, basil leaves detached from the bush in the corner and drifted down to land neatly in one of several boxes placed around the base. The rosemary was dicing itself in midair before settling in a large jar. Cinnamon shavings fell constantly from two trees, while the other five released periodic clouds of fine cinnamon dust, all falling at a precise, steady rate into a series of containers arranged around the pots.

And darting from one plant to another, clearly keeping every spell running in orderly fashion, was a flying squirrel around Bumble's size. Its fur was the faint pink color of dawn or new rosebuds, and it wore a gardening bonnet on its head, woven from golden straw.

Bumble leaped from the door handle just as this magic gardener was passing from ginger to rosemary. Lyra felt sure they would collide in midair, but instead, the two creatures caught each other by front paws and tail and swung around in a complicated dance. They landed on the table by the cinnamon trees. Sweeping off his chef's hat gallantly, Bumble planted a kiss on his companion's paw.

"Lyra," Chef Flax said with a smile, "meet Bumble's wife, Sprinkle."

Lyra took it all in stride as she bowed deeply. "It is an honor to meet you, Madame Sprinkle."

The rose-colored squirrel returned the bow, chattering in a pleased way.

"Sprinkle keeps the greenhouse in order, just like Bumble in the kitchen," Chef Flax said. "Except she's the one in charge here, far more than I am in the other room. As soon as we step through those doors, we're in her domain."

"What's that like?" Lyra gazed around at the various plants, all radiating perfect health while also harvesting themselves at a steady, even pace. "Running the greenhouse, I mean. What sorts of spells does she use?"

Both squirrels chatter-laughed. Even Chef Flax allowed himself a hearty chuckle.

"Sprinkle doesn't perform spells, Lyra. Neither does Bumble."

"But . . ." Lyra took another look at the very obviously magical greenhouse. "Then . . . how does it work?"

"Bumble and Sprinkle don't *do* magic. They *are* magic." Chef Flax pointed to the cinnamon trees. "Care to demonstrate, m'lady?"

Sprinkle leaped nimbly up to the top of one of the trees releasing intermittent clouds of cinnamon dust. Clinging with her two back paws to a branch, she twirled her tail twice, then tapped it lightly against the trunk. A pink shimmer, so faint Lyra wondered if she was imagining it, rolled over the tree. But the effect was immediate. The tree began releasing twice as much cinnamon, dust bursting from the trunk in double time and double-sized clouds.

Lyra pulled back expecting the explosion to coat them all in cinnamon, but Sprinkle was too much of an expert for that. The squirrel merely raised her hands and another pink shimmer erupted over the tree, which guided all the newly extracted cinnamon down into the jar Bumble was holding. Once the jar was full, Sprinkle's tail tapped once on the tree's trunk, and the cinnamon dust returned to its normal, slower rate of expulsion.

"She just . . . does all that? Naturally?" Lyra's voice came out as a squeak, but she couldn't help it. Her first day at the Royal Academy of Magical Baking had already filled her mind's wonder-banks to the limit, and the sun was only just beginning to rise.

"Naturally," Chef Flax confirmed. "That's how Bumble keeps things going in the kitchen too."

Lyra shook her head in admiration. "Are all flying squirrels like this?"

Bumble and Sprinkle broke into peals of chatter-laughter again.

Chef Flax hushed them, then explained, "Animals are like people. Some are good at baking. Some prefer painting, or weaving, or tailoring, or carpentry. Some are excellent winemakers, and others grow medicinal herbs. Bumble has a brother who brews the best ale I've ever tasted. These two just happen to be interested in food, both growing and preparing."

"But all are magical?" Lyra asked.

"Of course. In their own way." Chef Flax looked at her strangely. "Are you telling me you've never encountered an animal before?"

"Not many," Lyra confessed. "We've always lived here in the city."

"There are plenty of animals in the city."

Lyra shrugged helplessly. "My family doesn't get out much. We usually go from home to show venues and then back home for rehearsal. A few restaurants. I guess the bard world is pretty insulated."

Chef Flax nodded sagely. "So is the baking world, I'm afraid. But that's why it's grand to have worlds colliding! Each is enriched and expanded as a result. Sort of like yeast meeting flour."

"Or cinnamon meeting sugar," Lyra suggested.

"Exactly." Chef Flax winked. "Don't worry, Lyra. You're fitting in beautifully here."

Sprinkle chattered excitedly, then leaped to Lyra's shoulder.

"I think she wants to give us a tour." Chef Flax chuckled. "Quickly though, m'lady. We have cinnamon rolls on the go."

Lyra quickly lost all sense of time. Sprinkle gave them a whirlwind tour of the greenhouse, chattering rapidly about the various plants. It was mostly incomprehensible, but Lyra did find herself able to decipher some of the squirrel's chatters as the morning wore on. When they finally returned to the kitchen doors, for example, she could tell Sprinkle was reprimanding her husband for leaving his cinnamon rolls unattended for so long. Bumble answered only with a cheeky grin and a kiss upon his wife's cheek.

Once the three bakers were back in the kitchen, their work resumed in earnest. Chef Flax let Lyra help him fill, shape, cut, bake, and frost the cinnamon rolls. He even invited her to take the lead in some of the magical components.

"You might think that a Texture spell would be most helpful here," he said, demonstrating how to sprinkle cinnamon and brown sugar over the smooth rectangle of dough. "But I find it best to emphasize Flavor at this stage. Especially when you're rolling and cutting. A deepening charm ensures this filling really permeates the dough, so every bite has the same sweet, cinnamony taste."

Having used Madame Hazelnut's Deepening Spell for the Flavor component of her entrance exam cake, Lyra felt secure enough to perform it while rolling up the rectangle of dough into a log. It helped that she now knew she could hum while working. She even sang a bit, fitting the words of the spell to a simple tune as she cut the log into individual rolls and arranged them on a baking sheet.

It also helped her confidence that the spell was clearly working. Not only was each roll emanating the soft green glow of Flavor magic, but the air around the tray vibrated with the rich smell of cinnamon and sugar. Something deep inside Lyra resonated with the aroma, as if her own magical baking instincts were waking up to say, *"Yes. That is Flavor."*

She flatly refused, however, to attempt the Texture charm Chef Flax called for while the rolls were in the oven.

"It serves a double purpose," he coaxed. "Keeps the rolls from getting too hard or dense while baking, and since we're making the frosting at the same time, the spell works on that element also. Any fluffening charm will do. Didn't you use one for that incredible cake you made?"

"Master Pavlova's," Lyra confirmed. "But at the beginning level, and I worked out the equations specifically for a three-tiered cake. Pace, number of repetitions . . . Took me forever to get it right."

Nothing Chef Flax said could change Lyra's mind. She was content to observe while he whipped cream cheese, brown sugar, and vanilla together to form a frosting. As a compromise, he recited the Texture spell out loud, and she promised to take note of his rhythm so she could practice later.

Once the cinnamon rolls were out of the oven, it was Bumble's turn to perform some baking magic. Lyra watched, fascinated, as the flying squirrel leaped about six inches into the air. He soared back and forth over the tray so rapidly that he resembled a furry red blur. Ten seconds later, the cinnamon rolls were cool enough to be frosted.

Chef Flax insisted Lyra take over again. She obliged without hesitation and performed one more round of the Presentation spell as she covered each roll with a thick layer of frosting. Madame Temper's Chant of Precision resounded effortlessly in her mind and sent waves of efficient agility into her fingertips. Purple light sparkled around the icing spatula, guiding her hands to distribute the frosting evenly and neatly.

Bumble dusted the top of each perfectly frosted roll with a pinch of nutmeg before arranging them on plates. Then, with a simultaneous twist of Bumble's tail and Chef Flax's wrist, the plates rose into the air. The doors into the dining hall opened, and the laden plates soared out to land at their intended tables.

As soon as the second batch of cinnamon rolls went out, it was time to start another, and then another. Chef Flax was not kidding about the school's love for these particular treats, especially the second years. The kitchen walls seemed to be soundproof, so Lyra had no idea what was happening in the dining hall, but Chef Flax and Bumble seemed magically attuned. Every so often, one or both would pause, glance towards the doors, nod, and turn to accomplish whatever task was required.

Lyra was so lost in a happy baking daze that she jumped a few inches in the air when a knock sounded on the dining room doors.

"Come in, Hyacinth," Chef Flax called, not looking up from his final batch of frosting.

The doors opened to admit the tall, elegant figure of Hyacinth Roulade, third-year Texture apprentice. She crossed directly to Chef Flax, holding out a small jar with a warm smile.

"Good to see you, Chef. I brought you one of my vacation experiments, as you requested."

"Welcome back, my dear!" Chef Flax took off his hat to give Hyacinth a courtly bow, then accepted the offered jar with a grand flourish. "It's far too quiet around here without you students. What's this? Some sort of jam?"

"Preserves." Hyacinth flushed slightly. "It's a blend of mulberry, whortleberry, and raspberry. Strong, but surprisingly pleasant."

"Mulberry, whortleberry, raspberry . . . A daring combination." Chef Flax removed the jar's lid and gave an appreciative sniff, raising one eyebrow at Hyacinth roguishly. "Spent some time at the Berry household over break, I gather?"

Hyacinth flushed further, but she was saved from replying by Bumble, who leaped to her shoulder and wrapped his arms around her neck in a hug.

"I missed you too, Sir Bumble." Hyacinth laughed. "How's Lady Sprinkle?"

Bumble chattered excitedly, pointing his tail at Lyra.

"Oh! You're Lyra, right?" Hyacinth extended a hand, which Lyra shook. "It's a good thing I found you. The tour's about to start. The other first years are all gathered outside. No one was sure where you'd got to."

"Is it that time already?" Lyra scrambled to remove her apron. "Sorry. I didn't mean to keep anyone waiting! I've been here all morning."

"It's my fault, Hyacinth," Chef Flax said. "So exciting to find another kindred spirit. She's been a grand help to me. In fact, thanks to her assistance, I was able to make enough cinnamon rolls to cater the first-year tour."

He nodded at Bumble. The flying squirrel leaped from Hyacinth's shoulder down onto the counter, where the final batch of cinnamon rolls was arranged on two trays and ready for transport.

"Time well spent." Hyacinth smiled at Lyra. "And no need to apologize. We'll be right on time. See you soon, Chef! Sir Bumble! Many thanks for the snacks!"

The chef and sous chef bowed the ladies out as Lyra gave both her assurances that she would be back soon with her guitar.

As they crossed through the dining hall, each bearing a tray of cinnamon rolls, Lyra saw empty plates rise from tables and float back towards the kitchen, no doubt summoned by Chef Flax's deft magic.

Lyra smiled to herself. What was it Caramelle had said? *Bakers don't concern themselves with the service side of the industry?*

Apparently, there was no true distinction between "creation" and "service." At least, not in the case of Chef Peppercorn Flax.

And Sous Chef Bumble, of course.

CHAPTER NINE

CAMPUS TOUR

The first years were gathered outside the main hall with Razz Berry, Boysen's brother and the third-year Flavor apprentice. They were all thrilled with the gift of cinnamon rolls Lyra and Hyacinth brought, though it seemed to Lyra that Razz was mostly thrilled with the arrival of Hyacinth herself.

"You gave Flax the preserves?" he asked her as the trays passed around. "What did he think?"

Hyacinth blushed, but she was smiling. "He said the combination was . . . 'daring.'"

"He's not wrong." Razz winked at Lyra. "So, you had quite a morning! How do you like our dear head chef?"

"He's amazing," Lyra gushed. "So is Bumble. And Sprinkle."

Razz whistled. "You got the full Peppercorn Experience. Good for you. Took me weeks to get properly acquainted with those three when I first got here."

"You spent the whole morning in the kitchens, Lyra?" Boysen sounded wistful. "Wish I could've been there."

"Don't you know Chef Flax?" Lyra asked. "He said he's a friend of your family."

"Oh, sure. I've known Flax my whole life, but I've only met Bumble and Sprinkle a few times. And I've never gotten to *bake* with them."

"The kitchen is one of the first stops on the tour, Poison," Razz said cheerfully. "You'll get your chance soon enough."

Boysen threw a piece of cinnamon roll at his older brother, who managed to catch it in his mouth.

"I'll be visiting them again," Lyra told Boysen. "With my guitar. I'm sure you could come along."

"Really?" Ginger, standing next to Boysen, perked up. "What about me? Could I join?"

"And me?" Mac asked, his eyes wide and hopeful behind his glasses.

Lyra smiled. "I don't see why not. They seem to enjoy company."

"I'm sure Lyra will be too busy to spend much time in the kitchen." Caramelle accepted the tray of cinnamon rolls Hyacinth offered her and passed it to Mac without taking one. "We all will. If we want to still be here for a second term, of course."

"I don't know about that," Hyacinth said. "Chef is a great friend to have if you want to succeed in baking. Bumble too. I've learned just as much during my visits to the kitchen as I have in class."

Caramelle's eyebrows rose, but instead of replying, she pulled Lyra to one side.

"I was trying to cover for you," the auburn-haired girl whispered, while Boysen and Razz argued noisily over the largest cinnamon roll. "Remember what I said about making a good impression? You do *not* want to be known as the girl who spends all her time in the kitchen. People will start thinking of you as staff, or even"—Caramelle dropped her voice even lower, forcing Lyra to lean in close to hear the final words—"a *servant*."

"Chef isn't a servant," Lyra replied indignantly, careful to keep her voice low. "He's a chef. Isn't that what we're all hoping to be?"

Caramelle shook her head vigorously. "Not in a school. In the palace, ideally. Or in your own restaurant. But not slaving away over a hot stove, year after year, for a bunch of *students*. Have some pride, Lyra."

Before Lyra could respond, her eyes caught on the one person who could make her forget all about Chef Flax, Bumble, and even the amazing Lady Sprinkle.

"Cinnamon rolls?" Cardamom Coulis III smiled at the sight of the nearly empty trays. "I guess the tour started without me. Been to the kitchen already?"

Razz waved the third-year Presentation apprentice over. "You're right on time. These are a gift from Flax, courtesy of his new apprentice, the amazing Lyra Treble."

"Lyra's not his apprentice," Caramelle rushed to say, giving Cardamom a radiant smile. "She just agreed to help the chef out this once. She's awfully kindhearted."

Cardamom's dark eyes sparkled at Lyra. "Indeed. Very selfless of you to work all through your first morning, Miss Treble."

"It was fun," Lyra heard herself saying, then blushed at the unusually high pitch of her voice. Bringing it down to a more natural register, she went on, "Chef is incredible. I hope to go back soon."

Hyacinth held out one of the trays. "Cinnamon roll, Cardamom?"

"No, thank you."

"C'mon, Hyacinth," Razz chided her. "You know Coulis doesn't really *eat* food like the rest of us. He prefers *looking* at it."

"I eat plenty, I assure you," Cardamom said mildly. "Though, I do think looking at something beautiful is its own sort of nourishment."

"Is the tour going to begin soon?" Aniseed's icy voice rang out imperiously through the crisp midmorning air. She was standing three feet away from the group, arms folded, her raven hair as straight and still as her rigidly perfect posture. "Or shall I find a more efficient way to spend my time?"

"Of course." Hyacinth's calm tone and gracious smile smoothed over the sudden awkwardness. "We're all here, so let's get started."

She nodded to Razz, who darted up the main hall's three broad, shallow steps. Pulling one door open, he ushered the first years inside.

"This, as you know, is the main hall," Hyacinth said once they were all assembled in the foyer. She pointed at the magnificent double doors directly across from the entrance. "I'm sure you've also heard of the Great Room. Used only for graduation and a few other very special occasions. We won't be going in, I'm afraid."

Catching the look of disappointment on Lyra's face, Hyacinth smiled apologetically. "Only professors have a key. But work hard this year, and you'll get more than a glimpse. You'll get to attend our graduation ceremony."

"Not all of us," Ginger said under her breath. Lyra elbowed her, but the dark-haired girl shrugged. "Just speaking the truth."

Razz banged the two empty trays together. He had apparently polished off all the remaining cinnamon rolls single-handedly. "But who can work hard without sufficient fuel? Next stop on the tour: the kitchen. I'm sure Flax and Bumble are missing Lyra already, and I need to return these trays."

As Chef Flax had warned Lyra, the first years made only a brief pass through the kitchen and greenhouse. Still, it was a pleasant beginning to the tour. Chef Flax complimented Lyra on her exceptional baking instincts, and everyone except Aniseed was delighted with Bumble. Even Caramelle couldn't resist the furry red sous chef's charm, especially after he chattered out a lengthy sentence, which Chef Flax translated as praise of "Miss Meringue's exquisite entrance exam cake."

Sprinkle was an even bigger hit. Ginger, in particular, was fascinated by the gardening squirrel's work and by the greenhouse in general. She vowed to learn as much squirrel language as possible so she could come back and interview Sprinkle properly about the various kinds of plants and their magical care.

The only new information Lyra picked up from this part of the tour was about the Royal Academy orchard, which stood between the greenhouse and the stone wall surrounding the campus.

"It's not really fair to call it an 'orchard,' though," Razz mused, looking around the small enclosed space. "I think 'tiny collection of functional trees' would be more accurate."

"It doesn't seem tiny when you have to work in it," Cardamom said glumly.

Caramelle went very still beside Lyra. "Work? Students have to work in the orchard?"

"It's not that bad," Hyacinth assured her. "Once a term, we come out here on a Saturday to harvest. It doesn't take long at all with everyone working together. And then Chef always picks one fruit to invent some spectacular new dessert with that night, in celebration."

Razz sighed happily. "Remember the peach illusion cake, second term last year?"

"The one that looked like a peach but tasted like a blueberry cheesecake?" Cardamom frowned. "Not my favorite. I found it . . . confusing."

Razz ignored him, lost in a blissful memory. "It *floated*. Flax claims he was using Bumble's magic, but I'm pretty sure it was just the cake. Lifted by its own deliciousness . . ." He sighed again.

"Excuse me?" Mac raised his hand.

Boysen smacked his roommate on the back of the head. "Just speak, Macaron. You don't need permission."

Razz, in turn, gave Boysen a shove that nearly sent him sprawling. "Don't hit your fellow students, Poison. Bad manners."

"I was just wondering," Mac said nervously. "I see apple trees, peach trees, lemon, orange, lime, banana—and lots of different berry bushes."

"Five," Razz broke in. "Blueberry, blackberry, strawberry, cranberry . . . and, of course, everyone's favorite: *Razz*berry." He winked at Hyacinth, who rolled her eyes with an indulgent smile.

"But they're all blooming at the same time," Mac went on determinedly. "How is that possible? And who takes care of them?"

"The plants are magical, so everything's always in season," Hyacinth explained. "That's also why they don't need a lot of care. One of the royal gardeners comes around every few weeks to check on them, but that's it." She turned back to Caramelle. "Harvesting may sound like a lot of work, but it's really fun, not to mention rewarding. Trust me."

Caramelle clearly did *not* trust the third year on this particular point, but she forced her lips into a tight smile. "It will certainly be a . . . new experience."

"It's only once a term," Cardamom said, turning back towards the greenhouse as if he couldn't bear the sight of the orchard any longer. "Shall we move on to the parts of campus where they'll actually be spending most of their time?"

"By all means." Hyacinth smiled encouragingly. "Who's ready for some classrooms?"

Following Cardamom, who couldn't seem to get away from the area fast enough, the group passed back through the greenhouse. Lyra waved at Chef Flax and Bumble as they trooped through the kitchen. Pausing in the dining hall just long enough to give a brief history of the academy's first set of professors, who had held the first class *in* the dining hall centuries before, Hyacinth led the group back into the foyer and up one of the staircases to the second floor.

Rushing ahead, Razz opened the first door on the left and stood back with a bow. "Behold, the Flavor classroom!"

Lyra looked around the airy room, caught between excitement and apprehension. The Flavor lab was a miniature version of the exam hall. Two rows of three workstations each took up most of the space and faced a larger teacher workstation elevated on a small platform at the front. Behind the professor's counter, a vast blackboard covered the entire wall. Large windows lined the wall across from the door, letting in plenty of bright sunshine.

"You'll be starting your classes here tomorrow." Razz jumped onto the teacher's platform and perched nonchalantly on the workstation counter. "With all three professors. First years begin and end the week in a full tribunal."

Hyacinth didn't have to move. All she did was glare at the irrepressible Berry, and he hopped down from the platform with a sheepish grin.

"It's not a tribunal," she said. "Monday mornings, the professors meet with you all together to explain what the week's focus will be. Then you have a class with each professor individually."

"Flavor, Texture, and Presentation," Cardamom inserted. He turned a dazzling smile on the first-year group, making Lyra's heart spin faster than an electric whisk. "Save the best for last."

Razz booed loudly. Hyacinth ignored both boys and continued, "Tuesday, Wednesday, and Thursday will be full lab days. You'll spend all of Tuesday in this room working on Flavor with Professor Honeycomb."

"And me," Razz added, rubbing his hands together as if devising all manner of mischief. Before Hyacinth could reprimand him, he pointed to the ceiling. "Wednesdays are Texture days. Third floor, with The Puff . . . and the great Apprentice Baker Roulade, of course."

"And every Thursday," Cardamom said grandly, "Professor Genoise and I will guide you through the mysteries of Presentation. On the *top* floor."

Hyacinth shook her head, but persevered. "Fridays are for debriefing. You'll go to Flavor, Texture, and Presentation. Then all the professors will meet you in the Presentation classroom to share any final thoughts on the week and give you homework assignments for the weekend. Any questions?"

Mac started to raise his hand, then caught Boysen's eye and quickly lowered it.

"My roommate has a question," Boysen announced.

"If there's only one classroom per floor," Mac said, "then what are all those other rooms for? I saw a lot of doors."

"Practice kitchens," Hyacinth replied. "Lots of them, on every floor. Between this building and the dorms, you'll never be in want of a free workspace. And the bottom floor has a library." She smiled at Mac. "Excellent question."

Emboldened by her smile, Mac launched another query. "Are all the class-rooms alike?"

"Yes, but don't take our word for it." Razz headed to the door, waving for the group to follow. "This is a tour, isn't it? Let's get a move on. We've got two more floors to cover."

Most of the group turned back towards the door, but Aniseed didn't move. She stood by the teacher's platform, arms still folded, surveying the room like it was a lump of dough she couldn't wait to knead into submission.

"My ancestor was the first royal chef of Flavor," she announced to no one in particular. "Before the academy was even founded. Lord Saline Mint. I believe they named this room after him."

"Really?" Hyacinth sounded genuinely interested. "I didn't know any of the classrooms had names."

"They don't," Razz said. "Not anymore. Or if they do, no one uses them."

"It's still an incredible accomplishment," Hyacinth said hastily. "But I can see why we started referring to the rooms according to the discipline. It's easier to say 'the Flavor classroom' than . . ."

She looked at Aniseed questioningly.

"The Lord Saline Mint Space for the Education of Magical Flavor," Aniseed supplied, her voice clipped and cold.

"Doesn't that just roll off the tongue?" Caramelle smiled sweetly. "I can't imagine why we don't use the full title. Perhaps no one associates the name 'Mint' with Flavor these days."

The temperature in the classroom seemed to drop by several degrees. Aniseed sneered at Caramelle, but before she could deliver whatever verbal missile she was concocting, Cardamom raised his hands.

"History is important," he said smoothly, his rich voice even more effective than Hyacinth's at dispelling tension. "Not to mention fascinating. But baking is also about the future. Let's move on to the other floors, shall we? I've prepared a small demonstration in the Presentation classroom of how my chosen discipline can help you break new ground in the baking world."

Hyacinth's eyebrows rose. "A demonstration? Well done, Cardamom. Going above and beyond for our first years."

"Better make it quick, Coulis." Razz led the group out the door, then stopped in the hall to turn back and wiggle his eyebrows conspiratorially. "Because after the classrooms . . . it's time to meet Queen Penelope."

CHAPTER TEN

QUEEN PENELOPE

W ho's Queen Penelope?" Lyra whispered to Boysen as the group left the Flavor classroom.

"No idea," he replied.

"Didn't your brothers ever tell you?" Lyra persisted, following Razz upstairs to the third floor. "Or your parents?"

He shook his head. "They talked about her, sure, but always in hushed tones. I think my parents gave my brothers strict instructions to preserve at least some of the academy's mystery. They want all their boys to have the full first-year experience."

"All those who get in, of course," Caramelle said sweetly.

"Four out of four so far," Ginger pointed out. "I'd say the Berry parents have cause to be confident."

"Didn't your parents come here too, Caramelle?" Lyra asked.

The auburn-haired girl tossed her head. "Of course."

"Did they ever mention Queen Penelope?"

"Never. Perhaps it's a new addition to the academy? A portrait of a royal benefactress, long deceased?"

Ginger laughed. "Wrong on both counts, Meringue. Queen Penelope is very much alive, and she was here during my dad's time. He told me all about her."

"Then who is she?" Lyra persisted.

"Not a word!" Razz called to Ginger, apparently having overheard the whole conversation. "Your name is Crumble, right? Don't spoil this day for me, Crumble. I've been looking forward to this for two long years: Poison meeting Queen Penelope. Ruin it, and I will *crumble* you."

Ginger nodded solemnly. "My lips are sealed."

"Traitor," Lyra and Boysen said in unison.

"What?" Ginger shrugged. "He's been waiting for two years. And he threatened to turn me into a disappointing baked-fruit dessert. No, thank you."

"I like rhubarb crumble," Mac said suddenly. Unlike Razz, he appeared to have been only half listening to the rest of the group. Staring at Caramelle, he went on, "But only with a meringue topping. Meringue makes everything more elegant . . ."

By this time, the tour had reached the third floor. Boysen took the opportunity to "accidentally" step on Mac's foot, calling him back to reality just in time for Razz to usher them all inside the Texture classroom.

"Behold the domain of The Puff," Razz said grandly. "As you can see, exactly identical to the domain of The Honeycomb."

"But the door is blue," Boysen observed. "The door on the Flavor classroom is green."

Razz applauded. "Poison knows his colors. Good boy, Poison."

Hyacinth silenced him with another look, then turned to the rest of the group. "I'm sure you are all aware of the baking discipline colors. The doors are the main way we differentiate among the classrooms here. Flavor is green, Texture is blue—"

"And Presentation is purple," Cardamom finished. "Shall we proceed to the top floor?"

Another flight of stairs later, Lyra noted the Presentation classroom was an exact replica of its Flavor and Texture counterparts, except for two key differences. One was the bright purple door, which seemed to exude its own glow of refined luxury. The other was a display of six cupcakes arranged on the teacher's workstation at the front of the room.

These cupcakes were, without a doubt, the most elegant desserts Lyra had ever seen. They were all exactly identical, from the conveniently moderate size to the elaborate swirl of frosting on top. Somehow, they also all radiated the same polished air as the classroom's purple door.

Lyra knew at once that the primary cupcake flavor was vanilla and that the frosting was lightly spiced with cardamom. Not only could she tell by sight, but those same baking instincts that had started speaking to her in the kitchen with Chef Flax were still awake, giving her details about any baked goods she encountered. It was an exciting development, albeit rather overwhelming. She just hoped she could learn to control it soon.

"I've been experimenting with a particular category of Presentation spells," Cardamom explained as they all gathered around the cupcakes. "The one dedicated to *preserving*."

He already had Lyra's full attention, but at the word "preserving," she leaned forward. *Cakes, Magic, and You* had contained very little information about the higher levels of Presentation magic. She knew preserving spells were the final step, designed to lock in all other magic and keep the food fresh, and that they were desperately tricky. That was it.

Cardamom produced two long silver spoons from one of his apron pockets. Lyra noted rapidly that this apron, a pale lavender color to denote Cardamom as a Presentation apprentice, was as spotless as the rest of his attire. She also noticed the instruments he held resembled Professor Genoise's, though less elaborately carved.

"I baked these cupcakes this morning and layered in a variety of Presentation charms." Cardamom raised the two spoons over the cupcakes. "Now for the finishing touch."

Slowly at first, then with increasing speed, he began waving the spoons over the row of cupcakes. Streams of purple light instantly began pouring from the spoons. As Cardamom's movements grew faster, the streams wove together, creating an elaborate network of shimmering magic that nearly covered the entire countertop.

The spell went on for three solid minutes. By the end, Cardamom's hands were moving so fast that Lyra couldn't track their pattern. The dome of shining purple magic was so thick and bright that she could barely see the cupcakes anymore.

Finally, Cardamom brought the two spoons together and tapped the top of the glowing purple dome. Everyone gasped and turned away, blinking at the resulting flash of light. When they could see again, they realized each cupcake was now encased in its own orb of shimmering translucent purple radiance.

Cardamom picked one up, and everyone gasped again. His fingers weren't making contact with the cupcake at all. The orb itself sat in his palm, while the cupcake hovered inside, untouchable and perfect.

"The ultimate preserving spell," he announced in a voice brimming with pride. "Nothing can ruin this cupcake. Most of these charms only last a day or two, but I'm developing mine to last for months. Years, even. Forever is the goal."

He began distributing the cupcakes to the first years, who all received them with suitably grateful awe.

All except Boysen.

"Can you *eat* it?" he asked, staring dubiously at the inaccessible dessert he'd just been handed.

"Not while the spell lasts," Cardamom replied. "Like I said, nothing can get through this spell. Not hands, nor utensils, nor teeth."

"But . . ." Boysen looked around at his classmates for support, but they were all engrossed by the orbs of purple magic in their hands. "Doesn't that kind of miss the point?"

Cardamom paused in his cupcake distribution to give Boysen a condescending smile. "Depends on what the 'point' of baking is for you. To me, baking is an art. I got tired of spending hours creating masterpieces that were then devoured in seconds. I decided to make something both beautiful *and* durable so it can be seen and enjoyed by more people."

He handed the final cupcake to Lyra with a wink. "True art should be appreciated."

"I couldn't agree more," Caramelle said quickly.

Boysen shook his head. "I still don't see the point of making food that no one can actually eat."

"Spoken like a true Flavor nut," Cardamom said dismissively, depositing the silver spoons back into his apron pocket.

"Spoken like a true Berry, you mean." Razz clapped his brother on the shoulder. "Don't try to understand Coulis, Poison. Or any Presentation paragons. You'll strain something."

"Every discipline has its own focus," Hyacinth said calmly. "Cardamom, that was truly impressive. Thank you for the demonstration."

Hyacinth led the first years in a round of applause, to which Cardamom responded with a gracious bow. Then she turned to the door, smiling at Razz. "Looks like the wait is over. Care to lead the way?"

"Would I?" he crowed. "Follow me, firsties!"

The group could barely keep up as Razz bounded down the hall and up the stairs, which ended at a large wooden door. The door had no lock or handle that Lyra could see. Reaching into his pale green apron, Razz pulled out his own long silver spoon and performed a series of rhythmic taps.

The door swung open noiselessly. Stepping through, Lyra found herself on the roof of the main hall. She blinked at the influx of bright sunshine, then blinked again, hardly able to process what she was seeing.

They had emerged inside a large glass dome that dominated the center of the roof. Lyra knew there was a dome, of course, but she had always assumed this area served as a conservatory-type lounging area, or perhaps even another greenhouse for the academy kitchens.

This glass dome, however, was neither greenhouse nor conservatory.

Instead, it appeared to be the residence of one enormous chicken.

Lyra blinked a third time. Yes, that was definitely a chicken, though it was so large that Lyra didn't see how it could move. Then again, perhaps it never had to? It certainly looked like it was comfortably settled on the raised dais at the center of the dome, surrounded by silken pillows and soft fleece blankets. Its feathers, ranging in color from bright orange to rich mahogany brown, gleamed with cleanliness and health. This was clearly a creature who wanted for nothing.

The massive bird, which was at least five feet tall even when roosting, looked up when they entered. It made a loud squawking noise, something like a combination of a normal chicken clucking and the bellowing of a foghorn.

Razz responded with a deep, formal bow. Then he turned to face the group, spreading his arms wide.

"First years, meet Queen Penelope."

The bird nodded regally. Lyra now saw that there was, indeed, a tiny crown on its head, as befitted royal poultry.

Most of the first years copied Razz's bow. Aniseed, however, seemed frozen in shock.

"Queen Penelope is . . . a chicken?" she asked, her tone shrill with incredulity.

Queen Penelope squawked again, at a lower pitch that resonated with displeasure.

"Queen Penelope is not a chicken," Razz exclaimed indignantly. "She is a *treasure*. A legend." He nudged his brother. "What do you think?"

Boysen was staring at the giant bird with wide-eyed wonder. "Better than anything I imagined."

"But what does it do?" Aniseed asked, dropping her voice to a whisper. "Does it lay eggs?"

"*She* doesn't have to 'do' anything," Ginger said hotly. "She is a *queen*. Just by existing, she contributes more to this school than any stuffy Lord What's-His-Face."

"And she *does* lay eggs." Once again, Hyacinth stepped in before the tension could reach a breaking point. "The best eggs in the kingdom. Queen Penelope supplies all the academy's eggs, both for baking and consumption."

Hyacinth went on to explain that Queen Penelope had been residing on the academy roof for as long as anyone alive could remember. No one knew how old the bird actually was, or if she even aged. Year in, year out, she produced top-quality eggs at a consistent daily rate. She required no compensation or care other than a steady diet, which the academy was glad to provide.

"What does she eat?" Caramelle had been uncharacteristically quiet, but Lyra could tell even The Meringue was impressed by the magical bird.

Razz grinned. "Sweets. Cookies, cakes, pies, candied fruit—as long as it's full of sugar, she gobbles it down. Flax keeps her well contented, but she loves gifts from students as well. Bring a sufficiently sweet tribute, and she'll reward you with a dozen *extra*-premium-quality eggs for your own personal use. Speaking of . . ."

He winked at Hyacinth, who crossed the room to kneel by the dais. Pulling a jar from her sky-blue apron pocket, she presented it to the magnificent bird.

"Some preserves for you, Queen Penelope. Thank you again for those eggs at the end of last year. They made all the difference in my final exam custard."

Queen Penelope cooed graciously, then swept up the jar in one massive wing. After removing the top with surprising dexterity, she poked her beak inside. Every single feather shivered once as she made a jubilant squawking sound.

"I think she likes it," Razz said, giving Hyacinth another wink. "Told you."

Boysen turned to Lyra. "Amazing, huh?"

Lyra nodded slowly. "Incredible. This whole place . . ." She sighed, her shoulders suddenly drooping.

"What's wrong?" Boysen asked, catching the shift in mood.

"It's just . . ." Lyra struggled to find words, resisting the impulse to sing her thoughts. "This morning has been so wonderful. Chef Flax, and Bumble, and Sprinkle, and now Queen Penelope. And the baking. I got to *bake*! In the kitchen!"

"At the Royal Academy of Magical Baking." Boysen smiled. "Imagine that."

"I love it here," Lyra confessed. "Already. I don't want to leave. But tomorrow there's class. Including *Texture*." She shuddered. "Today's been so great, but the scary part is coming."

His smile widened. "Is that all? No need to fear tomorrow, Treble. Remember what we're here to do?"

"Become better bakers?" she suggested.

"Exactly. We're here to learn. Sure, tomorrow's going to be a lot of work. So is every day after that. But work isn't scary." His brown eyes shone with so much cheery warmth that she couldn't help but return his smile. "Tomorrow, Lyra . . . tomorrow is when the *real* fun begins."

CHAPTER ELEVEN

Gut, Mind, Heart

Thanks to Caramelle, Lyra was fifteen minutes early to her first class at the Royal Academy of Magical Baking. The two girls had rushed through breakfast at the first-year table in the dining commons before dashing to claim the prime workstations in the Flavor classroom. After that, there was nothing left to do but stare out the window and wait.

By the time the other students began to arrive, Lyra was so deep in a daydream that Boysen had to snap his fingers in front of her face to get her attention.

"There you are," he said cheerfully, leaning against her counter. "Missed you at breakfast."

Lyra smiled. It was nearly impossible *not* to smile when Boysen was smiling. "Caramelle wanted an early start."

Boysen nodded. "Aha. So, other than short, how was your second night in the hallowed halls of the academy?"

"Splendid. Surprisingly restful."

"And what's so surprising about a good night's sleep?"

"I didn't think I'd be able to sleep at all," she confessed. "Big day today, you know."

He nodded again, his eyes full of understanding. "But you managed it? No doubt thanks to Chef Flax's excellent meal. I, for one, dreamed about that mushroom gravy all night."

"Me too." Lyra neglected to add that Cardamom Coulis III had also featured prominently in most of her dreams the night before. Somehow, that just didn't seem like something to share with Boysen. Instead, she swiftly went on, "The dessert was a nice touch. I didn't expect them to serve our entrance exam cakes."

"They do that every year the night before classes start," Boysen said. "But I agree. Real confidence boost. Even if my brothers did ruin the surprise for me."

A bustle sounded at the door, and Boysen groaned. "And speaking of the ruin of all good things . . ."

Razz Berry strolled into the classroom, followed shortly by Professor Honeycomb.

"Good morning!" the professor trilled cheerily. Her gray curls were tied up in a green scarf to match her green Flavor master's apron. "Glad to see you are all getting off to a good, punctual start. They'll keep us on our toes, won't they, Razz?"

Razz folded his arms, giving the six first years a mischievous grin. "I'm sure they will, Professor."

The other two professors and their apprentices all arrived moments later, and Lyra's first day at the academy was officially underway.

"Flavor, Texture, and Presentation." Professor Genoise's rich voice filled the airy room, commanding attention without any need for strident force or obnoxious volume. "The three principles of baking. They are the foundation of this academy and also its guiding lights."

Professor Puff spoke even more quietly, but Lyra felt every crisp word vibrate in her bones. "We aim to help you discover which principle is your specialty while shoring up any deficiencies you may have in the other two."

"The first step in this journey of discovery is understanding where each principle lives in you," Professor Honeycomb concluded cheerily. "This is where we start putting our new apprentices to work. Apprentice Baker Berry, could you tell me where in the body Flavor lives?"

Razz didn't hesitate. "The gut. It's that feeling you get when you put two ingredients together. You can't always explain why they do or don't work together, but you just know."

"Exactly." Professor Honeycomb's blue eyes twinkled merrily at him as she turned back to the first years. "Flavor is a matter of instinct."

"Texture, on the other hand, is a primarily intellectual discipline," Professor Puff said. "Apprentice Baker Roulade, where does Texture live?"

"Texture lives in the mind," Hyacinth replied, her voice calm and confident. "Science and math come into play as much as magic."

Professor Puff nodded, and Professor Genoise took up the thread. "That leaves Presentation, of course. Apprentice Baker Coulis, tell us about your chosen discipline."

"Certainly, Professor." Cardamom gave Professor Genoise a small bow, then flashed a dazzling smile at the room in general. "Presentation lives in the heart. Each baker brings their own unique personality to every creation. If three bakers, all with equal aptitude, use the same Presentation spell, they will have three very different outcomes. Presentation is where your style can truly shine through."

To Lyra's astonishment, Cardamom looked right at her. His eyes were smiling. "This is where you make your mark."

"Just be careful to keep those marks on the baked goods, not yourself," Razz cut in dryly. "How many times last year did you accidentally dye your nose pink, Coulis?"

Cardamom didn't even miss a beat. "Fewer times than we had to evacuate the dormitory thanks to your noxious Flavor experiments, Berry."

Professor Genoise chuckled, and even Professor Puff smiled delicately.

"As you can see, we have a lot of fun here." Professor Honeycomb's grin was so wide that it reminded Lyra of Chef Flax. "But we also take our work very seriously."

Professor Puff nodded. "The Royal Academy of Magical Baking has a historic commitment to excellence. All of you have won a place here by demonstrating your own commitment as well as a determination to grow."

"You worked to attain the seats you now occupy because you want to become better bakers," Professor Genoise said, taking up the thread. "Not just better, but the best. Our pledge is to help you achieve that goal."

"We pledge to help you become the best bakers you can possibly be." Professor Puff raised her long silver Texture spoon as if actually taking an oath. "We will do all in our power to cultivate your growth in the three principles of baking."

Professor Genoise produced his own elaborately carved tools and pointed at each first year in turn. "Today, and indeed this entire first week, is about laying a foundation for that growth. We will be starting at a very basic level, but I adjure you to give each task your utmost."

"That's right," Professor Honeycomb said brightly. "My colleagues and I need to assess your current levels in the three disciplines so we may know how best to guide you beyond those levels. Any questions?"

The Flavor professor looked around, but Lyra and her classmates all remained silent.

"Then, my esteemed colleagues, I bid you farewell." Professor Genoise bowed deeply to the other two professors and then to the first years. Cardamom followed his example. "We shall see you this afternoon."

Professor Puff merely nodded at the group. "And I shall see you later this morning."

As soon as the Texture and Presentation professors had left the room with their apprentices, Professor Honeycomb turned to the first years with another broad grin. "Well then, Aspiring Bakers. After our little speech, all of you should be able to tell me, as one: where in the baker does Flavor live?"

Six voices responded, "Gut."

"That's right." Professor Honeycomb beamed at them. "Gut is instinct. That's the primary skill you must develop to master this baking principle. Which is tricky because instinct can't exactly be taught. The best we can do is give you plenty of opportunities to practice. Right, Apprentice Baker Berry?"

Razz nodded. "Lots of repetition. That's the only way to cut through all the other noise and consistently hear what your gut is saying. It's true that you can't learn instinct, but you *can* learn how to listen to what you already have."

"Very well put, Berry. Thank you." Professor Honeycomb turned back to the class, her kind face suddenly stern. "Lots of repetition. Learning to recognize the instinct you already possess and to act upon it. That is why we will not be using any magic in Flavor this first term."

A collective gasp went up from the six first-year students. Caramelle's hand shot into the air at the same time as Aniseed's.

"Save your breath." Razz chuckled. "She's not going to change her mind. And you don't want her to. Trust me. This method works."

"No Flavor spells?" Aniseed's voice rang out anyway from the back row. "You are refusing to teach us magic?"

"Magic can only get you so far in Flavor," Professor Honeycomb stated. "In this baking principle, think of spells as decorative icing. They enhance the finished product but cannot mask any underlying structural errors. You must have something to build upon first."

"Trust me," Razz repeated. "Or, rather, trust her. Professor Honeycomb knows what she's doing."

"Thank you for the vote of confidence, Berry. Now, all gather round." The professor waved a hand, inviting the group towards her workstation. "We're starting up here today."

She inspected them all as they made their way to the front of the room. Lyra straightened her light-brown tunic and smoothed the crisp white apron that marked her as a first-year student, wondering how long the outfit would stay in its pristine condition.

Not long, she thought ruefully. *And we're all responsible for our own laundry. I wonder if there's a special class on getting out cooking stains?*

"Grand," Professor Honeycomb said, nodding in approval. "All in your uniforms, I see. Hopefully, we won't do too much damage to them today."

She winked at Lyra, as if she had read her anxious laundry thoughts. Then she indicated six small bowls of identical brown powder arranged neatly on her workstation.

"To begin, I'll need a volunteer. I have used a spell of my own invention to distill six distinct flavors into powdered form. Who can tell me what flavors we have here?"

"I can," Aniseed's voice rang out imperiously.

Without waiting for confirmation, she stepped forward. Lifting the first bowl, she sniffed delicately. Her face went blank. She dabbed her smallest finger into the powder and touched it to her tongue. She closed her eyes.

Several long seconds passed.

"Rum," she announced finally, opening her eyes. "Infused with toasted brown sugar."

Professor Honeycomb shook her head. "Wrong. You're overthinking this. A good effort, though. Anyone else?"

Razz pointed at Boysen. "My brother can do it, Professor."

"Very well." Professor Honeycomb nodded at Boysen. "Aspiring Baker Berry?"

Boysen stuck his hands in his pockets, shifting awkwardly from foot to foot beside Lyra. "That's all right, Professor. I'm sure someone else would like to try."

"Come on, Poison." Razz thumped the countertop. "Don't be shy. Give the good people what they want."

Professor Honeycomb shot Razz a warning glance, but she was smiling as she turned back to Boysen. "I do insist, Aspiring Baker Berry."

Boysen took a deep breath, then smiled. "Sure thing, Professor."

Keeping his hands in his pockets, he leaned down and took a quick whiff of the bowl Aniseed had sampled.

"Vanilla," he said instantly.

Professor Honeycomb beamed. "Correct!" Her blue eyes, surrounded by a network of laughter wrinkles, swept over the other five students. "First lesson," she announced. "The most popular flavors are popular for a reason. Don't let the contempt of familiarity blind you to those flavors' complexity and potential."

She turned back to Boysen with a small bow. "Proceed, Aspiring Baker Berry."

Boysen took one more whiff of vanilla. "It's my favorite," he said, winking at Lyra. Then he leaned over the next bowl and inhaled deeply. "Almond."

Professor Honeycomb nodded. "Correct."

He walked around the table, keeping his hands in his pockets. He had barely tilted his head towards the third bowl before he quickly stepped back, wrinkling his nose. "Star anise. Whew, that's strong."

"It is an intense flavor," Professor Honeycomb agreed.

The fourth bowl, also, seemed overpowering when Boysen announced the answer without even inclining his head towards it. "Ginger." Boysen looked at Professor Honeycomb, his eyes twinkling. "I think I'm on to you, Professor."

"Is that so?" Professor Honeycomb's eyes widened innocently. "Well, why don't you finish the course properly, just in case you're wrong."

Grinning broadly, Boysen rounded the table to examine the final two bowls. He inhaled deeply from both.

"Caramel," he said, removing his hands from his pockets to point at the fifth bowl. "And the last, of course, is yours truly: the humble boysenberry." He bowed, then began clapping vigorously. "Brava, Professor! You've captured the flavors of *us*!"

"What?" Lyra asked, startled out of her nervous first-day-of-school silence. "The flavors of 'us'?"

Boysen pointed at each bowl, then to the corresponding classmate. "Boysenberry for me. Caramel for Miss Meringue. Ginger for our own Ginger Crumble. Almond for Macaron. Star anise for Aniseed. And the vanilla is for you, Lyra Treble."

"Since you used vanilla in such exemplary fashion in your cake, my dear," Professor Honeycomb explained. "I've been starting the first term with this little exercise for years now. It's usually easy, what with the silly baking names in abundance these days. I thought choosing a flavor for you would be difficult, but then I remembered that cake of yours . . ." Professor Honeycomb lifted her eyes in a silent moment of exultant memory before continuing on, "Recognizing flavors is a vital skill for any baker. I shall be working to develop all of your palates this year. And speaking of developed palates, let's all give a round of applause to Aspiring Baker Berry for that impressive demonstration."

Five students, Razz included, clapped dutifully. Aniseed folded her arms.

"But recognizing flavors is only the first step," Professor Honeycomb went on. "The next is much trickier: *combining* flavors. That is the task for the rest of today's lesson."

She nodded to Razz, who opened a cupboard and began pulling out small trays, each laden with six bowls full of identical powder.

"I have a set of first-year flavors for each of you. These bowls are clearly labeled, to avoid confusion." She smiled at Aniseed, who scowled in return. "Over the next hour, I expect you to make me a batch of cookies containing all six flavors."

"All six?" Ginger squeaked. "Together?"

Professor Honeycomb continued as if she hadn't heard. "You'll find the ingredients for basic shortbread at your workstations. Your proofing drawers have all been enchanted to chill your dough in thirty seconds. Apprentice Baker Berry is distributing the flavor trays. I encourage you to start by just mixing the powders in different ratios before jumping straight to the shortbread dough. You'll move faster, and you'll also get to practice listening to your gut instead of relying on taste. Experiment. Keep an open mind."

She smiled winningly at the six students. Lyra didn't know about minds, but everyone's mouth was certainly hanging open.

"In one hour, we'll all try everyone's cookies, and we'll learn how these unlikely friends can work together."

"If," Ginger said under her breath. "*If* they can."

Caramelle's lips were pursed so tightly together, her mouth had almost disappeared. Mac was sweating. Aniseed was practically vibrating with discontent. Only Boysen seemed unconcerned.

Professor Honeycomb winked at them. "Apprentice Baker Berry and I will be circling to watch your progress, but don't ask us for any help. You are, of course, free to consult with each other. One hour on the clock, and—go!"

CHAPTER TWELVE

PERSONALITY POWDERS

The six students scurried to their workstations. Lyra could hear Aniseed muttering to herself as she swept by, something about "disgrace" and "amateur." Across the aisle, Caramelle was standing at her counter, staring at the six powders as if they were about to sprout tentacles.

"Scared?"

Lyra glanced around to find Boysen at the workstation behind her, grinning.

"Terrified," she admitted. "Which you wouldn't understand, being the Flavor King and all."

"Flavor King? Salts, I hope not." He leaned forward across the counter, beckoning her to come closer. "Combining flavors is tricky, but it's also subjective," he whispered conspiratorially. "It's all about finding something you *like*. Mix a bit of this and a bit of that until you have a combination you'd actually enjoy eating."

Lyra stared at him. "Simple as that?"

"Simple as that. Remember: at the end of the day, we're all just trying to make something for people to eat. Something they'll *enjoy* eating." Boysen leaned back, rolling up his sleeves. "Start with yourself. Make some cookies *Lyra* would enjoy, and you're home free."

She glanced down at his collection of powders and scrunched her nose. "Lyra would not choose to include star anise in any form."

"Hey, Professor Honeycomb only said we have to use all the flavors." Boysen pulled a medium-sized bowl from one of his drawers. "She didn't say how much."

Lyra turned back to her own workstation and her own collection of personality powders.

Experiment. Keep an open mind.

It's all about finding something you like.

Make some cookies Lyra would enjoy.

She took a deep breath. "Here goes nothing." Then she pulled out her own mixing bowl and started trying out ratios.

Her first idea was to include equal amounts of all six flavors. She knew it was a disaster by the fourth personality powder. Vanilla and caramel and almond worked fine together, but ginger overwhelmed everything. Lyra almost felt her nose hairs burning. She couldn't even bring herself to add the boysenberry, let alone the star anise. She discarded the powders, washed out the bowl, and tried again.

For the second attempt, she tried starting with a tiny bit of boysenberry and ginger, then layering the milder flavors in moderate amounts. This worked well until she got to star anise. Even the most minuscule pinch of Aniseed's personality powder soured the entire bowl. Lyra threw the mixture out with a sigh and started again.

At least she knew her instincts were working. She had noticed them most strongly in the kitchen with Chef Flax, but now that she knew what they were, Lyra realized they had always been there. Even before the academy trials, when she was just baking for fun, she had felt her gut nudging her towards certain combinations and proportions.

Now, every time she tossed a bit of powder into the mixing bowl, she felt a stirring deep inside her, registering varying degrees of approval or dismay. There was no spell to communicate Flavor progress in shades of green light, but Lyra's gut was speaking. Her instincts were singing.

Maybe I really can be a baker, after all.

These instincts were emphatic in their rejection of Lyra's third attempt, which involved pitting spoonfuls of ginger and star anise against each other. They were even more horrified by her fourth effort. She had thought a healthy dose of boysenberry could drown out the harsher qualities of star anise, but the result made her skin crawl. Her gut actually shuddered as she washed the offensive mixture down the drain and began again.

Time began to fly by as her workstation gradually deteriorated into a powdery mess. Lyra was deep into failed attempt number twelve when a voice at her ear made her jump.

"What are you humming?"

Razz was standing by her workstation, looking at her curiously.

"W-was I humming?" Lyra stammered. "I'm sorry. Habit. Didn't even realize it. I can stop. I don't want to disturb—"

Razz waved his hand. "No worries. The Honeycomb didn't say anything about working silently. I just thought I recognized the tune. Boysen mentioned you're part of the Any Weather Bards, right?"

Lyra nodded. "With my parents and three brothers."

"I love your shows," Razz said. "My whole family goes whenever we can. Maybe that's where I heard . . . What were you humming?"

"It's a song about singing," Lyra told him. "How fun it is to get together with a group of people and sing. It's called 'All Gather Round.'" She laughed. "I just realized—Professor Honeycomb said that earlier. Must've put the song in my head."

"Well, don't let me stop you." Razz backed away. "I only got one bite of that cake you made for your entrance exam. Cardamom hogged it all."

Lyra's heart leaped up to her throat. She tried to speak around it. "He-he did?"

"Greedy fellow. He usually prefers *looking* at food, but he scarfed that cake down. Can't blame him, though." Razz turned, waving his hand. "Back to work with you. I can't wait for another Lyra Treble creation."

Lyra looked down at the collection of powders in her experiment bowl, wrinkling her nose. "Don't hold your breath."

Still, the words "Cardamom hogged it all" were fluttering around her head like overexcited baby birds. They made her heart race, but the adrenaline boost was invigorating.

She could keep going. She had to. She wasn't going to crumple under the weight of her first real Royal Academy of Magical Baking assignment. Not when there was someone who had hogged her creation.

After washing out her bowl for the twelfth time, Lyra tried again.

The thirteenth experiment was even worse than the twelfth. Fourteen through sixteen were just as foul. But the seventeenth brought a smile to Lyra's lips.

I could eat that, she thought, her gut purring in agreement. *I could eat a whole plate of that.*

Humming, she turned to the much easier task of whipping together shortbread dough.

"That's an hour!" Professor Honeycomb called some time later, just as Lyra's shortbread came out of the oven. "Everyone, bring a plate of your Flavor creations up here. We'll all sample together."

Lyra hastily transferred her cookies to a plate and joined her five classmates at the front of the room. Professor Honeycomb looked around at them, beaming her usual cheery smile.

"I see you've all managed to produce a batch of shortbread. Well done. Now, let's see how you've got on with your flavors. Ginger, would you pass your plate around, please?"

Compared to the judging process from the final entrance exam, Lyra found this communal cookie-tasting remarkably enjoyable. They all agreed Ginger's cookies were pleasant, but the star anise and boysenberry flavors were conspicuously absent. Mac's cookies were all over the place. "Feels more like a battleground than a dessert," Razz commented. "Six flavors all fighting for their position."

Caramelle's cookies, on the other hand, were a hostile takeover of one overwhelming flavor.

"Far, far too much caramel," Professor Honeycomb said. "Cloyingly sweet. Your namesake is a lovely flavor, my dear, but a little goes a long way."

At the first bite of Aniseed's cookies, the professor's face grew stern.

"Aspiring Baker Mint, what was the assignment?"

Aniseed nibbled daintily at her cookie. "To bake a batch of shortbread."

"And incorporate all six of the provided flavors," Professor Honeycomb added. She held up the cookie to Aniseed. "This is shortbread. Plain and unflavored. Did you use any of the powders?"

"Those flavors would never go together," Aniseed said calmly. "As a student of Flavor, I took the lesson as a test of my judgment. I judged the best flavor would be pure shortbread. So I made shortbread."

Professor Honeycomb's blue eyes hardened. The corners of her mouth drew down in an uncharacteristic grimace. Her usually warm voice became so cold, Lyra shivered.

"In the future, Aspiring Baker Mint, I strongly encourage you to take the lesson as given. My instructions are not open to interpretation. You have failed to complete today's assignment in the allotted time. As such, I expect you to complete it this evening. Bring your batch of fully flavored shortbread to my office first thing tomorrow morning." Without another word, the professor turned to Lyra. "Aspiring Baker Treble, what do you have for us?"

Lyra passed around her plate. She could barely swallow her own bite of cookie as she watched Professor Honeycomb chew, waiting for her response.

A startled look flashed across the professor's face, followed quickly by a suffusion of delight.

"That is . . . unusual," the professor said. "A bit off on your proportions—heavy on the ginger and not quite enough caramel to cut that spice—but . . . I *can* taste all six flavors. Barely. And . . ."

Professor Honeycomb looked to Razz.

"And I like it," he said simply. "Can't really explain why, but I enjoy it. I would eat more."

Boysen was standing next to Lyra. He nudged her shoulder and whispered, "What did I tell you?"

There was a general round of applause for Lyra's mysteriously likeable cookies, and then it was Boysen's turn.

"Transcendent," Professor Honeycomb announced immediately, still chewing her first bite. "Absolutely exquisite."

The verdict was unanimous. If Lyra's cookies were sufficiently enjoyable, Boysen's were life-changing. All six flavors were perfectly balanced, complementing and supporting each other in delicious harmony.

"And you didn't kill anyone." Razz clapped his brother on the back. "Good job, Poison."

It was Lyra's turn to nudge Boysen's shoulder. "Flavor King," she whispered. He rolled his eyes, but his grin was wider than ever.

A magical chime rang through the halls, signaling the end of class.

"See you all back here tomorrow for our full Flavor lab day," Professor Honeycomb called. "We'll continue laying this foundation in identifying and combining flavors. No homework, except for Aniseed. Class dismissed!"

Caramelle made a beeline for Lyra. "Aren't you glad that's over?" she demanded. "Sweet and savory, what a way to begin."

"I liked it," Lyra said honestly.

"At least we have Texture next." Looping her arm through Lyra's, Caramelle dragged her towards the door. "Trust me, roomie," she said, her voice as determined as her stride. "You got a bit lucky with Professor Honeycomb, but Texture . . . this is where Pestle really starts to shine."

Caramelle's prediction came true as soon as she and Lyra entered the Texture classroom.

"Aspiring Baker Meringue! And Treble!" Professor Puff greeted them warmly. "I am glad to see you both. Meringue, might I have a word? I was hoping to speak with you before class."

"Of course," Caramelle replied with her most gracious smile. She squeezed Lyra's arm, then darted up to the teacher's workstation, where she and Professor Puff began a whispered conference.

Caramelle had put them both in the front row for Flavor class. Left to her own devices, Lyra opted for the second row, choosing the workstation by the window. She had just settled herself on the stool to wait when Boysen and Ginger entered supporting a rather dejected-looking Mac between them.

"I'm sure it's not as bad as all that," Ginger said soothingly. Catching Lyra's eye, she waved. "Give us a hand here, Treble."

Lyra hurried over and helped deposit Mac in the front right workstation. He slouched on the stool, staring glumly at his shoes.

"Macaron here is convinced he's failed already," Boysen explained. "Which is a load of spun sugar. Tell him, Lyra."

Lyra patted Mac's shoulder. "That's a load of spun sugar."

"We've only had one class," Ginger pointed out. "One beginning assignment."

"Which I made a mess of." Mac buried his face in his hands. "You heard Boysen's brother. 'More like a battleground than a dessert.'"

"My brother is also a load of spun sugar," Boysen replied. "Sometimes. Mostly he's all right. But I'm with Ginger here. It was one assignment, on the first day."

Mac groaned.

"It's true," Lyra coaxed. "Like my mom always says, one sharp note doesn't ruin the song."

This made Mac look up, but his eyes were puzzled.

Ginger patted his other shoulder. "My dad's version is 'One burned cookie doesn't spoil the whole batch.' Same principle."

"Except in this case, I'm the burned cookie," Mac said sadly. "And the burned cookie gets tossed out at the end of term."

Boysen pushed himself between Mac and the counter. Rather than a gentle pat, he gave the other boy's shoulders a very ungentle shake. "We are weeks away from any tossing," he said firmly. "And your shortbread was not toss-worthy."

"It was the worst in the class," Mac said.

Ginger smirked. "Not quite. Aniseed didn't even do the assignment right."

"Exactly," Boysen agreed. "If anyone is up for tossing after only one lesson, I'd say it's Aspiring Baker Mint."

Mac shook his head. "Her shortbread was still amazing. Flavor is my weakest point."

"Then it's a good thing you're rooming with the Flavor King," Lyra said, winking at Boysen.

"I reject the title but agree with the concept." Boysen gave Mac's shoulders one more shake, then released him. "We all have our strengths and weaknesses, right? I saw your cake. Your Presentation is miles beyond mine."

"And it tasted good too," Ginger added.

Lyra nodded. "The ratio of coffee to marzipan was just right. No Flavor issues there."

"The point is that the judges chose each of us for a reason," Boysen said, finishing the combo. "We all deserve to be here, and we all have areas we can grow in. So, let's help each other out." He held up his hand as if taking an oath. "The Aspiring Bakers of the Whisk room do hereby offer to host daily study sessions for any who might wish to join."

"I wish," Ginger said instantly.

Lyra raised her hand. "And me."

"Oh, please." Aniseed was standing in the doorway. "It's only 'let's hold hands and help each other' until the first exam. We all know someone's going to be cut. This school is about rising to the top."

Ginger put her hands on her hips. "We'll rise a lot faster if we work together. Why do you think Professor Honeycomb gave us that assignment?"

"That assignment was an abomination," Aniseed sneered. "Believe me, 'Professor' Honeycomb won't be pulling anything like that again. My mother is very close with the royal chefs."

She swept by in a haze of perfume to the back row.

"Like Boysen said," Ginger muttered, "if anyone is up for tossing . . ."

"Forget her." Boysen patted Mac on the back so heavily, the other boy almost fell off his stool. "Daily study sessions. Starting today. After dinner. Deal?"

Mac looked from Boysen to Ginger to Lyra. His eyes drifted to the front, where Caramelle and Professor Puff were finishing their conversation.

"Deal," he said wistfully.

A magical chime rang out, and Professor Puff clapped her hands. "Let us begin! If you would all please take your seats, Aspiring Bakers?"

CHAPTER THIRTEEN

Master Chiffon's Advanced Aeration Charm

Once everyone was settled, Professor Puff crossed to the blackboard.

"I was very impressed by all of your entrance exam cakes," she said, "but one in particular demonstrated a remarkable grasp of a very complicated spell. Aspiring Baker Meringue, would you join me?"

Caramelle had chosen the workstation in front of Lyra's, but she hadn't even bothered sitting down after class started. She glided up to the platform.

Professor Puff waved her hand, and a piece of chalk rose into the air, hovering over the blackboard as if held by the professor's own nimble fingers. "Meringue, what Texture spell did you use for your entrance exam cake?"

"Master Chiffon's Advanced Aeration Charm," Caramelle replied.

Another wave of the professor's hand and the chalk was moving across the blackboard, spelling out Caramelle's words.

"A wonderful choice," Professor Puff said as the chalk made its final marks. "Wonderful but daring. Audacious, even, especially for a first year. What made you choose that spell?"

"It's the one I'm most familiar with. You see, Master Chiffon is my tutor." Caramelle paused to let that weighty detail sink in. "But I also believe it is the best possible Texture spell for cakes. The only reasonable choice."

Professor Puff raised her eyebrows, but she seemed pleased. "Bold words. Do explain."

"Texture is on display in a cake. Mistakes have nowhere to hide. Even the best Flavor or the most beautiful Presentation won't save a cake if it's too dry, or too moist, or stodgy, or crumbly. Especially if you have to stack many layers, you need a sponge interior that will support weight while also remaining light and fluffy."

"That is the age-old problem." Professor Puff nodded. "So how does Master Chiffon's spell provide the best solution?"

Caramelle spoke without hesitation, as if she were reading from cards. "Other Texture spells focus too much on moisture. Master Chiffon understands that air is the most important element here. He knows that lightness and stability don't have to be at odds in a well-made cake. His charm doesn't try to fight the air but works with it, letting the cake rest on its strength."

"Like a glider riding the wind," Professor Puff said with a smile.

"Yes!" Caramelle's whole face was alight with enthusiasm. "So instead of sinking or growing too rigid, the cake floats . . . when the spell is done correctly."

"Indeed." Professor Puff looked out at the other first years as the chalk continued moving behind her. "I trust you all had the chance to sample Aspiring Baker Meringue's cake yesterday?"

Everyone nodded. Lyra had only gotten one bite, but she didn't think she would ever forget it. While the Presentation and Flavor had both been polished, the Texture was absolutely the star of the show. It had been like biting into a decadent cloud.

Professor Puff went on. "That cake was an excellent demonstration of this spell done correctly. Thank you, Aspiring Baker Meringue, for providing that demonstration and for speaking so eloquently on the subject. It is clear that you have a passion for this baking principle."

"Oh yes," Caramelle said. Her eyes were sparkling. "Texture is so exact. It requires total precision. It is absolutely my favorite subject."

Lyra was struck by the change in her roommate's demeanor. It wasn't like she was a different Caramelle, but a more authentic Caramelle, as if a few extra layers had been removed.

Professor Puff, too, seemed to notice. "You will have no arguments from me about the wonder of Texture. Thank you again, Meringue. You may return to your seat for now."

As Caramelle made her way to the front row, Hyacinth rushed into the room, looking frazzled.

"I apologize, Professor," Hyacinth said, trying in vain to brush some powdery stains off her light-blue apprentice apron. She handed a scroll to the royal-blue-aproned teacher. "Here is the report from Professor Honeycomb's class, with Apprentice Baker Berry's compliments."

Professor Puff's usually placid eyes twinkled mischievously. "Oh, yes. I'm sure Apprentice Baker Razz Berry detained you so long because he was sending compliments to a wrinkled old lady like me."

Hyacinth blushed furiously, but she was smiling.

Professor Puff unrolled the scroll. Scanning it quickly, she nodded. "Thank you, Roulade. You are just in time for our spell instruction. Would you hand out these cards?"

As Hyacinth moved quickly through the room and deposited a small notecard on every counter, Professor Puff took her place behind the teacher's workstation.

"Today, we will be learning a modified version of Master Chiffon's Aeration Charm," she announced. "Apprentice Baker Roulade is giving you a copy of the spell for reference. Now, this is not the advanced spell that Aspiring Baker Meringue used so effectively on her cake. This is a beginner-level spell, intended for use in cookie recipes. For the next hour, I would like you to implement this spell in a batch of basic shortbread."

Lyra heard a faint whimper from Mac.

Professor Puff continued, "Some of you may think this task overly simplistic. I urge you to think again. Shortbread has a very distinct consistency, which even highly experienced Texturists can struggle to achieve. Look for the challenge. Even if your first batch goes well, make another. Build the muscle, and always seek to improve. It is a good rule for all your classes this term: approach every task with the questions, 'What can this teach me? What do I need to learn?'"

In the back of the room, Aniseed huffed. Professor Puff pretended not to notice.

"As in your Flavor class, we will not be offering you any assistance. Unlike Professor Honeycomb, though, I ask you not to consult with each other." Her gray eyes swept the room, zeroing in on each student with a keen glance. "I am quite serious about this. There will be a time for collaboration, but today, I wish to get a sense of your individual skill levels. The room should be silent for the next hour. Understood? Excellent. You may begin."

Lyra knew she was in trouble as soon as she looked at the spell. It seemed like a simple combination of words, but she couldn't get them to flow straight in her head. She wasn't used to learning something without setting it to music. Even after reading it through several times, she kept jumbling words or switching out entire phrases.

To make matters worse, this was a spell where tempo mattered. A baker was supposed to say each line at the same speed as their hands were moving. That meant the dough should finish coming together when the baker recited the last line of the charm. A wave of blue light would then roll out from the baker's hands and sink into the dough, signifying that Texture magic was at work.

Try as she might, Lyra just couldn't get the rhythm of her words to match her hands. She wasted bowl after bowl of ingredients. Sometimes, she moved too quickly through her mental recitation of the spell; her fingers couldn't incorporate the butter fast enough, and the flour crumbled to dry dust. Other times, she recited the spell too slowly, resulting in a dough that was both mushy and stodgily overworked. And not once did even the faintest shimmer of blue light appear over her hands.

Feeling a strange sense of déjà vu, Lyra washed out her bowl for the sixth time and started again.

"Aspiring Baker Treble?"

Her head snapped up, and Lyra found herself staring into the stern gray eyes of Professor Puff. The Texture headmistress was standing by Lyra's workstation. Her voice was quiet, but to Lyra, it seemed to echo around the otherwise silent room.

"Are you aware that you were humming, Aspiring Baker Treble?"

Lyra's heart sank down towards her stomach. "I was not, Professor Puff. I am so sorry."

"That is quite all right." The professor's gaze softened slightly. "We all have nervous habits to grow out of. When I first arrived at the academy, I was a foot-tapper."

"Really?"

"Oh yes. Professor Chiffon threatened to glue my feet to the floor with royal icing." Professor Puff gave Lyra a smile as quiet and firm as her voice. "I trust you will require no such alarming threats."

Lyra shook her head vigorously. "No, Professor."

"Very well. Carry on, then, Aspiring Baker Treble. *Silently.*"

"Yes, Professor."

Tears stung the corner of Lyra's eyes. She was aware of Boysen trying to get her attention from across the aisle, but she ignored him, focusing with all her might on adding flour, sugar, and butter to her mixing bowl.

What was it Chef Flax had said? *Hum, sing, scream if you need to.*

Apparently, Professor Puff operated under her own set of rules . . . or maybe it was Texture in general.

I knew this class would be the hardest, Lyra thought with a sigh. Pressing her lips together as tightly as she could, she dug her fingers into the bowl for another attempt.

It was no use. The reprimand from Professor Puff, though delivered as gently as possible, had popped the small bubble of confidence Lyra had managed to construct in Flavor class that morning. Between trying not to cry and maintaining constant vigilance on her vocal cords to keep them silent, Lyra could barely concentrate on the actual task. It was difficult to get through Master Chiffon's spell at all, let alone at the exact tempo required for perfect shortbread.

Too soon, but also not soon enough, Professor Puff announced the hour was up. Lyra's apron was covered with flour, and her hands were slick with butter. She was fairly certain there was a whole tablespoon of sugar in her hair. But the messiness of her appearance was nothing compared to the absolute disaster of the cookies she was pulling out of the oven.

This final batch was simply the last attempt Lyra had been able to squeeze in before running out of time. Desperate for one more chance, she had recited the charm with slow, deliberate care, only to feel the dough solidifying like concrete around her fingers. It was far too dense, but she had no choice but to bake it. Having nothing to present would be worse than failure.

At least we're not all *sampling everybody's work,* she thought glumly as she waited for Professor Puff and Hyacinth to reach her for private assessment. *Only two people will know just how bad this shortbread is.*

Considering one of those two was the single person in the room she most wanted and needed to impress, this was not a very comforting thought.

Also not comforting was the obvious praise Professor Puff was lavishing on Caramelle's cookies. Lyra's workstation was right behind Caramelle's, but the professor and Hyacinth kept their voices so low that Lyra couldn't hear their exact words. Still, their glowing smiles proclaimed Aspiring Baker Meringue had proven her Texture skills once again.

Then it was Lyra's turn.

For all her prim appearance and severe manner, Professor Puff was surprisingly kind. Her eyes did widen with surprise at the first bite of Lyra's concrete-like shortbread, but she recovered swiftly, speaking warmly of the cookie's enjoyable flavor.

"Learning a new spell is always difficult," she said. "I don't believe you've received much formal instruction in baking magic, have you?"

"No," Lyra admitted. She thought about adding, "*None at all,*" but decided this was not a time for such extreme honesty.

"Yet you have proven yourself capable. We all tasted your entrance cake, and Professor Honeycomb had high praise for your shortbread in her class this morning." Professor Puff looked to Hyacinth, who nodded vigorously in confirmation. "So, give yourself time. Keep practicing this spell. When you come for your full-day Texture lab the day after tomorrow, bring another batch of shortbread with you that represents your best effort and progress between now and then. That is your homework."

Lyra's heart was still sitting in her stomach, feeling as heavy as her rock-solid cookies, but she tried to smile. "Thank you, Professor."

Hyacinth gave Lyra an encouraging smile, then followed Professor Puff to Ginger's workstation.

The rest of the class was a blur. Lyra sat on her stool, fighting desperately to keep the tears back for a few more minutes. If she could just hold out until the chime rang and hide in her room through lunch . . .

The chime did ring, but before Lyra could make her escape, she found her way blocked by Boysen and Ginger.

"Not a word." Boysen held up his hand as Lyra opened her mouth to protest. "I couldn't hear what Puff was saying, but it's clear you've had a rough go. I think we all have, this morning."

Ginger nodded stoutly. "Texture is terrible. I don't see how anyone can like it."

"Caramelle seems to," Lyra pointed out. She looked around, but her roommate was already gone.

"Further proof that The Meringue is not human." Ginger sighed. "In any case, we've been kneaded like dough this morning. We all deserve lunch."

Mac joined them. To Lyra's surprise, his warm brown skin was glowing.

"That was amazing!" he gushed. "Professor Puff said I've got a good grasp of the shortbread variant for the spell. She wants me to experiment with the Florentine version!"

Boysen laughed. "If we've been kneaded like dough, Mac has *risen*. Still, we all deserve lunch."

Lyra hesitated. "I thought I'd just go back to my room, maybe rest up . . ."

Boysen picked up her bag. "Not a chance. I'm taking your supplies hostage, just to be safe."

"I need to practice," Lyra protested. "Professor Puff—"

"You can tell us all about it over lunch," Ginger said, linking her arm through Lyra's.

"This is a school for baking, Treble." Boysen smiled. "Can't start the term by skipping meals. You'll forget the whole point of why we're here."

Mac scrunched his eyebrows. "To become better bakers?"

Boysen kept his eyes on Lyra. "Almost. Why are we really here, Treble?"

She sighed. "To make things people want to eat."

"Exactly." His smile widened into a grin. "So, let's eat."

Against her will, Lyra felt the Berry grin working its contagious magic. The corners of her mouth turned up slightly, and her heart made a feeble lurch back towards its normal place in her chest.

"Okay," she said. "Let's eat."

CHAPTER FOURTEEN

MAKE YOUR MARK

It didn't take long for Lyra's friends to detect that she was not in the mood to discuss Texture. Instead, they spent lunch telling funny stories in a remarkably unsubtle attempt to cheer her up. The greatest contribution was Mac's account of his pet fox's exploits. Apparently, "Fortescue the Foppish Fox" was a fashion aficionado who aspired to turn Mac into a gentleman-about-town. By the time he was finished detailing Fortescue's ever-growing collection of silk cravats, Lyra's heart was light enough to chuckle along with the group.

Her spirits rose further with the arrival of dessert. While everyone else at the table received an elegant custard tart, Lyra's floating plate contained a cinnamon roll and a brief note from Chef Flax explaining that he had managed to save and magically preserve it from the last batch she had helped him make. Lyra dug in gratefully as she wondered again how the chef seemed to know exactly what his guests needed. Whatever the magic was, it seemed to relay information about hearts, not just stomachs.

Every part of her strengthened, Lyra was able to hold her head high as they trooped upstairs to the fourth floor. Only one class left, and then her first day at the Royal Academy of Magical Baking would be behind her . . .

"Oh, my auntie's rolling pins." Ginger stopped in the doorway of the Presentation classroom, stifling a laugh. Turning quickly, she pretended to brush some imaginary stains from Lyra's apron. "Behold The Meringue at work."

Boysen whistled. "So that's why she skipped lunch."

Lyra peered around Ginger. Caramelle was sitting at one of the workstations in the front row, her auburn hair shimmering in the afternoon sun that streamed through the nearby window. And there, leaning over the counter to speak to her, was Cardamom Coulis III. They were both smiling as they talked, clearly enjoying each other's company.

Lyra's stomach twisted in a way that had nothing to do with the excellent lunch she'd just consumed. Trying to keep her voice light, she asked, "You think she's been here the whole time?"

"Only a few minutes, I'd say." Ginger coughed to cover another round of giggles. "Depends on how long it took her to do that spell before coming here."

Lyra's stomach twisted further. "What spell?"

"She's cast a Presentation charm on herself," Boysen explained quietly while Ginger continued coughing. "Rather unsubtly too. Can't you see that faint shimmer in the air around her?"

Lyra stole a furtive glance at the cheerfully chatting pair as the group proceeded into the classroom. If she looked closely, she could just catch the outline of a golden glow emanating from her roommate, like an aura.

"Is that . . ." Lyra swallowed. She knew there was a whole magical profession dedicated to Self-Presentation enhancement, but she had never seen one of the spells in action. "Is that allowed?"

"Sure." Boysen shrugged. "It's not really doing any harm. Most people don't bother with it."

"Because it's pointless," Ginger said. She plopped her bag down on one of the back row workstations, as far from the Caramelle-and-Cardamom show as she could get. "It takes forever and then wears off fast. I would rather be practicing my flavors." Looking back towards the door, she sighed. "Best go fetch your roommate, Berry. He might need some smelling salts. Or a bonk on the head with a wooden spoon."

Macaron was frozen in the doorway. He was staring at Caramelle, his eyes wide behind his glasses. Lyra and Boysen scurried to retrieve him.

"She looks amazing," Mac breathed.

"I know, bud," Boysen sighed as he helped Lyra guide his friend towards the other third row workstation. "I know you think that."

Lyra looked at him curiously. "Don't you think so?"

"Sure." Boysen shrugged again. "But it's all sparkle and no substance. Personally, I prefer a bit of both."

Mac nodded. His eyes, still fixed on the back of Caramelle's head, were glassy. "Sparkle . . ."

Boysen shook his head, smiling at Lyra. "He's probably gone for the next few hours. Maybe ask your roommate to go a little lighter on the allure-factor next time?"

Before Lyra could answer, Professor Genoise swept into the room, clapping his hands once.

"Welcome, Aspiring Bakers!"

Everyone hurried into place. Aniseed was already settled at the other front row workstation, so Lyra and Boysen took the second row. Out of the corner of her eye, Lyra saw Cardamom Coulis (*the Third,* her brain insisted on adding) give Caramelle one more smile before strolling to join the professor on the teacher's platform.

"I trust your first day has been stimulating thus far." Professor Genoise's piercing gaze landed briefly on each student, as if he could read the tale of their morning in their faces. Lyra thought she saw a slight quirk in one of his manicured eyebrows when he got to Caramelle, but she couldn't be sure.

"As my colleagues and I explained this morning," the professor went on, "the goal for this week is to set a baseline. With that in mind, over the next hour and a half, I would like you to produce a batch of your best shortbread."

An audible groan rippled around the room. Professor Genoise ignored it.

"Remember that Presentation is a matter of heart. Of *personality*. As such, this afternoon, I do not just want to see your best shortbread. I want to see your best *decorated* shortbread. At your workstations, you each have the ingredients to make various kinds of frosting. Coloring has also been provided. Bake, shape, and decorate your shortbread however you desire."

Caramelle raised her hand.

Professor Genoise nodded. "Yes, Aspiring Baker Meringue?"

"How many spells are we allowed to use, Professor?" Caramelle asked, her voice as sweet as her namesake.

"Excellent question, Meringue. The answer is none."

"None?" she repeated.

"No magic today, please," Professor Genoise said firmly. "Remember, we are setting a baseline. Presentation is a chance to display your style. 'Make your mark,' to quote Apprentice Baker Coulis. I wish to see *your* individual style shine through before we begin layering spells on top of it. Coulis and I will be circulating and observing. Feel free to talk amongst yourselves or to us." After a moment of stunned silence, the professor chuckled. "Look at these faces, Coulis. You would think I just announced a ban on chocolate instead of giving them all free rein to express themselves. This is the best part of baking! Enjoy it. That is an order. Starting"—he held up his pocket watch—"now."

Lyra sighed. The no-magic rule was actually a relief, but she was not at all confident in her style. *What does that even mean?* she thought, automatically pulling out the shortbread ingredients. *And how am I supposed to "let it shine through"?*

"And to think," Lyra muttered under her breath as she measured sugar into a bowl, "I used to *like* shortbread."

"Oh, don't worry. You will again."

Cardamom Coulis (*the Third!*) was standing by her counter. Lyra dropped the measuring cup into the bowl, sending up a cloud of sugar directly into his perfect olive-skinned face. He sneezed.

"I'm so sorry!" she squeaked.

"Not at all." He sneezed again, then gave her a rueful smile. "It is I who should apologize. I broke a terribly important rule: never startle a baker during the measuring process. Do you forgive me?"

"Of course!" Her voice was an octave higher than usual. She coughed, then tried again. "I mean, no worries."

He bowed with mock formality. "Many thanks, Aspiring Baker Treble. As I was saying, don't despair. I swore off shortbread after my first day too, but it didn't last long. That's the first important lesson of the Royal Academy of Magical Baking."

"Which is?" she asked. Sharps and flats, he smelled good. It was hard to think straight with him standing right there, his dark eyes resting on her, but she gripped the edge of the counter and tried to listen.

"We're all here to become better bakers," he said. "Correct?"

She nodded.

"But that comes with rules, as well as pressure to follow those rules. If you focus on the pressure, you stop trying to break new ground. And that way, Aspiring Baker Treble, lies defeat. In baking, as in life, the ones who forge their own path are the ones who win. Understand?"

She nodded again. That was all she could do, considering her heart and stomach were flopping around in their own bizarre dance. Forming coherent sentences was out of the question.

"Excellent." He smiled. "I'll let you get back to it. But first, let me say what I came over here to say. Thank you."

"Thank you?" she heard herself echoing.

"Yes. Thank you for that exquisite cake you made for your final entrance exam." Cardamom raised his eyes to the ceiling, as if searching for some elusive thought. "It was . . . I have no words."

She stammered, "I-I thought—just vanilla. Too simple, really. Not—"

He held up one long, delicate hand to silence her. "Simplicity can be perfection when done well. And that cake was perfect." He leaned in, dropping his voice to a whisper. "You'll have to teach me your secret, Treble."

Then he was gone, leaving her with a wink and the lingering scent of cinnamon and honey.

Afterward, Lyra had trouble remembering the rest of class. She was dimly aware of the shortbread coming together with shocking speed. She had vague memories of whipping up a chocolate frosting as delicious as it was effortless. When Boysen told her later that she was singing softly to herself for the entire hour and a half, she wasn't surprised, but she couldn't tell him the name of the song.

It was only when Professor Genoise clapped his hands to signal their time was up that she rejoined the land of the living in earnest.

"Admirable effort today, Aspiring Bakers," Professor Genoise said. "Coulis and I agree that it is already a privilege and an inspiration to witness your styles at work. In the time remaining, you will inspire each other by sharing the results of your labor. We will also take this opportunity to make an initial assessment of your baseline style."

He then began calling them up, one at a time, to present their decorated shortbread to the class.

After the two classes that morning, Lyra felt she had a good grasp of her classmates' abilities. Nothing about the first few presentations surprised her. Professor Genoise and Cardamom assessed Aniseed's style as "elevated," while Caramelle's was "virtuosic."

Cardamom gave Lyra another wink as they labeled her style "joyful." Her head was spinning so much that she almost missed Boysen's evaluation as "welcoming." She did manage to pull herself together enough to give the Flavor King a warm smile as he returned to his seat.

Ginger provided the first real hiccup. Both Professor Genoise and Cardamom were noticeably unenthusiastic about her bold geometric design. Still, she seemed pleased with her assessment of "daring."

Lyra gave her a thumbs-up, then let her eyes drift towards the window, her mind already elsewhere. The first day was almost over. Sure, Texture had been abysmal, but . . . Cardamom Coulis (*the Third!*) adored her entrance exam cake. He wanted *her* to teach *him* the secret.

She needed a few moments alone to process all of this. Or a few hours. That conversation with Cardamom kept replaying in her head, demanding reflection and analysis. Maybe if she beat Caramelle back to the room, she could pretend to be napping and just think until dinner . . .

Behind her, Ginger drew in a sharp breath.

"Sweet and *savory*, Mac!"

Lyra's eyes and attention snapped back to the present. Mac was standing at the front of the room, placing his decorated shortbread on the professor's counter for inspection.

It was a crown.

Lyra felt herself echoing Ginger's gasp. Even from several feet away, Mac's creation was resplendent. Dozens of tiny shortbread cookies, cut and colored like jewels, were shaped into a tiara. It was all held together by the fluffiest, silkiest buttercream frosting Lyra had ever seen. Mac managed to position his masterpiece on the counter directly in a shaft of golden sunlight so the whole thing actually shone.

"Well done, Mac!" Boysen called. He began a class-wide round of applause, which Professor Genoise joined in enthusiastically. Even Aniseed gave a few soundless claps, not daring to turn up her nose at something the headmaster of Presentation so obviously approved of.

"I echo Aspiring Baker Berry," Professor Genoise said. "Well done, Fondant!"

"And without magic." Cardamom's voice was surprisingly cool. "You didn't manage to sneak in a spell, did you, Aspiring Baker Fondant?"

Professor Genoise shook his head before Mac could answer. "He did not. I would know in an instant if he did."

"All the more impressive, then." Cardamom smiled tightly. "Please do share your wisdom with us, Fondant."

"It's the buttercream," Mac said immediately. "My special meringue buttercream. It brings everything together and makes it . . . sparkle."

His eyes landed on Caramelle.

"Indeed, it does." Professor Genoise gave Mac a deep bow. "I am sure Coulis will agree with my assessment of your style, Fondant. Majestic."

Mac's whole being glowed, as if he had performed a top-tier Presentation spell on himself. He returned the professor's bow, then stumbled back to his seat, stealing several glances at Caramelle along the way.

Professor Genoise spread his hands. "An auspicious first day, Aspiring Bakers. I reaffirm my words from the welcome feast. This will be a year of special excellence at the academy." He turned to Cardamom. "Any parting thoughts, Coulis, before we dismiss them to their well-earned rest?"

"I agree with you, Professor, as always. This is a most . . . stylish group of personalities." Cardamom's gaze swept over the room, catching and holding on to Lyra's for two definite beats. "I encourage them all to remember that Presentation is a living discipline. Forge your own path."

"Forge your own path." Professor Genoise nodded sagely. "With that, I bid you all adieu. I look forward to our full lab day together, three days hence. Now that we have identified your baseline style, come prepared to challenge that style, stretch it, and build upon it. Class dismissed."

CHAPTER FIFTEEN

WHISK WHIZ REVIEW

Hear ye, hear ye!" Boysen clapped imperiously in a perfect imitation of Professor Genoise. "I hereby call this first meeting of the Whisk Whiz Review to order!"

"Whisk Whiz?" Ginger echoed, snuggling further into the corner of the couch she was sharing with Lyra and Caramelle.

Boysen winked from his position on the floor by the fire pit. "Host room gets to pick the name. Right, Mac?"

"What?" Mac, sitting on the edge of the cushy armchair, was staring at Caramelle. He snapped back to attention when Boysen clapped him on the shoulder. "Oh, right. Whisk room. We're the hosts. Whisk Wizard Review."

"Whisk *Whiz*," Boysen corrected. "If the group takes issue with this title, we can always rotate hosting duties and rooms."

"Or use the common area," Lyra pointed out. "There's more space."

Boysen placed a hand on his heart. "You cut me to the quick, Treble. Are you saying you prefer that soulless, exposed laboratory setting to the cozy cheer of Whisk?"

"Cozy is one word for it." Caramelle shifted uncomfortably at her end of the couch. "Lyra is right. I don't know why we're not in the common room."

"Privacy," Boysen replied. "Think about it, Meringue. In the common area, the second and third years could waltz in at any moment, or just eavesdrop from the foyer." He spread his arms, indicating the "cozy" living area they were crowded into. "Only in the safety of our own rooms can we speak freely about the day's events. Starting with the beginning and moving through the day. That means Flavor class. Any thoughts on the 'powders of personality'?"

Mac groaned. "How about 'forget it ever happened'?"

"Don't be a stodge, Macaron." Ginger tugged the cushion from behind Lyra's back and threw it at him. "We've got to mess up in order to learn. That's the whole point of being here."

Caramelle sniffed. "I thought it was a bit heavy-handed, honestly. An object lesson too obvious to be effective."

"It can't have been too obvious," Ginger said innocently, "since you failed and all."

Caramelle opened her mouth, but Boysen held up his hands. "I call foul, Crumble. Rule number two of the Whisk Whiz Review: no snark-bombs against fellow Whisk Whizzes."

"And you didn't fail," Mac said, gazing at Caramelle. "Your cookies were amazing."

"If you like caramel." Ginger's voice was sweet, but Lyra elbowed her anyway.

"If anyone failed, I did." Mac hung his head. "'More like a battleground . . .'"

"At least you completed the assignment," Ginger pointed out. "Unlike my roommate."

"Speaking of, where is Aniseed?" Boysen looked at the door as if expecting her to walk in. "I'm happy to help her with that homework batch for The Honeycomb."

Ginger sighed. "She's not doing it."

There was a moment of silence.

"Not doing the homework?" Caramelle squeaked.

"Nope." Ginger rolled her eyes. "Says it was not a legitimate assignment, and they can't force her to waste her time."

Caramelle's voice was tight with anger. "If she thinks baking is a waste of time, then why is she here?"

Ginger shrugged. "Maybe she assumed her ancestry would put her on some kind of 'elevated' track."

"Elevated." Boysen shook his head. "That's the word Professor Genoise used for her style, right?"

"He's quite the diplomat," Lyra said, smiling.

Boysen returned her smile. "Or full of spun sugar. But that's Presentation, at the end of the day. Let's not get ahead of ourselves." He glanced at Ginger. "I take it Aspiring Baker Mint will not be joining us Whisk Whizzes?"

"She'd rather be baked into a failed soufflé," Ginger said. "That's a direct quote."

"How poetic." Boysen turned his attention to Mac. "We'll work on the Flavor stuff later," he promised. "Professor Honeycomb let me take a set of personality powders. That'll be the lab portion of tonight's Whisk Whiz Review, for anyone who wants to join. Sound good?"

He looked around, including the group in the question.

"Sounds great," Lyra replied. "Thanks, Boysen."

"Don't mention it. Any other thoughts on Flavor?"

"I have a question," Caramelle said. "Lyra, how did you do it?"

"Do what?" Lyra asked, startled.

"I was wondering the same thing," Ginger confessed. "It's like Professor Honeycomb said. Your shortbread wasn't balanced, flavor-wise, but it was good. Just *good*. I enjoyed eating it."

"Exactly." Caramelle sounded wistful. "How did you do it?"

"I . . . um . . ." Lyra looked at Boysen, but he just grinned. "I-I don't know."

"You don't know?" Caramelle repeated shrilly.

Lyra shrank back into the couch. "Boysen told me to make something I'd enjoy eating. So . . . I did."

"You did," Boysen affirmed. Then, as if sensing Lyra's discomfort, he turned briskly to Caramelle. "Speaking of a how-to, Meringue, care to let us in on how you managed that bit of Texture wizardry?"

"You had Puff in your pocket before class even started," Ginger marveled. "How many years have you been practicing that aeration charm?"

Caramelle smoothed her apron, which was somehow still spotless after the day's labors. "A fair few."

"Can you help me?" Lyra asked. "I have to bring another batch to Texture lab the day after tomorrow. She's expecting to see progress."

Caramelle nodded graciously.

Ginger patted Lyra's hand. "I'm sure you weren't that bad."

"Oh, but I was. I don't know what it is about that spell." Lyra shut her eyes, trying to block out the memory of Professor Puff's look of surprised concern. "I just couldn't get the words straight."

"Was that it?" Boysen's surprise was almost as bad. Lyra might have made a run for it if she wasn't trapped between two girls on a very squishy couch.

"Yes," she said defensively. "I mean, I hope so. Either that or I'm just fundamentally hopeless at Texture."

Boysen shook his head. "Not possible. I just thought . . . Didn't you have to do a lot of memorizing for shows? With the Any Weather Bards?"

"That's different," Lyra said. "Everything's easier to remember when you set it to music."

"You'll be fine," he assured her. "Your brain's already trained for memorization. You just need practice. We all do."

"Not Caramelle." Lyra smiled at her roommate. "Not for this charm. Seriously, Caramelle. You're really, *really* good."

Caramelle returned Lyra's smile with elegant modesty. "Master Chiffon is an excellent tutor."

"Mac was great with it too," Ginger pointed out. "Didn't Puff tell you to work on the Florentine version of the spell, Fondant?"

Caramelle's eyebrows shot up. "Really?"

"Yeah," Mac said softly. "Professor Puff said my shortbread was—"

"Smashing," Boysen finished. "That's what you told me. And Hyacinth said the same. Yes, with Fondant and Meringue here, I'd say we're well set for Texture."

"And Presentation." Lyra looked from Mac to Caramelle and back. "'Virtuosic' and 'majestic' are pretty great for baseline style assessments."

Caramelle blushed. "Cardamom was too kind, really. He's such a generous baker."

"He was generously chummy with you, for sure," Boysen said. His smile went a little rigid as he turned to Lyra. "And with you, Treble. Whatever he said to you at the start of class certainly put you in a great mood."

Lyra felt a flush spreading over her own cheeks. "He liked my entrance cake."

"As would anyone with a brain." Boysen's eyes bored into her. "Anything else?"

"Only what he said to everyone at the end of class," she said quickly. "Forge your own path. Don't let the pressure get to you."

"Is that all?" Caramelle's gaze was even more intense than Boysen's. "You did keep him at your workstation longer than he spent at anyone else's. It felt a bit . . . unprofessional to me."

Ginger huffed. "Listen to the salt calling the sugar white."

"And what's that supposed to mean?" Caramelle demanded.

"*You* certainly commandeered plenty of his time," Ginger said. "Just how early did you get there?"

Caramelle half rose from her seat, but Boysen held up his hands.

"Rule two," he said sharply. "No snark-bombs against fellow Whizzes. Second offense, Crumble."

"I would like an apology," Caramelle said between gritted teeth.

Ginger's dark eyes narrowed. "Are you serious?"

"I was on the fence about this 'study group' anyway." Caramelle tossed her head, but her auburn curls stayed perfectly in place. "Lyra and I can do quite well on our own if we're not welcome here."

"Of course you're welcome," Mac said hastily.

Boysen nodded. "Absolutely. All Whizzes welcome in Whisk." He looked sternly at Ginger. "Right, Crumble?"

Ginger opened her mouth as if to protest, then glanced at Lyra.

Lyra mouthed, *Please.*

Ginger sighed. "Sorry, Meringue. Twice."

Caramelle glared at her, then sat back, crossing her arms. "Fine."

"Excellent," Boysen said. He drew in a deep breath. "So, that's the day. Flavor, Texture, Presentation. We've all got our strengths and things to work on."

"What do you have to work on, Boysen?" Lyra asked.

He hesitated. "Presentation. Professor Genoise was being generous when he said my style is welcoming. 'Homey' would be a better word. That charm I used for the entrance exam is the only Presentation spell I really know. I'm halfway decent at it only because I've just kept using it, over and over. That's not going to fly with Professor Genoise."

Lyra leaned forward so she could place a hand lightly on his shoulder. "You're better than you think," she said. "At all of it."

He looked up at her, his brown eyes flickering with gold in the firelight. "So are you."

Out of nowhere, a wave of anxiety rose up in Lyra's chest. It wasn't just from Texture class or from her parents' sneak-attack doubt fest when they said good-bye. It was the culmination of the whole past year, since the first Royal Academy of Magical Baking entrance trial she had somehow passed. That was when the question had first popped up.

What am I doing here?

Lyra had no formal training. No connections in the magical baking community. Why was she, a Treble from the Any Weather Bards, moving forward when more experienced bakers were not?

She could give herself no answer. Every subsequent trial, she expected to fail. But every shocking success only added questions to the list.

How am I still here?

But she was. She made the cut at every trial. She was an Aspiring Baker. She had just finished her first day of classes at the Royal Academy of Magical Baking.

Still, the questions kept coming.

What if it's all a mistake?

And then, even more terrifying:

How long until they all find out?

Suddenly, sitting on the couch in the Whisk room with four incredibly talented bakers, Lyra wanted to open her mouth and let it all pour out. She wanted to tell them that she was a fraud, that the professors had made a mistake, that she didn't belong and couldn't do it, and what sort of twisted cosmic joke *was* this and—

Boysen's golden-brown eyes flashed dark with concern.

"Lyra? You all right?"

She was still leaning forward, her hand on his shoulder. The room had gone very quiet.

"I—" She took a shaky breath. "Um, I—"

"It's been a long day." Boysen smiled, taking Lyra's hand from his shoulder and holding it lightly. "I think we could all use a break before we dig into the practice sessions. How about some music, Treble?"

"Music?" she repeated.

Ginger clasped her hands together. "Oh, yes please. Never fails to calm my nerves."

"I thought we were here to study," Caramelle said, her ramrod posture somehow becoming even stiffer.

"A quick break would be helpful for all of us," Boysen insisted. "Cleanse the palate, so to speak."

Lyra hesitated. "I-I do have my guitar. In my room."

"Perfect!" Boysen stood, helping her up with him. "Make haste to Pestle, Aspiring Baker Treble, and return with your lyre. Ha!" He grinned. "Lyra. Lyre. I get it."

"Ha ha." She rolled her eyes, but the smile spreading across her face was genuine. The wave was retreating, pushed back by the warmth of the fire and the sincere enthusiasm in Ginger's voice and the gentle pressure of Boysen's hand, still holding hers.

Lyra squeezed his fingers, then let go.

"One song," she said. "Then we do some serious studying."

Boysen looked at the group. "What say you, Whizzes of the Whisk Whiz Review?"

Ginger snorted. "We get a vote? So this is a democracy now?"

"The Whisk hosts are generous tyrants," Mac said softly but with an unmistakable twinkle behind his glasses.

"What did I tell you?" Boysen crowed. "Life of the party is our Macaron Fondant."

Lyra turned to her roommate, raising her eyebrows in a silent question.

"Fine." Caramelle pursed her lips. "Quick break for singing. Then let's get to the real work, please? Some of us are here to learn."

"All of us," Boysen corrected. He winked at Lyra. "You heard the council. Off with you."

"Be right back," Lyra promised, then practically skipped to the door. It was hard to feel weighed down in this room, with this particular collection of "personality powders." The wave of questions could wait a little longer.

If only she could push aside Professor Puff's homework assignment so easily . . .

Lyra sighed.

One day at a time, Treble. One day at a time.

CHAPTER SIXTEEN

Set It to Music

The first Flavor lab day was a smashing success. Lyra's attempts to complete her Texture homework, on the other hand, were a dismal failure. Despite Boysen's encouragement in Whisk Whiz Review and Caramelle's private coaching in Pestle afterwards, Lyra still went to bed Tuesday night without any confidence in the shortbread she had made to present to Professor Puff.

The next morning, her stomach heavy with dread, she decided to forego breakfast in favor of an early visit to the kitchen.

"Lyra!" Chef Flax's eyes lit up when she came through the door, then immediately filled with concern. "What's wrong? Tough day in class yesterday?"

"Not at all," she assured him. "Flavor lab was great. It's today that I'm worried about."

Bumble leaped from the counter over to Lyra's shoulder, chattering excitedly. Chef Flax tilted his head to one side.

"I think he's saying you should tell us all about it while you help us with this bread for lunch. Or something like that," the chef said.

Bumble launched from Lyra's shoulder. Flying to a cupboard, he produced an apron and soared back to her, chattering all the while.

"Close enough." Chef Flax chuckled. "Even if that wasn't his original idea, he approves. Step up to the counter, Lyra. I always think better while kneading."

Lyra obeyed, tying on the apron over the uniform version she was already wearing. "You actually knead your bread physically? Aren't there spells for that?"

"Of course there are." Chef Flax turned a lump of dough onto the counter for each of them. "But I've been up for hours, running multiple spells at once. At this point in the morning, right before the breakfast rush, I find it soothing to bake without any magic at all."

Bumble chattered something emphatically, and Chef Flax nodded. "Soothing and also important. After all, we don't want to be completely dependent on magic. Got to keep those baking muscles nimble. Literally." Flouring his hands, he winked at her. "Now, dig in, Lyra. With your hands and your words. First, tell us what made yesterday great. We'll start with the sweet and build up strength for the sour."

Lyra needed no further encouragement. Dusting her own hands with flour, she plunged them into the dough, punching and turning and punching again. Then she lifted the whole lump into the air before throwing it back down onto the counter with a loud, satisfying *thud.*

"You're right." Lyra shared a grin with the large red-faced head chef. "That is soothing."

While she worked, she told Chef Flax and Bumble about her first full lab day in Flavor. The first years had spent the morning in an exercise Professor Honeycomb called FIT: Flavor Identification Training. Razz brought a tray of twelve jars to every student, and Professor Honeycomb led them through the recognition of the flavor contained within each jar. After lunch, they practiced combining those flavors, starting with two at a time and gradually building up to six-flavor dough.

Lyra had thoroughly enjoyed the day. Her nose was tired, and she never wanted to smell that much rosemary at once ever again, but she could feel the results. She was learning to recognize that gut voice and feel more confident in following it.

"And that's after only one day," she gushed to Chef Flax, her fingers locked into the kneading rhythm. "I mean, I'll never be as good as Boysen, or any of the Berrys, but I can at least be competent."

Bumble tapped Lyra's arm with his tail, forcing her to stop kneading and look at him. He chattered one short, firm sentence.

Chef Flax grinned. "More than competent, Bumble says. We agree that you have splendid instincts, and we're glad you're starting to trust them."

"Thanks, Bumble." Lyra smiled at the flying squirrel, and he returned to his task of keeping the counter well dusted with flour.

"So, yesterday was a grand success in learning new things." Chef Flax performed a complicated twist with his dough that sent it flying three feet into the air before it landed on the counter with impressive precision. "That was the sweet. Now for the sour. What about today fills you with dread?"

Lyra paused, letting her hands sink into the dough with a sigh. "Texture."

Briefly, she recounted her disastrous first class with Professor Puff, taking out all her frustration upon the hapless lump of dough.

"The classroom can be an intimidating environment," Chef Flax said soothingly, once she had pounded out the last humiliating detail. "Especially Professor Puff's classroom. I'm sure you'll get the hang of that spell after some practice in less stressful circumstances."

"It's not just the classroom." Lyra gave the dough a particularly violent toss that only just managed to avoid hitting Bumble. "I tried the spell again last night, back in the dorms with my roommate. She's a Texture expert. Even with her help, I couldn't get the tempo right."

Bumble suddenly froze, then delivered a series of particularly high-pitched chattering noises.

"He says you're done kneading," Chef Flax interpreted.

Bumble shook his head, chattering derisively. Chef Flax held up his hands in surrender.

"All right, I missed that one. But I do think you should stop, Lyra. I'm not sure that dough can take much more."

Bumble stretched himself to his full height and width and repeated the chatter -squeak statement, taking off his chef's hat and waving it for emphasis. Then he proceeded to tap his foot deliberately on the counter, pointing alternately at Lyra and at his foot.

"Something about . . . rhythm?" Lyra suggested. "Because I said I was having a hard time with the tempo of the spell?"

Bumble nodded emphatically, then sang a few short notes in his surprisingly rich baritone.

"That's it!" Chef Flax smacked his hand on the counter, sending up a cloud of flour that made Bumble sneeze. "Set the charm to music!"

"Music?" Lyra echoed.

"Of course! You've set other baking spells to music, yes?"

"Yes . . . in preparing for my entrance exam. But—"

"And you sang that Flavor spell the other day, when you helped me with the cinnamon rolls. And they came out perfectly."

"But that was Flavor," Lyra protested. "And it wasn't for class. It was just for fun."

"All baking is just for fun," Chef Flax said stoutly. "Or it should be. If you stop having fun, you stop growing. And it shows in the finished product. Trust me. It's hard to enjoy eating something the baker did not enjoy creating. And that misses the whole point, doesn't it?"

"What point?"

Chef Flax spread his arms wide, indicating the whole kitchen with its array of delicious smells. "The point of baking. I love eating, and I love making things that other people love eating. That's why we all got into this business, right?"

"That's why *I* got into it," Lyra replied. "Or why I'm trying to. But didn't you come from a baking family? Didn't you—I don't know—*have* to become a baker? Because you're a Flax?"

The head chef laughed, while his sous chef erupted in a fit of chatter-giggles.

"There's a lot of variety in baking families," Chef Flax explained through lingering chuckles. "We're not all Mints or Chiffons or Glazes. The Flaxes are a rather laid-back bunch. Sure, my parents were delighted when I became a baker, but they would have been equally happy if I had gone into politics like my brother. Or took up the trapeze and joined the circus, like my sister. No, Lyra Treble, I got into baking for one thing: joy. The joy of making food, and the joy of the person eating the food. Simple as that."

He offered Lyra a bowl, and she dumped her well-kneaded lump of dough into it with a sigh. "I don't see how anyone can enjoy Texture. Except Professor Puff, maybe, and geniuses like Hyacinth. Or my roommate."

Bumble covered both bowls of dough with pieces of cloth and scampered away. Lyra glumly watched him leap about the kitchen as he pulled ingredients from various cupboards and deposited them on the counter.

"Some bakers are more inclined to certain disciplines than others," the head chef admitted, setting the covered bowls in the proofing drawer to rise. "But there's joy to be found in each part of baking. You just have to find your own way into that joy. For you, that seems like music."

"But shouldn't I just be able to *do* the spell?" Lyra asked. "That's what Professor Puff is expecting. She wants me to focus on getting it right, not finding the fun."

Chef Flax placed a floury hand on her shoulder. "All the professors here are deeply invested in your growth as a baker. They just each have their own style. Professor Puff may seem a bit severe, but she really does want to see you all succeed. I'm sure she'll be thrilled with your progress however you go about achieving it."

Lyra shook her head. "She wasn't thrilled on Monday in class. When I was humming, I mean. I got the feeling that any noise is frowned upon in Texture."

"That's mostly personal preference. Professor Puff is a quiet soul and therefore enjoys a quiet baking environment."

Bumble tugged on Lyra's hand. Chattering in what she took as an encouraging yet firm tone, he pointed at the array of ingredients he had collected.

Chef Flax beamed. "Our sous chef has prepped your workstation, Aspiring Baker Treble. Everything you need for shortbread. Let's do some musical baking!"

Lyra stared at him. "You mean . . . sing the Texture charm? Now?"

"Yes, and yes."

"I . . ." Lyra swallowed. "I have class."

"There's plenty of time until then," Chef Flax said firmly. "And you have homework to finish, right?"

"I-I made some shortbread with Caramelle last night. With the spell."

"But you're not satisfied with it." Chef Flax shook his head. "So, let's use that as a backup and see if you can't whip up something better now."

Tugging on Lyra's hand again, Bumble stared up at her, his bright eyes full of pleading.

"Okay, okay." Lyra mustered a tiny smile in answer to the flying squirrel's irresistible charm. "For you, Bumble."

Ever since the disastrous class, just thinking about Texture made Lyra's heart sink and set her mind buzzing with nerves. So she was absolutely amazed at how pleasantly the next half hour flew by. It took her only three minutes to invent a catchy tune for Professor Puff's beginner-level version of Master Chiffon's Aeration Charm. After singing through it a few times with both Chef Flax and Bumble, she was ready to try the spell with actual ingredients.

The first attempt exceeded all Lyra's expectations. Granted, her expectations were dismally low, but it was still heartening to finish singing the charm only ten seconds after the shortbread dough came together around her fingers. Even better, a faint blue shimmer washed over her hands with the final words, rippling out across the bowl before fading away.

Chef Flax inspected the dough with an expert eye and confirmed Lyra's assessment. The charm had worked, though only at half strength. These cookies would have a clumsy, labored texture, but they would be dimly recognizable as shortbread and not altogether unpleasant to eat. Compared to the bricks she had produced the day before, Lyra considered this a huge win.

The second trial was even more encouraging. Determined to wean herself from dependence on music, Lyra only whispered the spell-song, but it was still effective. The tune guided her through the word-maze and kept her tempo steady. The dough came together two seconds before the final word was sung, and the blue shimmer that rolled out from Lyra's hands shone brighter and longer than before.

For the third attempt, Lyra asked Chef Flax to do the singing so she could focus on the mental recitation. He obliged eagerly. To Lyra's delight, Bumble contributed his baritone, singing the tune wordlessly under Chef's strong tenor. Even better, the greenhouse door opened after only a few measures, and Sprinkle herself came soaring in. She landed on the counter beside her husband and joined in with gusto, singing a wordless descant in a sweet soprano voice.

Some may have considered this song, performed by a large human chef with two flying squirrels for backup, as more distracting than helpful. Lyra was almost certain that's what Professor Puff would say, and probably Caramelle too.

But she didn't care. The trio's music coursed through her whole being, engraving the charm's words onto her brain and sinking its tempo deep into her muscles. She closed her eyes, feeling even her Flavor-focused instincts perk up at the magic unfolding beneath her hands.

The result was an undeniable success. Lyra actually felt the ingredients snap together into a fully cohesive dough at the exact same moment the trio finished singing the charm. A wave of blue light, warm and bright and vivid, erupted from her hands. It pulsed over the bowl for a few seconds, sparkling and shimmering. Lyra felt like it was winking at her.

"Well done!" Chef Flax applauded as the light sank down into the dough. "I can tell you right now, that's a batch of shortbread I would enjoy eating."

Bumble and Sprinkle clapped their hands and tapped their tails on the table, chattering their agreement.

"Thank you," Lyra exclaimed. Her veins were thrumming with the kind of fluttery excitement she usually associated with an especially successful Any Weather Bards performance. Stepping back from the bowl, she gave her own round of applause. "Seriously. Thank you. That was some excellent singing!"

Bumble bowed low while Sprinkle bonked his head lightly with her tail, chatter-laughing affectionately.

"No thanks necessary," Chef Flax translated. "We are honored to assist you, Aspiring Baker Treble. I think you'll make a fine Texturist."

Lyra sighed, but she was still grinning. "I wouldn't go that far. I eventually have to try it without any music at all."

"Repetition and review. That's all you need." Chef Flax pulled a pocket watch from his apron. "Let's get this batch in the oven and get you some breakfast. Bumble and I can handle the cleanup. You mustn't keep Professor Puff waiting."

Lyra protested about the cleanup, but Bumble and Chef staunchly waved away her offers of help. She had to content herself with another fervent round of thanks, along with a promise to bring her guitar for a proper concert soon. Then, after scarfing down a quick bacon croissant, she was off to the Texture lab, freshly baked shortbread in hand.

It was time to present her homework to Professor Puff.

CHAPTER SEVENTEEN

Pasta Confessions

Professor Puff, as Chef Flax had said, was a quiet soul. She would never be as voluble in her praise as Professor Honeycomb, nor as elegantly lavish as Professor Genoise. But when Lyra turned in her homework shortbread before Texture lab, the professor's satisfaction was clear.

It was a good day for Pestle all around. Professor Puff called Caramelle up again at the beginning of class, praising her excellent use of the simplified aeration charm. The professor also called up Mac, who looked like he could die happy right then, standing side by side with Caramelle as the Texture headmistress congratulated them.

"I know you are both already experienced Texturists," Professor Puff said, her short gray hair shining silver in the morning sunlight. "Sometimes, bakers who have advanced as far as you have, especially at a young age, grow careless with the basics. But you did not fall into that trap. You approached this 'simple' charm with the same care as a high-level spell, and for that, I commend you."

She dismissed them to their workstations with a round of applause, which everyone but Aniseed joined enthusiastically.

"And speaking of this 'simple' charm," Professor Puff went on, "we will be spending the rest of today reviewing it. I believe Professor Honeycomb discussed the importance of repetition?"

Six students nodded.

"Excellent. Then I need not repeat my colleague's wise words." She then instructed them to produce another batch of shortbread using the same aeration charm. "We'll spend the morning in review. After lunch, we can begin applying the spell to other recipes. Remember: repetition is key."

Just like her practice session in the kitchen with Chef Flax, Lyra was astounded at how enjoyably the dreaded Texture lab day flew by. Whenever she felt herself getting lost in the words or rhythm of Master Chiffon's Aeration Charm, she merely shut her eyes and let the music play in her mind. Not only did the song help keep her locked in to the spell, but the mental image of Bumble and Sprinkle crooning in perfect harmony never failed to bring a smile to her lips.

Better still, even a silent mental use of the song produced pleasing results in her spellwork. With friendly voices chorusing in her mind, Lyra was able to stay relaxed in the tense silence of the classroom. The dough came together around her fingers with the same precise timing as the night before, and the blue light danced even more vibrantly around her hands. Professor Puff was just as pleased with Lyra's morning batch of shortbread as with her homework.

The afternoon was increasingly fun. Lyra had no trouble adapting the tune to other versions of the charm. Careful not to let a sound escape her lips, she sang on the inside as she whipped up multiple versions of pastry and rolls, each batch slightly fluffier than the last. By the time they all left for dinner, Master Chiffon's Simplified Aeration Charm was rolling off her mental tongue with relative ease.

"Congratulations, Lyra!" Boysen gave her a high five as they took their places at the first-year table in the dining hall. "And congratulations to all of us. The Whisk Whizzes did themselves proud today."

Lyra sighed happily. "I didn't know Texture could be so much fun."

"It was our first full-day class with magic," Ginger pointed out. "Magical baking is fun. Who knew?"

"Which makes it all the more surprising that we're not doing any magic in Flavor." Caramelle sat as primly at the table as she always did in class, her white apron still spotless. "One week I could understand. Maybe even two. But the entire first term?"

"Flavor is a tricky discipline," Boysen said, sounding remarkably like his brother. "You can't hide behind magic like in the other two."

Caramelle's eyes flashed. "Texture is an exact, demanding principle. It requires far more precision than Flavor."

"Sure. Of course." Boysen held up his hands in surrender. "I'm just saying that everyone has to learn the basics. We'll get to the magical shortcuts and enhancements later, but for now, Honeycomb's trying to get everyone on a level playing field."

"Baking is *not* a level playing field," Caramelle protested. "Some people have what it takes, and some don't. I thought if anyone would understand that, it would be the teachers at the Royal Academy of Magical Baking."

"Careful, Meringue," Ginger teased. "You're beginning to sound like my poor persecuted roommate."

Aniseed had not made an appearance in the dining hall since the welcome feast, apparently determined to take all her meals in the haughty seclusion of her room. The other first years all went silent as they remembered the brief but intense scene between Professor Honeycomb and Aspiring Baker Mint the previous morning.

"I still can't believe she actually threw Aniseed out," Lyra said, her voice hushed with awe. "Missing an entire Flavor lab day . . ."

Ginger snorted. "I can't believe Aniseed didn't do the homework. I know her ego is more puffed up than over-proved choux pastry, but I didn't think she was that dumb."

"Do you think Professor Honeycomb will get in trouble?" Mac asked. "Aniseed did threaten to get the royal chefs involved. Her family has a lot of clout."

Boysen shook his head. "The royal chefs are all former academy students. They all adore Honeycomb. Aniseed won't get anywhere with that."

The arrival of floating plates heaped with food interrupted the conversation. Boysen actually yelled in excitement at the sight of Chef Flax's special homemade pasta and meatballs swimming in a decadent creamy tomato sauce. Lyra felt a bit like yelling herself after the first luxurious bite. The meatballs were spiced to perfection. The sauce contained just the right hint of sweetness to balance the acidic tomatoes. Even the pasta was flavorful. Winding one particularly long strand around her fork, Lyra breathed in and could have sworn she detected a whiff of caramelized garlic.

And Chef Flax says he's not a Flavor specialist, she thought with a happy sigh, her taste buds and stomach uniting in a chorus of delight.

For a few minutes, the first-year table was silent except for the sounds of clinking silverware.

Caramelle, though, was clearly not finished with the topic. After one or two delicate bites, she put down her fork and said, "Aniseed has to learn that family connections don't mean anything here."

"Really?" Ginger sounded incredulous. "You actually think that? As a Meringue?"

"I know I have been fortunate," Caramelle said evenly, dabbing at her lips with her napkin. "Being a Meringue is inspiring. It motivates me to work harder. I am sure that helped get me here—but now I'm here. At the academy, all that matters is talent . . . and training."

She fell silent, but Lyra could tell her roommate was still brooding about Professor Honeycomb's "no magic" curriculum.

"And hard work," Boysen added. "Like the Whisk Whizzes demonstrated today."

"Especially Lyra." Ginger speared a giant meatball with her fork and took a large bite, somehow managing to speak intelligibly while chewing. "How'd you do it? I know you were dreading today, but you clearly managed to impress The Puff."

Caramelle smiled at her roommate. "I knew those extra coaching sessions would help. We've been hard at work in Pestle, on top of the study group."

Lyra concentrated on winding another long strand of pasta around her fork. She hadn't told anyone about her time in the kitchen or the musical strategy she had worked out with Bumble and Chef Flax. It felt like confessing a weakness, one that would make her feel even more like a fraud than she did already. But she also didn't want to be dishonest.

Surely anything that involved a duet between flying squirrels couldn't be truly bad . . .

Lyra took a deep breath. "I set the charm to music, actually. That's what made the difference."

Beside her, Caramelle inhaled sharply.

"You sang the charm?" Mac looked confused. "I didn't hear anything."

"I didn't sing it aloud," Lyra explained. "I just set it to a tune to help me learn the words. And then I sang it in my head to keep me on beat."

Ginger clapped her hands. "Oohhh, that's a great idea! I bet that would help us all, especially when we have loads of these spells to keep straight."

"You took Master Chiffon's Aeration Charm," Caramelle said slowly, "and set it to *music*?"

"Why not?" Boysen began tapping on his knees, already feeling out a rhythm. "Like Ginger said, we're going to be learning a lot of magic this term. Wouldn't it help to have a system going in, to help us memorize them all?"

"But—it's—" Caramelle seemed to be struggling for air as well as words. "It's math! An exact science. You can't just add in a new element, like melody or singing. It's . . . That's cheating!"

"Cool your cakes, Meringue," Ginger said. "We're not saying to *do* the spell with music. We just want to use music to help us *memorize* the spell at the right tempo. Learn the words, so we can say them. Internally. Without singing."

"I sing them," Lyra reminded her. "Internally, of course, but I'm not just reciting."

"And it worked," Ginger observed.

Lyra nodded. "It did. It's the only way I could get the spell to work for me."

"That is not right," Caramelle said, her voice low and tight with anger. "The baking world has traditions. They have been developed over generations, and they exist for a reason. Spells are meant to be spoken, not sung. That is how things have always been done."

Ginger rolled her eyes. "Give it a rest, Meringue. You're just mad that Lyra doesn't need your help in Texture. She can succeed on her own."

"That's not true," Lyra protested. She turned to Caramelle pleadingly. "I need lots of help. I only tried the music thing because Chef Flax suggested it, and then he and Bumble helped me practice. But I was just building on our practice sessions from last night. I needed all that repetition and support for today."

"She's right, Meringue," Boysen said. "We're grateful for each Whiz's contribution to the group. We wouldn't truly be 'Whizzes' without your Texture skills." He grinned at Lyra. "Or without Treble's ability to set charms to music."

Mac had one eye on Caramelle, whose face was still scrunched into a scowl. "Are we sure that's not cheating?" he asked.

"It's not," Boysen said flatly. "My brothers used all kinds of tactics to help them memorize stuff." Lyra caught his eye, and his voice softened. "We can double check with the professors if it'll make you feel better, Meringue."

"It would," Caramelle replied stiffly. "Thank you."

Without another word, Boysen rose and crossed to the professors' table, then returned a moment later with Professor Puff.

"We have a question, Professor," he said politely. "And, as it is a matter of academy ethics, I thought it best not to wait."

"Of course." The professor's keen gaze swept over the table. "I am at your disposal."

Four students looked at Lyra, who suddenly wished she could roll herself in a strand of pasta and drown in tomato sauce.

"I-I set the charm to music," she confessed. "To help me learn the words and stay on tempo. I don't sing it when I'm baking—not out loud, I mean. I sing it in my head, instead of . . . reciting it mentally. Is that okay?"

Professor Puff's eyes widened. She was silent for so long that Lyra added "being baked into a meatball" to her list of preferable activities for this particular moment.

Finally, the Texture headmistress spoke.

"That is okay, Aspiring Baker Treble." She paused again, choosing her words with care. "I cannot say that I wholly approve. My desire for each of you is to rise to the level of the challenge, not adapt the challenge to suit your preferences. But baking is a long journey through the self, discovering one's own strengths and weaknesses. The academy's aim is to help you hone your strengths and shore up your weaknesses. As a rule, we encourage you to employ any tool you possess in this pursuit."

Lyra's hands were shaking under the table. She clasped them together tightly, trying to keep her voice steady as she whispered, "Thank you, Professor. I will keep trying to . . . rise to the level of the challenge."

Professor Puff nodded gravely. "I am sure you will, Aspiring Baker Treble. I am sure all of you will."

Caramelle was quiet for the rest of the meal and all through Whisk Whiz Review. When the group urged Lyra to teach them the aeration charm song, Caramelle voiced no objection, but she didn't participate. She also excused herself shortly thereafter, saying it had been a long day and she wanted to go to bed early.

As she left, Lyra couldn't bring herself to look at her roommate, sure that she would see disapproval in the auburn-haired girl's eyes. Another conversation was coming, sooner or later, and Lyra was not looking forward to it. But when she tiptoed into the dark room later and climbed into her own bed, it was hard to be apprehensive. It had been a good day. A *great* day.

And tomorrow was their first Presentation lab. A full day in the Presentation classroom.

A full day with *Cardamom.*

Lyra buried her face in her pillow to stifle a sudden gleeful giggle.

Vaguely disquieting roommate issues aside, her first week at the Royal Academy of Magical Baking was turning out to be an unqualified success.

Two days later, Lyra collapsed on her bed in Pestle after dinner, burying her face in her pillow. The Friday Whisk Whiz Review would be starting soon, but she needed to close her eyes, even just for fifteen minutes.

Lyra heard the door opening. Caramelle was coming in.

Fifteen minutes, Lyra promised herself. *Just pretend to be asleep. You can talk later.*

She scrunched her eyes tightly shut and tried to breathe slowly and steadily. Thankfully, Caramelle went straight to the bathroom, slamming the door behind her.

Lyra sighed. They would have to talk it out at some point.

Pestle was too small a room for this kind of trouble to go unaddressed.

CHAPTER EIGHTEEN

BREAKING GROUND

Sighing again, Lyra burrowed further into her pillow. She wished she could block out the events of the day before in the Presentation lab, but it was no use. The memories had been simmering for over twenty-four hours. Her mind felt like a mixing bowl left unwashed, with bits of dough hardening around the edges.

At least she'd managed to arrive at Professor Genoise's classroom at the same time as Caramelle on Thursday. Her roommate had tried to shake her the whole morning and get there first, but Lyra had stuck to her like . . . well, caramel. She was not about to give up the chance of some private conversation with Cardamom before lab day.

It turned out they needn't have been in such a rush. Apprentice Baker Coulis didn't appear until the magical chime rang, and then there was no time for even an exchange of greetings. Professor Genoise began the class with exact punctuality.

"Welcome, Aspiring Bakers," the Presentation professor said graciously. "As we shared with you on Monday, the tone of this first week is *foundational*. We must master the basics so we can build upon them. Aspiring Baker Treble, will you come up here, please?"

Startled, Lyra hopped down from her stool and joined Professor Genoise at the front of the room.

"Would you be so kind as to share with your classmates what Presentation spell you used for your final entrance exam cake?" the professor asked.

"A-a cleanliness spell," Lyra stammered. "Madame Temper's Chant of Precision."

Professor Genoise clapped his hands. "Exactly! I remember asking you on the day why you chose that particular spell. Do you recall what you said to me?"

Lyra glanced at Cardamom, standing inches away on the teacher's platform. He smiled encouragingly.

She took a deep breath, inhaling the exotic scent of cinnamon and honey.

"I'm a messy baker," she confessed. "It was an important cake, so . . . I wanted it to be neat."

"Indeed." Professor Genoise dismissed her with a wave, and she scrambled back to her second row workstation in relief as the professor went on, "Neatness is a virtue oft overlooked by Presentation specialists, to their detriment. Would you agree, Apprentice Baker Coulis?"

"Absolutely. The principle of Presentation lives in the baker's *heart*." Cardamom's eyes caught Lyra's again, and he gave her another smile that seemed to be just for her. "But if your final result is messy, how can your heart's intent shine through? Style cannot disguise sloppiness."

Lyra was aware of Caramelle glaring at her from the front row. Her roommate was tracking every look exchanged between Lyra and Cardamom. The air around the auburn-haired girl was practically vibrating with displeasure.

Oblivious, Professor Genoise beamed at Lyra. "Today, we shall be taking a page from Aspiring Baker Treble's book. Over the next hour, I wish you to bake a batch of shortbread—"

The entire class groaned.

"—using Madame Temper's Chant of Precision." The professor chuckled. "Such woeful expressions! Embrace repetition. Bake as many batches as necessary to give me the neatest, cleanest shortbread you can in one hour."

He reviewed the chant while a delicate piece of chalk moved rapidly through the air on its own and wrote the spell on the board in neat, flowing script. Then, holding his pocket watch in one hand, Professor Genoise instructed them to begin.

Lyra found the next hour more pleasant than tedious. She had spent so much time with this particular spell in preparation for the entrance exam that it felt a bit like coming home. There was also something relaxing about the now familiar ritual of shortbread. Butter, sugar, flour . . . Mix the dough . . . Wait thirty seconds while the dough chills in the enchanted proofing drawer . . . Cut and bake the cookies . . . Especially when combined with Madame Temper's simple chant, the whole process became like an exercise in meditation.

It helped that Cardamom kept stopping by her workstation. He rarely said more than a few encouraging words, but they did share a laugh over Lyra's returning enjoyment of shortbread. Even better, she couldn't help thinking that he did visit her more than any other student, a suspicion confirmed by the number of times she caught Caramelle turn and glance at her from the row ahead.

All in all, Lyra felt thoroughly refreshed when the hour was up. Twelve pieces of pale gold shortbread sat on a plate in front of her. Each one measured two and a half inches long, one and a half inches wide, and a quarter inch tall, with a tiny ridged border surrounding the top. The same pattern of three dots adorned the smooth, buttery surface of each cookie.

Lyra's fingers were still tingling from the purple light that had swirled around them with each of the four batches, trimming the shortbread to be precise and identical. The magic seemed to have been at work inside her also, smoothing the rough spots leftover from the week, leaving her heart clean and neat.

These happy feelings vanished as soon as Professor Genoise began his evaluation rounds.

"Aspiring Baker Meringue!" The professor's smooth, polished demeanor nearly cracked. He stood by Caramelle's workstation, mouth hanging open in disbelief at the dizzying array of shortbread in varying states of neatness. "You have certainly exceeded the requirements of this morning's assignment. I take it Madame Temper's spell was not . . . sufficiently challenging for you?"

Caramelle smiled radiantly, raising her voice ever so slightly to be heard across the classroom. "Not at all, Professor. I found it quite challenging. But once I had completed it to my satisfaction, I began thinking . . . how might this spell be improved?"

Professor Genoise's eyes widened even further. "Improved?"

"Innovated upon," Caramelle amended. "As you so rightly said, we are laying a foundation this week. Madame Temper's work is an important part of baking history, so of course it should be included in that foundation. But isn't baking also about the future? Breaking new ground to lay an even stronger foundation? Then anything built upon it would necessarily be improved."

"Your . . . passion is to be commended, my dear." Professor Genoise pulled out a monocle and leaned in to give one particularly exact plate of shortbread a closer inspection. "I take it you indulged in some experimentation with Madame Temper's spell?"

"I did indeed. Only after completing the original assignment, and meaning no disrespect to Madame Temper, of course. Or to you." She waited for Professor Genoise's nod of acknowledgement, then went on. "I found the exercise increased my understanding of the spell's fundamental nature. I would like to continue these experiments, if I may."

Professor Genoise tapped his monocle against the counter thoughtfully. "I have no doubt of your baseline abilities, Aspiring Baker Meringue. And I do wish your class time to prove both beneficial and stimulating." He hesitated. "But I would prefer such experiments to be supervised, and I do have a room full of other students to attend to."

Cardamom broke in. "Professor, haven't you often said that the most advanced bakers are those who dare to think outside the box? Clearly, Miss Meringue is quite advanced for an Aspiring Baker. I can work with her today."

Professor Genoise considered for a moment, then nodded. "Please do, Coulis. The rest of the day, if you please. We will be moving on to rough puff pastry next, so see how you can 'innovate upon' Madame Temper's Chant of Precision in that medium. *After* a few run-throughs with the original spell." He turned back to Caramelle. "Never you fear, Aspiring Baker Meringue. You are in excellent hands with Coulis."

"Thank you, Professor." Caramelle's eyes shone as she returned Cardamom's smile. "I'm sure I am."

The rest of the morning was a blur to Lyra. For reasons she couldn't explain fully, even to herself, she found it difficult to focus. She kept stealing glances at the workstation in front of her, where Cardamom and Caramelle were hard at work.

They seemed to be having a splendid time. Caramelle was certainly laughing a good deal. The sound grated on Lyra's nerves, drawing her gaze again and again from her own bowl of ingredients to the sight of the two heads, one auburn and one dark, bent over pieces of parchment.

Thankfully, the cleanliness spell was ingrained enough in Lyra's muscles that she still managed to complete the required batch of pastry. But this time, the wave of purple light that rippled out when the spell took effect was faint and flickering. Not only did it fail to smooth her own rough edges, but it left the pastry uneven and lopsided.

Even then, Lyra couldn't concentrate. She barely registered Professor Genoise's disappointed sigh. His constructive criticism and encouragement did lodge vaguely in her subconscious, and she heard herself assuring him she would do better after lunch.

But the afternoon was no better. Cardamom spent the whole day at Caramelle's workstation, scribbling spell variations on parchment and whipping up batch after batch of full-puff pastry. Lyra, meanwhile, could barely produce the minimum requirement. Her thoughts were wandering as much as her gaze, and all in the same Coulis-ish direction. Try as she might, she could not force them into the soothing cadence of Madame Temper's chant.

Professor Genoise was gracious in his assessment. He seemed to attribute Lyra's poor performance to "first full-day lab jitters," and was confident she would find her stride soon. After assigning her a redo of the puff pastry as homework, he dismissed the class with a smile and elegant bow.

The first years returned to the dorm to freshen up before dinner. Caramelle was practically floating.

"Wasn't that a wonderful day?" she sighed. Standing in the middle of Pestle, she spun around twice and landed gracefully on her bed with a happy giggle. "Texture will always be my first love, but *Presentation.* What an invigorating discipline!"

Lyra sat on the edge of her own bed, her posture as rigid as Caramelle's usually was. "I had no idea you were so passionate about . . . innovation."

"Apprentice Baker Coulis is very inspiring," Caramelle said, sitting up. "And so gallant! Besides, we understand each other. He knows what it's like to advance so far that you get bored with the old way of doing things."

"But you didn't get bored," Lyra said, fighting down the urge to yell. "I thought you *love* 'the old way of doing things.' You don't even want me to sing the spells mentally because that's not how it's always been done."

Caramelle tossed her head. The auburn coils remained firmly in place. "That's different. This is sanctioned experimentation. Professor Genoise allowed it."

"Professor Puff sanctioned my singing," Lyra pointed out.

"Not fully," Caramelle shot back. "I was there, Lyra. Anyone could see she was uncomfortable with the idea."

"But she still allowed it," Lyra persisted. "She said it was okay."

"Which surprised me." Caramelle folded her hands, her spine and shoulders back to their customary rigid position. "Honestly, I didn't expect the academy to be so lax. I guess she feels sorry for you."

Lyra felt her face turning as red as Caramelle's perfectly styled hair. "Sorry for me?"

"That's one explanation for her indulgence of your deceitful behavior."

"Deceitful?" Lyra echoed, her hands shaking. "You're the one being deceitful."

Caramelle's voice was as brittle as her posture. "I beg your pardon?"

"It's Cardamom, isn't it?" Lyra demanded. "It's not enough to put Presentation spells on yourself—and you just *can't* hog the bathroom like that in the morning, by the way—but now you have to pretend to be some kind of innovator? You lie about wanting to 'break new ground,' just so he'll notice you?"

"You're just jealous," Caramelle sneered. "Did you really think you could monopolize him all day? Cardamom is far too advanced a baker to find you interesting for very long, Treble."

Lyra clasped her hands together, tensing every muscle to keep her voice steady. "It's not . . . that. It's not *just* that. I care about baking, Caramelle. And honesty. I thought you did too."

"Honesty? You?" Caramelle voice rose shrilly. "Don't make me laugh. You claim to have no training, but you're here. You passed every entrance trial. Maybe Professor Puff's not sorry for you. Maybe she's bewitched."

"Bewitched?" Lyra echoed weakly.

Caramelle pressed on, each word as heavy and hard as a blow from a rolling pin. "You can't even perform the most basic Texture spell, but you got into the Royal Academy of Magical Baking. That's just . . . not possible." She narrowed her eyes, studying Lyra. "What are you hiding?"

"Nothing!" Lyra felt like a ball of risen dough someone had just punched down. "I studied and practiced on my own. I worked hard."

"Oh, please," Caramelle scoffed. "You expect me to believe that a bard with no baking genes and no formal education got into the most exclusive magical baking academy in the kingdom just on sheer *grit*?"

Lyra stared at her, unable to speak.

After a heavy moment of silence, Caramelle stood and stormed to the bathroom door. Wrenching it open, she turned and hissed over her shoulder, "I'm watching you, Treble. Maybe you really are a prodigy, or maybe there's something else going on. Either way, I'm going to find out."

Then she had flounced into the bathroom and slammed the door behind her.

Lyra had wandered through that evening in a daze. She couldn't remember what Boysen, Ginger, and Mac talked about at dinner. Caramelle was conspicuously absent from the Whisk Whiz Review that night. When Lyra returned to the room afterwards, The Meringue was already in bed. She had also managed to avoid Lyra all throughout Friday, taking her meals early and slipping out of every class as soon as the chime rang.

Now Lyra lay curled up on her bed, trying to block out the sounds of bottles being banged around in the bathroom.

I just need a nap, she thought dully. *Fifteen minutes, and I'll feel better . . .*

But she knew no nap would be enough. Caramelle's words kept bouncing around in her head, jarring her nerves as roughly as the angry noises from the bathroom: *Maybe you really are a prodigy, or maybe there's something else going on. Either way, I'm going to find out.*

"When you do figure it out," Lyra whispered to the empty room, "maybe you could clue me in?"

Sitting up, she began gathering her books. She could wait somewhere else until Whisk Whiz Review started . . . In fact, maybe it was time to pay Chef Flax and Bumble another visit. Caramelle might emerge from the bathroom any minute, and Lyra was in no mood for another confrontation.

She tiptoed to the door, slipping out just as a particularly loud *BANG* sounded from the bathroom and sent her scurrying across the first-floor common area.

CHAPTER NINETEEN

Serious as a Soufflé

Pushing open the door into the kitchen, Lyra found herself face to face with Chef Flax.

"Lyra!" he exclaimed. "I didn't expect to see you this evening. Shouldn't you be with the other Whisk Whizzes, celebrating the successful end of your first week?"

"I'm heading there soon. Just looking for a place to . . . wait until then." Suddenly, she noticed he was wearing an overcoat, and his chef's hat had been replaced by a worn fedora. "Oh, Chef. Are you going out?"

"I am indeed. Annual reunion dinner with a few chef colleagues of mine. Bumble and Sprinkle are out as well." He winked at her. "Fridays are their date nights, you see."

She nodded glumly. "Of course."

"They will be sad to have missed you," he said, sounding sincerely regretful. "As am I at my inability to host you properly."

"It's fine." She felt the head chef's kind eyes peering at her and tried to force her lips into a smile. "I couldn't stay long, anyway."

At that moment, Boysen's voice sounded behind her.

"Thought I'd find you here, Treble."

"Mister Berry!" Chef Flax grinned. "Right on time. Come to whisk our Lyra away to Whisk?"

"I'm not sure," Boysen replied. "Looks like it's just the two of us tonight. That's why I came to find you, Lyra."

"Oh?" Lyra tilted her head. "I know Ginger's having dinner at home. Where's Mac?"

"Something about private practice," Boysen said darkly. "Probably code for writing secret poems of unrequited love."

She stared at him. "Really?"

"He's a Fondant." Boysen shrugged. "Fondants are hopeless romantics. They fall fast and hard. Your roommate's proclivity for Self-Presentation spells didn't help."

Lyra's shoulders tightened at the mention of Caramelle, then drooped. "Poor Mac."

"I've got my eye on him," Boysen assured her. "I'll help him keep his head above water. But for tonight, it looks like you and I are the only committed Whisk Whizzes."

"Right." Lyra swallowed, trying to keep her tone bright. "Well, if you want an off night or some solitude, I can—"

"An off night?" Chef Flax clapped a hand to his heart. "Perish the thought!"

"It is technically the weekend," Lyra pointed out. "Last day of classes for the week. No class tomorrow or the next day."

Chef Flax kept his hand on his heart, the picture of injured nobility. "This is the Whisk Whiz Review, Aspiring Baker Treble. From my understanding, it happens every evening during the week."

"He's right," Boysen said with equal enthusiasm. "Our comrades may be lazy slackers, but someone must uphold this noble tradition."

Lyra tried to match his energy, but she couldn't muster the strength. "Sure. Sounds good."

Chef Flax studied them both for a moment. Then he waved his hand, and the candles in all four iron chandeliers burst into light, casting cozy shadows flickering over the walls.

"I suggest a change of scenery for tonight's review," he announced. "I had planned to make some frosted brownies for Queen Penelope tomorrow. You'll see Bumble has already laid out all the ingredients." He waved his hand, indicating the laden island countertop. "But I am sure she would be delighted to receive a visit from two 'whizzes' such as yourselves."

"You would let us bake in your kitchen?" Lyra squeaked. "Unsupervised?"

"Why not?" The head chef's eyes twinkled. "I trust you. And Queen Penelope really shouldn't have to be kept waiting. You can collect the weekend eggs while you're up there too, which will be quite a help to me and Bumble."

Boysen's whole face was alight with joy. "Thank you, Flax!"

"Y-yes," Lyra stammered. "Thank you!"

The head chef waved off their gratitude. After instructing them where to put the eggs they collected, he gave them another wink and then vanished into the dining hall.

Lyra and Boysen fell into a baking rhythm with surprising speed and ease. She moved instinctively to melt chocolate with butter over a double boiler, while he went for the dry ingredients, using his Flavor instincts to add just the right amounts of salt, cocoa powder, and even a pinch of cinnamon to the flour and sugar. Lyra thought she saw a few flashes of vivid green light out of the corner of her eye, proving that Boysen Berry was far more advanced in Flavor magic than he might readily admit.

For a few minutes, they worked in peaceful silence. Lyra felt the weight on her shoulders slowly start to lift.

"Since we're the only Whizzes present, we get to make the rules," Boysen eventually said as he cracked eggs into a mixing bowl. "If we want to make tonight a 'review' of non-baking matters, it shall be so."

"Non-baking matters?" Lyra echoed, bringing the melted chocolate over to the island counter.

"Indeed. Such as . . . oh, off the top of my head . . . roommate relations?"

Groaning, Lyra covered her face with the spatula she'd been using to stir the chocolate.

Boysen pulled her arm down, forcing her to look at him. "I take it you have not yet reconciled with Aspiring Baker Meringue?"

"I mean, I guess it's nothing. It's fine." Lyra shrugged. "We can get by without speaking."

Boysen raised a single eyebrow.

"We can!" Lyra insisted. "Nothing in the rules says we have to be chummy. She certainly didn't come to the academy to make friends."

"No one did, technically," Boysen said dryly. "But friends make it easier to do what we *did* come here to do."

Lyra picked up the whisk lying beside the bowl of eggs. "I don't need her. I have you and Ginger and Mac. That's friends enough, right?"

In response, Boysen snatched the whisk away and softly hit her with it.

"Hey!" she protested, grabbing for the tool. "Whose side are you on?"

He held the whisk out of her reach. "Hard to say, since you won't tell me exactly what you two were fighting about."

"It's . . . We . . ." Lyra flushed. "It's boy stuff."

"Boy stuff." Using the stolen whisk, Boysen began beating the eggs with somewhat unnecessary force. "You mean Cardamom."

Lyra flushed brighter. "How did you know?"

"Remember, my brother is in the same class with him," Boysen replied. "I've heard a lot about 'The Coulis' over the past couple years."

Something about his tone prickled at Lyra's nerves. She began buttering the brownie pan, her voice decidedly sharper. "I take it Razz doesn't think very highly of 'The Coulis'?"

Boysen shrugged. "Razz doesn't think about Cardamom much at all, really. My brother's got limited room in his brain. At the moment, it's all being taken up by Flavor and Hyacinth. Or Hyacinth and Flavor. The order of importance depends on the day."

"Then how can you say you've heard a lot from him about Cardamom?" Lyra demanded.

"It was mostly their first year." Boysen stopped whisking, apparently realizing the eggs were quite beaten enough. "Razz brought stories home every week. He said all the girls were in love with Cardamom, but not as in love as Cardamom was with himself."

"Sounds like he was jealous," Lyra said. "And that was two years ago."

"Doesn't seem like much has changed. Remember what I told you about sparkle and substance? Cardamom strikes me as lots of the former with very little of the latter." Boysen smiled bitterly. "Maybe he and Caramelle are perfect for each other."

Lyra's voice was shrill. "No one makes it to the third year of the academy on sparkle alone. And you've only just met him! How can you claim to know that—"

Boysen held up his hands in an "I surrender" gesture. "Hey, I don't claim to know anything. I just . . . I have eyes, okay? It doesn't take a genius to see how Caramelle's been throwing herself at The Coulis all week." He lowered his hands, staring moodily at the thoroughly whisked eggs. "I guess I'm just surprised *you* got caught up in it."

Out of nowhere, Lyra's rising anger vanished. She slumped against the counter, her insides caving like a cake removed from the oven too soon.

"It wasn't just Cardamom," she said. "My fight with Caramelle, I mean. That's how it started, but . . ."

She trailed off. After a few moments of silence, Boysen nodded to himself and stepped back from the counter, wiping his hands on his apron.

"Let's start over. We have both just arrived to keep the time-honored tradition of the Whisk Whiz Review." He held out his hand, which she shook with mock formality. "I, Aspiring Baker Berry, do hereby pronounce said review to be in session. All matters, baking or non-baking or otherwise, are up for discussion."

"What would be counted as otherwise?" Lyra asked, smiling in spite of herself.

"I believe your word for it was 'boy stuff.'" Boysen squared his shoulders as if bracing for a fight. "Out with it, Treble. Your argument with The Meringue, from start to finish."

Lyra took her own deep breath. Then, while Boysen slowly stirred the melted chocolate and butter into the eggs with a dash of vanilla, she recounted the previous day's angry conversation with Caramelle, from her own accusations about Cardamom to her roommate's not-so-veiled threats.

"And she hasn't spoken to me since," Lyra finished, handing Boysen the bowl of dry ingredients. "It caught me off guard, to be honest. I thought we were getting along pretty well."

"You were." Boysen glanced sideways at her as he carefully folded the dry ingredients into the chocolate and egg mixture. "Surprisingly so. I know you're new to the baking world, so you're not familiar with the Meringues, but 'friendliness' is not one of their famous qualities."

Lyra rubbed her eyes. "Ginger told me. Our first day. But Caramelle's been so nice. I thought . . ." She trailed off again, letting her gaze drift to the finished brownie batter.

"I thought so too," Boysen said. She could feel his gaze on her, radiating concern as warm and comforting as the preheated oven behind them. "But that's not what's really bothering you, is it?"

"How did you know?" She sighed.

"I have eyes." Suddenly, he clapped her on the back, snapping her out of her gloomy trance. "You can't let all that nonsense about 'hiding something' get to you. You're not hiding anything."

"Are you sure?" she asked. "I don't know how I got into the Royal Academy. I really don't. What if it's so bad, I'm hiding it even from myself?"

"Then I'd say you deserve a Stellar Enchantment Pin for all those psychological layers."

"I'm serious!" She buried her face in her hands. "Maybe she's right. I don't belong here, and it's only a matter of time before everyone knows it."

"You can't spout nonsense like that," Boysen chided her. "I'll have to take that pin back."

"Boysen—"

"Listen, Lyra." He pulled her hands down from her face and held them. "The professors know what they're doing. They say you belong here. Are you saying you know more than Professor Honeycomb?"

"No," she said immediately.

"Are you saying Professor Puff doesn't know what she's talking about?"

"Of course not."

"And do you think Caramelle Meringue is a better judge of baking talent than Professor Genoise?"

"No, but—"

"No. Full stop. The authorities of the Royal Academy of Magical Baking chose *you*, Lyra Treble. That's all that matters."

"I wish I knew why," she said in a small voice.

"Don't we all?"

She actually snorted. "You're a Berry! I may be new to the baking world, but even I know why you got in, Flavor King."

"Exactly." He stared at her hands, seemingly unaware that he was still holding them. "How do I know they didn't pick me just because I'm a Berry?"

"No one who has tasted anything you've baked would think that," she said flatly. "You've got the best Flavor instincts of anyone in our class. Period."

He shook his head. "I'm just saying . . . you don't have the market cornered on insecurity, Treble. It's practically an admissions requirement for an academy like the Royal Academy of Magical Baking. Everyone here has a reason to doubt themselves."

"Even The Meringue?"

"Especially The Meringue." He finally let go of her hands and began pouring the brownie batter into the prepared pan. "The more Stellar Enchantment Pins attached to your hat, the heavier it gets. Same with legacy. I'm surprised Caramelle can even walk around upright."

Her eyebrows raised. "Are you defending her?"

"It doesn't excuse what she said to you," he said wearily, transferring the pan to the oven. "But I do think she's under a lot of pressure. Just . . . don't let her get to you, and maybe cut her a break."

Anger flashed in Lyra's gut again, but it was drowned out by a sneak-attack wave of concern.

"What about you?" she asked in a much softer tone. "What's the Berry pressure like?"

Boysen was silent for a while, his gaze now firmly fixed on the oven timer. "Manageable," he replied after a few moments. "More of an annoyance than anything, most of the time. Nothing like a Meringue." He shuddered. "Or a Mint. I'm afraid Aniseed's headed for a rough awakening."

He was trying to deflect. She wasn't going to let him.

"We're not talking about Aniseed. Or Caramelle. Do you . . ." She hesitated, then pressed on. "Do you even want to be here? I mean, do you actually like baking?"

"I do, alas." He finally looked at her, grinning ruefully. "I wish I could tell you I'm the family black sheep and have a deep longing to run away and be a shoemaker or something. It'd make me much more interesting, I'm sure."

She gave him her own rueful grin. "Being the black sheep isn't nearly so fun as it's cracked up to be. Trust me."

"But it *does* make you more interesting."

"Thank you," she said, not entirely sure why she was blushing. She shook her head and got back to the point doggedly. "So, you *do* want to be here? You'd want to even if you weren't a Berry?"

"Absolutely." He spoke in the solemn air of someone making a great confession. "I love Flavor. I nearly failed math three years in a row because I kept doing Flavor experiments when I was supposed to be doing my homework."

"Seriously?"

"Serious as a soufflé." He spread his hands helplessly. "I'm a total baking nerd, and Flavor is the focus of my nerdy obsession. I'm everything a Berry should be, in the most boringly Berry of ways. You still want to be my friend?"

"Nope. I'm only friends with *interesting* people. Non-nerds."

He sighed. "Yeah. That's a good call."

"But . . ." She smiled. "I guess since there are no interesting non-nerds around, you'll have to do. For now."

CHAPTER TWENTY

The Caramelle Experience

All academy ovens worked at a magically charged high speed. Five minutes later, Lyra took the brownies out and popped them in an enchanted cooling drawer. Boysen whipped up a vanilla cream cheese frosting with a decadent raspberry swirl and asked Lyra to promise solemnly never to breathe a word to Razz about the choice of berry.

At Boysen's urging, Lyra performed the cake version of Madame Temper's Chant of Precision that she had used in her entrance exam. She had doubts about the spell's efficacy with brownies, but Boysen assured her it could work as a general finishing touch. He also insisted that Queen Penelope would appreciate the extra effort.

Sure enough, as Lyra hummed the song she had written for the spell during her entrance exam prep, streams of purple light began flowing from her fingertips. The magic danced around the pan, elevating Boysen's already tidy frosting job. Simultaneously, a sparkling, clean feeling washed over Lyra.

If only relationships could be transformed so easily, she thought.

The finished brownies were not just neat. They glowed, as if remnants of Boysen's Flavor magic and Lyra's Presentation spell were still lingering in every molecule. Surely, this was a dessert fit for a queen.

The giant chicken accepted their offering with all the gracious poise one would expect of royalty. Bowing her head in thanks, she clucked appreciatively about the pan's special shimmer. She then abandoned all restraint and gobbled up every morsel of brownie in seven seconds, leaving her feathers flecked with raspberry and chocolate.

While Queen Penelope reveled in the sweet treat, Lyra and Boysen turned to collecting the weekend's eggs. Hyacinth had shown them how the system worked. Within a few minutes, Lyra and Boysen each had ten massive trays in their arms, all hovering in a protective floating enchantment. After the eggs were safely deposited in the kitchen and the baking mess was cleaned up, Boysen suggested returning to Whisk for hot chocolate.

"What about you, Treble?" he asked, once they were settled by the fire with their steaming mugs. "We learned earlier that I'm a Flavor nerd. Hopelessly so. But what's the focus of your nerdy obsession?"

She shrugged. "Baking."

"Yes, but which principle?" He was studying her again, his brown eyes dancing in the firelight. "I've been trying to figure it out all week. Are you more gut, mind, or heart? What's your favorite part of the baking process?"

"I don't know," Lyra admitted.

He raised his eyebrows. "Seriously?"

"As a soufflé," she said. "Honestly. I've been trying to figure it out too. I didn't realize it was such a big deal here. I mean, I knew they picked six people and only three were left at the end of the year. I just didn't realize it was so . . . specific. That they weren't just picking the top three bakers, but one for each principle."

"It's not always so clear," Boysen said. "You can't get through the academy without being really good at all three. Most of the time, someone will demonstrate a particular strength in one of the three, but not always. Sometimes it's a matter of preference. Which principle interests the student the most? Then they *choose* that principle to focus in, rather than being selected by the professor. That's what happened with Hyacinth."

Lyra's eyes widened. "Really?"

"Oh, sure. Hyacinth . . . she's phenomenal. Once-in-a-generation baker, and I'm not just saying that because she's probably going to be my sister-in-law someday."

"So she could have picked anything?" Lyra asked. "She was that good in all three?"

Boysen nodded. "And she chose Texture. Razz says she likes math. A lot. Like, it's scary."

"Caramelle likes math," Lyra observed.

"Which proves Caramelle is a born Texturist. And also scary." Boysen's intent gaze didn't waver. "And you? Do you like math?"

"It's all right."

"So maybe Texture isn't your nerdy focus."

"But Texture isn't *just* math," Lyra protested. "I loved the Texture part of my final entrance exam. Master Pavlova's Spell of Fluffening is so fun. I wrote two whole songs about it."

Boysen's smile widened. "So, Texture is a definite maybe. What about Flavor? You enjoying Honeycomb's class?"

"So much. I can't wait for more FIT."

"As I said, you've got great instincts." He spoke the next words carefully, keeping his voice light. "And Presentation? Does that class have any . . . special appeal for you?"

She kept her own voice light, refusing to acknowledge the blush spreading across her face. "Sure. I do like the idea of style and getting to express myself."

"Got it. You like all three disciplines equally and have so far shown plenty of aptitude in each." Boysen nodded sagely. "Congratulations, Treble. You are officially an enigma."

She gave him another shove. "Thanks for nothing, Berry."

He laughed and rolled off the couch. "Don't thank me. Thank the Whisk Whiz Review! If anything can sort out your magical baking woes, it can."

"What can?" asked a voice from the door.

They both whirled around. Caramelle Meringue was standing in the doorway, her posture and auburn curls as perfect as ever.

"I apologize for my lateness," she said, her voice surprisingly shaky. "And for my absence last night. I . . ." She trailed off, looking around the room. "Did I miss it?"

"Not at all." Boysen stood, ushering her to sit in his spot on the couch. "Lyra and I were holding down the fort. I'll get you some hot chocolate. Treble, how about a refill?"

Without waiting for a reply, he took her still mostly full mug and walked quickly to the kitchen portion of the room, leaving the two roommates in relative privacy.

Caramelle perched primly at the edge of the couch. Lyra curled further into her corner, gazing determinedly at the fire. They sat in awkward silence for a few moments.

Inwardly, Lyra was spiraling. She had spent the past twenty-four hours thinking of all she wanted to say to Caramelle. She lost track of the number of conversations they'd had in her head. Now, she couldn't remember a single one of the biting, witty remarks she'd imagined herself delivering.

Before she could concoct a new one, Caramelle took a deep breath.

"I'm sorry, Lyra."

Lyra blinked. "Beg your pardon?"

"I'm sorry," Caramelle repeated. "I snapped at you yesterday. I shouldn't have said . . . what I said."

The spiral inside Lyra continued, just in reverse. She wrapped her arms around a pillow for support. "Do you still think I'm hiding something?"

"I was just stressed." This wasn't really an answer, but Caramelle did look incredibly harried, so Lyra let her continue. "I've been under a lot of pressure, this first week. I know we all have, but I don't respond to pressure well. It's not an excuse. I just wanted you to know . . . I'm sorry."

She looked up at Lyra. With a start, Lyra saw her roommate's eyes were filled with tears.

"Being a Meringue is not easy," Caramelle said, keeping the tears in check with admirable self-control. "Every advantage it brings has an expectation attached. There must always be precision. Perfection. I have a legacy of excellence to uphold and centuries of tradition from which I can never deviate. It's . . . so heavy, Lyra. Sometimes I can actually feel it. Right here."

She pressed one hand delicately to her chest. Lyra noted the perfectly manicured fingers were trembling.

"It's like this bag of wet flour," Caramelle continued, "pressing down on my heart. Sometimes it's so heavy, I can hardly breathe."

Lyra could feel her own heart softening. It was impossible to see The Perfect Meringue in this state and maintain the sense of bewildered outrage that had dominated her thoughts for the past twenty-four hours. Still, she tried to steel herself.

"You said I bewitched the professors. You basically accused me of cheating," she said, as coldly as she could manage in the face of Caramelle's fragility.

"I don't want to fall back into old habits," Caramelle said, her voice rising to a quietly hysterical pitch. "I want us to be there for each other this term. Help each other, like I said that first day. Can you help me, Lyra? Can you forgive me?"

For a moment, Lyra hesitated. Caramelle hadn't taken back anything she'd said yesterday. She hadn't owned up to her deceit in Presentation class. She hadn't mentioned Cardamom at all.

The memory of Ginger's warnings from their first day echoed in Lyra's head:

The Meringue must always be first and best.

The Meringue is not a person. The Meringue is a force of nature, and as such, ought to be treated with the same reasonable fear.

Tangle with The Meringue, and you end up with egg on your face. And all over your clothes, and in your hair, most likely.

But then another memory broke in, much more recent, tinged with the delicious smell of baking brownies and the warmth of genuine concern.

The more Stellar Enchantment Pins attached to your hat, the heavier it gets, said Boysen's voice in Lyra's mind. *Same with legacy. I'm surprised Caramelle can even walk around upright.*

Lyra studied the girl sitting beside her on the couch. Her roommate did, indeed, look exhausted, like it took all her strength to keep that perfect posture under the burden of her family name.

Boysen's voice continued, *I do think she's under a lot of pressure. Just . . . don't let her get to you, and maybe cut her a break.*

Lyra sighed. "I forgive you."

Caramelle's eyes widened. Then she threw her arms around Lyra, burying her face in her startled roommate's shoulder.

"Thank you!" she squeaked into Lyra's hair. "Just . . . thank you."

Lyra pulled back, holding her roommate's shoulders. "On one condition. No more games. Do you actually *want* to experiment with spells in Presentation?"

Caramelle's shoulders tensed for a moment, then slumped. She shook her head slowly. "I don't know what came over me. My parents would be horrified. If they hear I was *innovating . . .*"

She shuddered.

"Then don't," Lyra said simply, forcing her lips into an encouraging smile. "Let's just both focus on doing the best we can in class. Deal?"

Caramelle mustered her own shaky smile. "Deal."

"All well?" Boysen asked gaily, arriving from the kitchen with three mugs at just the right time. Caramelle sat back, wiping her eyes, and accepted the drink he handed her.

"Better," she said, beaming at Lyra. "I hope."

Lyra nodded, ignoring the broad wink Boysen was trying to give her. All wasn't quite well just yet. She wasn't sure, at least. But compared to the past twenty-four hours, her internal "texture" had definitely improved. She took the mug Boysen offered her and flashed him a tiny, quick private smile.

"Better," she agreed.

"Thank the seasonings for that," he said cheerily. "The magic of the Whisk Whiz Review strikes again." He raised his mug. "To the Whisk Whiz Review!"

The girls raised their mugs.

"The Whisk Whiz Review!"

Over the next several weeks, Lyra began to wonder if the Whisk Whiz Review *was* magic. Either that or Boysen had performed some sneaky wizardry on their hot chocolate, spiking them with an enchantment to promote goodwill.

Regardless, after that evening with Boysen and the following reconciliation with Caramelle, the term really did get . . . better. The first years settled swiftly into the rhythm of the Royal Academy of Magical Baking and of their communal life. Each week rolled thrillingly into the next, more difficult and yet equally more fulfilling than all its predecessors.

Professor Honeycomb sharpened their instincts. Professor Puff demanded exactitude that was, somehow, as comforting as it was rigorous. Professor Genoise encouraged each of them to embrace their unique style. And always, in the evening, every first year except Aniseed gathered around the fire in Whisk, challenging and encouraging each other through that day's trials. Lyra fell into her bed in Pestle every night exhausted and yet happier than she had ever been.

A big part of this happiness was due to Boysen. He was, without question, the soul of their group, holding them all together with hot chocolate and smiling wisdom. Ginger was practical and refreshingly no-nonsense. Mac was whimsical and funny, often brightening a dull moment with a sneak-attack morsel of wit. Lyra tried to contribute by sharing her music and the joy of someone from outside the baking world.

Still, Boysen was the anchor. He always seemed to know when Lyra was spiraling, and he had a special smile seemingly designed to pull her back from the brink every time. Lyra didn't know where she . . . where *any* of them would be without him. She didn't *want* to know.

The other primary happiness factor for Lyra was Caramelle. Being on good terms with one's roommate really did make a difference. Lyra had suspected that from the beginning, especially when she first saw the size of Pestle.

But this happiness was more than just a lack of tension in small living quarters. Caramelle's presence *enhanced* Lyra's experience at the academy. For one thing, she was an incredible student, both conscientious and creative. No one worked harder than Caramelle. She made it clear every day that she was not interested in coasting on her family name. She had earned her place at the academy, and she was going to earn the right to keep it, no matter what.

It was stimulating to be around someone who cared so much all the time. Lyra felt herself growing by sheer proximity. In fact, as the weeks went by, Lyra found herself singled out by the professors nearly as much as Caramelle. Even Professor Puff called Lyra up once or twice for public praise.

Caramelle extended this same determination to her relationships with her peers. She seemed to take Professor Honeycomb's personality powders lesson as an educational mandate. The professors worked together well and clearly expected their students to do the same. So Caramelle Meringue was going to be the best team player anyone at the academy had ever seen.

Lyra was the primary target of Caramelle's camaraderie efforts. Caramelle took the "roomie" title as seriously as she took every aspect of academy life. Just as she had promised Lyra on their first day, and reaffirmed by the fire in Whisk at the end of the first week, the girls of Pestle had each other's back. Caramelle was the most faithful study buddy, meal companion, and accountability partner anyone could ask for.

There were downsides to the Caramelle Experience, of course. She spent longer in the bathroom every morning than the other three girls combined, layering herself in Self-Presentation spells. True to her word, she eased off her innovation craze in Professor Genoise's class, but she still took every opportunity to ask for Cardamom's help, calling him over to her workstation and flirting so shamelessly that Lyra blushed on her behalf.

Even Caramelle's single-minded devotion to excellence could be a trial. Lyra had to argue her into sleeping sometimes or remind her that things like "breaks" existed. As the term drew to a close and the professors made no mention of what their final exam would be, Lyra had to talk Caramelle down from many a stress-induced ledge. There were also times when Caramelle's smiles at the Whisk Whiz Review felt a little forced, as if "cooperation with colleagues" was just another assignment she was checking off her Perfect Aspiring Baker list.

But in the grand scheme of things, Lyra couldn't complain. In fact, she was grateful to whatever academy official or twist of fate had put her in Pestle with Caramelle. She chuckled to herself sometimes whenever Ginger's dire warnings floated back up to the surface of her memory.

Sure, a bad meringue can make a mess, Lyra thought as she and Caramelle headed towards the Flavor classroom at the start of the term's final week. *But a good meringue? A good meringue lifts up everything around it.*

Hopefully, the Caramelle Experience would be enough to get Lyra through the dreaded first-term exam. Surely, the professors would be sharing details about it soon.

Just thinking about it sent jitters coursing through Lyra's veins. The academy already felt like home. If she could just get through to the second term . . .

Professor Honeycomb clapped her hands as they walked through the door. "Welcome, Aspiring Bakers!"

CHAPTER TWENTY-ONE

PESTLE GIRLS STICK TOGETHER

rofessor Honeycomb's cheery greeting never got old to Lyra. The plump teacher's curly gray hair, always tied back carefully in a green scarf, shone in the morning light as she nodded at each student in turn.

"Come in, come in. Meringue and Treble, it does me good to see you arm and arm. That's the congenial Royal Academy spirit! Looking particularly sharp this morning, Fondant. Crumble, congratulations again on that inspired use of chili pepper last week. I look forward to your next icing endeavor with great anticipation. My my, Aspiring Baker Mint, how *do* you keep your apron so clean?"

Boysen tried to slip past with a friendly wave, but she snagged his apron strings and pulled him to the front.

"Not so fast, Berry. Your brother tells me you have a flair for the experimental. Is this, indeed, the case?"

"I-I like to play around with new combinations sometimes," he admitted, trying to extricate himself politely from her grasp. "But I wouldn't call that flair."

"Don't be modest, Poison." Razz placed a heavy hand on each of his little brother's shoulders, trapping him firmly in place. "Regular mad scientist, this one. Has his own private laboratory at home and everything."

"It's a shed out back," Boysen protested weakly.

"Which you spent hours in every day after school." Razz was obviously enjoying his brother's discomfort and just as obviously proud of his accomplishments. "Hours and hours, Professor Honeycomb. We had to drag him in for dinner. And he's kept it up here at the academy."

"Oh?" Professor Honeycomb raised her eyebrows.

Mac nodded. "It's true. You should see the state of the Whisk kitchen on the weekends."

"Traitor," Boysen muttered softly.

"Can confirm," Razz said. "I get samples sometimes when I'm on dorm duty. You should taste some of the combinations he dreams up!"

"I should indeed." Professor Honeycomb's blue eyes twinkled as she pointed a finger in Boysen's face. "No more holding out on me, Berry. Do you hear? I want your favorite recent experiment on my counter when you come in for Flavor lab tomorrow. Is that understood?"

Boysen's face was as red as his namesake, but he managed his genuine good-natured grin. "Yes, Professor."

"Excellent. Now, off with you."

Boysen scurried to his workstation just as Professor Genoise swept grandly into the room followed by Professor Puff at a more demure pace. The three teachers stood together on the platform and surveyed the first years.

"As I am sure you know," Professor Genoise began, "this is the final week of our first term. Your first term evaluation will take place this Saturday morning in the exam hall."

"For this evaluation, we ask that you repeat your final entrance exam cake, with a few key differences," Professor Honeycomb said.

Professor Puff took up the thread. "This exam should be a showcase of your growth in this first term. As such, you may only use techniques or spells you have learned in class." A murmur ran through the room, but the Texture headmistress continued unperturbed. "The same rules from the final entrance exam apply. You may choose only one spell each for Texture and Presentation, and they must be spells from the first term curriculum."

"For Flavor, of course, we haven't been using magic this term." Professor Honeycomb smiled. "So you are not permitted to use any Flavor spells. But I ask that you include one additional ingredient in your exam cake as a flavor combination. Review the many flavors we have covered this term and choose one that will harmonize well with the taste of your original recipe. This will demonstrate the development of your Flavor instinct . . . or lack thereof."

Professor Genoise stroked his neat gray beard with delicately manicured fingers. "I am sure we do not need to explain to you the importance of this exam. Only five of you can advance to the second term. At the end of this exam, we will announce who will be leaving us. We will also award the year's first Stellar Enchantment Pin to the Aspiring Baker who most distinguishes themselves with their cake."

"Then we will all gather that night for our annual winter holiday feast, before you leave for break." Professor Honeycomb beamed at the class. "We look forward to celebrating your growth!"

"And to tailoring your instruction for the second term," Professor Puff added. "The first exam allows us to identify the strengths and weaknesses of the foundation you have laid thus far, that we may build upon it efficiently for the rest of the year."

"We shall be spending this week in review, to ensure that you may approach Saturday's task with confidence." Professor Genoise surveyed the first years. "Any questions? Yes, Aspiring Baker Meringue?"

Caramelle's hand stayed frozen in the air after she was called on, as if she'd forgotten she had raised it. "Professor, may I ask why we are only hearing about this now, with not even a full week to prepare? Why the secrecy?"

"Secrecy is a strong word." Professor Genoise chuckled. "We are not setting you up to fail, Aspiring Baker Meringue. We simply want the most accurate assessment possible of what you have learned this term. If you have been applying yourself each day in class, you have nothing to fear."

He smiled graciously, and Caramelle slowly lowered her hand.

"Any other questions? No?" Professor Genoise turned to the Flavor headmistress, giving her a deep bow. "As always, thank you for hosting, Professor Honeycomb."

"Of course, Professor Genoise. Professor Puff."

The Texture and Presentation teachers nodded formally to the class, then departed.

Professor Honeycomb rubbed her hands together briskly. "Time for some Flavor Identification Training! Razz, distribute the powders, if you please."

This kicked off a whirlwind week for the first years. Each day, they pushed themselves in class, straining every nerve to absorb as much foundation-building "growth" as possible. Each night, all but Aniseed gathered in Whisk, pooling their resources from the day and comparing strategies. They then spilled out into the dorm's first-floor common area, making full use of the larger kitchen as they each baked practice cake after practice cake.

Despite the stress of the looming exam, it was one of the happiest weeks of Lyra's life. She received a personalized compliment from each professor on their respective lab days, which was better than even her roommate. Though Caramelle was singled out once by Professor Genoise and several times by Professor Puff, only Lyra and Boysen were called up by Professor Honeycomb for public praise.

The one small lump in Lyra's batter that week was, in fact, Caramelle's behavior in Presentation. The auburn-haired girl was positively frantic for help in preparing for the exam. And since, of course, Professor Genoise had to divide his attention equally among all six students, the task of assuaging Caramelle's anxiety fell entirely to Apprentice Baker Coulis. She kept Cardamom at her workstation all through class on Monday and Friday and for most of Thursday's lab.

Lyra tried not to let it bother her. It helped that she knew Caramelle well enough by now to understand that this was not a game . . . At least, not entirely. The Meringue's exam-induced panic was all too real. Lyra kept reminding herself of that all through the hours spent in Professor Genoise's classroom that week, keeping her eyes determinedly focused on her own work and making a valiant effort to ignore the faint scent of cinnamon and honey wafting towards her from Caramelle's workstation.

Still, on the whole, Lyra reveled in the sense of fulfillment and accomplishment simmering in her chest through every long day. When the roommates arrived back in Pestle Friday night after the final Whisk Whiz Review of the term, Lyra felt tired but as ready as she would ever be.

"Time for a good night's sleep." Lyra yawned as she took off her apron and surveyed it ruefully. It was covered in stains from the week's practice sessions. "Thanks again for recommending that I get the extra apron," she said to Caramelle. "It makes a difference to head into a big event with a clean outfit, and I'm not up for laundry tonight."

Caramelle didn't seem to hear her. She was leaning against the door, staring off into the middle distance.

"Caramelle?" Lyra threw the apron at her roommate, who caught it reflexively. "You all right?"

Caramelle looked down at the apron in her hands. "I'm just . . . nervous. About tomorrow."

"You don't say." Lyra crossed the room and wrapped the auburn-haired girl in a hug. "I know you probably won't agree with me here, but if anyone has reason *not* to be nervous, it's you."

"It's dangerous to think that way." Caramelle pushed the apron into Lyra's hands and moved away, perching on the edge of her bed. "My mother always warned me that if I don't take baking seriously, I'll get complacent. That's . . . not an option in my house. Nothing less than the absolute best. Ever."

"You do take it seriously," Lyra insisted. "And you work hard. Complacent is not the word anyone would use to describe you."

Her roommate just stared at the floor, eyes wide in her pale, strained face.

Lyra placed a hand on the girl's rigid shoulder. "Everyone knows you have done *absolutely* everything you can to succeed tomorrow. All that's left to do is rest."

Caramelle kept her gaze on the floor. A few long silent moments ticked by. Then she nodded, as if she had made a decision.

"There is one more thing I can do." She stood, grabbed Lyra's hand, and started dragging her to the kitchen area. "Put that apron back on. We're not done practicing."

Lyra groaned. "Yes, we are. We have our recipes for tomorrow. We've each made our cake at least a dozen times this week. Now we need *sleep*."

Caramelle took the apron and started putting it on Lyra. "Remember what I told you at the beginning of term? I wanted us to be there for each other. Have each other's back. So this is me having your back."

"How?" Lyra demanded as Caramelle tied the apron strings firmly. "By practicing solidarity in sleep deprivation?"

"By giving you an edge." Caramelle leaned in, dropping her voice to a whisper. "I've been getting some extra help from Cardamom in Presentation class this week."

Lyra's heart flip-flopped. "I . . . I noticed."

"It's not like that first week," Caramelle assured her. "I actually do need the help. My style is virtuosic, remember? I can put on a great show. But we've been focusing so much on basic neatness this term, and that's my weak spot. Cardamom has been so helpful. This week, he gave me a great tip to get the most out of the Presentation spell you and I are using in our exam cakes."

"Madame Temper's Chant of Precision?"

"That's the one." Caramelle gripped Lyra's arm, her hands shaking. "I know you used that spell in your final entrance exam, and it was great, so I've been telling myself all week that you don't need this tip. That I could keep it to myself. But that's not fair. Pestle girls stick together, right?"

"Sure," Lyra said slowly. "But . . . special help? Isn't it cheating?"

Caramelle's eyes widened. "Not at all! We're supposed to use what we've learned in class. This is what I learned in class, from Professor Genoise's official assistant. And it's not like he gave me a different spell to use or anything. It's just a slightly better technique for the spell we're using already: a shift in inflection to two words and an extra repetition of the last line."

Lyra hesitated. "I appreciate it, Caramelle. I really do. But if it's such a subtle adjustment . . . will it matter? I mean, will it make that big a difference?"

"This is our first exam at the academy," Caramelle said fervently. "We're up against a group of incredibly talented bakers, and one of us won't be here next term. We have to use every resource at our disposal to make sure we're not that one."

"I guess . . ."

"Just let me show you once, and then you can decide if you want to use it or not," Caramelle pleaded. "I think . . . I *know* Cardamom would want me to share this with you. He talks about you quite a bit, you know."

Lyra's flip-flopping heart gave a great leap, lodging somewhere in her throat. "He does?"

"Oh yes. He thinks it's great that we're roommates. He believes in both of us so much." Caramelle gazed at Lyra, her eyes large and shining with intensity. "Will you go through the recipe once with me?"

"Okay," Lyra relented. "One more practice run, with Cardamom's adjustment to the Presentation spell. But then we sleep. Deal?"

"Deal!" Caramelle clapped her hands. "Oh, Lyra! Tomorrow is going to be a grand day."

She smoothed her perfectly coiled auburn hair, then twirled in place before dancing towards the kitchen. Lyra laughed and followed, caught up in her room-mate's sudden burst of spirits.

"A grand day indeed," Caramelle sang under her breath as she quietly got out bowls and pans. "I can feel it, Lyra. You mark my words. The Stellar Enchantment Pin is coming to Pestle tomorrow."

CHAPTER TWENTY-TWO

A Bard's Best Effort

For the first time in her baking career, Lyra was excited about an exam.

True, her baking career had been remarkably short so far, especially compared to her classmates. But as she stood in the exam hall, watching the early dawn light filter through the windows and waiting for the professors to arrive, Lyra was struck by how good she felt.

The year of trials leading up to her academy acceptance had been . . . well, a trial. Lyra loved the baking part, but baking in public rattled her nerves. Being *judged* in public was even worse. She remembered keenly the jangled state of her insides the last time she had stood in this exam hall, waiting for the final entrance exam to begin.

But now?

Lyra glanced around at her friends. Ginger caught her eye and made a face. Mac gave her two thumbs up. Boysen just smiled, his whole face lighting up in one of his special Lyra-only grins.

They had made it through the first term. Together, they had survived and overcome everything the Royal Academy of Magical Baking could throw at them. Thanks to their support, Lyra could confidently say that she was the best baker she could currently be.

Lyra returned Boysen's smile. How could anyone be sad or stressed when surrounded by such warmth?

As usual, the only one who worried her slightly was Caramelle. The ladies of Pestle had stayed up late with their final practice run. Lyra knew they were both exhausted, but they had ended the night in remarkably good spirits. The sense of congeniality and partnership seemed to fill the room; Lyra could still feel it in the air when she woke up that morning.

Caramelle, on the other hand, did not appear fueled or inspired. She perched on her stool, hands folded, posture and hair both savagely perfect. She had barely said a word to Lyra all morning. In fact, she didn't seem able to look anyone in the eye.

Lyra could only imagine the pressure her Meringue roommate was under for this first final exam. She ached to help her friend, to return the support given so generously the night before, but it was impossible with Caramelle in this closed-off state.

"Aspiring Bakers!"

The imperious voice of Professor Genoise cut across Lyra's thoughts. She abandoned her attempts to catch Caramelle's eye and turned to face the professors.

"You have your instructions," Professor Puff called out. "Your final entrance exam cake, using only spells and techniques you have learned in class this term."

Professor Honeycomb's eyes were sparkling so brightly, Lyra could see them all the way across the room. "You have been practicing diligently," the professor said warmly. "We are proud of your progress this week and across the whole term."

"Now let us see that progress in action." Professor Genoise spread his hands. "Two hours on the clock, and . . . begin!"

Lyra's hands moved faster than thought. The recipe was like a familiar tune, and her muscles sang it expertly, weaving through each step with effortless rhythm. That familiar rush of performance adrenaline coursed through her whole body, setting all her senses alight with the joy of knowing she could do this. She was *good* at this.

She, Lyra Treble, was an Aspiring Baker. She belonged at the Royal Academy of Magical Baking.

And this cake was going to prove it to everyone.

Step one was mixing the cake batter, which meant the Texture spell came first. Lyra was glad. She was feeling more confident than ever before about this particular baking discipline, but she still remembered a time when she had stumbled over the spell. It was good to know she could get it over with at the beginning.

All five members of the Whisk Whiz Review had chosen Master Chiffon's Aeration Charm for the exam's Texture component. This was largely due to Mac's enthusiastic advocacy during their Monday night meeting. Eyes shining behind his glasses, he had recited the entirety of Caramelle's speech from week one about this particular charm's efficacy for cakes. Boysen, Lyra, and Ginger applauded raucously, and even Caramelle let her exam-week severity crack for a moment, giving Mac a rare smile that rendered him speechless for the remainder of the evening.

Lyra had contributed by reworking the tune she'd created for the spell, adapting it for each of her classmates. She even obliged them by singing it during their first few practice rounds. Caramelle declined this offer but with such grace and gratitude that Lyra couldn't be offended. It made sense, after all. If any of them could truthfully claim not to *need* Texture help, it was The Meringue.

All the other Whizzes had been thrilled with the song. Boysen claimed Mac had even invented accompanying dance moves, a claim Mac denied so violently that Lyra felt sorry for him. So when his foot started tapping and wiggling during one of his musical practice rounds, she pretended not to notice.

The memory made Lyra smile as she stood in the exam hall, steeling herself to launch into an intermediate level of Master Chiffon's Aeration Charm. Caramelle had worked with her tirelessly on the equations to work out pitch, tempo, and number of repetitions. It was a fairly short spell, but Lyra had to get through it exactly twenty-seven times and at varying speeds for each stage to guide the magically powered beaters.

Lyra had never accomplished this without singing the charm in her head. In fact, she was still unable to perform any Texture spell without any mental singing, a fact she was careful to hide from her roommate.

Whatever Professor Puff might say, Lyra knew Caramelle did not approve of such musical "tricks." The Meringue barely tolerated her classmates' use of songs to *learn* the spells. Lyra didn't want to rock the mostly peaceful boat of their relationship by admitting she still needed music to have even a hope of *accomplishing* those spells.

Lyra took a deep breath. Keeping her lips pressed tightly together, she began creaming butter and sugar together, kicking off round one of the charm's jaunty tune in her head at the same exact moment. The song surged through her fingers into the handheld mixer, locking the beaters' movements into a swift, steady rhythm and infusing every ingredient with an extra shot of airy lightness. Thirteen rounds later, she added the eggs and vanilla, slightly moderating her pace for the next six rounds.

Then came the trickiest part. Setting the handheld mixer aside, she slowed the song down to a gentle lullaby, using a spatula to painstakingly fold in alternate additions of dry ingredients and buttermilk. Eight agonizing rounds later, she was rewarded with a wave of vivid blue light. It poured from her hands in one radiant wave, encompassing not only the batter, but the entire bowl. The glowing blue orb pulsed softly once, twice, three times, once for each cake layer. Then it shrank rapidly and disappeared into the silky-smooth batter, as quiet and demure as Professor Puff herself.

Lyra allowed herself a single sigh of relief once the cakes were in the oven. The batter looked exactly as it had the previous night, except maybe even a tad fluffier and more glistening. She glanced around, wanting to give Caramelle a grateful smile, but her roommate's auburn head was bent over her own batter.

Lyra sighed and turned her attention to frosting. No spells needed here. This was where the Flavor instinct was supposed to kick in, informing her if the flavors she wanted to combine were sufficiently balanced.

Shaking out the lingering tension in her shoulders, Lyra found herself singing

"All Gather Round" under her breath as she measured out a small dose of dried boysenberry powder. The juicy, sweet, slightly tart berry paired so well with her vanilla cake that it was a natural addition for her flavor combination. Boysen's delight with her plan had been a lovely bonus. It was like she had unlocked a whole new category of private Boysen smiles to savor for the coming term.

Lyra whipped heavy cream until stiff peaks formed. Still singing in her head, she added vanilla, sugar, and the measured boysenberry powder. Then she beat cream cheese into airy heights, carefully folded in the boysenberry whipped cream, and sampled.

Not enough.

Her gut wasn't whispering. It was singing as loudly as the "All Gather Round" song trilling through Lyra's thoughts. She smiled and added a few more pinches of boysenberry powder to the frosting.

TOO MUCH, complained her Flavor-attuned gut.

Lyra stifled a giggle. She whipped up some more heavy cream, adding just vanilla and plain sugar this time. Then she folded it into the frosting, a tiny scoop at a time, until she guessed the boysenberry had been sufficiently mellowed. She tried a tiny taste, and her gut broke into a chorus of delight.

Just right! Just right! Just right!

Lyra sighed happily. She could practically see the green light that would have danced over the frosting if she had been performing a spell. Even better, she could almost hear Chef Flax's delighted laugh rolling underneath the chorus of instincts in her gut.

He and Bumble were going to *love* this cake. Sprinkle too.

By this time, the layers were ready to come out of the oven. Lyra set them in the magical drawer specifically enchanted to cool cakes down at an even rate without collapsing them, and set about final preparations for assembly. This involved hand painting a few dozen boysenberries with a shiny vanilla-based glaze. It was tedious, but when she arranged them on her intricately piped frosting, the effect would be marvelous.

The task slipped by merrily as Lyra hummed to herself, surrounded by the pleasant background noise of bakers hard at work. Everything was going well—very well. Better than any practice session that week. All that remained was decoration, and with Caramelle's tip from Cardamom about the Presentation spell, Lyra could move quickly without fear of sloppiness.

She was practically dancing as she removed the perfectly cooled cakes from the drawer. Holding her hands over the cakes and decorative materials, she mentally recited Madame Temper's Chant of Precision, taking great care to implement the modified inflection and extra line repetition Cardamom had shared with Caramelle. Then, her heart singing, she began the fun, though nerve-wracking process of assembly.

That was when everything started to go wrong.

Perhaps "wrong" was an exaggeration. The frosting did go on the cake. The layers stacked nicely and showed no sign of caving. Piping did occur. Berries were arranged.

But no streams of purple light appeared to pull the decorative elements together. Everything felt slightly off, as though the cake was missing some key factor to draw all the separate parts into a cohesive whole. Some *magical* factor.

But that's what the chant is supposed to do, Lyra thought desperately. Her fingers itched, strangely heavy without the light of successful magic, but she didn't dare recite the chant again. Presentation spells were notoriously volatile when performed too many times.

Looking around, she saw that all her classmates were putting the final touches on their cakes. There was a definite glow to each finished product, a quiet brilliance that made Lyra's senses sing. These cakes were beautiful examples of a simple Presentation spell executed to perfection.

Lyra looked back at her cake. It wasn't ugly or messy by any means. The frosting was smooth and creamy. The piping was mostly neat. The glazed boysenberries were a pleasantly shiny addition to her original design of red and pink roses. The cake looked all right, actually, but it was definitely lacking that exquisite glow.

It looks like a bard made it, Lyra realized, her heart plummeting down to her shoes. An enthusiastic bard with no formal training in magical baking. A bard's best effort, sure, but . . . just a bard. Not a baker.

There was no time to change it. Even as Lyra reached for the piping bag, hoping vainly to add a bit more pizzazz, Professor Puff's voice rang out calmly through the hall.

"Time is up, Aspiring Bakers. Please place your cake at the end of your counter."

Without another word, the three professors moved as one to Mac's counter and began their silent perusal of his cake.

The first term final exam judging had begun.

CHAPTER TWENTY-THREE

Madame Temper's Chant of Betrayal

Lyra slumped on her stool. In the corner of her eye, she saw Boysen trying to get her attention, but she pretended not to notice.

She couldn't look at him. She couldn't look at anyone.

The judging proceeded as silently as it had during the final entrance exam. Before, the lack of noise had made Lyra jittery. Now, it pressed down on her shoulders like a fifty-pound bag of flour, giving her the strange feeling that she was sinking into the stone floor.

The cheerful morning sunlight streaming through the windows felt oppressive. Like all rooms at the academy, the exam hall's temperature was magically controlled, but Lyra was uncomfortably warm. No matter how many times she wiped her hands on her apron, they remained slick with perspiration.

When the three professors reached her counter, Lyra wasn't sure what to hope for. Would the Flavor and Texture be so amazing that they would break their silence and compliment her, like before? But if Professors Honeycomb and Puff spoke, that meant Professor Genoise would also have to speak.

Lyra did *not* want to hear what he had to say.

She tried to rally. Sitting up, she folded her hands in imitation of Caramelle and smiled. She hung on to that smile and clenched her hands in her lap as each professor's eyes widened at the sight of her lackluster cake. Professor Genoise glanced at her, raised a single eyebrow, but said nothing.

That first moment was the worst. The cake cut beautifully, and though Professor Puff's face was habitually unreadable, Lyra was fairly confident she saw approval in the Texture headmistress's gray eyes. She also could have sworn she saw Professor Honeycomb's shoulders wriggle in delight at the first taste of Lyra's vanilla-boysenberry flavor combination.

All three professors nodded. They had a silent moment of communication, exchanging a series of meaningful looks with each other and the cake. Then they nodded again, bowed to Lyra, and moved on.

That was it. No words, no winks, no smiles. No message of any kind.

Lyra clenched her hands even tighter, digging her nails into her palms. The smile melted off her face like buttercream frosting on a cake still warm from the oven. She glared at her okay-looking cake, silently demanding that it answer the question screaming repeatedly through her brain.

What did I do wrong?

She went back over every step. Point for point, the recipe and execution were identical to the dozens of practice sessions she had squeezed in over the past week. The only new element was the slight tweak to Madame Temper's Chant of Precision, but that had gone perfectly the night before.

Squeezing her eyes shut, Lyra replayed that final late-night practice session with Caramelle, urging her memory to analyze each moment in slow motion. It was tricky, both because of her still tingling nerves and her bleary-eyed exhaustion. Still, when she reached the point when Caramelle had demonstrated Cardamom's pro tip, Lyra paused.

She remembered something.

She had been distracted at the time, making notes of the adjustments and cleaning up in preparation for bed. But she distinctly remembered Caramelle's hands moving in a complicated pattern over the cake just before the streams of purple light appeared to confirm the chant's magic was at work.

The movement happened so fast, Lyra had barely caught it. But it did happen. Caramelle recited the altered spell, then performed some intricate motion with her fingers. At the time, in her weariness, Lyra had dismissed this as a careless gesture, like someone dusting off their hands at the end of a long day's work.

But Caramelle was never careless. Every move she made was purposeful. She had done something to that cake . . .

Lyra's blood felt sluggish, like ice was forming along the insides of her veins. Her heart seemed to be taking longer and longer between each beat. But her thoughts moved rapidly, pounding along with terrible clarity towards an even more terrible conclusion.

Caramelle had sabotaged her.

Once her mind formed the words, there was no reclaiming them. She could only watch, helpless, as the reasoning played itself out on her mental stage.

Caramelle was a Meringue. She had told Lyra many times that failure at the Royal Academy of Magical Baking was not an option for her. And for a Meringue, failure meant anything below first place. Absolute perfection was the only true definition of success.

Caramelle's words from the night before echoed in Lyra's memory: *We're up against a group of incredibly talented bakers, and one of us won't be here next term. We have to use every resource at our disposal to make sure we're not that one.*

Caramelle had been living by that principle all term. It seemed so obvious to Lyra now. Caramelle had joined the Whisk Whiz Review not for camaraderie's sake, but to glean every advantage she could from her classmates' strengths—and to analyze their weaknesses. Then, last night, she must have decided she needed one more "edge" to guarantee she would be at the top of the pack.

She needed to trick Lyra.

There was no tip from Cardamom. Lyra was sure of it. Caramelle had invented the slight adjustments to the chant, then practiced them with Lyra to prove their efficacy. That hand motion must have canceled the detrimental impact of the altered spell or perhaps infused the whole cake with an extra boost of glamour to cover any gaps. Only then had the purple light appeared, confirming to Lyra's naive eyes that the chant had worked.

Caramelle was an expert at Self-Presentation spells, after all.

Lyra realized with a start that her whole body was shaking. Her blood wasn't frozen anymore. It was boiling, making her cheeks flush as her heart pounded in her ears.

She forced her eyes to look in Caramelle's direction, only to find the three professors gathered around her roommate's counter. Their judging was nearly complete. As she watched, Professor Genoise bowed low over Caramelle's hand, kissing it, while his colleagues gave Caramelle a silent round of applause.

In that moment, Caramelle glanced up and caught Lyra's gaze. She froze. A shadow passed over her eyes. Lyra couldn't help but think of her younger brother Rondo, whose face had worn the same expression when Lyra caught him stealing bites from one of her practice cakes.

Then Caramelle's face twisted. Her mouth hardened. Her chin tilted up. She stared boldly at Lyra over their professors' shoulders, raising her eyebrows in an unmistakable message.

Well? What are you going to do about it?

Nothing. Lyra knew she could do nothing. Regardless of Caramelle's deception, it was Lyra who had decided to use the altered chant. Lyra knew she hadn't been in the baking world long, but she was pretty sure that blaming someone else for your own mistakes was a bad idea at the Royal Academy of Magical Baking.

She stared at Caramelle until the auburn-haired girl dropped her eyes. Then Lyra turned away. Boysen was still trying to get her attention, but she fixed her gaze on the professors as they returned to the front of the room.

It was judgment time.

"This has certainly been a fascinating day," Professor Honeycomb said. "Your hard work over the past term is on full display, here in this room. Each of you has something to be proud of."

She looked directly at Lyra as she said this, lingering on her in a rather obvious fashion. Lyra felt like she was glowing and shriveling at the same time.

Professor Puff took up the thread, speaking in the same cool, even voice she always used. "Unfortunately, only five of you may carry on at the Royal Academy for the second term. The student who will not be joining us is Aniseed Mint."

Lyra blinked. She hadn't even had time to panic thoroughly. Despite her Presentation disaster, she was safe.

She was a second term student at the Royal Academy of Magical Baking. Just like that.

Of course, "just like that" did not sit well with Aniseed.

"*What?!*" the dark-haired girl shrieked. She stood, knocking over her stool, and actually stamped her foot in rage. "I demand a recount!"

"This is not a vote, Miss Mint," Professor Puff said coolly. "Our decision is final."

Aniseed tossed her head so violently, Lyra wondered how she didn't give herself a neck spasm. "Your reasons, then! Or do you have any, other than a jealous grudge against me and my family from the very beginning?"

"Reason one." Professor Honeycomb's voice was flat, hard, and so very un-Honeycomb-ish that Lyra shivered. "You disregarded the rules of this exam by using a Flavor spell, not to mention advanced charms from Texture and Presentation that were not covered in this term."

"It is not my fault that your curriculum is so amateur," Aniseed sneered. "This term has been a joke. I chose spells I have mastered on my own and made a cake that demonstrates my abilities as an excellent magical baker. The Royal Academy of Magical Baking is supposed to value excellence!"

"Excellence in the discipline of baking," Professor Genoise said coldly, peering at Aniseed over the tops of his spectacles like she was some tacky over-decorated pastry. "Discipline, Miss Mint. Discipline requires us to follow rules and to sacrifice our own ego for the sake of growth. Humility is a necessary ingredient in excellence, and it is an ingredient you clearly do not possess."

"Lack of humility and a lack of discipline," Professor Puff agreed. "That is what you have demonstrated, Miss Mint." The professor turned away from the fuming girl. "And your so-called mastery of spells leaves much to be desired. That is, without doubt, the most boring cake I have ever had the displeasure of consuming."

Aniseed stood for a moment, absolutely rigid with fury.

"You will be hearing from the royal chefs about this," she hissed. Then she stormed out, throwing her apron on the floor as she went.

"I do hope so," Professor Honeycomb called mildly after her. "It has been too long since I've seen dear Nougie—I mean Master Nougat. I would love a catch-up."

Professor Genoise ignored the sounds of Aniseed's angry exit from the hall. He smiled at the remaining students.

"A most interesting day indeed. It is now my distinct honor and delight to conclude the morning's activities by awarding this year's first Stellar Enchantment Pin. As my esteemed colleague said, each of you has reason to be proud of your efforts this term. Choosing one distinguished baker from such an admirable group is always a difficult task. Today, it was a markedly high standard in Presentation that tipped the scales in favor of this particular student."

He held up a small pin shaped like a glowing star.

"For demonstrated excellence in Master Glaze's Shine Spell, I hereby award this Stellar Enchantment Pin to Aspiring Baker Caramelle Meringue!"

Lyra's mouth dropped open. Her thoughts were on a rapid downwardly spiraling loop.

We were both supposed to be using Madame Temper's Chant of Precision. That's what she said she was working on with Cardamom. She claimed the Glaze spell was too complicated. But—

Caramelle walked to the front amidst enthusiastic applause from her professors and fellow students. Her pace was sedate and her manner as poised as always, but Lyra could see her fingers trembling as she accepted the pin from Professor Genoise and pinned it to her crisp chef's hat.

Lyra joined in the applause. She even forced her face into a smile. The last thing she wanted was for the professors to see her grimace and form a negative opinion of her "collegial spirit."

Another memory from the night before flashed across her mind: Caramelle's cheerful voice, pealing like a welcome bell, *You mark my words. The Stellar Enchantment Pin is coming to Pestle tomorrow.*

Lyra rose from her seat along with her fellow students, continuing the applause as Caramelle walked gracefully back to her seat.

You were right, Caramelle, Lyra thought. *But the pin isn't the only thing coming to our room.*

Pestle was a small space. There was nowhere to hide, and Lyra was done mincing words to save her "oh-so-pressured" roommate's feelings.

The Meringue was headed for a reckoning.

CHAPTER TWENTY-FOUR

LIKE A LEMON DRIZZLE SPONGE

Lyra managed to escape the exam hall without encountering anyone. She didn't particularly want to be alone, but she wasn't ready for conversation yet. There would be time for that later. For now, she just wanted to be quiet and get her thoughts in order.

Without thinking, her feet took her to the one place on campus where she wouldn't be alone but wouldn't be required to talk or listen: Queen Penelope's rooftop throne room.

Despite Lyra's lack of a sweet offering, the giant chicken was pleased to see her. Evidently, Queen Penelope had been at the Royal Academy of Magical Baking long enough to know when a student needed some thinking time. Clucking amiably, she made room for Lyra to curl up beside her on the pillow-laden dais and even offered the dejected first year a plate of vanilla walnut scones. Lyra took one out of politeness and decided after the first nibble that the royal fowl was on to something.

Maybe we all just need a little more sweetness, she thought. *Might even change Caramelle's disposition for the better.*

By lunchtime, Lyra still didn't feel like talking, but her fingers were beginning to itch for some kind of activity. Idly, she wished she had grabbed her guitar on her way up to the roof. Queen Penelope might have enjoyed some Any Weather Bards tunes. And what better way to clear the head than a little music-making?

Suddenly, Lyra sat up.

"I'm still thinking like a bard," she said out loud.

Queen Penelope clucked inquiringly.

"But I'm not a bard," Lyra went on. "And I don't want to make music right now. I want to *bake.*"

After giving the royal chicken a deep curtsy of thanks, Lyra bounded down the back staircase that connected the rooftop abode directly to the kitchen. Chef

Flax and Bumble were delighted by her arrival and even more delighted by her offer to help in the holiday feast preparations. Like Queen Penelope, they seemed to understand Lyra's mood and didn't push her to talk more than she wanted. After congratulating her on making it through to the second term, they simply let her roll up her sleeves and focus on the work.

Despite her inner turmoil, Lyra enjoyed the afternoon. She stirred the béarnaise sauce for the roasted vegetables and rolled the pastry for the beef Wellington. She toasted pecans for the baked brie and ran out to the greenhouse to collect ginger for the carrot soup. She even swallowed her recent bad experience with Presentation and helped Chef pipe frosting onto twenty-four miniature yule log cakes, making each one resemble a snowy tree branch.

All the while, she didn't say a word. But at Bumble's insistence, translated by Chef Flax, she did sing.

When relevant, she sang whatever spell was required for the task at hand. Otherwise, though, she just sang. By the time Chef Flax ordered her to go join the first years at the feast, she had made it through most of the Any Weather Bards' repertoire, with a few Lyra originals thrown in. Even without any guitar accompaniment, both the head chef and the sous chef declared she had fulfilled her promise of a concert. She left the kitchen to the sound of Chef Flax's applause and Bumble's chattered praise.

The first-year table welcomed her with joy. Thankfully, Caramelle was at the professors' table for her victory dinner, so Lyra did not have to face her just yet. Also thankfully, the other Whizzes accepted "helping Chef Flax in the kitchen" as sufficient explanation for Lyra's absence throughout the day, so she didn't have to endure any probing questions. Best of all, the time with Chef Flax and Bumble had refreshed Lyra enough to let her put on a convincing show of joining in her friends' jubilant mood.

"Any big plans over break?" Ginger asked as the main course floated over to replace the soup.

"Practice," Mac sighed. The steam rising off the beef Wellington fogged up his glasses. He took them off, rubbed them clean on his apron, and continued, "Second term is going to be even harder. I don't want to get behind."

"You'll have to set aside at least one night for fun," Boysen said firmly. "Specifically, next Wednesday night. My parents want to have all of you over for dinner. Berry tradition." Once they had all gladly accepted this invitation, Boysen clapped Mac on the shoulder. "And sure, second term is going to be hard, but it can also be better. We know the ropes now."

"And we don't have to deal with dear Lady Mint," Ginger added. Pausing to breathe in the savory aromas of roasted vegetables, creamy béarnaise, and pastry-wrapped beef, she smiled at Lyra. "Speaking of, want to switch rooms? Join me in Zester?"

Lyra paused with a laden fork halfway to her mouth. "Seriously? Don't you want the room to yourself?"

"No, thanks." Ginger grinned, spearing a particularly juicy brussels sprout and dunking it in béarnaise sauce. "I share a room with my sister at home. It would be weird not having a roomie."

"What about Caramelle?" Mac's gaze drifted over to where Caramelle sat at the professors' table, the light from the chandeliers glinting off her Stellar Enchantment Pin. "Won't she be lonely?"

Lyra kept her eyes down, pretending to be fully absorbed in arranging the perfect bite of pastry, beef, and gravy on her fork.

"No," she said, marveling at how light and carefree her own voice sounded. Past experience with performance did have its benefits. "No, I think Caramelle will be just fine on her own."

Lyra was ready and waiting when Caramelle returned to Pestle that evening.

Well, maybe not *ready*. But she was waiting.

"How was dinner?" Lyra asked coolly. "Did you enjoy the celebration?"

Caramelle hesitated for a moment, hand still on the open door, as if she were contemplating making a run for it. Then she tossed her head in a very Aniseedesque fashion.

"Yes, thank you." She entered the room and closed the door firmly behind her. "Professor Puff was eager to hear of my parents' restaurant. She was a year ahead of my mother here at the academy."

Lyra stood slowly from her bed, crossing her arms. "I bet your parents were so very proud when they heard about your win. Really living up to the Meringue potential, aren't you?"

"No more than expected," Caramelle replied evenly. "For generations, no one in my family has ever failed to earn the first-term Stellar Enchantment Pin at the Royal Academy of Magical Baking."

"That's not what I meant. Meringues will do anything to get ahead, right?" Lyra could feel her voice rising with her anger and made no attempt to stop it. "It doesn't matter who gets hurt or what dirty, underhanded method you use, so long as you win. Today, you truly became a Meringue."

Caramelle's eyes flashed. "So you're suddenly an expert on the baking world? You have no idea what this business is like, Treble. You're not a baker. You're a . . . a . . . *musician!*"

"And performers know *nothing* about cutthroat competition." Lyra rolled her eyes. "I've tried to give you a break, you know. I've tried to imagine the pressure you're under and how hard it must be. But I'm done. Pressure doesn't give you an excuse to commit sabotage."

"Sabotage?" Caramelle repeated shrilly. "How dramatic! You really are a performer. I didn't *sabotage* you. If anything, it was a test. You would have been fine if you stuck with your recipe. But you jumped at the chance to 'get ahead,' didn't you? Climb down off your pedestal, Treble. You're as desperate to win as any of us. You're just mad that I outsmarted you this time around."

"I trusted you!" Tears stung in Lyra's eyes, but she tried to hold them back. She was *not* going to give Caramelle the satisfaction of seeing her cry. "That's why I'm mad. Sure, the pin would be great, but I was just happy to stay for another term. I would have been thrilled for you to win, you know. You've worked hard. You deserve it. You could have won fair and square. But you didn't."

Caramelle laughed harshly. "You would have been happy for me? Who's lying now? You're lying to yourself."

"I'm not," Lyra insisted. "I would have been happy for you."

"Really?" Caramelle folded her arms. "All right, Treble. Look me in the eye, right now, and swear that you didn't secretly hope to win this term. Swear that not even the tiniest part of you wanted to get the pin."

Lyra opened her mouth, then closed it.

Caramelle nodded. "I thought so. Because you wanted to win, didn't you? Not just because you wanted to prove something, but to impress Cardamom."

"Cardamom?" Lyra repeated, trying not to sound like she'd been punched in the gut.

"That's what this is really about, isn't it?" Caramelle spat, her face flushing nearly as red as her hair. "You wanted to catch his eye. Make him notice you. Admit it, Lyra. You're not mad at me all of a sudden because you think I sabotaged you or betrayed your trust. You've been mad all term because of the attention I've been getting from Cardamom. He's taken an interest in me, and you can't stand it."

"I can't stand that you're a liar!" Lyra was shouting now. She wondered briefly just how thick the walls in the dorm building actually were and how many students might be listening in to the Pestle Roomie War. Then anger drove out every other thought, and she bellowed, "All you do is lie! You've been lying to Cardamom. No way you need *that* much help in Presentation. But you know that's the only reason he's spending time with you, so you just keep right on lying. It's sickening!"

"You're just jealous you didn't think of it first." Caramelle smirked.

Lyra ignored her. "You've been lying to all of us, all term. Flattery for the professors. Self-Presentation spells for Cardamom. Speeches about community for the rest of us. You stood right here, in this room, and told me you wanted us to work together."

"And you went right along with it." Caramelle seemed to puff up with each sentence, like an over-whipped choux pastry. Even the chef's hat pinned carefully to her head was quivering with rage as she hissed, "You were happy to take advantage of all my expertise, weren't you? Just a poor innocent bard with nothing to contribute and *everything* to gain. What could you possibly have done to help *me*?"

"I was always grateful—" Lyra began, but Caramelle plowed right ahead.

"And you just soaked up everything like a lemon drizzle sponge, didn't you? I could see your game, Treble. Learn everything you can from me and then cut me down at the first opportunity." Caramelle took a deep breath, smoothing her hair with one trembling hand. "I just got there first."

"If you really believe that," Lyra countered, "then you're the one lying to yourself. Do you really think all bakers are that awful? Did you think everyone at the Whisk Whiz Review was just waiting to stab each other in the back?"

At the mention of the Whisk Whiz Review, Caramelle wilted. She rallied back in the blink of an eye, but Lyra was sure she hadn't imagined the pang of sadness in her roommate's eyes.

"We had a great time together," Lyra continued softly, hoping to get through to whatever part of Caramelle had produced that pang. "All five of us. We got each other through the term, and we made it *fun*. That wasn't all a lie, was it?"

For a moment, Caramelle froze. Her careful mask of poise cracked. Then her mouth set in a firm line. She smoothed her hair again, caressing the brilliant Stellar Enchantment Pin on her hat with the same gesture. When she spoke, her voice was cold and brittle.

"The Whisk Whiz Review contributed nothing to my experience this term. I gave it a try for the sake of professional courtesy. But I shall not be attending in the future," Caramelle said.

Lyra boiled over.

"Fine!" she snapped. "We will get along just fine without you. And you won't need to worry about me 'sponging' off you anymore, because I'm moving in with Ginger after the break. We confirmed it with Professor Honeycomb after dinner. You'll have the room to yourself."

"I'm sure Ginger was fascinated by your account of my 'betrayal,'" Caramelle scoffed. "Bet you had a sympathetic audience all round. What did the other Whisk Whizzes have to say?"

Suddenly, Lyra felt as deflated as an under-proofed loaf of bread. She sighed. "I didn't tell them anything."

Caramelle raised her eyebrows. "Oh?"

"No. And I'm not going to." Lyra swung her bag, already packed, over her shoulder and picked up her guitar. "For your sake and mine. Since you have no shame, I'll just have to be ashamed for both of us."

She walked to the door. Caramelle stepped aside to clear the path.

"Enjoy the break," Caramelle said coolly. "See you in two weeks."

"I hope not," Lyra replied. Wearily, she opened the door, stepped through it—and ran straight into Cardamom Coulis III, who was just raising his hand to knock.

CHAPTER TWENTY-FIVE

SOMETHING SPECIAL

"Lyra!" Cardamom exclaimed, stepping back and examining her anxiously. "Sorry about that. Are you all right?"

"Hi!" she squeaked. Then, realizing that wasn't the proper response, she tried again. "I mean, fine. I'm fine. How are you?"

Before he could answer, Caramelle appeared at Lyra's shoulder. "Cardamom!" she said, her eyes and voice shining with delight. "What a lovely surprise. I thought I wouldn't get to see you until after the break!"

Cardamom smiled. "Congratulations, Aspiring Baker Meringue. Winning the Stellar Enchantment Pin is quite an achievement."

"I couldn't have done it alone," Caramelle purred. She put a friendly arm around Lyra, using the gesture to maneuver herself around the other girl. "My colleagues provided wonderful support, of course, but most of the credit belongs to you." Cardamom started to protest, but she held up a hand. "I mean it. I don't know where I would have been this term without your help. And how kind of you to come by and congratulate us before break! It gives me the chance to repay you. I could make some dessert for us, and we—"

"That's not necessary," he interrupted smoothly, matching her smile. "You have nothing to repay me for, Caramelle. You earned that pin."

"At least let me thank you," she insisted. "If you must rush off for break, I can whip up some cookies for—"

"I'm actually here to see Lyra."

"Lyra?" both girls echoed.

Cardamom's smile hit Lyra like a searchlight. "Yes. I wanted to catch you before you left for break. Looks like I'm just in time." He stepped backwards with a bow, gesturing gallantly to the couches in the common area. "Might I have a word?"

"Of course," Lyra said weakly. She brushed past Caramelle, who seemed to have been shocked into paralysis, and followed Cardamom over to the couches.

He waited until she sank down beside him, still clutching her bag and guitar, then began. "First of all, congratulations on surviving your first term. Well done, Lyra."

"Thanks." She blushed, wishing the couch would open up and swallow her. "It didn't end well, though. Today was . . . awful."

"I wouldn't use the word 'awful,'" he said kindly.

Lyra looked down, cursing inwardly at the sight of her stained, wrinkled apron. *Why didn't I take this off earlier?*

"You didn't see my exam cake," she pointed out. "It was awful."

"Professor Genoise showed it to me." He shook his head. "Not awful. Not nearly so terrible as some of my creations my first term."

"I find that hard to believe."

"Believe it," he said grimly. "In comparison, your cake was more than acceptable. But it could have been better. That's why I'm here."

Lyra blinked. "You're—"

"I spoke to Professor Genoise," Cardamom went on. "He agreed that your exam cake, though it excelled in both Flavor and Texture, did not live up to your potential in Presentation."

She blinked again. "I have potential?"

"Absolutely. Your work in class has been solid, but the professor and I both know you can go beyond solid." He placed one of his hands on hers. "We think you're something pretty special, Lyra."

"Oh," Lyra managed to get out. It was difficult to form coherent thoughts, let alone words. She felt like she was simultaneously floating and drowning.

"So we want to make sure you succeed." Cardamom's dark eyes radiated warmth. "That's why I would like to be your tutor next term. I could meet with you Wednesday and Thursday evenings, after dinner. Wednesday, we would be preparing you for your Presentation lab the next day. Thursday, we could go over what you did in lab. Professor Genoise thinks it's a grand idea, so long as you're interested."

He paused long enough that Lyra realized he was waiting for a response.

"I'm—yes," she stammered. "Yes, please. And thank you."

His smile broadened, and he gave her hand an encouraging squeeze. "Excellent. I look forward to working with you, Lyra." He winked as he stood up. "Maybe you can finally teach me that secret we talked about all those weeks ago. Whatever makes your style so joyful, as Professor Genoise puts it."

"Sure," Lyra said faintly.

"Have a wonderful break, and I'll see you in two weeks."

"Sure," she repeated.

With one final bow, he was gone.

Lyra sat there on the couch for a long time, too dizzily happy to move. Not even the sound of Pestle's door slamming could burst her bubble.

Caramelle heard the whole thing, she thought with an uncontrollable surge of mean satisfaction. *Serves her right.*

Lyra's heart felt like it might leap out of her chest at any moment. Her fingers were numb from clutching her guitar case. Her face hurt from smiling. She didn't care. All she could think about was the pressure of Cardamom's hand on hers and the warmth of his eyes as he smiled at her.

We think you're something pretty special, Lyra.

Cardamom remembered details from a brief conversation with Lyra from the beginning of term, along with the style-word Professor Genoise had given her. He had gone to Professor Genoise on her behalf. He was looking forward to spending time with her.

He sees me.

Finally, noises from Whisk and Zester broke Lyra out of her reverie. She darted out the main lobby door before any of her friends could emerge from their rooms. There would be time later to tell them the news. For now, she just wanted to keep all this beauty to herself.

He sees me. The thought kept sparking in her mind like a magical flame as she floated down the path outside the dorm, keeping her warm in the bitingly cold winter air. *Cardamom Coulis the Third sees me. And he thinks I'm special.*

Me.

Lyra Treble.

Special.

Lyra danced through the main academy gate, singing as she made her way home, carried on a dream-wave of cinnamon and honey.

Still riding the dream-wave, Lyra found it difficult to sleep that night. It also felt strange to be back in her own bed. After three months in the focused quiet of Pestle, she had forgotten how loud her house was, even at night. Each Treble child had their own room, but her brothers still found a way to snore in three-part harmony.

Lyra crept downstairs with the first light of dawn the next day. Humming to herself, she began whipping up pancake batter, smiling as she added a liberal dash of cinnamon to the dry ingredients.

These would go well with honey, she thought, her heart giggling at the secret joke.

"Smells good," sang a rich tenor voice behind her.

Turning, Lyra found her oldest brother Canto standing in the doorway.

"You're up early," they said in unison, then laughed.

"Baking hours," she explained. "Dawn is like midmorning for a baker."

Canto yawned a perfect A minor arpeggio. "Sounds like a terrible existence."

"You get used to it." Lyra poured buttermilk into the bowl of flour, salt, baking soda, and cinnamon, stirring carefully so as not to overmix them. "What's your excuse? You all got in so late last night, I didn't expect anyone to be up for another hour or so."

"We're playing a brunch gig." Canto helped himself to one of the bananas Lyra had set out to serve with the pancakes. Biting off half, he winked at her. "You should join us."

"Play a show?" Lyra's eyebrows rose. "Today? With no rehearsal?"

"It's just the old set," Canto wheedled, somehow managing to speak clearly around the banana. "For Thespy's cousin's birthday party. He requested all our biggest hits. You don't need rehearsal for those."

Lyra shook her head, turning to melt butter over the griddle. "I haven't played in weeks. Really played, I mean."

"You're a pro." Canto filled the kettle and set it on the stove's back burner with a decisive *clang*. "And a Treble. You'll be great. Besides, it'll mean a lot to Mom and Dad."

Lyra paused, a spoonful of batter halfway between the bowl and the griddle. "Really?"

"Really, truly, surely," Canto sang. Leaning down from his noble height of six feet three inches, he planted a kiss on top of her head. "It'll mean a lot to all of us. We've missed you, Lyra-lee."

A sweet ache rose up Lyra's chest. Dropping the spoon back into the bowl, she wrapped her arm around her brother's waist in a quick side hug. "I've missed you too. All of you."

He returned the hug, then reached above her head to retrieve six mugs from the cupboard. "Think you'll go back? Or was one term enough?"

"Of course I'll go back." She paused and turned around to stare at him. "Why wouldn't I go back?"

"Mom said it's really stressful."

"Sure, but . . . it's school. Stress is normal."

"For baking?" Canto's naturally high voice rose half an octave. "What's there to be stressed about?"

"There's a lot to learn," Lyra shot back. "It's a three-year program."

"Don't they cut people throughout the year or something?"

"One person at the end of every term. But I made it through."

Canto yawned again, this time in a descending chromatic scale. "I repeat: sounds like a terrible existence. Why put yourself through all that?"

"Because . . ."

Lyra turned around and took a moment to gather her thoughts. She poured four spoonfuls of batter onto the griddle and watched until tiny bubbles began to appear on the surface. Then, in a series of deft movements, she flipped, buttered, and stacked the pancakes, putting the plate in the oven at a low temperature to keep warm.

"Because I love baking," she said simply. "And I want to learn how to do it better."

Canto inhaled, grinning with appreciation at the aromas circulating through the tiny kitchen. "But you're already a great baker. Do you really need that school?"

She paused again as more butter melted over the griddle's smooth surface, then asked, "How's your painting? Working on anything new?"

"Not really new," he replied, wrinkling his eyebrows at the change of subject. "That same one I started just before you left. *The Joy Song*, I'm calling it."

"You haven't finished yet?"

He shrugged. "There's not a lot of time. We've got that day gig at the café, then rehearsal at night for the weekend shows. And Rondo has started songwriting, so we spend whatever free time we have workshopping his stuff."

"Really?" Lyra exclaimed, momentarily distracted from the main point. "Is he any good?"

Canto nodded solemnly. "Mom and Dad think he might reach Uncle Clef's level someday. We'll play you one of his new ones later."

"Little Rondo. Who knew?" Lyra sighed happily. Then the smell of browning butter recalled her to the present, and she ladled four more spoonfuls of pancake batter onto the griddle, returning the conversation to the original topic. "So, when do you paint?"

"A little here, a little there." Canto shrugged again. "Sometimes after rehearsal or if I need to unwind after a show."

"Doesn't it bother you? Not having time to paint?"

"Nope. It's no big deal." Canto grabbed the whistling kettle from the stove and filled the teapot. "Painting is just for fun. Music is what matters, remember?"

"Didn't you ever want to do anything else?" Lyra persisted. "When you were my age?"

"Afraid not, Lyra-lee."

"You always wanted to be part of the Any Weather Bards? Forever?"

"Always *always*, forever and a day." Leaning against the counter, Canto smiled at her, his round face full of settled peace. "I enjoy other things, but music is home."

"Home . . ." Lyra flipped the pancakes, spread them with butter, and added them to the warming plate in the oven. Gazing at the empty griddle, she felt another sigh building up in her chest and let it out softly. "Home is a tricky tune at the moment. I can't seem to find my part."

With a speed and grace that belied his hefty tenor build, Canto opened the oven, snatched the top two pancakes, and devoured them both before Lyra could protest.

"Come and play the gig with us today," he said, silencing her indignant squeak with a *boop* on the nose. "See how it feels. Maybe now that you've been away for a while . . . you'll find that home was here all along."

CHAPTER TWENTY-SIX

A Nice Place to Visit

Lyra was surprised at the simultaneous ease and difficulty with which she slipped back into her old life.

Just as Canto had predicted, she had no trouble joining the Any Weather Bards for the brunch gig. Her fingers picked out the well-known chords of each song effortlessly, and her brother Largo was grateful for her support on the melody line. She even remembered the old descant she had written for herself on "All Gather Round."

And since the party was at the home of a longtime family friend, Lyra soon found herself surrounded by people who had known her since she was born. This was both comforting and disorienting. After three months in the baking world, she had to keep reminding herself that no one else in the room cared about the correct use of Master Chiffon's Aeration Charm or even knew of Master Chiffon's existence.

As the day wore on, Lyra found herself growing weary of this once well-loved scene. She tried to muster appropriate levels of interest for all the old conversational topics, but it was difficult with her mind and heart still so full of the academy.

Even her old school friends didn't want to hear about Bumble and Sprinkle, or marvel at the idea of personality powders, or speculate which Presentation spells had been used on the elaborate birthday cake Thespy had purchased from a local bakery. Everyone at the party was consumed by the same neighborhood issues Lyra remembered, as if from another life: the community's monthly talent show at the café, if the traveling Dawn Dancers might visit again this spring, and rumors about a new kind of magical fire for theatrical lighting, designed to change color according to the play's thematic progression. Mostly, of course, the party was abuzz about the next possible collaboration between the Any Weather Bards and Thespy's theater troupe, the Constant Company.

When people did ask about the academy, their inquiries always followed the same tired track, and Lyra was tired of repeating the same tired answers. Yes, she was glad to be home. No, she wasn't home for good, just on break until second term. Yes, the Royal Academy of Magical Baking was a wonderful school, though rigorous. No, she didn't sit around eating cake all day. Yes, she was making friends with the other bakers. No, she didn't miss music all that much. Her family, sure, but music . . .

This was the point where the other person's eyes usually glazed over with total incomprehension. Again and again, Lyra heard the same basic idea, uttered with little variation and always with the same blank, vaguely disapproving stare: "But you're a Treble. Trebles are bards. How can you not miss making music?"

Thankfully, Thespy had requested "The Joy Song" to close out the party. This was Lyra's all-time favorite of the Any Weather Bards' repertoire. Like a perfectly executed Texture spell, it left one feeling both secure and lighthearted, anchoring the feet while sending the soul soaring. She could understand why it had formed the inspiration for Canto's latest painting. In fact, she had sung it frequently to herself while practicing her cake for the academy's final entrance exam.

As all six Trebles took their places once more on the permanent "stage" in Thespy's living room, Lyra breathed an inward sigh of relief. It *did* feel good to be making music again. Not only was it simply fun to play and sing with her family, allowing herself to get swept up in their expert flow, but she always thrilled at the showcase of their signature spells. Bardic magic was so very different from baking magic, and the Trebles stood out even among other bards.

Most bards focused all their training on pre-performance spells. They spent hours learning how to gauge an audience's mood, casting charm after charm at a dizzying rate until they had formed a mental map of each listener's surface-level emotions. Then they would tailor the performance to that map, constantly shifting the program to suit the audience's changing whims.

Lyra had heard her father rant against this practice so many times, she knew the speech by heart. She recited the climactic point to herself now as Largo tuned his violin and Canto settled himself behind his cello.

A bard's first responsibility is not to the audience—not to cater to them, anyway. It is the music that holds our allegiance. We use magic to get inside each song so we may reveal that song's truest nature. True music is what the audience needs. A performance of pure music will soothe anxiety, comfort sorrow, and deepen gladness. Be true to the music, Treblette, and you will serve the audience well.

Instruments tuned and ready, Lyra waited with her brothers, watching their parents carefully. Harmon Treble sat at the piano while his wife stood behind him, her hand on his shoulder. Their eyes were closed. Lyra knew they were breathing in unison, mentally reciting the preparation spell to unlock the heart of "The Joy Song."

Then, as if some invisible signal had passed between them, Melody squeezed her husband's shoulder and stepped back. He lifted his hands, all seven Trebles took a breath, and—as one—they began to play and sing.

Lyra felt the familiar wave of magic instantly. Unlike baking magic, bardic magic did not manifest visibly. There were no streams of colored light, no lingering shimmery afterglow. Yet the effect was no less tangible.

The music activated and continued the spell Lyra's parents had begun in that silent shared moment, sending a tide of magic across the stage. It flowed on every side, without and within, pouring from her mother's voice and her brothers' hands and her own faltering heart. The tide swept out into the room, swirled around each listener, and caught them up in a moment of carefree wonder.

This was the spirit of "The Joy Song," its truest nature, discerned by magic and revealed by performance. For a bard, this was the highest possible achievement. This moment was the fullest expression of life's deepest meaning.

Lyra was aware of the moment and appreciated it—even enjoyed it deeply. Simultaneously, she found her eyes and thoughts wandering to the kitchen, where the remains of the birthday cake were just visible on Thespy's long table.

Maybe Master Glaze's Shine Spell? Or something even more advanced . . .

Canto caught her gaze and raised his eyebrows, silently reminding her to stay focused. She nodded, smiling, as she forced herself back into the Treble groove.

For now, anyway.

It doesn't feel quite right to be here, she acknowledged to herself, lifting her voice to join Canto's high harmony for the chorus. *But it's a nice place to visit once in a while.*

"Friends! Aspiring bakers! Victorious conquerors of the first term!" Boysen stood on his front doorstep, spreading his arms to greet Lyra, Ginger, and Mac. "Welcome, all, to the house of Berry, for—"

His grand tone was immediately drowned out by the laughter of his older brother.

"The house of Berry?" Razz appeared in the open door and clapped Boysen on the shoulder. "You missed your calling, Poison. You should have been a ringmaster for the circus. Or a maître d' at a particularly pompous restaurant."

Mull and Whortle, the younger Berry twins, poked their heads around Razz.

"I dunno," Mull said, his face serious. "Our house is pretty grand."

Whortle nodded, mirroring his twin's solemn expression. "I'd say it's *Berry* grand."

Then they, too, burst into raucous laughter.

"All right, all right." Boysen waved them away good-naturedly. "I'm *Berry* certain Mom ordered you lot to clear out before my guests arrived."

Razz, Mull, and Whortle groaned.

"That sounds Berry lame," Mull pouted.

"And Berry boring," Whortle chimed in. "Which one of you is Lyra?"

"We want to meet Lyra," Mull agreed. "Boysen says—"

Boysen covered Mull's mouth with his hand. "Boysen says you both better scoot or you'll be Berry sorry."

"C'mon, little seedlings." Razz grabbed a twin with each hand and hauled them down the front steps by their shirt collars. "Let's leave Poison in peace. Hyacinth is making us dinner."

"Yay, Hyacinth!" Mull and Whortle cried simultaneously. They wrenched themselves from Razz's grip and took off down the sidewalk, waving and calling over their shoulders, "Bye, Boysen! Bye, Lyra and Not-Lyra and that other guy!"

Razz chuckled. "You guys have fun. Better head on in soon so Mom can meet . . . everyone." He winked at Boysen, then ran to catch up with Mull and Whortle.

Ginger raised her eyebrows. "Not-Lyra?"

"That other guy?" Mac protested.

Boysen shook his head. "If you don't have brothers . . . be grateful." Turning, he motioned for them to follow him inside. "Come on. Razz was right about Mom wanting to meet all of you."

The Berry household reminded Lyra of her own home. It was another townhouse, long and narrow, with multiple floors to provide living and sleeping spaces for a big family. But there was one key difference. While the Treble house was always full of music, the Berry home was full of *smells*—the rich and wonderful aroma of constant culinary creation.

Lyra breathed in deeply as they followed Boysen down a hallway and past a flight of stairs.

"I hope your mom didn't go to too much trouble," she said.

Ginger agreed. "I'm sure she's busy enough with six Berry boys to cook for. Seven, including your dad."

"Straw and Cran have their own place now." Boysen paused before a closed door at the end of the hallway. Cheerful sounds of bubbling, steaming, and stirring emanated from the room beyond. "With me and Razz away at school most of the time, Mom's been coming out of her frame. Dad too, though he won't admit it. They miss cooking for a crowd." He pushed through the door, standing aside to let them all enter. "Trust me. You're doing them a favor."

They stepped into the room, and Lyra caught her breath.

The Berry kitchen was . . . well, Berry amazing.

Directly in front of the door, a long dining table stretched nearly half the length of the room, with benches pulled up on either side. Dried vegetables, fruits, and flowers hung from the ceiling. A fire blazed merrily in a large brick fireplace halfway down the right-hand wall.

Beyond the fire was the kitchen portion of the room. A wide counter wrapped around from the left wall, jutting across towards the fireplace. It divided the room neatly but left ample space for dishes to be carried back and forth. The counter continued along the back wall, breaking only for a door in the back right corner before resuming along the right wall.

Above the counter, the back wall was dominated by three tall windows. Lyra noted they must be facing north. The early evening glow streamed in, mixing beautifully with the hanging light fixtures to ensure sufficient illumination, but the room would never be in danger of getting too warm.

It was an incredible setup for cooking. Still, what made the room truly special was the activity happening inside it and the person performing that activity.

"Welcome!" Boysen's mother bustled around the corner and practically skipped the length of the room, holding her floury hands out in greeting. "So glad you could join us. We are honored to have the academy's future here in our home!"

Lyra adored her immediately. In fact, Lyra adored the whole house. She felt instantly at ease in this new environment.

That's how I felt the first time I visited Whisk, she reflected as Boysen's mother shook hands with each of them. *Maybe that's just the Berry power. They carry the welcome with them wherever they go.*

"Thank you for having us, Mrs. Berry," Ginger said.

Mrs. Berry beamed at them. Her green apron marked her as a Flavor expert, like Professor Honeycomb, but her wavy brown hair was tied back in a multicolored scarf embroidered with wildflowers. She had Boysen's dancing brown eyes and the same kind of grin that lit up her whole face. She was also nearly as tall and lanky as her son, though she moved about her kitchen with a graceful confidence that would send The Meringue into spasms of violent envy.

"Thank *you,*" she insisted. "And thank your parents. The break between terms is a precious time. Only two weeks! We are sorry to take you away from your families for even a single night, but I did so want to meet Boysen's friends and express our gratitude. You made the first term so wonderful for him." Somehow, her smile grew even wider and brighter, lighting up the room as well as her face. With a look in her eye that told Lyra exactly where Razz had gotten his sense of humor, Mrs. Berry exclaimed, "The least we can do is give you a *Berry* wonderful evening!"

CHAPTER TWENTY-SEVEN

A Berry Wonderful Evening

Lyra glanced at Boysen, who was trying hard not to look self-conscious. He was failing.

She grinned at him, then at Mrs. Berry and said, "He made the term wonderful for us. I don't think I would have survived the first *week* without the Whisk Whiz Review, let alone all the weeks that followed."

"He does have a gift for bringing different elements together." Mrs. Berry ruffled her son's hair fondly. "Flavors and also people. Razz has more technical know-how, but Boysen has the gift."

Boysen turned the color of his brother Razz's berry namesake. "Thanks, Mom."

She tweaked his ear, then turned back to her guests. "Now, let's see. Macaron Fondant, yes?"

Mac smiled, his customary shyness evaporating in the warmth of Mrs. Berry's welcome. "That's me."

"Roommates are a crucial part of your first year," Mrs. Berry said. "They can make or break a term. Thank you for making this term a great one for my son, Macaron."

"The pleasure's all mine," Mac said grandly. "And please, call me Mac."

"Mac it is. And this must be Ginger Crumble."

"Guilty." Ginger grinned. "How'd you know?"

Mrs. Berry winked. "You have your dad's nose. He came in during my second year at the academy. I was so sorry to see him go at the end of that year. He was a fantastic baker. I trust he's still at it?"

"Oh yes," Ginger assured her. "Has his own little pastry shop across town. We live above it."

"Meaning he took the downstairs of your home and turned it into a public bakery?" Mrs. Berry chuckled. "Sounds about right. Your mother must be a most understanding woman."

"She loves it," Ginger said. "She never made it to the academy, but she specialized in icing at a different school. He bakes, she decorates. They make a good team."

"That's like Mom and Dad," Boysen said. "They have their own restaurant. But it's a couple blocks over, not in our house."

"And we don't have those lovely complementary strengths." Mrs. Berry sighed. "I am a Flavor nerd, and I married a Flavor nerd. We produced six other Flavor nerds. It's all 'gut' in this household. Rather one-note."

Ginger laughed. "You don't make it through the academy without being strong in all three principles. I'm sure you're amazing at Texture and Presentation too."

"She is," Boysen affirmed.

"And so is Mr. Berry," Mac added. "My family goes to their restaurant at least once a month. Not a bad thing on the menu. The Berrys make a great team."

Mrs. Berry curtsied, then turned to Lyra. "And speaking of good teams, you must be Lyra Treble. I'm sure Boysen told you we've been to see your family perform many times?"

"He did," Lyra said with a smile. "So you understand that the Trebles know all about a 'one-note' household. All music, all the time."

"Until you," Mrs. Berry pointed out. "Really, it staggers me to think of it. To get into the Royal Academy of Magical Baking without any extra help or formal training? You are remarkable, my dear."

Lyra felt like she had entered a blushing contest with Boysen. And she was winning. She managed to keep her voice level as she stammered a thank-you.

Mrs. Berry was still shaking her head in awe. "Unprecedented. In my lifetime, at least. Your parents must be very proud."

"Shocked is more like it," Lyra confessed. "They thought baking was my hobby, right up until the end. To be honest, I think they'd be happier if I just stuck with the Any Weather Bards."

Boysen's right eyebrow rose. "Even now? When you've made it through the first cut?"

Lyra nodded. "They keep asking if I'm sure I want to go back."

"But that's just . . . That's wrong!" Boysen exclaimed. "Don't they know how amazing you are? How special this is?"

"Hush," Mrs. Berry said, laying a hand on her son's arm. "It's a hard thing for a parent to see their child grow and change, especially if that change takes them outside the family circle quicker than we'd like. I can't imagine how I'd feel if one of you boys wanted to do something other than baking."

Boysen was still fuming. "You'd support us, of course."

"Hopefully. Eventually. But it would be difficult." Mrs. Berry squeezed his arm. Then, suddenly, she wrapped Lyra in a hug. "I'm sure your parents are very proud of you."

Lyra was torn between the desire to break down into tears or giggle from sheer delight. Mrs. Berry's embrace was like being inside a loaf of bread fresh from the oven—nourishing and so wonderfully warm.

She settled for returning the hug and whispering, "Thank you."

Mrs. Berry pulled away, dotting at her eyes with her apron. "Pleasure having you in our home, dear. All of you." She clapped her hands, rubbing them together in a way that reminded Lyra forcibly of Professor Honeycomb. "Well! Let's all sit down, then. Don't want the food to get cold."

When the three guests were arranged on the benches, she employed Boysen to help her carry dishes to the table. First came a giant cauldron of stew, heartily full of meat and vegetables in a rich, creamy broth. The intoxicating curlicues of steam were still glowing a bright green, revealing that a high-level Flavor spell was in effect. Then came a massive bowl of salad, followed by two loaves of sourdough bread. Lyra didn't need the faint shimmer of royal blue disappearing into the loaves to tell her the texture would be light and joyfully springy. There were two cutting boards with different kinds of cheeses, three different varieties of herb butter, and an assortment of pickles and olives.

Lyra surveyed the table, her heart shining in the reflected warmth of that spread. It was all simple fare, lacking any of the fancy finishing touches so valued by Professor Genoise and Cardamom. Yet, Presentation magic was definitely at work. No streams of purple light emanated from the food, but the whole table seemed to glow like a cozy hearth fire. It was like Mrs. Berry had distilled all the comfort of home into a chant and cast it over the entire kitchen. Every sight, sound, smell, and touch was like a mini hug, and Lyra could only believe the taste would be the same.

She breathed in deeply. What was it Boysen had said about his deficiency in Presentation, way back during that first Whisk Whiz Review? *Professor Genoise was being generous when he said my style is welcoming. "Homey" would be a better word.*

Lyra shook her head at the memory of his gloomy tone.

"Homey" is nothing to be ashamed of, she thought as Mrs. Berry brought over a platter of fresh fruit. *It's something to aspire to.*

"Save room for dessert," Mrs. Berry warned, taking her place at the head of the table. "Mr. Berry made it with me this morning. He very kindly agreed to cover the restaurant tonight so I could host you all, but he is thoroughly glum about missing it. He made me promise to tell you that his presence is with us in dessert form and that you'd best partake so he can feel like he participated."

"Deal," the friends chorused.

"First, a toast." Mrs. Berry raised a glass of cider, and all followed suit. "To the Whisk Whiz Review!"

"The Whisk Whiz Review," everyone echoed before taking a sip of the deliciously crisp cider. Then they dug into the food with all the goodwill of culinary-minded teenagers.

"This stew," Mac said dreamily. "The memory of it will sustain me for many a long stressful day next term."

Lyra fervently agreed, then turned to where Boysen was seated on her right. "Did you make the stew?"

He shook his head. "Mom wouldn't let me make anything."

"That's right," Mrs. Berry said firmly. "No baking on break. That's the household rule for academy students."

Mac stared at her blankly. "No baking . . . at *all?*"

"Baking is like exercise. Each principle uses a different set of 'muscles,' so to speak," Mrs. Berry explained. "If you push the muscles nonstop, they stop growing, and fatigue sets in. Best case, you plateau. Worst case, you hurt yourself. I know how intense a workout the academy can be. That's why no Berry boy does any baking between terms."

"She's serious." Boysen sighed. "They even put a padlock on my shed out back."

Mrs. Berry sipped her cider, unperturbed. "There will be plenty of time for your experiments at the end of the year, Boysen."

"She's right." Lyra patted Boysen's hand. "At least it gives you a reason to look forward to going back to school."

"*Another* reason," Boysen corrected her. He winked. "I've got plenty."

"This bread is amazing, Mrs. Berry," Ginger gushed. "How did you keep it so light? I knew you must be a Texture genius."

Mrs. Berry smiled ruefully. "Not a genius. Just a hard worker. Flavor always came easy to me, but Texture . . . Let's just say I spent many an hour practicing spells in that lab and many hours in my own kitchen since."

"That's encouraging, really," Lyra said. "That you can get this good by working hard. Putting in the hours. It's good to remember that it's not all down to innate talent."

Mac nodded. "I was a Texture disaster at first. Still am, sometimes. It's hit or miss."

"But you're putting in the work." Boysen high-fived him from across the table. "And you've been recognized by Professor Puff more than once as a result."

"Thanks to you," Mac said. "All of you, really. The Whisk Whizzes." He turned to Mrs. Berry. "Lyra's been setting all the spells and charms to music, to help us memorize them. It's made a huge difference."

Beside him, Ginger spoke up. "All hail Lyra Treble and her bard baking skills!"

"Hear, hear!" Boysen joined the silent clapping, then nudged Lyra with his elbow. "I can't wait to see what you come up with next term. We're taking Whisk Whiz Review to a whole new level."

"Absolutely," Lyra said, but her heart sank when she remembered that

Cardamom's tutoring sessions meant she'd miss two out of every five review sessions.

But that's a good thing, she argued. *I'm getting some extra help. They'll be happy for me.*

She struggled one moment longer, then took a deep breath.

"Next term is going to be a little different for me, actually. In a good way, I think. I hope."

"Different how?" Ginger asked. "Other than the incredible gift of having me as a roommate."

Lyra smiled. "A gift indeed. I'm . . . Well, Cardamom came to see me Saturday night. After the feast."

"Cardamom Coulis?" Mrs. Berry asked, her right eyebrow rising just like Boysen's. "The Third?"

"That's the one." Lyra focused on selecting a piece of cheese from the cutting board. "He talked to Professor Genoise, and they agreed that he should tutor me privately next term."

"Professor Genoise is going to tutor you?" Mac asked.

"No," Lyra clarified. "Cardamom."

Five full seconds of silence followed. Lyra tried to ignore it, taking a bite of cheese and chewing far longer than was necessary.

"Tutoring you . . . how?" Ginger asked finally. "And when?"

"In Presentation, Wednesday and Thursday nights," Lyra answered. "After dinner."

Boysen's voice was very even. "So you'll miss our review those nights."

"Afraid so." Lyra looked around, forcing a laugh. "Come on, all of you! Professor Genoise thinks I have potential. I'll still be with you the other three nights of the week, and I'll be able to pass on everything I'm learning from Cardamom."

"Not everything," Ginger muttered under her breath.

Lyra stared at her. "Huh?"

"Never mind." It was Ginger's turn to force a smile. She reached across the table to give Lyra an awkward but genuine high five. "Presentation training! Maybe you'll be able to give Mac a run for his money."

"Ah yes," Mrs. Berry said, apparently eager to change the subject. "From what I hear, you're quite a Presentation virtuoso, Mac."

Mac looked down, but he was smiling. "Professor Genoise called my style 'majestic.' Caramelle was the 'virtuosic' one."

Another few beats of silence followed the mention of Lyra's former roommate. Lyra glanced up to see that Mrs. Berry was watching her son keenly. Boysen had gone still. The air around him felt thick, heavier than the stew, and yet vibrated at some unpleasantly dissonant frequency.

"Well, Your Presentation Majesty," Mrs. Berry said, turning the attention back to Macaron. "Mr. Berry will be eager for your notes on his four-tiered sticky toffee gâteau. I'll bring it out once we clear all this away, and you can give me your opinion to pass on to him."

Mac gave some humble affirmative, and the meal resumed with Mrs. Berry maintaining a steady flow of cheerful chatter.

Lyra kept eating automatically. It was hard to enjoy the food with Boysen silently vibrating beside her, but she pressed ahead, determined to recapture the comfortable ease of the evening.

He's just annoyed about the Whisk Whizzes, she told herself in between bites of stew, cheese, and bread. *But I'll be there more than half the time. It doesn't have to be that different. Nothing important is going to change.*

But something about that out-of-tune frequency at which Boysen was vibrating told her otherwise.

Everything was about to change.

CHAPTER TWENTY-EIGHT

Second Term Begins

All three professors were waiting in the Flavor classroom when the students arrived on the first day after break.

"Greetings, Aspiring Bakers!" Professor Genoise waved them in. "Take your seats."

"No time to dilly-dally in the second term," Professor Puff said dryly as the five first years hurried to their workstations.

Professor Honeycomb was as cheerfully welcoming as ever. "It is delightful to see you all. I look forward to hearing about your time away, but alas, my esteemed colleagues are correct. Time is precious this term." The magical chime rang, and she bowed to Professor Genoise. "Please begin, Basil."

He returned the bow, then faced the class. "Congratulations to you," he said, each word as clipped and precise as his neatly trimmed beard. "You have successfully completed your first term at the Royal Academy of Magical Baking. I hope you used the break to savor that accomplishment because this term will provide no chance to do so."

Professor Puff took up the conversational baton smoothly. "Whatever carried you through the first term will not be sufficient for the second. You cannot rest on your accomplishments. Instead, you must build upon them. Growth is the only way forward."

"And our job is to help you grow," Professor Honeycomb joined in. "First term was about setting a baseline. We now have a thorough understanding of your individual strengths and weaknesses and can structure this term's curriculum accordingly."

"The schedule will be a tad different," Professor Puff explained. "Each Monday morning, in this room, we will hold a mini exam."

Caramelle drew in a sharp breath. Lyra pretended not to notice or care that her former roommate already looked more stressed than ever.

"We spent a good deal of first term talking about community," Professor Honeycomb reminded them. "I trust you were listening. This term, your ability to work with others will be an important factor in your progress, or lack thereof."

Professor Genoise nodded. "Each of us will be assigning you a major project every week, due on Monday morning. But we do not expect you to complete three projects a week on your own."

"We have put you in two groups," Professor Puff announced. "Each group will work together on these three projects and present the results on Monday mornings. The third years will cast preservation spells on Sunday nights as part of their rounds."

Professor Honeycomb beamed at the class. "We took care, when assigning these groups, to put you with partners who would complement your unique baking skills."

"Aspiring Bakers Crumble and Fondant are one group." Professor Genoise gestured to Ginger and Mac. "Berry, Meringue, and Treble are another."

Lyra turned around to look at Boysen, who winked at her with one of his signature whole-face grins. She grinned back, then glanced across the aisle at Caramelle.

The Meringue was staring pointedly straight ahead. Her posture was so rigid, Lyra thought a strong gust of wind might snap her in half.

Slowly, icily, Caramelle raised her hand.

"Yes, Aspiring Baker Meringue?" Professor Genoise said.

Caramelle's voice was as frosty as the air around her. "I would prefer to work alone."

The professors were silent for a moment.

"Is that allowed?" Lyra asked.

"It is." Professor Honeycomb shook her head. "Though, we do not recommend it. I call it inadvisable."

"But not impossible," Caramelle countered. "I know there is precedent. Didn't Apprentice Baker Coulis work alone in his second term of the first year?"

"He did," Professor Genoise replied slowly. "I trust he shared with you how difficult it was."

Caramelle reached up to stroke the Stellar Enchantment Pin attached to her hat. "I am not afraid of hard work."

"You will be expected to complete all three projects every week," Professor Honeycomb warned her. "There will be no extensions or grace given because you are working alone."

"I understand."

Professor Puff studied Caramelle, her gray eyes unreadable. "Are you absolutely certain, Meringue?"

"I am." Caramelle held Professor Puff's gaze steadily. "I can do it, Professor. I need to. I believe it will be important for my growth. Please allow me to try."

Another beat of silence followed, then Professor Puff nodded. "Very well. Aspiring Baker Meringue will be her own group and will complete all the assignments alone each week."

Lyra was torn between relief and concern. She was excited to partner with Boysen, and she certainly didn't relish the prospect of working closely with Caramelle ever again. But she had been Caramelle's roommate for three months. She knew exactly how the auburn-haired girl responded to stress and how hard she pushed herself.

Even in her anger, Lyra had been a little worried over vacation thinking about Caramelle alone in Pestle this term. Now, with three major projects to complete every week, completely on her own . . . Lyra honestly didn't know how Caramelle would survive.

Lyra shook her head.

Not my problem, she told herself firmly. *Not anymore.*

"Very well." Professor Honeycomb wiped her hands on her apron, as though ridding herself of any guilt for Caramelle's imminent demise. "Any other questions or concerns?"

The other four students shook their heads.

"Excellent," Professor Genoise said. "Since there is no project due this morning, we will spend this time going over your first-term exam cakes."

"We put a preservation spell on all of them immediately after the exam, to ensure they would survive over the break," Professor Puff said. "The Apprentice Bakers are bringing them up from the kitchens as we speak. Ah, here they are."

Razz appeared at the door, bearing a cake in each hand. Lyra recognized Boysen's globe and Ginger's honeycomb instantly. Hyacinth followed with Caramelle's resplendent creation and another, equally impressive, which must have been Mac's. Finally, Cardamom entered, carrying Lyra's vanilla disappointment reverently in both hands.

"Thank you, Apprentice Bakers." Professor Honeycomb directed them to line the cakes up on her teacher's workstation counter. "Let's take these one at a time, shall we?"

"Beginning with Aspiring Baker Fondant," Professor Genoise said, waving a delicate hand at Mac. "Please join us, Fondant, and tell us which flavors and spells you used from first term to recreate your final entrance exam cake."

Mac shuffled forward, pushing his glasses up his nose.

"The original was a coffee genoise sponge with marzipan filling. Fondant on top with a drizzle of tempered chocolate." He glanced at Caramelle, cleared his throat, and looked at his shoes. "For flavor, I added a coating of caramel buttercream and caramel drizzle with the chocolate."

"Inspired choice," Professor Honeycomb said approvingly. "The caramel's richness enhances the delicacy of the marzipan, and the coffee keeps it from being too sweet. Though, you still need to work on your ratios, Fondant. That's my goal for you this term. You've learned to listen to your instincts regarding *which* flavor to add. Now you can start refining *how much* flavor to use."

Mac nodded. "Thank you, Professor."

"For Texture, I believe you used Master Chiffon's Aeration Charm?" Professor Puff inquired.

"Yes." Again, Mac glanced at Caramelle. "The advanced version."

Professor Puff's stern mouth curled up in the slightest of smiles. "You came a long way last term, Fondant. There is still ample room for improvement, but this was a competent demonstration of that spell."

"Thank you," Mac said again. "I'll keep practicing."

"I know you will." Professor Puff turned to Professor Genoise. "But the Presentation was the real star of the show. Right, Basil?"

"Absolutely." Professor Genoise gestured to the three perfect tiers covered smoothly in fondant. An intricate network of chocolate and caramel was drizzled over the whole thing, like a draping of lace. "I believe you employed Master Glaze's Shine Spell?"

"That's right," Mac said. "Fondant can be a bit . . . boring. I like the extra sheen the spell provides, especially with the drizzle."

Professor Genoise waved his hand again over the cake. "Stunning. And considering this was the only spell you were allowed, even more impressive. No cleanliness spells, but still fairly neat. And I agree: Master Glaze does provide that extra shot of glamour to elevate your choice of ingredients. Well done, Fondant."

Mac was so pleased, he couldn't speak. His eyes shone behind his glasses as he shook Professor Genoise's hand.

"Not to say you can't still grow," Professor Genoise admonished him. "You are quite talented, but as Professor Puff said earlier, we cannot rest on our accomplishments. Knowing what you are capable of, I expect you to push yourself even further this term."

"Of course, Professor. And thank you." Mac returned to his seat while the other students, led by Boysen, clapped raucously.

The round of applause for Caramelle was more subdued, though still very polite. Lyra forced her face into an expressionless mask as Professor Puff praised the cake's peerless Texture. She managed not to look smug when Professor Honeycomb observed that the Flavor was adequate but imbalanced, due to an overabundance of caramel.

Tell me about it, Lyra thought.

But then Professor Genoise said, "Am I correct in deducing that you used Master Glaze's spell also, Aspiring Baker Meringue? Like Aspiring Baker Fondant?"

"Yes," Caramelle said, without a glance at Mac. "Apprentice Baker Coulis advised it and worked with me to master the execution."

During two weeks of vacation, Lyra had managed to forget this particular detail of deception. Now, stomach roiling, she struggled to maintain her calm mask.

How many times had the Pestle roommates practiced Madame Temper's Chant of Precision together? How many times had Caramelle sworn that Master Glaze's spell was too fiendishly complicated for her taste?

How many times had she lied?

Cardamom's smooth voice cut across Lyra's inner rant. "Aspiring Baker Meringue has made wonderful progress." He smiled at Caramelle. "I am confident in her abilities to excel this term."

"Only thanks to your excellent tutelage," Caramelle said sweetly.

Lyra's head felt like a tea kettle on high boil. She managed to join in on the second round of applause as Caramelle returned to her seat, but she kept her eyes on the professors, her posture as rigid as any Meringue.

Why are you still surprised? she asked herself. *The Meringue is not to be trusted. And to think you were worried about her!*

In that moment, Lyra vowed not to waste any more emotional energy on Caramelle's wellbeing. If The Meringue wanted to run herself ragged and let her ambition literally drive her into the ground, so be it.

Lyra was *done*.

Her inward fuming made it difficult to concentrate on Ginger's cake. She was dimly aware that the reviews were mixed. Professor Honeycomb loved the flavor, but the other two professors had grave concerns. Apparently, Ginger's "daring" style was a bit *too* audacious for Professor Genoise, while Professor Puff lamented her lack of attention to Texture details.

Lyra refocused just in time to hear Professor Puff say, "Baking is, indeed, a creative endeavor. But it also requires exactitude."

"And discipline," Professor Genoise added. "One must learn to make the box before one can think outside it."

"Was it fun?" Ginger asked. She was, Lyra saw, taking it all like a champ. "I mean, fun to look at? And tasty?"

"Very tasty," Professor Honeycomb said. "No complaints about the flavors you chose or their ratios. Your instincts are spot-on."

"And the design is . . . fun," Professor Genoise admitted. "Alas, fun is not enough."

To Lyra's surprise, Professor Puff gave Ginger a warm, encouraging smile. "Fret not, Crumble. You and Fondant will be a great help to each other this term. You can coach him in Flavor, and he can do the same for you in Presentation. And you can both work together on your Texture."

Ginger returned the smile bravely, her head held high. "Mac is great. We'll work hard."

All three professors began the round of applause this time. Lyra was starting to feel better until she saw Caramelle roll her eyes as Ginger passed. That sent another wave of rage crashing into Lyra. She spent most of Boysen's turn floundering between indignation and anxiety on Ginger's behalf, only emerging when Boysen returned to his seat amidst general acclaim.

It's fine, she thought, fighting against a stab of guilt. *I'm sure everyone loved him.*

Turning around, she caught his eye. His grin confirmed her suspicions.

Yup. Another huge success for the Flavor King. Not sure why they don't just move Boysen right along to the second year. He's definitely good enough.

She gave him a thumbs-up, promising herself she'd get the details from him later.

"Aspiring Baker Treble," Professor Genoise called, snapping Lyra's attention back to the front of the room.

Her heart sank. There was her cake, sitting frumpily on the counter like a textbook example of failure. She couldn't stand the thought of that sorry excuse for a dessert being evaluated privately, let alone publicly.

Not that she had a choice in the matter.

Sure enough, the Presentation headmaster indicated the spot on the platform Boysen had just vacated, his gracious voice only emphasizing the impossibility of refusal.

"Aspiring Baker Treble, would you join us?"

CHAPTER TWENTY-NINE

BETTER THAN BEST

As she walked to the front of the room, Lyra could feel the warmth of Boysen's gaze behind her, along with Ginger's and Mac's. They propelled her forward, allowing her to push through Caramelle's frigid presence across the aisle.

"Remarkable flavor, Treble." Professor Honeycomb's cheerful smile added to her classmates' support. Lyra stood a little straighter as the professor continued, "Your original vanilla was already marvelous. But the addition of boysenberry, at just the right amount?" Professor Honeycomb lifted her eyes as if searching for adequate praise in the air above her head.

"Exquisite?" Razz suggested, giving Lyra a wink.

"Yes. Thank you, Berry." Professor Honeycomb took Lyra's hand and shook it. "Exquisite. You've got quite a gut there, Treble."

Caramelle snickered, turning it quickly into a cough. Lyra ignored her, focusing instead on Professor Honeycomb's sparkling blue eyes and the sight of Boysen in her peripheral vision.

"Thank you, Professor," Lyra said.

"Remarkable growth in Texture this term, also." Professor Puff's voice was always demure, but Lyra could now recognize the subtle notes that indicated particular approval. "You did credit to Master Chiffon's Aeration Charm."

"Only the intermediate version," Lyra confessed.

The right corner of Professor Puff's mouth quirked up. "And at the beginning of the term, you were struggling with the beginner level. As I said, excellent growth. If you continue to apply yourself, and with Aspiring Baker Berry's help, I have no doubt you will advance even more remarkably this term."

Lyra glanced over at Boysen, whose arms were pumping up and down in a *"let's go!"* gesture. She stifled a laugh.

"Thank you, Professor. I look forward to getting better," Lyra said.

"Speaking of getting better," Professor Genoise said gently, "I believe

Apprentice Baker Coulis already spoke to you about the Presentation aspect of this cake?"

Lyra forced herself to look the professor in the eye. "Yes, sir. Allow me to apologize. I hate submitting subpar work. It won't happen again."

Professor Genoise's green eyes were kinder than she expected. "I confess I was surprised. You performed Madame Temper's Chant of Precision to great effect during your final entrance exam. May I ask what was different last week?"

Lyra could feel Caramelle tensing up in the front row, only a few feet away. She ignored her.

"I think I let my nerves get to me, Professor. I got stuck in my head. It's such a simple spell, and I ruined it by overthinking it."

"Of course." Professor Genoise nodded, along with the other two professors. "We've all made such mistakes. Everyone can have a bad day."

"It won't happen again," Lyra repeated.

Professor Genoise smiled. "Oh, but it will, my dear. You can be sure of that. Our job is to equip you with the skills that will enable you to push through such bad days so your quality level remains high, regardless. That is where Apprentice Baker Coulis comes in. He went over your tutoring plan for this term?"

"Yes. Thank you. Both of you." Lyra was blushing and knew she was blushing, which made her blush more. "I am so grateful for Apprentice Baker Coulis's help."

"I haven't done anything yet." Cardamom chuckled. "But I'm excited to work with Aspiring Baker Treble. I think we can learn a lot from each other."

"Indeed. Thank you, Coulis." Professor Genoise gave Lyra a small bow. "And thank you, Treble. I know I don't need to urge you to work hard."

She shook her head fervently, still blushing. Then Boysen started clapping, and she floated back to her seat, carried along by the applause and the glow of Cardamom's smile.

And by the furious glare coming from The Meringue.

That was a nice bonus.

"Lyra!"

Cardamom's eyes lit up as she entered the Presentation classroom. Her heart jumped into her throat and stuck there, making it difficult to speak or think or even breathe.

Pull it together, Treble, she admonished herself. *If just the way he says your name turns you into a catatonic mess, you'll never make it through the term.*

At least she had the smiling part of social interaction covered. Her face felt frozen into a happy grin that almost certainly made her look ridiculous.

She swallowed hard. "Hi, Cardamom!" Then, before she could stop herself, she dropped into a curtsy.

Cardamom laughed gaily. "We should have more musician bakers," he said, stepping backward into a deep, grand bow. "They understand the etiquette of performance."

"What does that have to do with baking?" Lyra asked, wondering if the flush on her cheeks would prove as permanent as her delirious grin.

"Everything." Cardamom spread his hands, looking for a moment just like Professor Genoise when he was about to judge a cake. "First lesson, Aspiring Baker Treble: all baking is performance."

Lyra looked around. She'd never been in a classroom at night before. Darkness poured through the massive windows, but the room was cozily lit by the same magical fire that operated in her dorm's fire pit. Torches were set in sconces around the wall, and two massive chandeliers hung from the ceiling, holding row upon row of magically burning candles. She could easily imagine them as stage lights and the teacher's platform as a stage, waiting for the next culinary tale to be told.

"That makes sense," she said slowly. "I get the same sort of nerves before an exam that I used to have before shows with the Any Weather Bards. More, actually. Singing in front of a crowd never scared me as much as baking for Professor Puff."

"The Puff?" Cardamom sounded incredulous. "She's not that scary."

"Not her, exactly." Lyra hesitated. "Just . . . her disapproval. I want to impress her. All of them, really. I guess I'm scared of failing."

"Every baker is, deep down." Cardamom put a hand on each of Lyra's shoulders, looking her in the eye. "What sets you apart is how you handle that fear. You can let it cripple you, or you can use it for fuel." His dark eyes, inches from her own, danced in the magic candlelight. "Ready to fuel up, Lyra?"

Her heart was now pounding against the walls of her throat so loudly and painfully that she was sure he must hear it. Speaking was out of the question, so she just nodded.

That was enough for Cardamom. "Excellent. Let's get started."

Lyra saw that he had pulled two stools behind the teacher's counter. Sitting on one, he motioned for her to sit beside him.

"I thought we'd begin each session with a conversation," he said, perching on the stool as elegantly as The Meringue, but with much less rigid effort. "In future weeks, we'll have Presentation labs to prepare for and look back on, but for now, we can just talk. How's the term so far?"

Lyra finally managed to swallow, pushing her heart back down to its rightful place. In a remarkable imitation of a calm voice, she answered, "It's going well, I think. No complaints yet. I mean, the professors haven't found a reason to complain about me yet."

He smiled. "Flavor and Texture labs all right?"

"Great," Lyra said fervently, and she meant it. The past two days had been lovely. She was amazed at what a difference it made *not* to be rooming with Caramelle. Sure, she missed The Meringue's expertise in Texture, and Mac was moping through the Whisk Whiz Reviews like a lovesick puppy, but Lyra was determined to focus on the positive. "I love Flavor. I enjoyed the first term, just learning how to combine different tastes. Listening to my gut. Trusting my instincts."

"Like a performer," Cardamom said with a wink.

"Yes!" Lyra beamed, her heart fluttering delightfully. "Exactly. And this term, we're using *magic*. We started Madame Hazelnut's Deepening Spell in lab yesterday. It's the one I used in my entrance exam. I love how it doesn't pile magic on top but just brings out the good that's already there. Makes the food taste more *real*—more like itself. And the spell felt *easy*. Even easier than it was in my entrance exam after all the months of practicing I did. Not just easy . . . Fun. It was fun."

She was suddenly aware that she had been talking very fast and rambling. But Cardamom didn't seem to mind. He was still watching her, listening patiently.

She let her ridiculous grin relax into a genuine smile. "Texture can hurt my brain sometimes," she confessed. "But Flavor just . . . flows."

"Especially with a Berry as your partner," Cardamom observed.

For some reason, her heart stuttered. She felt heat creeping back into her cheeks.

"Boysen is amazing," she managed. Then, with more ease, "I mean, the Berry boys are Flavor Kings, right?"

Cardamom's face was impassive. "Absolutely. And from what I've seen, Boysen is the best of the bunch."

"Really?" Lyra's eyes widened. "Better than Razz?"

"Hands down. And Razz knows it too. But he's a Berry, so he's not mad about it. Not even a bit jealous. Just proud, and rightly so."

Lyra shook her head in wonder. "They're an incredible family."

"No one can beat them in good nature or in Flavor." Cardamom waved a hand dismissively. "For what that's worth, anyway."

"For what that's worth?" Lyra repeated.

"Flavor is all well and good," Cardamom said airily. "So is Texture. But when it comes to measuring the true worth of a baker, nothing matters more than Presentation."

Lyra felt her own eyebrows lift. "What do you mean?"

"Think about it." Cardamom leaned forward, his voice eager. "Where do all the top bakers go? They work at the palace, or they open their own restaurants. Ever been to a royal banquet?"

Lyra shook her head.

"Take my word for it," Cardamom said. "Exquisite Presentation. Beyond exquisite. As for restaurants, I've never seen one with shoddy Presentation. Have you?"

"No," Lyra admitted.

"Because they don't exist. A baker with poor Presentation skills isn't going to succeed in any public position. It doesn't matter how good the Flavor is or whether they're experts in Texture spells. Presentation is what sets you apart. It's the dividing line between the best and the *better* than best."

Lyra giggled. Involuntarily, nervously, stupidly. "Better than best?"

"That's right." Cardamom's face was serious. "So don't worry about Boysen always winning in Flavor or Caramelle dominating in Puff's class. Presentation is how you win."

To her own amazement, Lyra heard herself voicing a contrary opinion. "But isn't the opposite also true? No matter how good something looks, if it doesn't taste good, the restaurant won't stay open. Right?"

Cardamom shrugged. "Sure. But unless the food *looks* good, the restaurant will never open in the first place."

"Doesn't that just mean the three principles have to work together? Like the professors said at the beginning of the year?"

Cardamom rolled his eyes. "And all principles are equal, and no one discipline is more important than the others. They all say that, but deep down, every baker believes their area of expertise is chief. Including our three professors." He winked. "But only Professor Genoise is correct."

The wink sent a jolt of electricity through Lyra's insides. The rich scent of honey and cinnamon was all around her, making her feel pleasantly dizzy. Still, she couldn't quite bring herself to agree wholeheartedly.

"It's a tough lesson," Cardamom said, watching her closely enough to note her uncertainty. "But an important one. It's also why I asked Professor Genoise to let me work with you this term."

"You-you asked?" The jolt of electricity must have started a fire deep within Lyra. Her heart was beginning to feel like a pot of chocolate chips over a double boiler. "I thought you two decided together."

"I asked. And I wouldn't take no for an answer."

Leaning forward even further, he balanced gracefully on the edge of the stool.

"Flavor instincts can be trained," he said softly. "Texture spells can be learned. But style? The unique part of each baker that shines through in Presentation? That can't be taught, or bought, or memorized. You either have it or you don't. And you . . ."

He gave her one of his most dazzling smiles, briefly removing her ability to breathe. Was her heart actually melting?

". . . you, Lyra Treble, have it."

CHAPTER THIRTY

In the Meantime, Cookies

Yep. Lyra's heart was definitely melting. Somehow, though, the pile of goo was still pounding away, hammering blood through her veins at breakneck speed. When she managed to form words, her voice came out as a whispered squeak.

"I do?"

"You do. And in a different way than I've ever seen in any other Presentation expert." Cardamom smiled, his teeth white and gleaming against his dark olive skin. "You are quite an enigma."

"I'm certainly . . . different," she said, trying not to yell over the roar of her own blood rushing in her ears. "From my family, anyway. And I haven't had the right training. I think . . . some of the other students think I'm an imposter."

Cardamom frowned. "An imposter?"

"That I pulled some kind of trick to get in. That I'm a fraud." To Lyra's horror, her eyes filled with tears. She looked down at her hands, clenching them in her lap to keep herself steady. "That I . . . that I shouldn't be here."

She blinked rapidly, trying to banish the tears before they could fall. *Where is all this coming from?* she thought desperately. *I thought I was over this. I thought I was settled. I thought—*

Suddenly, Cardamom's hand was covering both of hers.

"Old baking families are the worst," he said softly. "Believe me, I know. The Coulis name is brand-new compared to some of your classmates."

Lyra tore her eyes away from the delightful sight of Cardamom's hand on hers to stare at him in shock. "Really? I thought—I mean, you're 'the Third.'"

"Exactly." His tone was grim and edged faintly with bitterness. "Only 'the Third.' If you can count the generations on one hand, or even still keep track of them, that's too few. The Mints lost count ages ago. So did the Meringues."

"And the Berrys?" Lyra guessed.

"Oh, yes. Not that you'd know. They're so terribly nice, the Berrys." Cardamom sighed. His hand was still covering hers, just resting, as if it had been designed to fit there. "I'm saying that I understand what you're feeling. I've been through my share of it."

"But everyone respects you," Lyra protested. "Professor Genoise can't speak highly enough of you. You're . . . you're incredible!"

"I worked hard for it," he said flatly. "So did my dad and my grandfather. Our name is good now, but we've had to break the path every step of the way with the old families laughing at us the whole time. And I'm here to tell you, Lyra, that you can't let them get to you. You can't listen, not for a second. Understood?"

She nodded, unable to speak but grateful that the tears were still contained within her eyes.

"You belong here," Cardamom whispered. Then, louder, "You belong here. Say it."

"I belong here," she repeated.

"That's my girl."

He smiled. It didn't light up his whole face, like Boysen's grin, but his dark eyes sparkled with their own inner flame, which was far more exciting.

"And we're going to make sure you stay here," he went on, giving her hand an encouraging pat before leaning back and crossing his arms. "We just have to build up your skills to match. You're in a good place with Flavor. What about Texture?"

With great effort, Lyra pulled her attention from the bewildering mixture of emotional "flavors" swirling inside her and tried to match his professional tone. "It's off to a good start, I guess. An okay start. I think I could really like Texture if I gave it a chance. Setting spells to music helps a lot."

"Music?" Cardamom's eyebrows lifted delicately, and the faint distaste in his tone sent Lyra's stomach into a nosedive. "You . . . *sing* the spells?"

"N-no," Lyra stammered. "We just use music to memorize the words. The Whisk Whi—I mean, my friends and I find it helpful."

Cardamom nodded, but his serious expression did nothing to reverse the course of Lyra's plummeting stomach. "Interesting. And Puff approves?"

"Well . . . sort of. She said she would prefer it if we just did the assignment as it's written. Rise to the challenge, I think. But she also said that baking is a journey, and bakers should use any tool at their disposal to help them along the journey."

"Of course." He looked at her for a few moments, his face full of thoughtful concern. The silence lasted long enough for Lyra's stomach to finish its descent, landing somewhere near her toes with a pathetic *thud.* When he did speak, though, his voice was gentle. "I think you need to be very careful with this music element, Lyra. As your tutor, I feel it is my responsibility to warn you against bad habits."

Lyra's heart slipped loose and began to follow her stomach's recent downward course. "Is music a bad habit?"

"It could be if you become dependent on it. And even if not . . ." He hesitated. Then, in a tone that was somehow equal parts kindness and bitterness, he continued, "The baking world can be hard to break into. If you don't show them you can play by their rules, they'll never take you seriously. They'll never let you in."

"But . . ." She floundered, her internal temperature dropping faster than a magically controlled cooling drawer. "Aren't we supposed to forge our own path? Make our mark?"

"Absolutely. But first you have to prove yourself. Not by bending the rules, but by following them better than anyone else. And along the way, you infuse each tradition with your personality. The strongest personalities are the ones that stand out. Beat them at their own game. That's how you make your mark." Before Lyra could reply, Cardamom gave her another dazzling smile. "But that's what I'm here for. Thanks to these tutoring sessions, you won't need any more shortcuts. Right?"

"Right," she echoed automatically.

"I have a feeling you're going to make quite a mark, Lyra Treble. With my help, you could change Presentation forever. That's the reason I wanted to work with you." His hand reached out to rest on hers again. "Well . . . that's one of the reasons, anyway."

Lyra's insides chose that moment to start singing. The song was loud inside her head and shaky with nerves, but she couldn't stop it.

In fact, she had no desire to.

The only problem was to keep her actual voice from joining in.

Bring it on, second term, sang Lyra's soul as she perched on her stool. This time it wasn't her heart melting like tempered chocolate in the hot sun. It was her doubts and fears from only a few days ago. In fact, to borrow a word from Professor Puff, it was shaping up to be an "exquisite" few months.

Private lessons with Cardamom? Boysen for a partner in group projects? Rooming with Ginger and laughing with her and Mac at the Whisk Whiz Review?

The song of Lyra's soul changed keys, coming around for another triumphant chorus.

Bring it on, second term. Bring it on, Royal Academy of Magical Baking.

I am so ready.

Cardamom gave her hands a squeeze, then released them and stood. "Ready to make your inimitable mark on the discipline of Presentation?"

She rose from her stool, hoping he wouldn't notice the hand she placed on the counter to keep from falling over. "Ready and willing."

"Then we're off." He strode to a nearby bookshelf and returned with a stack of books, placing them on the counter with a *thump*. "Let's forge the Treble path."

Two hours later, Lyra found herself standing in the foyer of the dormitory, unsure what to do next.

Cardamom had gallantly walked her back to the dorm building, taking his leave in the foyer with a deep bow before heading upstairs to the third floor. But Lyra wasn't interested in returning to her own room yet. Nor did she want to check if the Whisk Whizzes were still reviewing.

As much as she loved her friends, she wasn't ready for *people* yet. Her internal ingredients shelf was far too jumbled. She needed time to sort through it all and get some of those tricky spices back in their jars.

It was the perfect time for another visit to Queen Penelope, but she was loath to show up in the chicken's throne room empty-handed again . . .

And with that, clarity struck.

I want to bake, Lyra thought, marveling at how quickly she had forgotten this simple truth. *That's what I need. I'll make some cookies and take them to Queen Penelope.*

She retraced her steps to the main hall. All nine of the practice kitchens were kept fully stocked with basic ingredients, magically preserved and checked daily for any replenishment needs. Lyra had done all her practicing in the dorm during the first term, so she'd never had to use one of the large, brightly lit rooms.

Now, though, she was grateful for the academy's abundant provision of space. With three practice kitchens on each of the second, third, and fourth floors, an Aspiring Baker had plenty of options for some alone time.

Lyra went straight up to the fourth floor. Every practice kitchen was empty, so she chose the one closest to the stairs and began pulling out ingredients for her favorite cookie recipe: browned-butter chocolate chip.

As she measured out the butter into a pot on the stove, she considered using a spell or two. It wouldn't hurt to get in another rep of Madame Hazelnut's Deepening Spell for Flavor, and she could always use more Texture time. Since she was technically in a practice kitchen, shouldn't she . . . well, *practice?*

But then Chef Flax's voice pealed through her memory, accompanied by Bumble's cheerful chatter: *Sometimes, I find it soothing to bake without any magic at all.*

So do I, Chef, Lyra thought fervently. *So do I.*

Pushing aside all thoughts of Flavor charms and gray-eyed Texture professors, Lyra set the butter to brown and began measuring the two kinds of sugar. Next came the flour, sifted into a separate bowl with baking soda and salt. Then it was time to check the butter, giving it a brief stir so it wouldn't burn . . .

Before Lyra knew it, she was singing her "Chocolate Chip Cookie Song," the first baking song she had ever written.

Let the butter simmer now,
Not too hot.
Wait until it starts to brown,
Then move the pot.

While it's cooling, sift together
Salt, soda, flour:
A trio fit for any weather,
Full of power.

Join the sugars in the bowl,
Brown and white.
Add the butter, sweet and whole-
-some: happy sight!

Whisk until it's light and fluffy;
Eggs are next;
Cure for every brain that's stuffy,
Or perplexed.

Vanilla: pour it in, friend, by
The tablespoon.
Though we're near the end, cry
Not: sweet comes soon!

Fold the flour and chocolate in,
Gentle, slow,
Feel that special glow begin;
Breathe, and know:

When the oven's done its job,
You will feel
Gladness none can ever rob,
Joy that's real.

Lyra couldn't remember the last time she had felt so peaceful. Not even the merry warmth of the Whisk Whiz Review could rival the simple bliss of just *baking*, the movement of her hands falling naturally into the rhythm of the song on her lips.

Singing and baking fit together so perfectly, she thought as she placed the cookie sheet in the magically powered oven. *How could it be wrong to combine them?*

Chef Flax would say it wasn't wrong at all. So would Ginger, and Boysen, and maybe even the whole Berry family. But were they in the minority? Cardamom's concerns had been even stronger than Professor Puff's, and they certainly weighed more heavily on Lyra's mind.

And, of course, Caramelle had made her opinions clear . . .

Lyra shook her head. *No Meringue tonight.*

But even without the Caramelle factor, the question of "music in baking" was still trickier than choux pastry. Lyra sensed all her confusion from earlier returning in a flood. Her insides were suddenly back to feeling like a chaotic kitchen with too many projects going on at once and dirty dishes piling up faster than she could clean them.

What was the best way to ensure she survived to the third term? Whose counsel should she prioritize? Between the Flax/Berry viewpoint and the Coulis/Puff warnings, what was a Treble to do?

To her surprise, it was her mother's voice that pierced through the gathering mental haze.

One note at a time, Lyra. Don't think too far ahead. One note, then the next, then the next. Just keep on singing and you'll be fine.

Lyra smiled; her rising spirits timed perfectly with the *ding!* of the oven.

One day at a time, she thought. After pulling the cookies out, she set them to cool and quickly finished clearing away her mess. *Keep on singing—or baking, rather. Maybe both sometimes.*

Lyra arranged the warm cookies on a plate and gave her tidy workspace a final glance of inspection. Then she was off to the roof, stopping once or twice to breathe in the rich nutty aroma of browned butter and chocolate chips fresh from the oven.

She would figure it all out eventually.

And in the meantime . . . there were cookies.

CHAPTER THIRTY-ONE

WHISK WHIZ RECREATION

One week down." Mac collapsed into the chair in Whisk with a groan. "Eleven more to go."

Ginger threw a pillow at him from her corner of the couch. "Not so fast," she warned. "We still have our first weekend of mad baking ahead of us followed by the first of several Monday morning exams. I wouldn't call the week over until *that's* done."

Mac groaned again, covering his face with his hands. "Is Friday no refuge anymore? Is nothing sacred?"

"Of course Friday is a refuge," Boysen said, arriving from the kitchen with a tray of mugs. "And the Whisk Whiz Review is sacred." He handed Lyra a mug of hot chocolate. "Speaking of, welcome back to the fold, Treble. How were your two evenings away?"

His voice was carefully light, and Lyra responded in kind. "They were good. Tutoring is going to be a big help to me this term. Though, I missed you all, of course."

"Ha!" Ginger swatted Lyra with the remaining pillow. "No way you missed us *that* much. You were happier than an over-proofed lump of dough when you came home last night and the night before."

Lyra wrapped her fingers around the mug, concentrating on the steam rising from its creamy surface. "Both things can be true."

"Of course." Boysen finished handing out hot chocolate and sat back on his heels. "We're glad you're back and also glad the time away is proving . . . beneficial."

"It really is," Lyra insisted. "And not just for me. I'll soak up all the insight I can and bring it back to Whisk."

Mac wrapped his arms around the pillow Ginger had thrown at him, hugging it to his chest. "Could you maybe ask Cardamom how the professors expect us to do this every week? This first round of projects feels . . ."

"Unmanageable?" Ginger suggested. "Cruel? More ridiculous than Professor Genoise's monocle?"

"You're just miffed about Genoise's evaluation of your exam cake," Boysen said. "So what if you're too 'daring' for his particular tastes? You shouldn't take it so personally."

Lyra looked at her roommate curiously. "That happened Monday. I thought you were over it."

"It comes and goes in waves." Ginger sighed.

Lyra persisted, "But why didn't you say anything? The last time we talked about it—"

"Was Tuesday," Ginger reminded her. "I've barely seen you since." She smiled dryly at Lyra's sorrowful expression. "It's okay, roomie. You've had a lot going on. We'll find a rhythm soon."

"Speaking of rhythms," Boysen said, "how about we set ourselves a schedule for the weekends?"

Mac raised his hand. "Could this schedule include some downtime? Y'know, to avoid keeling over and hating the world?"

"My partner is wise," Ginger said solemnly. "When building a work schedule, always prioritize *not* working."

Boysen nodded, copying her grave tone. "Of course. That is the only way to ensure you have sufficient energy when the time does come to work. Otherwise, as my esteemed roommate so rightly observed, you run the risk of hating the world."

"And baking most of all," Ginger added.

"Exactly." Boysen, too, raised his hand. "All in favor of setting aside most of our Friday evening sessions for Whisk Whiz Recreation?"

Mac raised his other hand. Ginger gave a thumbs-up.

"I guess," Lyra said cautiously. "Are you sure we won't get behind?"

"You haven't heard the rest of the schedule yet." Boysen took a sip of hot chocolate, as if to brace himself. "I further propose that each team use Saturdays as practice days for the weekly project assignments and Sundays as 'performance.'"

"Bake all day Saturday *and* Sunday?" Ginger asked, her tone incredulous.

"Makes sense." Mac nodded fervently. "Work out the issues on Saturday, then do a clean run through on Sunday. But if disaster strikes on Sunday, we would still have the results from Saturday as a backup."

Lyra's eyebrows crinkled. "How will it all stay fresh?"

"Remember the preservation spells," Boysen replied. "We could ask the third years to perform them Saturday nights as well as Sundays. I'm sure Razz or Hyacinth wouldn't mind."

"Or Cardamom," Lyra said. "He would be glad to help."

Ginger rolled her eyes. "Glad to help *you*, maybe."

Lyra ignored her. "So, we use Friday night to cool off from the week, then hit it hard Saturday and Sunday?"

"That's the idea." Boysen raised his hand again. "All in favor, say 'sweet.'"

The other three chorused, "Sweet."

"And *savory*." Ginger shook her head. "That's still a ton of baking."

Lyra patted her shoulder. "That's why they put us in teams. It won't be nearly so bad with a partner."

"That's right." Boysen caught her eye and flashed her a grin. "Could even be fun."

"What about Caramelle?" Mac's voice was anxious. "She has to do it all by herself."

"Serves her right," Ginger said grimly.

Lyra had kept her promise to Caramelle and hadn't told her new roommate any details about the Pestle breakup, but Ginger seemed to have guessed exactly what happened. She also didn't need any encouragement to think the worst of The Meringue.

Mac, on the other hand, was still viewing the world through Caramelle-colored lenses. "Don't say that, Ginger. Think about handling all this work alone. And it's only going to get tougher from here."

"Serves her right," Ginger repeated. "She's the one who asked to work alone."

"And she's not even coming to the Whisk Whiz Review anymore." Mac stared despondently into his hot chocolate, ignoring the steam as it fogged up his glasses. "Did she say why, Lyra?"

Lyra gazed into her own mug, avoiding everyone's eyes. "I think . . . she's gone as far as she can with us. That's what she believes, anyway. She wants to be able to move at her own pace."

"Can't you try to talk to her?" Mac persisted. "Make her see sense?"

"Lyra has wasted enough breath on that particular lost cause," Ginger said heatedly. "Seriously, Macaron. What is it with you and The Meringue?"

Mac froze. "What do you mean?"

"I mean she's an arrogant, puffed-up lump of over-enriched dough." Ginger spread her arms as if to indicate the size of Caramelle's ego. "What do you see in her?"

Mac opened his mouth, then closed it. He looked at Boysen helplessly.

"Point of order, Crumble," Boysen said, his calm voice instantly defusing the tension. "We do not investigate matters of the heart. 'Tis far too . . . layered for the Whisk Whiz Review. And we don't speak ill of other Whisk Whizzes."

"The Meringue is not a Whiz anymore," Ginger shot back. "She has forfeited the right to—"

"You can't stop being a Whiz," Boysen said firmly. "It's a lifetime membership, guaranteed. If Caramelle ever wants to return, she'll be welcomed back with open arms."

Ginger shook her head but said nothing.

Mac studied Ginger over the top of his mug. "What do you have against her, anyway?"

"She was mean to my friend," Ginger said. Lyra started to object, but Ginger cut her off. "I don't know the whole story, but she did something to hurt Lyra. Isn't that enough?"

"Lyra doesn't seem to be taking it as hard as you are," Mac observed.

"Lyra's a better person than I am," Ginger said.

"That's not true," Lyra protested.

"And you've hated Caramelle from the start," Mac went on. "You were sniping at her all first term. Why?"

Ginger looked at Boysen. "Does this count as 'matters of the heart,' or do I have to answer?"

"I think it's a valid question," Boysen replied. "Especially since you and Mac are going to be spending a lot of time together this term. Best to clear the air."

"Fine." Ginger sighed. "I guess . . . to me, Caramelle Meringue represents everything that is wrong with the baking world."

"Is that all?" Boysen asked dryly. "Easy fix, then."

Ginger stuck her tongue out at him, then continued, "What are we always saying in these review sessions? That baking is about creation. *Shared* creation. That's the whole point of this academy. We're here to make good food so we can share it with others. Right?"

"I'll drink to that," Lyra said, taking a sip of hot chocolate.

"But creation requires creativity," Ginger went on. "Not just doing the same old thing over and over, but trying new things. Pushing boundaries. Taking risks."

"Creativity is 'daring,'" Boysen suggested innocently.

"Exactly." Ginger nodded. "That was one of the founding principles of the academy. This school was supposed to be like an incubator for creativity, raising new generations of bakers who would keep moving things forward."

"Oh yeah . . ." Lyra closed her eyes in an effort to remember. "I did some research into the academy when I was going through the trials. That was a big part of the founding charter. I think the book I read even used the phrase 'incubator for creativity.'"

Mac's eyes squinted at Ginger behind his glasses. "What does this have to do with Caramelle?"

"It's her whole family, really," Ginger said. "And others like them. We're the Royal Academy of Magical Baking, right? But somewhere along the way, people stopped caring about the 'academy' part, or even 'magical baking.' They only care about 'royal.' About getting ahead and moving up in the world."

"Being the best, no matter what," Lyra muttered, thinking of her last conversation with Caramelle.

Ginger pointed at her. "That's it. That's the mantra. Baking isn't about experimentation anymore. It's about doing the same things everyone has always done, but better. So you can beat everyone else out of that exclusive royal chef job or get the best restaurant space. Competition has replaced creativity."

"So . . . you don't really hate Caramelle?" Mac said. "Not personally, I mean. You just hate her whole family on principle?"

"Hate is a strong word." Ginger took a determined sip of her hot chocolate. "Let's call it cordially dislike. But it *is* personal."

Boysen looked at Ginger curiously. "Did she steal your favorite rolling pin in kindergarten or something?"

"Sweet and savory, no." Ginger chuckled. "The Meringue didn't go to my school. She had private tutors all the way. But we still ran into each other plenty over the years, at competitions and dinners and such. The baking world is small. You know that better than most, Berry Boy."

Boysen shrugged. "I knew *about* Caramelle, sure. I knew about all of you before we started here. Except for Treble, of course." He winked at Lyra. "But I didn't know anyone well enough to form an opinion, let alone a 'cordial dislike.'"

"Well, I did." Ginger drained the rest of her cocoa and set the mug down on the floor. "Let's just say . . . Caramelle is a true Meringue. The whole family are Texture experts, which means they are obsessed with rules. Formulas. The baking world should be structured just so, according to 'how things have always been done.' And, of course, that includes the Meringues at the top. Can't have structure without hierarchy."

"Cardamom was saying something pretty similar the other night." Lyra instantly felt the air in the room start spinning a tad bit faster as tension whipped up again, but she tried to ignore it. "That old baking families are damaging the profession, making it harder for new ideas to take root."

Ginger whistled. "Well, isn't that the honey calling the sugar sweet?"

"Coulis is not an old name," Lyra said, carefully avoiding everyone's eyes. "He's only 'the Third.' It's been rough for him and his family."

"I'll bet." Ginger snorted. "Do they collect all their tears in crystal bottles or diamond?"

Lyra couldn't help glancing at Boysen. He was studying his hot chocolate with unnecessary intensity.

Meanwhile, Mac was still on the subject of auburn-haired Meringues. "I don't think she's really like that," he insisted. "That old-family nonsense. We all spent a lot of time with her last term. She didn't talk that way."

"I was surprised," Ginger admitted. "I tried to give her the benefit of the doubt. I thought maybe Lyra could be a good influence. But it turns out . . . a Meringue is a Meringue, through and through and always. You can't un-whip those egg whites."

"What do you think, Treble?" Boysen asked. Lyra looked up to find him watching her closely. "You two spent the most time together. Do you think Ginger's right? Or should my poor roommate continue to hold out hope?"

Lyra's hot chocolate had gone cold in her hands. She clutched the mug anyway, trying to draw support from its smooth surface as she chose her words carefully. "I think . . . *you're* right."

"Me?" Mac and Ginger asked at once.

"Boysen." Lyra smiled at his look of surprise. "I was really . . . disappointed in Caramelle at the end of last term. But I also saw how hard she worked. If she chooses to come back to the Whizzes, we should let her."

Mac and Boysen cheered as Ginger groaned. Lyra held up a hand. "I'm not saying I think she *will* come back. Honestly, I'm with Ginger on that. I don't have a lot of hope that Caramelle will change any time soon. But . . . creativity is all about being open to change, right?"

"Exactly." Boysen beamed at Lyra, which somehow warmed her heart far more than the hot chocolate could have. "Besides, it sounds to me like Crumble's problem is more with Professor Genoise than any particular student."

"Mac, throw that pillow at Boysen," Ginger commanded. "I don't have any missiles left."

Mac hugged the pillow she had thrown at him earlier. "You can pry it from my cold, floury hands."

Ginger nudged Lyra. "Roomie, take that pillow from Fondant."

"Is a pillow fight really the best way to begin the term?" Lyra laughed.

"It's Friday, isn't it?" Ginger lunged across Lyra, snatched the pillow from Mac, and used it to swat Boysen on the head. "Fridays are for cooling off!"

"Watch the hot chocolate!" Mac yelped, cradling his mug.

"Watch the fire!" Boysen rolled to the side and managed to empty the dregs of his hot chocolate into the flames rather than onto the rug. In the same fluid motion, he grabbed the pillow from Ginger's hands and threw it back, catching her squarely in the nose. "Mac! Battle stations!"

With that, the first ever Whisk Whiz Recreation kicked off to muffled shrieks of pillow-faced laughter.

CHAPTER THIRTY-TWO

Scones and Tricky Spices

It was early Saturday morning when a knock sounded on the door of Zester.

"Coming!"

Still tying a red scarf around her hair, Lyra rushed from the bathroom and opened the door.

"Boysen!" she exclaimed. "I was just about to swing by Whisk and see if you wanted to head down to breakfast. Ginger's already there."

"That's why I'm here." He grinned. "But not to head down to breakfast. To invite you to Whiz." Stepping back into a bow, he gestured grandly towards the door of his and Mac's room. "Breakfast is served."

That was when Lyra noticed his apron was already dusted with flour.

"We're going to be doing a lot of baking today," she said, trying to contain a smile. "Don't tell me you—"

Boysen held up his hands in surrender. "Guilty as charged, I'm afraid. But it's always a good idea to get the ovens warmed up. And this way we can get an earlier start."

Shaking her head, Lyra let the smile spread over her face. "At least tell me you didn't do anything too elaborate?"

"Just blueberry scones," he assured her. "Easy and fun. Didn't use any magic, either. No fuss."

"Fine. You win this round." She stepped through the door, closed it behind her, and followed him across the common area. "But tomorrow I make breakfast. Deal?"

"Or you could just promise to burst into song throughout the day," he suggested. "Sing for your supper. Or breakfast, in this case."

"Sing for my scones?"

"That's the ticket."

"Me bursting into song at some point is basically guaranteed." Lyra stopped in the open doorway, breathing in the delicious aroma of blueberry scones fresh from the oven. "But it's not sufficient payment. I make breakfast tomorrow, and that's that."

"You're on." He led her to the kitchen portion of the room, where a variety of ingredients, bowls, and utensils were already laid out on the counters. Pulling out a chair by the table, he indicated the tea tray and platter of scones, each the size of Lyra's fist and bursting with blueberries, placed neatly between two sheets of parchment and pens. "Working breakfast. We can make a plan while we eat. Help yourself to tea."

Lyra didn't hesitate. She sat down and poured a cup of tea, adding plenty of cream and honey. Then she chose a particularly massive scone and took a bite, closing her eyes.

"These are perfectly scrumptious," she managed to get out while chewing. "Weren't we supposed to make three different kinds of scones for Flavor?"

"Not these." Boysen sat next to her. Choosing a scone, he held it up to the light for examination. "Secret Berry family recipe. Not for public consumption."

Lyra took another bite. "And blueberries weren't part of the assignment."

"Exactly. If I'm going to make scones for breakfast, you'd best believe they'll be blueberry." He tore off half the scone and popped it into his mouth.

"Your favorite?" Lyra guessed. He nodded, mouth too full to speak. "I wonder why. Perhaps because you don't have a brother named Blue?"

Swallowing, he gave her a rueful smile. "Probably. I'm also quite fond of bilberries."

Lyra laughed. "I hadn't thought of that! Bill is actually a normal name. Why don't you have any brothers named Bill?"

"You've met my parents." Boysen shrugged as he poured himself a cup of tea. "They're a bit odd."

"I met your mom," Lyra corrected him. "And she's lovely."

"Lovely people are often odd, and vice versa." He winked. "Present company included, of course."

She considered throwing a blueberry at him but took another bite instead. "Aren't we supposed to be making a plan?"

"Yes. To business!" Taking another scone with one hand, Boysen used the other to begin writing their assignments on his parchment. "Flavor: three batches of scones. One plain, one with cinnamon, and one with garlic."

"Plain, sweet, savory," Lyra noted. "To practice Madame Hazelnut's Deepening Spell."

"Good ol' Madame Hazelnut." Boysen finished that column, then began another. "Texture?"

Lyra sighed. "Two loaves of bread. Each. With that proofing charm."

"Right." Boysen echoed her sigh. "Takes forever."

"Maybe we can start with that?" she suggested. "Get it out of the way?"

Boysen wrote a large number one by Texture and circled it. "Done. Then we can move right on to Presentation and get *that* out of the way."

Lyra raised her eyebrows. "I wanted to end with Presentation. Frosting is fun!"

"Sure, frosting is fun." Boysen ground his pen into the parchment as he wrote. "But five different colors of frosting to decorate five different batches of sugar cookies? That's a bit more 'fun' than I can handle on any given day."

"We have to practice Master Brûlée's Coloring Charm," Lyra said. "And each color is a little different. Besides, repetition—"

"Is the key to baking success. I know, I know." Boysen underlined the Presentation assignment five times to emphasize his understanding. "I would prefer to get all that repetition behind me as early in the day as possible."

Lyra sipped her tea primly. "You just want to end with Flavor because it's your favorite."

"You like Flavor too," he pointed out. "You couldn't stop raving about the deepening spell after lab on Tuesday. 'Soothing and satisfying,' I believe you called it?"

"Sure." Lyra concentrated on choosing another scone. "But that was before our Presentation lab."

"And before your tutoring sessions with The Coulis," Boysen added quickly.

"I didn't say that," she protested, her heart strangely heavy all of a sudden. The air around Boysen was vibrating again. For some reason, her own insides were churning in response, swirling around her heavy heart at uncomfortable speeds.

Trying to keep her voice light and even, she went on, "It's fine if you want to end with Flavor. Everyone thinks their discipline is the most important. There's nothing wrong with it."

He raised his eyebrows. "*Everyone* thinks that way? Who told you that?"

"It's true, isn't it?" She picked up her pen and began writing out their schedule, keeping her eyes determinedly on the parchment. "So, we'll start with Texture, then the coloring charm, then—"

"Hang on." Boysen grabbed her hand, forcing her to stop writing. Reluctantly, she looked up at him. "Let's get back to that sweeping statement you made about the entire baking world. *Everyone* secretly thinks their discipline is the most important? Did Cardamom tell you that?"

"Yes," she admitted. "What's the big deal?"

"And he also told you that old baking families are ruining the profession and persecuting poor 'new' bakers like him?"

She tugged her hand free, her cheeks flushing. "It's been tough for him. He's had to work really hard to get where he is."

"So has everyone here," Boysen said heatedly. "Old families don't get any special treatment. Remember Aniseed? The Mints are as close to baking elite as it comes, and she was out the first term."

"But a Meringue got the first Stellar Enchantment Pin," Lyra shot back.

"Because she worked incredibly hard. You know that better than anyone."

Lyra rolled her eyes. "That's not all she did."

"About that . . ." His voice softened. "You want to tell me what happened between you and Caramelle?"

She paused, then shook her head. "I would rather not."

"You sure?"

"Positive."

Boysen's eyes narrowed. "I suppose you've already been over it with The Coulis?"

"No," she said flatly. "Not with anyone."

He stared at her, one eyebrow raised incredulously.

"I mean it," she persisted. "Some notes should be left unsung or they'll spoil the harmony."

"Whatever you say."

She set her teacup down forcefully, nearly spilling tea across the parchment. "Sharps and flats, Boysen, what is your problem today?"

"Okay, okay." He lifted his hands in another gesture of surrender. "I'm sorry, Lyra. Truly. You're right. Some notes should be . . ."

"Left unsung," she finished. "Or they'll spoil the harmony."

"Yes. That. Some flavors are too strong, so you leave them out of the stew. I get it." Picking up a scone, he offered it to her with both hands. "I present you with this, the best of the batch, as a peace offering."

Lyra eyed the scone. "Best of the batch? How can you tell?"

"Instinct." He gave her his most winning grin. "Flavor's all about gut, right?"

She studied him and the scone for a few more seconds. Then, sighing, she accepted the peace offering and took a large bite.

"Yup," she said after swallowing. "Best of the batch."

He bowed his head with mock formality. Then his face took on an uncharacteristically serious expression.

"I don't want to argue, Lyra. I just want you to remember . . . Cardamom's perspective is just that. *His* perspective. It's not necessarily universal truth."

"So he's lying?"

"No." Boysen gritted his teeth in exasperation. "I'm only saying . . . his experience is his experience. It won't be the same for every baker. It might not be the same for you. And that's okay. You don't have to agree with him about everything automatically."

Lyra looked down at her hands, remembering the moment when Cardamom had covered them with his own.

"He believes in me," she said softly. "He thinks I could be something really special."

"That we *can* agree on." The warmth in Boysen's voice drew her eyes up to meet his. He smiled. "I amend my earlier statement. Anything nice The Coulis says about you, agree automatically. Everything else . . . maybe take it with a grain of salt."

"A grain of cardamom?" she said innocently.

He grimaced. "Sure. Actually, that's perfect. Tricky spice, cardamom. A little goes a *long* way."

"Ha ha."

They sat in silence for a few moments. Lyra finished her best-of-the-batch scone. Boysen took an inordinate interest in his tea, pouring another cup and adding cream with deliberate precision.

Slowly, Lyra's insides stopped their uncomfortably rapid swirling. She took a long time fixing her own second cup of tea, following his example and keeping her eyes on the table.

What was all that about?

Boysen was supposed to be a safe space. *He* was the magic of Whisk, no question. What would the first term have been like without the haven of his smile? Lyra couldn't imagine it. Frankly, she didn't want to.

She also didn't want to rock the boat again, but she wasn't quite ready to abandon their earlier conversation just yet.

"So . . ." She took a deep breath. "You really don't think Flavor is the most important? Not even a little bit, way deep down?"

Boysen thought for a while before answering, which she appreciated. It made it easier to believe him when he said, "No. Honestly, I don't. And I can't answer for Honeycomb, but I suspect she would say the same."

Lyra's eyes widened. "You think a master of Flavor wouldn't claim—"

"Nope." He shook his head firmly. "Why do you think the academy is structured the way it is? Because a true baker needs to know all three disciplines and respect their interdependence. The professors are experienced enough to understand that. Flavor is my favorite, and it comes the most naturally to me, but it can't stand on its own. Neither can Texture, nor Presentation."

"That's what I thought," Lyra confessed. "It's just . . . Cardamom seemed so sure."

"Which is why we take Cardamom's words with—"

"A grain of cardamom. I know." She gave him a determined smile. "Thank you."

Now it was his eyes widening in surprise. "For what?"

"For . . . listening. Talking. Making breakfast," Lyra answered.

CHAPTER THIRTY-THREE

The Proof Is in the Proofing

Despite its rocky start, that Saturday ended up being Lyra's favorite day at the academy thus far.

The proofing spell for Texture wasn't complicated. It was just tedious to stand over a lump of dough and recite the super-long incantation, silently and at a painfully slow pace.

"Ten pages . . ." Boysen groaned. "Ten pages of magic words with a breath between each one and three breaths between each sentence. Go too fast and the dough collapses. Miss a beat and the dough collapses. I love ciabattas and all, but just how amazing is this bread supposed to be for all of this work?"

"At least the spell makes proofing go faster," Lyra pointed out. "You can actually *see* the dough growing. And the words themselves kind of tell a story."

Boysen flipped through the pages of parchment. "A really boring story."

"It doesn't have to be boring." Lyra began measuring flour, salt, and yeast into a large bowl. "The spell's all about slow, steady growth, right? Encouraging the yeast to bloom faster but in a controlled way. So, we can just imagine the dough is some poor student discouraged by their lack of progress."

"They're the unlikely hero of the story," Boysen said, a grin spreading across his face. "A diamond in the rough. And we're the wise old mentor giving them that crucial pep talk before the big moment."

"Exactly."

Boysen grabbed his own bowl with a sigh and started measuring flour into it. "A really long, slow, boring pep talk."

"That's the spirit," Lyra sang, keeping her eyes on the water she was heating to a precise temperature. "But I only want to do this spell once this morning, Berry. No weird faces or trying to make me laugh, got that?"

"Who, me?" Boysen placed a hand to his heart, covering his apron with flour in the process. "I never engage in such childish activities."

Lyra flicked a pinch of flour at his face. "Behave."

"I will if you will, Treble."

They chatted pleasantly as they each whisked the dry ingredients together and used a spoon to create a well in the center. After adding a liberal dash of olive oil and a cup of warm water, they worked the liquid through the dough. Then they turned the oozing blobs out onto the floured counter for more kneading.

Lyra enjoyed every second of it. In fact, ciabatta was the first yeast bread she had ever attempted, so it held a special place in her heart.

She remembered vividly how terrified she had been of the proofing process when she first began baking. Her goal had always been to make cakes: light, fluffy, gorgeous dessert masterpieces. Yet, after mastering brownies and various kinds of cookies, she still hadn't felt ready to try a cake recipe. Only true bakers made cakes. And until she had successfully made bread, Lyra wouldn't feel like she could call herself a baker.

Cakes, Magic, and You had recommended soda bread as a good beginner recipe. Soda bread contained no yeast, went directly into the oven without rising, and barely required any kneading. Especially considering the endless list of flavors and fillings one could add, soda bread was the perfect tune for a scared little bard to practice on and build some confidence.

Lyra had tried every single one of the soda bread variations listed in *Cakes, Magic, and You.* She had then taken to inventing her own flavor combinations. "Peanut Butter Chocolate Soda Bread" had been a dismal failure, but "Sundried Tomato with Smoked Sweet Paprika" was a family favorite. Even after her long-suffering parents had declared a household ban on soda bread for the next decade, Lyra was still allowed to make what her oldest brother had termed "red bread."

After the ban, though, Lyra had known she couldn't delay any longer. She had flipped glumly through the rest of her already tattered cookbook's limited bread section, staring at the instructions for proofing times and water temperatures and kneading rhythms. Her heart had quailed at the many tables of complicated Texture spell equations. For one terrible morning, she had considered abandoning her cake dreams altogether.

Then, buried towards the end of the cookbook, she found the recipe for ciabatta.

Unlike enriched breads, which had to proof twice and took up the entire morning, ciabatta required only one proof and could be ready to eat in under two hours. The yeast went directly into the dry ingredients without needing to be bloomed in warm water. The only measurement listed for the olive oil was "a healthy splash."

The process itself also just felt more . . . casual. There was still kneading, but it mostly involved picking up bits of dough and slapping them back down to create air pockets. No finicky shaping, either. *Cakes, Magic, and You* assured Lyra that ciabatta dough was *supposed* to resemble a blob monster.

Lyra smiled as she and Boysen each rubbed olive oil around the inside of their bowls, then plopped their dough back in, ready for proofing.

Thank you, beautiful blob monster, she sang softly in her mind. *You gave me the courage to learn more complex songs.*

After arranging the stack of spell pages carefully on a clean patch of counter, Lyra spread her hands over the bowl and pressed down lightly into the dough. Next to her, Boysen did the same. They looked at each other.

"Ready?" Lyra asked.

He nodded. "Ready."

"Deep breath. Three, two, one, go."

Silently, they each began reciting the spell.

Pink . . .

Lyra inhaled, waited a beat, and exhaled, matching the rhythm of Boysen's breathing beside her.

Mauve . . .

Inhale. Beat. Exhale.

Red . . . Breathe. *Scarlet* . . . Breathe. *Orange* . . . Breathe. *Marigold* . . . Breathe. *Yellow* . . .

Slowly, silently, Lyra recited the colors of the sunrise. The page-long sentence culminated in the stirring words *Dawn . . . is . . . near.* Then, after three measured breaths, she and Boysen moved on to the next page.

It wasn't as bad as Lyra had feared. She felt herself being drawn into the rhythm, savoring each word as it rolled off her mental tongue. Every page described a different kind of rise, from morning dawns to ocean tides to the journey of a tiny acorn into a majestic tree. Lyra's favorite part was near the end, when the spell followed a baby bird through its first wondrous flight.

Throughout, the words seemed to fit perfectly with the tune Lyra had composed the first time she made ciabatta. She let that tune roll through her head automatically, its cadence keeping her breath and mental recitation steady. Far from being a distraction, the music wove effortlessly through the words and lifted her heart to join the sun and the bird in their rising.

Even better was the spell's effect on the proofing. Not only was the dough rising visibly with every phrase, but it felt softer and smoother beneath her fingers and gleamed with a satiny sheen. She could sense the spell binding the separate ingredients closer together, while simultaneously expanding them—a blob monster caught in an ever-expanding net. The whole experience was rather soothing, especially with Boysen standing beside her, breathing in unison as they helped keep each other locked in to the appropriate pace.

Finally, half an hour later, they reached the last word on the last page. Lyra paused, her hands still resting gently on the dough, hardly daring to breathe. Then Boysen's face slowly leaned into her peripheral vision. Darting a glance, she saw he had twisted his features into a ridiculous mask of pretend agony.

"I'm dead," he pronounced in hollow, sepulchral tones. "That spell has killed me."

Chuckling, she pushed him away and stepped back to survey their handiwork. "Didn't kill the bread, though. Both look pretty good to me."

"I just don't see the point," Boysen complained. "What normal baker would go through all this trouble to shave fifteen minutes off proofing time? Baking is all about multitasking. If we had just set the bread to proof normally, we could have been halfway through another assignment by now."

"The spell guarantees a good proof," Lyra reminded him, "and eliminates the risk of misjudging how long the dough needs, or something else going wrong. Wouldn't that save time in the long run?"

"Sure. But I don't think it's practical, overall. My mom never uses this spell."

"She doesn't need to." Lyra closed her eyes briefly, remembering the remarkable meal she had enjoyed at the Berry house. "I bet her proofing instincts are never wrong."

"That's not true," Boysen said slowly. "Everyone has their bad days. She and dad both have plenty of horror stories, especially from their early years. The thing is, they're so experienced, they can usually salvage a disaster."

Lyra turned on the kitchen's two ovens, setting them to the right temperature. "And the only way to *get* that experience is . . ."

"Repetition." Boysen drizzled olive oil over two baking sheets. "They're always telling us that. 'Practice, practice, practice. Learn the rules so you can break them responsibly later.'"

"Now that's incentive to keep using this spell," Lyra said with a smile. As one, they plopped their dough onto the prepared baking sheets and stuck them in the ovens. "Though, honestly, I don't need it. That was the most relaxing thirty minutes I've had all week."

"I always knew you were weird."

Lyra flicked another pinch of flour at him, scoring a direct hit on his nose. "I'm serious. I know baking is all about multitasking. That's why it's kind of nice to have an excuse to just do one thing for a while. I bet your mom would say the same."

"Probably." He rubbed the flour off his nose and started helping her wipe down the counters. "Next time you come over for dinner, you can ask her. Maybe you two can have a nice chat about meditation practices."

"That sounds nice, actually." Skipping over to the table, Lyra scanned the assignment list. "But for now, let's knock out those color spells for Presentation."

"Are you sure?" Boysen asked. "We can end with that, if you prefer."

"Nope. You made breakfast, so you get to pick. And I know you want to end the day with Flavor."

"I do, thanks." Boysen wagged his finger in her direction. "But don't think this lets you off the hook. I still expect you to sing for your scones at some point."

The first step was to whip up five small batches of buttercream frosting. With two stand mixers going at once, they were able to do this in record time. Lyra monitored the consistency of the butter and sugar, trusting Boysen's Flavor instincts to cover the dash of vanilla and heavy cream.

Then, spreading the five small bowls across the counter, it was time for the coloring.

"I'm actually a little excited about this," Boysen confessed. "Working with food coloring is a pain, especially when we're talking about frostings in five different colors."

Lyra's eyes widened in mock surprise. "The Flavor King is excited about *Presentation*? I thought you couldn't wait to get this out of the way."

"I can't. Presentation is a pain too. But it's less of a pain than synthetic food coloring. That stuff can seriously throw off Flavor and Texture."

"Whatever you say," Lyra crooned.

He narrowed his eyes at her. "I'm excited, but I'm not going to enjoy it. Got that?"

"Of course." She gave him a huge wink. "Your secret's safe with me."

"Watch it, Treble." He paused, as if struck by a sudden thought. "What about music? That would help me enjoy it."

"Music?" she echoed.

"Of course!" His whole face lit up in his usual grin. "Each color's charm is a little different, right?"

"Right . . ."

"That's because each color has a different personality. So why not give them each a little theme song?"

She hesitated for a moment, staring at the bowls. Then, in a very quiet voice: "I did."

CHAPTER THIRTY-FOUR

SOUNDS OF COLOR

You did?" Boysen repeated. "You already wrote songs for the colors?"

"Not whole songs. Just a little line of melody for each one. No words either," Lyra explained.

"That's brilliant!"

"No, it's not." Lyra shook her head firmly, talking almost to herself. "It's a bad habit."

"What is?"

"Music. Depending on it to learn the spells. I need to get out of it."

"Says who? Oh, wait." Boysen paused. Lyra was keeping her eyes on the frosting, but she could hear Boysen's grin dissolve into a scowl. "I know who."

She whirled on him, squaring her shoulders. "Look, it's not—"

"Save it." He held up his hands, half in defense and half in surrender. "No more grains of cardamom today, all right? My palate's overloaded."

"Fine," Lyra sighed. Turning back to the counter, she felt her shoulders slump a little at the sight of the five bowls of glaringly uncolored frosting. Suddenly, reciting the five different charms in total silence didn't seem quite so fun or exciting as Cardamom had made it seem in Thursday's tutoring session.

Boysen nudged her shoulder. "You're still going to share those songs with me, though."

She sighed again. "Boysen—"

"Hear me out. I have three most excellent reasons." He held up a hand over the bowls and counted on his fingers. "One, as my friend and partner, you are duty bound to help me get through this task using every tool at your disposal. Two, you promised to sing for your scones. Three, and most importantly, you *want* to sing these color songs. I can tell. So go for it."

Lyra hesitated a few seconds longer, but Boysen's arguments were as irresistible as they were logical. With a third and final sigh, she said, "All right. Just once, to help get the colors straight in our heads." Rummaging through a stack of parchment on the counter, she retrieved his copy of the color charm list. "It's like the proofing spell. Just think of each color as a different character. Starting with red."

Lyra sang a brief intense tune with lots of leaps to high notes and a few dazzling runs.

"Red is super passionate about everything," she explained. "A little strange, but bold about it."

"Like Mac," Boysen suggested.

Lyra raised her eyebrows. "Quiet little Macaron Fondant?"

"It's always the quiet ones," he said mysteriously. "Our Mac has hidden depths. Remember the word Professor Genoise gave for his style?"

"Majestic," Lyra said thoughtfully. "Red is a royal color."

Boysen nodded. "Exactly. And it's the color of heat too. I think Mac's got a fire in him. He's a slow burn, but when he ignites . . . he's going to leave us all in the dust. Wait and see."

Lyra smiled. "You're a good friend to him, Boysen."

"It's easy to be nice to Mac." Boysen smiled.

"Unless you're Caramelle."

"Don't remind me." He sighed. "So, red is Mac. Who do you have for green?"

"I wasn't assigning specific people," Lyra said. "Just personality. I thought of green as innovative. A scientist type, always pushing boundaries and trying something new."

Lyra sang a quiet melody that kept breaking out into different styles, changing key with each new theme. Then she and Boysen looked at each other for a moment.

"Ginger," they both said at once.

"Nice!" Boysen crowed. "You're right. Presentation *can* be fun. Who's next? What are your thoughts on yellow?"

In answer, Lyra trilled a simple, joyful tune.

Boysen cocked his head. "Someone who's just really happy?"

"That's the idea," Lyra said. "Think about it. When you're looking at something that's bright yellow, is it possible to be sad?"

"It is difficult," Boysen agreed. He studied her for a few seconds. "I think that's you, Lyra."

"Me?" she asked, startled. "I'm yellow?"

"Professor Genoise did say your style was joyful," Boysen reminded her. "And it *is* hard to be sad when you're around."

Lyra's heart suddenly filled with the same delicious warmth she usually associated with the first sip of hot chocolate. "Th-thank you," she stammered.

"I'm sure the other Whizzes would agree," he went on quickly. He made a great show of pointing at the list. "So, that's three colors. Can't wait to hear purple."

The delicious warmth was lingering, but she pushed it aside and made a face. "Purple was tricky. I couldn't quite seem to capture it."

Lyra sang a complex, vivid tune that wavered between major and minor intervals. It started out light and whimsical, then dove dramatically into a heavy, pondering cadence. The end was poignant, failing to resolve the two contrary styles.

They were both silent for a while.

Eventually, Boysen commented, "A lot going on there."

Lyra nodded. "That's what I was saying. I don't feel like I can get a hold of what it wants to be."

"No, you definitely captured it. That's absolutely purple. It's the color that can't figure out who it is, not you."

"There's so much to it," Lyra mused. "And I can only take so much of it at one time. You know? It's bright and dark and heavy and light and noble and overbearing and—"

"Caramelle," Boysen said flatly.

Lyra's breath came out in a *whoosh*, like she'd been elbowed in the gut. She locked eyes with him.

"Caramelle," she repeated.

For some reason, her eyes filled with tears. Boysen must have noticed because his voice was gentle as he rushed to change the subject. "I guess that makes me blue. Hope so, anyway. If it doesn't fit, we'll have to start over and rearrange everyone."

"Right." Blinking back the tears, Lyra took a deep breath. "Blue . . . That's perfect, actually. Listen."

The tune she sang was steady and straightforward but rich. It was the kind of melody that could both ground a person and inspire them to new heights, with a surprise chromatic run at the end.

When she finished, Boysen looked stunned.

"Well." He cleared his throat. "Blue. I like that a lot. You sure that's me?"

"Positive." Lyra smiled. "That was the first one I came up with, actually. It's my favorite."

"I see." He hesitated, as if torn between two dangerously different conversational tracks. Then he broke into a classic tension-diffusing grin. "Your favorite. Definitely me, then."

Lyra groaned, wondering why she suddenly felt so relieved. "Someone thinks very highly of himself."

"The music doesn't lie, Treble. Neither do the colors." Taking the parchment from her hand, Boysen spread it out on the counter. "I can't wait to see these in action. Singing them is going to make a huge difference."

"Oh no," she gasped. "That's not allowed."

"Not allowed?" He looked at her curiously. "I know Texture has very strict rules, but Presentation is different."

"It still has rules. They call it a baking *discipline* for a reason."

"It's all about style," he argued. "If you can't mix it up in a style-based discipline, when can you?"

"The style comes out in other ways," she insisted. "You follow the rules, infusing each one with your personality. The strongest personalities are the ones that stand out. That's how you make your mark."

He opened his mouth, then closed it.

"What?" she demanded.

"It's just . . . Nothing."

"Spit it out, Berry."

He sighed. "I told you. A little cardamom goes a long way, and I hit my limit at breakfast."

"This is something we discussed in our private sessions, yes. So what?" She folded her arms. "He *is* my Presentation tutor."

Boysen rolled his eyes. "Believe me, I know."

"And Professor Genoise's assistant."

"Sure, but—"

"So that means he knows what he's talking about," Lyra continued, her voice rising. "The 'grain of salt' rule doesn't apply here."

"Grain of cardamom," Boysen corrected, then held up his hand to forestall her retort. "Got it. Sorry. I just . . . I like those songs, Lyra. They're really good. *Better* than good. I was excited to try something new."

Lyra slowly unfolded her arms. "I understand. And thank you. I-I'm glad you like the songs."

He nodded, attempting a playful smile. "Maybe I can get Mac to wear more red from now on. Might bring out new notes in his personality."

"We can try an experiment," she said, joining him in the "determined fun" routine. "I'll encourage Ginger to wear green. See how they behave. Compile results next weekend."

"Experiment?" He threw up his hands in mock despair. "Now we really are acting like Crumble. Quick! Is my hair turning green?"

Lyra's laughter was interrupted by the ovens, whose timers went off simultaneously. They both ran to retrieve their bread, listening as they tapped the bottom of each loaf.

"Why does a hollow sound mean it's fully baked?" Lyra thought out loud. "The bread's not hollow."

"Not sure," Boysen replied. "Good question for Professor Puff on Monday."

Lyra reverently placed the loaves on the waiting rack to cool. "Or your mom, when I come over for that dinner."

"Absolutely. But I'm not sure she uses the tap test anymore. She'll probably just tell you it's a matter of instinct. And, of course—"

"Repetition." Lyra sighed. "Of course."

Boysen looked at the clock. "Salts, the day is going fast. Where were we? Oh . . . right. Colors." He stared at the parchment dejectedly.

"What's the matter?" Lyra asked, waving a palette knife in front of his face. "It's exciting, remember? Coloring without synthetic stuff that messes with Flavor?"

"I guess. But . . ." Boysen clasped his hands and turned to her. "Are you *sure* we can't use the songs? At least a little?"

His brown eyes were full of a woeful pleading Lyra usually associated with puppies. Combined with the sight of the breakfast remnants on the table, and the lingering effects of the soothing Texture spell, and the warmth that always permeated the air in Whisk . . . it was too much for Lyra's half-hearted defenses.

"A little," she relented. "We shouldn't sing them out loud, but . . . we can think about each melody when we're reciting the charm."

"You're the boss." He grinned, the pleading instantly replaced by mischievous glee. "For Presentation, anyway. But this afternoon—"

"I know, I know." She waved a hand dismissively. "All hail the Flavor King."

Boysen drew himself up to his full lanky height. "I shall have my coronation cake all in blue, if you please."

"I have created a monster."

"A monster with an incredibly deficient memory." Boysen relaxed, shrugging cheerfully. "I'm going to need to hear each of those tunes twice more if you want me to think them correctly. Don't want green leaking into purple, or some other combustible color conflict."

"And we definitely can't have that." Lyra opened her mouth to begin the red melody, then paused. "This does count as singing for my scones, right?"

He wrinkled his eyebrows, considering. "Yes. Partly. I still want one spontaneous musical moment some time after lunch. Surprise me, and your breakfast debt is paid."

"You are a kind and generous monarch." Lyra looked at the clock too, surprised at her own sudden sadness. Time was passing so quickly. As complicated as some of the moments had been, she didn't want the day to end.

Glancing around, she tried to capture the cheery kitchen as a memory she could revisit later. The freshly baked bread filled the air with a delicious aroma. The mahogany paneling gleamed in the morning sunlight pouring through the windows. Next to her, Boysen leaned over the counter, studying the parchment. He brushed a strand of brown hair out of his eyes with a floury hand, oblivious to the smudges this left on his forehead.

A smile unfolded inside Lyra. It diffused her melancholy with a sweet lightness, lifting her mood like yeast working its way through flour.

I know second term is supposed to be hard, she thought. *But if it includes days like this . . . I think we'll be just fine.*

"Listen up, Flavor King." She took a deep breath, focusing on the first notes of the red melody. "Let's see how this goes."

CHAPTER THIRTY-FIVE

GAAAAAARLIC!!!

When all was said and done, Boysen insisted that Lyra's color songs had been a huge help.

"Just look at that green." He pointed to each bowl in turn, highlighting the distinct shades. "And the red actually looks like red! I never got that close in class. Even at the end of lab day, my red was more . . . pink. Watered-down pink."

Lyra gazed at the bowls dejectedly. "They're not bright enough. Cardamom's purple was so much more vibrant when we practiced Thursday night."

"This was only our first run of the day," Boysen reminded her. "We'll try again after dinner."

"Maybe without thinking the songs?" Lyra suggested. "They didn't give quite the kick I was expecting."

"What were you expecting? Perfection?"

She poked at the yellow, which fell several shades short of the warm marigold she had envisioned. "I guess."

"Any Presentation expert would call that a ridiculous expectation. Any *baker*, for that matter." Boysen shook his head. "I'll keep thinking the songs. They help me visualize the colors I'm going for and keep them all distinct in my head."

"Really?"

"Really. I'm telling you, that is the most fun I have ever had on a Presentation task. Ever." Boysen paused. "Of course, it would be even more fun if we could actually *sing* the songs . . ."

"No way," Lyra said firmly. "They are a mental tool only. For focusing."

"Just as an experiment," Boysen wheedled.

"On your own time, if you want. Or get Ginger. We have enough work to do as it is."

He sighed. "You wrote them, so you're the boss. But I'm adding 'Spoilsport' to your official list of titles."

"I have a list?"

"Everyone has a list. Whisk Whiz rule."

Lyra smiled. "You love your rules, don't you?"

"When they're reasonable, sure," Boysen said. "I'm not crazy about all the academy rules, and Texture gets a little out of control sometimes, but the Whisk Whiz rules are great."

"*You* made all the Whisk Whiz rules," Lyra pointed out.

"Exactly." He winked. "So you know they are both reasonable and good. For example, it is getting dangerously close to lunchtime, and Whisk Whizzes never miss a meal. We should get a move on with the sugar cookies so all this frosting has a home."

"The sugar cookies!" Lyra groaned. "We should have made those first and worked on the frosting while they cooled. And doesn't the dough have to chill for a while?"

"No trouble at all, Treble." Swinging open the fridge door, he presented her with a roll of sugar cookie dough. "Made it this morning while the scones were baking. It's only enough for this first round, but we can whip up some more after lunch and leave it to chill until our second round after dinner."

Lyra threw her arms around him. "I am adding 'Savior' and 'First-Rate Forward Thinker' to *your* official list of titles."

He waved her aside with a laugh, but his grin was genuine as they prepped the cookie sheets. "We'll have to run those by the council for approval. Don't want to give me *too* much to live up to."

The sugar cookies only took ten minutes to bake. While they cooled, Lyra helped Boysen clean up from the morning's work. By the time they had finished frosting the cookies, the academy's lunch hour was nearly over. They rushed down to the dining hall, entering just as Ginger and Mac were exiting.

"Have you seen Caramelle?" That was Mac's only greeting as he scanned anxiously behind them for signs of auburn hair.

"Hello to you too," Boysen said dryly. "How was the morning in Zester?"

Ginger nudged her project partner. "Productive, once I got this one to stop listening for sounds of life in Pestle."

"Academy walls are enchanted," Boysen pointed out. "They're not entirely soundproof, but they do limit the spread of noise."

"That's what I told him." Ginger smiled at Lyra. "How's it going in Whisk?"

"Wonderfully." Lyra looked around the dining room. "You haven't seen Caramelle at all? What about breakfast?"

"No." Mac pushed his glasses up his nose. "That's what worries me. No breakfast, no lunch . . ."

"Maybe she's eating in her room," Boysen suggested. "That's what Treble and I did for breakfast."

"She already has so much baking to do on her own," Mac protested. He turned to Lyra. "Do you really think Caramelle would waste time on making something for herself to eat?"

Lyra's heart sank. "No."

"Exactly." Mac turned towards the teachers' table. "I'm going to say something to Professor Puff."

"Before that"—Boysen placed a hand on his roommate's shoulder—"why don't you go check on Caramelle first if you're so worried? I doubt she would thank you for reporting her to the teachers."

"Especially without verifying the facts," Ginger agreed. "Though, I don't know what you're so whipped up about, Fondant. The Meringue is a big girl. She can take care of herself."

Again, Mac turned to Lyra. "Can she? When she's under stress?"

Lyra sighed. "Caramelle does have a tendency to . . . lose track of things when she's on a deadline. Food, sleep—"

"Morals, conscience."

Lyra gave her new roommate a look. "Not helping, Ginger."

"Okay, okay." Ginger looped an arm through Mac's. "We'll swing by Pestle on our way back. You can even take her this." She held up a piece of spice cake wrapped carefully in a napkin. "I was saving it for an afternoon treat, but I guess The Meringue might need it more than I do. Deal?"

Mac took the piece of cake reverently. "Deal."

Boysen and Lyra wished him luck, then sat down just long enough to gobble up toasted cheese sandwiches and bowls of creamy tomato bisque. Taking their own pieces of cake to go, they returned to the dorm in time to see a dejected Mac entering Zester.

"No answer," he said glumly. "I've been knocking and calling . . . Ginger gave up and came in here to prep. I left the cake outside." He pointed back to the closed door of Pestle. "I can hear sounds through the door. She's definitely baking. But I still don't know if she's eaten anything today."

"We'll check on our way down to dinner," Lyra assured him. "If the cake's still there, maybe we can let one of the teachers know."

"Or the older students," Boysen suggested. "I bet she'd answer the door if The Coulis was calling."

Lyra's jaw tensed. "Hyacinth's the Texture assistant. She could relate to Caramelle better on that level."

"We'll figure it out." Boysen slapped Mac's shoulder encouragingly. "In the meantime, you've done all you can, Macaron. Go help Crumble."

Mac shrugged and disappeared into Zester without another word.

"Sharps and flats." Lyra shook her head. "He *has* got it bad, hasn't he?"

"Try living with him." Boysen sighed. "But, as I said, he's done all he can.

And so have we." He strode across the common area towards Whisk. "C'mon, Treble. Time for some more repetition."

Following their strategy from that morning, they kicked off the afternoon with their second round of the proofing spell for Texture. Boysen complained all the way up to starting the long spell, but afterwards, he had to admit it was growing on him.

"It can be soothing," he said as they prepped their loaves for the oven. "You were right."

"See?" Lyra grinned. "Did you think of it as a story?"

"A little. It's still a really boring story. I was focusing more on the breathing and the silence." He kept his eyes on the rising oven temperature. "I still think it's a waste of time if you're alone, but with the right company, it can be . . . nice. Just to be quiet together, for a while."

"Absolutely," she agreed. "Though, I think most bakers might cherish the quiet alone time. I'm still going to ask your mom the next time I see her."

He flashed her a quick smile in response, then they settled into easy silence again. Only when they each had placed their loaf of bread carefully in the oven did he clap his hands. "Right! That's Texture done for the day. You know what that means?"

Lyra bowed. "All hail the Flavor King?"

"That's right." Boysen handed her a bowl. "Three batches of scones. Plain, sweet, and savory. We can do the plain version together. Would you rather handle the sweet or savory this afternoon?"

"I'll start with sweet," Lyra said. "You can handle savory. Garlic is tricky."

"You'll still have to tackle it some time," Boysen warned.

"Of course. We'll switch for round two, after dinner." She gave him her most winning smile. "I just want to observe and take notes for now. Learn from the master and all that."

"The Flavor King is immune to flattery," Boysen replied loftily, "though musical tributes have been known to earn his good graces."

Lyra bonked him with her wooden spoon. "Let's see the royal instincts in action first, shall we?"

They started by whipping up a batch of plain scones. As the dough was coming together, Boysen demonstrated how to make the most effective use of Madame Hazelnut's Deepening Spell.

"It's a lot like the proofing spell, actually," he said, using his fingers to work bits of butter through the mixture of flour and sugar. "The words do matter with this one, but silence is equally important. You have to *listen* for the flavor."

"Listen?" Lyra repeated. "Like listening to your gut?"

"That's part of it. But you also have to listen to the ingredients themselves."

Lyra crinkled her eyebrows. "How does that work?"

"The spell actually helps. It deepens the flavor, which makes it louder. Easier to hear." Without taking his eyes off the dough, Boysen took Lyra's hands and placed them in the bowl, burying them in the floury mixture before covering them with his own. "Now recite the spell, then *listen*."

Lyra complied. After ten seconds, she felt a slight tingle in her fingertips, as if the dough were coughing. She jumped, knocking into Boysen and scattering a cloud of flour into the air.

"I heard it!" she squealed. "I mean, I felt it. The dough! It was talking to me!"

Boysen laughed. "Of course it was. And what did it say?"

"I-I'm not sure," Lyra confessed. "I got so excited, I didn't quite catch the details."

"Let's try again." Boysen took her hands again, returning them to the bowl. "This time don't just listen for the dough. Listen to your gut, like we've practiced in class. Recite the spell first."

Lyra repeated the short spell mentally, then closed her eyes. Only five seconds later, she felt that jolt of life in her fingers again. Keeping them steady, she strained her inner ear as she listened for a response from her inherent Flavor instincts.

"What do you hear?" Boysen asked.

"Something's off." Lyra stayed perfectly still, grateful for the stabilizing pressure of Boysen's hands on hers. "I hear the dough, and I hear my gut, but they're not . . . in tune. It's like they're trying to play in the same key, but one is just a half step off."

"That's great!" Even with her eyes closed, she could hear the smile in Boysen's voice. "That's how Flavor works. You keep doing the spell until the dough and your instincts are singing the same song."

"What if I go too far?" she asked. "What if I say the spell too many times and the flavor gets too intense? Is there a de-flavoring spell I don't know about?"

"Afraid not." He nudged her shoulder. "But that's what practice is for. Go ahead. Recite, listen, repeat. Until it's right."

After three more recitations of Madame Hazelnut's Deepening Spell, both Lyra's and Boysen's instincts declared the plain scones ready to go. Lyra then watched carefully as Boysen mixed up another batch. He added fresh garlic minced fine, one pinch at a time, taking long pauses to recite the spell and listen. Once he deemed it had reached peak garlic flavor, he stepped back and invited Lyra to confirm his assessment.

She buried her hands in the dough and waited.

"That's weird," she said after a few moments.

"What?"

"I can hear the dough, but . . . it's super faint. Much less clear than it was with the plain batch." Opening her eyes, she looked first at her hands, then at him. "Are you, perchance, some sort of Flavor instinct superconductor?"

He blinked. "Beg pardon?"

"I could hear so clearly when your hands were in the bowl too. Maybe you were accidentally sharing your Flavor royalty superpowers with me, by osmosis or something?"

"I don't think it's a *super*power—"

"Well, I can't imagine garlic is just a quieter flavor than plain butter."

"Garlic isn't quiet at all," Boysen confirmed. "It's one of the loudest flavors imaginable."

"Then I'm just not at your level yet." Lyra nodded towards the bowl, where her hands were still buried in flour. "Let's test the theory, anyway."

Slowly, Boysen placed his hands over Lyra's. "Any better?"

"*GAAAAAARLIC!!!*"

Lyra didn't just *say* the word; the flavor wasn't just *speaking* to her. She sang out the word at such a volume that both she and Boysen jumped back from the bowl in alarm.

"Salts, Lyra!" Boysen reached a shaky hand to poke her shoulder. "What the hollandaise was that?"

For a moment, Lyra was laughing too hard to answer.

"It's your own fault!" she gasped finally, still doubled over with merriment. "You *are* a superconductor!"

Boysen stared at his own hands. "I—it made that big a difference?"

"You can bet your ballads it did." Lyra straightened up and tried to swallow the last of her giggles. "And you were right. Garlic is plenty loud, not to mention showy. It's what we in the music business call a *diva*."

"I believe you." Boysen's awed gaze drifted from his hands to Lyra. "And . . . it *sings*? Like that? You heard it sing?"

She felt a flush creeping over her cheeks, but it was as much from delight as embarrassment. "You did say you wanted a spontaneous musical moment," she reminded him.

He nodded, his eyes still resting on her in wonder. "Consider your breakfast debt paid. Overpaid, really. I'll have to make something much fancier tomorrow to pay you back."

"I'm making breakfast tomorrow," she protested. "That was the deal."

"That was before the garlic sang the song of its people. Through *you*." Boysen nodded again. "Yep. Eggs Benedict, at the very least. I'll swing by Queen Penelope's first thing in the morning."

"Boysen—"

He held up a hand. "The Flavor Superconductor King has spoken. Besides, I have a feeling I'm going to have quite a debt to work off by the end of the day." Grinning, he handed her the third and final bowl of scone dough.

"If you think garlic is loud . . . I can't wait to hear what kind of song *cinnamon* has to sing."

CHAPTER THIRTY-SIX

FLAVOR KING FUMBLE

The rest of the afternoon flew by, even faster and more pleasantly than the morning. It was almost a shame to have to stop and run down to the dining hall for dinner, especially when a glance at Pestle's closed door showed the spice cake was still there, uneaten.

Thankfully, Boysen had an idea on the way down that cheered them both up.

"Why don't we swing by the kitchens after we eat?" he suggested. "I haven't seen Flax since we got back."

Lyra was stunned to find that she hadn't either. She gave her hearty assent to this plan, with the provision that they keep the visit short.

"We still have a lot of baking to do," she pointed out. "One more round of Presentation and Flavor after dinner."

They had lingered so long over the Flavor scones that the dining hall was deserted by the time they reached it. After bolting down their steaming portions of shepherd's pie, they dashed to the kitchen doors in time to grab the cookie tray floating out towards them.

"We'll have our dessert in here, thanks," Boysen told the cookie tray.

The cookies did not seem to agree. The tray kept tugging, determined to complete its journey to their table. It took all Boysen's and Lyra's strength to pull the platter of sweets back inside the kitchen.

"Bumble!" Lyra called as soon as they were inside the doors. "A little help?"

The flying squirrel glanced over and chattered a merry laugh. With a single wave of his tail, the tray went still, resting in Lyra's and Boysen's hands.

"Careful there." Chef Flax chuckled. "Line order magic is no small feat. Nothing for first years to be messing around with."

Boysen set the tray on the counter and gave Bumble a weary salute. "Noted. And hello, Flax."

"It's great to see you!" Lyra ran around the counter and threw her arms around the head chef.

"Second term greetings to you both," he said warmly, returning her embrace. "Salts, I'm glad you're all back. I know break time is important, and you lot certainly deserve it, but it gets too plum quiet around here in between terms."

Bumble chattered an affirmative. Scampering over to the cookie tray, he carefully selected a few varieties and delivered them to Lyra and Boysen.

"One peanut butter oatmeal and one white chocolate macadamia?" Boysen whistled. "Bumble, you know me too well."

Lyra closed her eyes, inhaling the scent of her own cookies. "Chocolate chip . . . and double chocolate chunk. Thanks, Bumble."

Bumble swept off his sous chef's hat and gave an elegant bow.

"So, how's the term going so far?" Chef Flax asked. "One week down, and you're both still standing. That's a good sign."

Boysen nodded, then said around a mouthful of peanut butter oatmeal cookie, "Still standing, still baking."

"I'm afraid we can't stay too long." Lyra cast a wistful glance around the pleasantly bustling kitchen. "These weekly projects are intense."

"It helps when you have the right partner," Boysen said with a wink.

She smiled. "Yes. Absolutely."

"They made you two partners, did they?" Chef Flax beamed. "Inspired pairing."

Boysen polished off his second cookie in two massive bites. "I'll say. You should hear the Flavor songs she's discovered, Flax."

"Flavor songs?" the head chef repeated.

"Just . . . what I hear when the Flavor spell is done." Lyra kept her eyes on her half-eaten double chocolate chunk treat. "It's not a big deal."

"And the color songs!" Boysen went on, raising his hands to express the immensity of his excitement. "Wow, Flax. That's the only word. A song for each color in Master Brûlée's Coloring Charm."

Chef Flax whistled. "Master Brûlée? I simply must hear these."

"They're not really songs," Lyra rushed to say, shooting Boysen a glare, which he cheerfully ignored. "It's just a short line of melody for each color."

"At least sing the red one, Treble," Boysen wheedled. "As a treat for Flax."

Bumble hopped onto Lyra's shoulder, chattering indignantly.

"And Bumble," Boysen added. "Of course. Especially Bumble."

Lyra sighed. "Fine. Just red, and then we really need to get back to work."

She sang the dynamic tune that expressed, for her, all the majestic passion of the color red.

"Brava!" Chef Flax and Bumble both applauded enthusiastically, the flying squirrel chattering praise for the head chef to interpret. "That's red, all right. Bumble and I agree. We can't wait to hear the other colors!"

"Maybe tomorrow?" Boysen suggested. "If we get an early start, we might be able to get through our final round of projects before dinner."

"That could work," Lyra replied cautiously. "We could do three in the morning and three in the afternoon . . ."

"And then spend the evening here!" Boysen exclaimed. "Is that all right, Flax?"

Chef Flax's broad face creased into joyful wrinkles. "More than all right. I can think of no better way to spend my Sunday evening . . . Especially if Miss Treble can be persuaded to bring her guitar and give us that concert she's been promising?"

"I can't believe I got through a whole term without managing to fulfill that promise." Lyra shook her head. "I'm so sorry, Chef."

"Not at all, my dear." Chef Flax waved dismissively while Bumble hopped down to the counter, chattering in a soothing tone. "We understand how much pressure you're under. First term in particular can be overwhelming."

"But now we're through," Boysen said, clapping a hand on Lyra's shoulder. "So we should take an evening to celebrate. Right, Treble?"

Lyra hesitated, but the combined pleadings of a Berry, a Flax, and a flying squirrel sous chef were irresistible. "Tomorrow night," she agreed. "Only if we finish our work."

After returning to Whisk, they whipped up another batch of buttercream frosting in record time. At Boysen's urging, Lyra sang through each color tune once, and then they took turns mentally reciting the charms. Purple was still barely recognizable, and green was proving tricky, but Lyra couldn't deny the marked improvement in red, yellow, and blue.

"Repetition is all we need," Boysen promised her. "Tomorrow morning will be even better. By the afternoon, we'll have something we can turn in with pride."

Then, as promised, they ended the day with Flavor. Boysen persuaded Lyra to try the garlic scones this time, while he handled the cinnamon. To her delight, Lyra realized she could hear the flavor better than she had in the afternoon. It was still much fainter when she was working alone than when Boysen put his hands in the bowl, but she could make out the tune clearly enough to guide her recitation of the spell.

"At least I know I can make it on my own," she said happily as they finally pulled the completed scones out of the oven. "Can't rely on your Berry superconductor superpowers forever."

"Superpowers?" The door burst open. Razz Berry strode in, followed closely by Hyacinth Roulade. "What's this about Poison having superpowers?"

"Just finishing up our practice run for Monday's exam," Boysen said quickly, before Lyra could explain. "Speaking of, mind doing an extra round of preservation spells? We don't want to let everything hang on tomorrow."

"Don't ask me." Razz collapsed into the sofa, putting his feet up on the edge of the fire pit and crossing his arms. "I'm not on duty. Hyacinth drew the short straw tonight, so I'm just keeping her company."

Hyacinth crossed to the counter, smiling warmly at the array of scones, ciabatta, and frosted sugar cookies. "You all have been working hard, I see. I'd be glad to get in some extra preservation spell practice. Are the other first years following a similar plan?"

"Ginger and Mac are on the same schedule," Boysen replied. "If you cast an extra spell or two when you stop by Zester, I'm sure they'd be grateful."

"Of course." Hyacinth turned to Lyra, her smile faltering slightly. "And . . . Pestle? Do you think Caramelle wants a preservation spell?"

For some reason, Lyra's heart sank.

"I'm not sure," she confessed. "I—we wanted to talk to you about that, actually. About . . . Caramelle." She paused, looking at Boysen.

"She's been locked in her room all day, as far as we know," he told Hyacinth. "Did either of you see her at dinner?"

Hyacinth shook her head. "Or at lunch, or breakfast."

"Exactly. We're concerned she's not eating." Boysen nudged Lyra's shoulder. "Treble says Meringue can get a little too . . . focused, sometimes."

Lyra braced her shoulders, forcing her voice to stay light and measured. "She works very hard. Might not be taking care of herself. We've all tried knocking, but she won't respond."

"We even tried to take her a snack earlier. Nothing." Boysen gave Lyra another encouraging nudge, then turned to Hyacinth. "Could you . . . maybe take her some food when you do your rounds? She might listen to you."

Hyacinth's golden eyes were full of concern. "Of course. I'll let you know how it goes."

Lyra swallowed a retort that she didn't want to know and just nodded her thanks. It had been such a lovely day overall. She was not going to let any troublesome thoughts about The Meringue ruin it.

Focus on the work, she told herself silently, marveling at the healthy glow emanating from the baked goods as Hyacinth completed the preservation spell. *Focus on the baking. That's why you're here, after all. And if tomorrow can be just like today . . .*

Catching Boysen's eye, she grinned, earning her a special Lyra-only smile in return.

She could deal with another day just like today. In fact, she was looking forward to it.

The next day certainly started off the same, only better. True to his promise, Boysen paid an early visit to Queen Penelope, giving her their first batch of cinnamon scones from the day before in exchange for some of her very best eggs. Lyra declared the resulting eggs Benedict "a breakfast fit for baking royalty."

This, of course, led to a discussion about what sort of crest would be appropriate for the Flavor King, and then for the other Whisk Whizzes. This brainstorming session carried them through their first round of ciabatta prep. After a half-hour break for the proofing spell, the banter resumed, lasting through all three scone varieties and the five different colors of frosting for the sugar cookies. They were still debating which animal would best represent Ginger's experimental "daring" when they ran to the dining hall for a brief lunch.

Lyra could tell they were both a little nervous when they returned to Whisk for their afternoon session. This was supposed to be the final round for each of the projects. If all went well, they would be presenting the fruits of this afternoon's labors to the professors in the morning.

Boysen endeavored to keep their spirits up by shifting the family crest design conversation to the three professors and finally to Chef Flax and his flying squirrel companions. His efforts paid off. The hours slipped by so pleasantly, Lyra forgot to worry about how much of her future was riding on the level of cinnamon in this scone or the shade of purple on that sugar cookie.

Finally, as the warm light of sunset was streaming through the window and both their stomachs were grumbling for dinner, they pulled the last batch of garlic scones out of the oven and stepped back.

"We did it," Lyra announced. "I really think this last round is the best."

Boysen grinned as he tried to wipe his floury hands with his even more floury apron. "Of course it is. Repetition pays off, right?"

"Indeed." Lyra returned his grin. "Repetition and good company. I think we make a great team."

"I think you think right." Giving up on his floury hands, Boysen reached behind a stack of towels on the counter and pulled out a small napkin-wrapped package. He presented it to her with a bow. "And, in the spirit of teamwork, I have to show you this."

Lyra unwrapped the package to find a frosted sugar cookie. Nothing fancy or peculiar about it except for the frosting. Even Cardamom hadn't produced such a brilliant shade of red in their tutoring session.

She looked at Boysen, eyebrows raised. "Where did this come from?"

He was watching her intently, his shoulders unnaturally tense. "You."

"Me?"

"It's from our first batch yesterday," he explained, speaking very fast and in a deliberately even tone. "I took it with me when we visited the kitchens. I had it in my pocket, and when you sang the song for red for Flax, I put my hand in my pocket and recited the spell. Mentally. Just to see what would happen. Later, after you left, I checked. And look!" He pointed triumphantly at the frosting's vivid hue. "That's way better than it was, right? Almost as good as Genoise did in class." Spreading his hands wide, he looked her directly in the eye, his voice suddenly serious. "It's the music, Lyra. Singing the song out loud made all the difference."

She stared at him. "Why didn't you show me earlier?"

"I knew you wanted to focus on the assignments." The low, rapid-fire voice was back, and Boysen didn't seem to know what to do with his hands. "I wanted us to get in a couple more good rounds today, so we could relax. And I know you said you didn't want to sing out loud, so I thought . . . you might get mad."

Lyra's stomach felt like an overpowered oven. The fumes were rising up through her throat, choking her.

"You thought right," she managed to say. "You tricked me."

"I didn't mean—"

"You tricked me, and you lied about it. All this time."

"I wouldn't call it a—"

"I told you I didn't want to use the songs. Repeatedly."

He held up his hands in mock surrender. "I know, I know. I just can't understand *why*. When it takes a spell to the next level like this, why wouldn't you—"

"I told you why," she shot back. "I gave you all my reasons."

Boysen's determined calm exploded.

"But your reasons are all wrong! The academy is about discovering your strengths. *Your* strengths, Lyra. What makes you special. And this is it. Your music could change baking forever! Why would you hide that kind of gift? Just because Cardamom says—"

Lyra couldn't take anymore. The smoke from her overheated stomach-oven was behind her eyes, stinging and producing a wave of tears. Blinking them back as hard as she could, she whirled around and stumbled blindly to the door.

"Lyra—"

Boysen was right behind her, but she didn't stop. She made it to the door, wrenched it open—and ran straight into Cardamom Coulis III, who was just raising his hand to knock.

CHAPTER THIRTY-SEVEN

THE SCENT OF PROGRESS

Lyra stumbled backwards to avoid running into Cardamom, only to collide with Boysen as he came up behind her.

"You!" she squeaked, staring wide-eyed at the Presentation assistant framed in the doorway.

Cardamom smiled. "Me. We have to stop meeting like this, Lyra."

A hysterical giggle bubbled out of Lyra's mouth before she could stop it. "It is turning into a habit, isn't it?"

"What are you doing here?" Boysen asked sharply.

Lyra jumped. For three seconds, she had forgotten Boysen was there. Not only there, but actually holding her upright.

She could hear the scowl in Boysen's voice as he steadied her on her feet and stepped back, releasing her. "It's a bit early for dorm rounds, Coulis. Though, our projects are ready if you want to get the preservation spells out of the way."

"I'm actually just here for Lyra," Cardamom replied, his tone smoother than perfectly whipped buttercream. "I tried Zester first, and they said I would find you here. But I don't want to interrupt your work—"

"We just finished," Lyra said quickly. "What do you need?"

Cardamom's dark hair somehow caught the last rays of the setting sun streaming through the window on the other side of the room. It shone like a halo as he explained, "Another pair of hands. I'm trying out the next level of my experimental preservation spell, and I would love to show it to you. Your thoughts would be invaluable."

Lyra's stomach, which only a few moments before had felt like an overheated oven, was now rising like well-proofed ciabatta dough. "My thoughts?"

"We were just about to head to dinner," Boysen cut in. "It's been a long day. Long weekend. Got to eat."

Cardamom kept his eyes on Lyra, his smile unmoving and yet alive. "I would also love to cook you dinner afterwards. As a token of gratitude."

"We have plans." Boysen tapped Lyra's shoulder. Reluctantly, she turned to look at him. "Flax and Bumble, remember? We promised them yesterday that we'd spend the evening with them after dinner."

"It sounds like Cardamom's project is time sensitive," Lyra said instinctively.

"It is," Cardamom affirmed. "I'm not sure when I'll get a chance to run this experiment again."

Boysen ignored him, keeping his eyes on Lyra. "You promised to bring your guitar. Didn't you say you owe Flax a concert?"

For a moment, they stared at each other. Lyra almost wavered. The distress in Boysen's normally cheerful face twisted her insides so uncomfortably that she had to drop her eyes.

Then she spotted the sugar cookie in her hand. The frosting's vivid red hue brought all her anger flooding back, and her will hardened.

"I'm sure Chef will understand the need to help a fellow baker." She met Boysen's gaze and even tossed her head in a most Caramelle-like fashion. "I think I've had enough music for one weekend."

Boysen opened his mouth, but no sound came out. He reminded Lyra of her brothers when they'd been roughhousing and "accidentally" punched each other in the gut.

Her resolve already failing, Lyra shoved the incriminating cookie into his hand. "See you tomorrow. Thanks for . . . everything. This weekend."

"Thank *you*," Boysen replied.

His voice sounded hollow. Lyra turned away, eager to leave before her anger ran out. She smiled brightly at Cardamom.

"Shall we?" Lyra asked.

"We shall." Returning her smile, Cardamom offered her his arm. She took it and left Whisk without a backward glance.

It turned out that Cardamom didn't need another pair of hands so much as *eyes*. For Presentation spells to be truly effective, he explained, they required an audience. Lyra was more than happy to fill this role.

Perching on a stool at the counter in Cardamom's kitchen, she watched as he held up his two elaborately carved silver Presentation spoons over a tray of truffles. The truffles were already a work of art. Each one was a perfect sphere, exactly an inch and a half in diameter. The chocolate coating ranged from pure white at one end of the tray through gradations of cream and tan to a brown so dark it was almost black. The smooth, shiny surfaces revealed the baker's mastery in the art of chocolate tempering. As if all this weren't enough, each truffle boasted its own unique design, hand painted in various shades of red and pink.

Lyra had gasped in awe at the first sight of this delightful tray, earning a smile and a bow from Cardamom. But then he'd held a finger to his lips, indicating a need for silence. Lyra swallowed her exclamations of praise. She felt songs bubbling up, a veritable cacophony of choruses for each of these truffles, but she forced them down with a deep, steady breath.

The truffles were certainly song worthy, but now was apparently not the time.

For a moment, Cardamom stood motionless, the spoons poised over the tray. Lyra counted nine full beats of her heart. Then, suddenly, he inhaled sharply and began waving the spoons over the truffles. His arms moved slowly at first, then faster and faster, following the steps of a complicated dance. Multiple streams of deep purple light poured from the spoons. They joined the dance, weaving nimbly in and around each other, sparkling so brightly that Lyra had to squint to keep looking.

As they swirled, the purple light streams formed a living dome over the tray. That was when Lyra became aware of a rich chocolaty scent filling the air. It emanated from the dome, as though the streams of light were drawing out and absorbing the very essence of the truffles.

Then, at the same moment Cardamom brought the spoons together with a clear-sounding *ping*, the speed of the swirling began to decrease. The dome of purple light shrank, swirling more and more slowly, before sinking into the truffles. Cardamom watched carefully, as if counting in his head. A few seconds later, he brought the spoons together with another, softer *ping*, and the purple light vanished.

Lyra stared at the tray. If the truffles had been a work of art beforehand, now they were a masterpiece. Each shimmered with its own special glow, as unique as the delicately painted designs, declaring that every single truffle had become a bit more fully itself. Yet the whole tray also shone, proving the various glows were cooperating to form a radiance greater than the sum of their parts. And the smell . . . That delicious aroma of chocolate filled the air around the tray so strongly that Lyra almost imagined she could *see* it.

A wave of wonder washed over Lyra. She found herself thinking of "The Joy Song," when she had last performed it with her family over break. The magic of that song lay in its ability to call forth the joy already dwelling deep in everyone's hearts. Even if one wasn't feeling particularly joyful, an accomplished bard could use that song to reveal, increase, and combine the joys of everyone present until the room was bursting with a sense of gladsome wholeness.

That's what baking can do, Lyra thought, gazing wide-eyed at the gloriously enchanted truffles. *Except even better. "The Joy Song" never made me feel quite like this . . .*

Looking up, she found Cardamom watching her closely.

"What do you think?"

Lyra couldn't speak. If she opened her mouth, one of the truffle songs her brain was still rapidly composing would come blaring out. Instead, she nodded fervently, hoping her face conveyed all the admiration she sincerely felt.

Thankfully, Cardamom seemed to understand.

"I knew you would appreciate this spell," he said, returning the silver spoons to his apron pocket. "Even if no one else here does."

With great effort, Lyra forced the songs to the back of her brain. "I don't see how anyone couldn't appreciate it," she gushed. "That glow—I've never seen anything like it. And the scent! How do I still smell chocolate?"

Cardamom leaned over the truffles, sniffing expertly. "Indeed. That's been my focus for this round of experiments. Preserving the look is one thing, but the aroma . . . Smell forms such a large portion of the culinary experience. If Presentation can capture the nose as well as the eyes, there'll be almost no need for taste."

Lyra couldn't fully agree with that last sentence, but she was not about to ruin this moment by quibbling. She just nodded again and held out a hand to hover over the tray, palm down.

"Is it like those cupcakes you showed us at the beginning of the year? Nothing can touch them?"

In answer, Cardamom placed his hand on top of hers and pushed down. Just before her hand encountered the truffles, a ripple of purple light emerged and buzzed against her fingers before disappearing back into the treats.

"Fully protected, like the cupcakes. This spell doesn't last as long, though." He sighed as he released her hand, almost scowling at the tray. "I had to sacrifice duration to get the aroma right. Next step is to put it all together. By the end of the year, I plan to have a round of preservation spells covering both sight and smell for any length of time one might require."

"I can help," Lyra said eagerly. "I mean, I'd love to help. If you want."

"You already have. As I said, Presentation requires an audience. That's one of the first things I learned from Professor Genoise." He spread his hands, indicating the tray of dazzling truffles. "Your presence and attention made tonight's breakthrough possible. Thank you, Lyra."

"Any time." Stifling a wayward giggle, Lyra tried to match his professional tone. "But I would love to help more actively. Even just as a sounding board? If you need to bounce ideas off someone or talk things out?"

Elegantly, he raised a single eyebrow. "That wouldn't be boring for you?"

"Not at all," she assured him. "I would find it . . . fascinating."

"I confess it would be helpful." Sighing again, Cardamom rested his hands lightly on the counter. Lyra wondered how he kept his nails so clean, even after working with chocolate. "Innovation requires secrecy. I don't have anyone here at the academy I can really trust, especially with the in-process experiments."

Lyra's eyes widened. "Not even Professor Genoise?"

"Oh, I can trust him. But his days are full already. He doesn't have time to show the proper interest."

"Then let me," Lyra begged.

He smiled. "Your days are full too."

"You're my Presentation tutor," she countered.

"Exactly. I'm taking up far too much of your time already." He paused. "Though, I do most of my experiments on the weekends. Sunday nights, like tonight—"

"Sunday nights are free," Lyra broke in. "I'll be getting my projects done in the afternoons. And I'm sure it would be beneficial for my education, participating in the work of a real Presentation expert."

"You've convinced me." Smiling even more broadly, Cardamom held out his hand across the truffle tray for a formal shake. "I accept your offer of assistance, Aspiring Baker Treble, with humble gratitude. Shall we begin at once?"

Lyra shook the offered hand. Was it just her imagination or were the truffles actually singing "The Joy Song" in twelve-part harmony?

"We shall, Apprentice Baker Coulis."

The rest of the evening was a happy blur to Lyra. Cardamom came alive before her eyes, theorizing recitation strategies and sketching out spoon movement patterns and speculating the necessary adjustments for different types of pastry. There didn't seem to be much need for Lyra to answer or to speak at all, which was just fine by her. She was content to sit at the counter, watching and listening with all her might, as Cardamom questioned the very limits of preservation magic.

Eventually, he remembered his promise to make her dinner. With a feast of apologies for the delay, he set to work, not allowing her to lift a finger. Soon they were sitting at the counter together, enjoying a selection of sweet and savory crêpes. He was just explaining the secret to his delicious lemon curd—a touch of cardamom, of course—when a sharp knock sounded on the open door.

Lyra froze when she saw the intruder, every muscle in her shoulders suddenly stiffer than overbeaten egg whites.

"I do hope I'm not intruding," Caramelle Meringue said coldly.

CHAPTER THIRTY-EIGHT

Crêpes, Comfort, and Confidence

Lyra could feel the tension rolling off her former roommate all the way across the room. Caramelle's habitually perfect auburn curls were slightly disheveled. Her apron was covered in a bewildering array of stains, and there were deep shadows under her eyes. But her posture was even more rigid than usual, and her tightly crossed arms felt like a warning.

Go ahead, they seemed to be saying. *Offer to help. I dare you.*

"Caramelle!" Cardamom stood and crossed to the door, his movements as smooth and disarming as his voice. "You're not intruding at all. What brings you to the third floor?"

"My projects are ready," Caramelle replied, her eyes lingering on Lyra before turning to Cardamom. "I need preservation spells put on them so I can go to bed. I believe you are on dorm duty this evening?"

"So I am." Pulling a pocket watch from his apron, Cardamom glanced at it and laughed. "Sweet and savory, is that the time?"

Lyra looked at the clock on the wall. "Flats," she gasped.

"My deepest apologies, Aspiring Baker Meringue." Somehow, Cardamom extricated one of Caramelle's tightly crossed arms and bowed low over her hand. "I have fallen behind in my responsibilities, but I assure you it was not intentional. Thank you for coming to look for me. I am sure the other first years will thank you also."

Caramelle's manner had softened during his apology, but the ice returned instantly at the mention of her classmates. "I don't know if anyone else is ready yet."

"Boysen and I were ready hours ago," Lyra announced. Stepping down from her stool, she gave Caramelle a gracious smile as befit the official assistant, and unofficial dinner companion, of Cardamom Coulis III. "But you can go first, Caramelle. We don't want to keep you from sleep. I'm sure you're exhausted."

Caramelle withdrew her hand from Cardamom's sharply. "I'm fine," she snapped.

"You can visit me last, actually. Take your time. I wanted to get in one more round of scones anyway."

"I'll be right down," Cardamom said. "It's no trouble."

"Take your time," Caramelle repeated. Her gaze passed scornfully over the remains of the crêpe supper, then lingered again on Lyra. "It looks like you have some cleaning up to do." Turning on her heel, she marched away, her heels clicking angrily against the hardwood floor.

Cardamom smiled ruefully at Lyra. "I hope I haven't offended her."

For some reason, Lyra felt as hollow as an under-stuffed éclair. "That's just Caramelle," she said, almost to herself. "She's easily offended."

"What's that?"

Shaking her head, Lyra tried to snatch back some of the elation she'd been swimming in only moments before.

"I think Caramelle's just tired," she said brightly. "She's been baking all weekend. In heels, no less. I never could get her to embrace the idea of comfort clothes."

Cardamom looked down at his own stylish shoes and pressed trousers with a mock groan. "I'm afraid I understand her there. We both have a lot to learn from you."

"We'll see." Lyra's eyes kept drifting to the spot in the doorway where Caramelle had stood. "You both have Stellar Enchantment Pins to back you up. Maybe I'm the one who needs to learn."

"Don't worry about that. This is going to be your term. I can feel it." Cardamom gave her one more quick smile, then drew out his long silver Presentation spoons. "For now, though, I should get going. Thank you again for a marvelous evening, Lyra."

She blushed, a tiny bit of delirious joy seeping back into her deflated heart. "Thank you too."

"I look forward to our tutoring sessions this week and to continuing next Sunday night—if you're still interested, of course."

The eagerness in Cardamom's voice swirled around her brain like streams of purple light, reawakening and preserving all the giddy sensations of the past several hours. So what if she still needed to work things out with Boysen? So what if Caramelle was all alone in Pestle, working herself into a stress-fury?

Cardamom Coulis (*the Third!*) wanted to spend every Sunday evening with *her*, Lyra Treble. He trusted her. He enjoyed her company. He had made her crêpes.

Lyra realized she was grinning.

"Absolutely, I'm interested."

Professor Honeycomb was unusually businesslike when class began the next morning.

"First weekly exam!" She clapped her hands once, briskly, to call the five students to order. "In future weeks, there will be written components. But for now, each group will present their projects for evaluation. Any volunteers to go first?"

From the corner of her eye, Lyra saw Caramelle's hand go up primly.

"Aspiring Baker Meringue," Professor Puff called. "Thank you."

Razz, Hyacinth, and Cardamom moved as one, each grabbing some of the trays spread out over Caramelle's workstation. Once the three platters of scones, four loaves of bread, and five plates of frosted cookies were arranged on the teachers' counter, Caramelle joined the professors at the front, and the evaluation began.

Lyra studied her former roommate. Caramelle's auburn curls were neatly arranged and shining with the obvious glow of a Self-Presentation spell. Her apron was spotless. The Stellar Enchantment Pin on her chef's hat sparkled so brightly, she must have polished it. All in all, The Meringue looked as savagely perfect as ever. The only trace of the previous night's dishevelment was a faint echo of dark circles under her eyes.

"Splendid," Professor Genoise announced. "Your mastery of Master Brûlée's Coloring Charm is impressive, especially after only one week. Still room to grow, of course, especially in yellow, but this is a commendable start."

Caramelle bobbed a quick curtsy. "Thank you, Professor."

"The scones are a little . . . weak." Professor Honeycomb took another bite and chewed reflectively before continuing. "Garlic is a bold flavor and should be treated boldly. You seem to be scared of it."

"I'm not—" Caramelle cut herself off with a sharp breath, then proceeded with a voice as carefully controlled as her hairstyle. "I thought Madame Hazelnut urged caution when working with stronger flavors."

Professor Honeycomb patted her on the shoulder. "Caution just means listening extra carefully to your instincts. The stronger the ingredient, the stronger your will has to be when working the magic. Don't let the flavor boss you around, Meringue."

Caramelle nodded shortly.

"Still, a good effort on the whole." Professor Honeycomb leaned down, giving the cinnamon scones another sniff. "Your instincts are solid. Confidence is all you need—confidence and boldness." She turned to the class, raising her eyebrows. "And confidence comes through . . . ?"

"Repetition," five voices replied in unison.

"Exactly." Smiling, Professor Honeycomb gave the floor to Professor Puff.

"The texture is flawless, of course." Professor Puff's gray eyes swept once more over the four loaves, perfect in their signature ciabatta-ish irregularity, before settling on Caramelle's face. "But I had no doubt it would be. My chief concern is your health. Did you find the solo work overly taxing?"

Somehow, Caramelle managed to stand even straighter. "Not at all, Professor."

"Is it sustainable?"

"Yes."

Professor Puff shared a look with Hyacinth. "Apprentice Baker Roulade told me you did not leave your room for meals and refused all offers of food."

Caramelle didn't even blink. "I have all the food I need in my room, Professor. I am in no danger of going hungry."

Lyra heard Mac stirring in his seat.

"Very well, Aspiring Baker Meringue." Professor Puff held the auburn-haired girl's gaze a few moments longer, then gave a slight nod. "Your work has certainly exceeded expectations. You may continue working in a solo group, but Apprentice Baker Roulade will be checking on you periodically. Understood?"

"Perfectly, Professor."

"Thank you. Well done."

"Yes, well done," Professor Genoise agreed. "Dismissed, Meringue. Aspiring Bakers Berry and Treble, please bring your projects forward."

Caramelle returned to her seat while the third years cleared her trays and ran to help Lyra and Boysen.

Lyra had been so swept up in preservation innovation with Cardamom that she had forgotten to be nervous about this morning. Still, she reasoned, she didn't actually need to be nervous. They had worked hard. She was confident in the results of that work.

She was less confident in Boysen himself. They hadn't spoken since she stormed out of Whisk the night before. For one terrifying moment, she wondered if he would produce the "deception cookie" and tell the professors about her illegal color songs.

Then she glanced over and caught him looking at her. His normally carefree face was so full of anxiety that her own fears evaporated and took most of her fury with them.

Sure, she was still angry. They would need to have a serious talk before she could work with him again. But after all . . . it was Boysen. However stubborn and infuriatingly opinionated he might sometimes be, he wasn't cruel.

He raised his eyebrows in a silent question. She couldn't bring herself to smile, but she gave him a bracing nod, which he gratefully returned. They could face the judgment together.

What mattered was the baking. Everything else could wait.

The professors were unanimous in their praise. Every single baked good demonstrated not only proficiency with the required spells, but a level of refinement only found through frequent repetition. Professor Puff inquired about their strategy and was impressed by Boysen's account of the methodical schedule they had devised.

"You are establishing a laudable routine." The Texture headmistress gave them a rare smile. "That is how to set yourselves up for success not just this weekend, but over the whole term. I commend you, and I urge your classmates to follow your excellent example."

Professor Honeycomb, of course, was even more effusive. The cinnamon scones sent her into such paroxysms of delight that Lyra wondered for a moment if there was such a thing as *dangerous* Flavor success. But the professor recovered soon after and gushed exuberantly about the powerful combination of instinct and magic.

"Madame Hazelnut would be proud," she said, her whole face beaming. "Garlic and cinnamon are two of the hardest flavors to control."

"It was important to . . . find their voice," Boysen replied, very carefully *not* looking at Lyra.

Professor Honeycomb smiled even wider. "That's it! Let them speak, but make them listen, also. Manage them without squashing them. The spell helps, but only if you're using it in conjunction with your own gut. Congratulations to both of you."

Professor Genoise was milder but no less appreciative. "These shades are exactly where I would expect them to be," he assured them, gesturing at the five different colors of frosting. "They may seem faint to you, but Master Brûlée's spell is particularly dependent on repetition. The secret is to capture the color's essence—to understand each hue's distinct personality. That takes time."

Now it was Lyra's turn to avoid looking at her partner. She kept her eyes fixed on Professor Genoise, refusing to acknowledge the five distinct color melodies playing all at once in her head.

"Overall, an auspicious beginning to the term," Professor Puff said graciously. "Just be sure to stay focused. Good beginnings only come to good ends through diligent effort."

Professor Honeycomb looked back and forth between Boysen and Lyra, her blue eyes sparkling even more brightly than Caramelle's Stellar Enchantment Pin. "I knew you two would make a good team."

For some reason, Lyra felt herself beginning to blush furiously. She managed to echo Boysen's respectful thanks and promises of continued diligence, then fled back to her front-row seat before Professor Genoise had finished calling on Ginger and Mac.

As she settled herself behind her counter, though, she found herself suddenly surrounded by a cloud of cinnamon and honey.

"Well done," Cardamom whispered. He gave her shoulder a quick encouraging squeeze before following Razz and Hyacinth to collect the final round of projects.

Smiling and blushing even harder, Lyra turned towards the front—and caught Caramelle's eye. The auburn-haired girl was glaring at her from across the aisle. For an instant, The Meringue's constant mask cracked and revealed a sliver of jealous rage.

Then, as quickly as it had appeared, the crack vanished. Caramelle faced the front again with all the appearance of lofty unconcern.

Lyra forced herself to focus on the third years bringing Ginger and Mac's projects to the front, but she couldn't help a small internal sigh.

She may have escaped Pestle, but clearly she was *not* done dealing with The Meringue.

CHAPTER THIRTY-NINE

Finding Our Rhythm

If Boysen and Lyra's evaluation was universally glowing, Ginger and Mac's was universally . . . mixed.

Surprisingly, Professor Puff's comments were the most positive. She praised the consistent structure of all four loaves, pointing out the many air holes so distinct to ciabatta.

"You both committed fully to the proofing spell," she said, her voice rich with unusual warmth. "The bread's density is a touch too high, but that can be worked out through practice. This spell requires a strong foundation, and you have laid it. I look forward to seeing how you build upon it in future weeks."

Professor Honeycomb, on the other hand, was less enthusiastic.

"The plain scones are lovely. Top-notch, in fact. But the sweet . . . I'm having a hard time finding the cinnamon." The Flavor headmistress held a scone directly against her nose, inhaled deeply, and shook her head. "It's there, but it's barely coming through in scent or taste. How many times did you recite the spell?"

Mac wilted visibly, but Ginger's voice was calm as she replied, "Seventeen."

"That many?" Professor Honeycomb's blue eyes widened. "Then why—"

"We only put in a pinch of cinnamon," Ginger went on. "At the beginning. We never added any more after that."

The professor looked from Ginger to Mac, then back again. "Whyever not?"

"It was an experiment," Ginger said smoothly. "Rather than just adding a bunch more cinnamon, I wanted to let Madame Hazelnut's spell carry the flavor. Or at least see how far the spell could go on its own."

"Not very far, apparently." Professor Honeycomb looked again at Mac. "Aspiring Baker Fondant, did you agree to this experiment?"

Mac swallowed hard. "S-sort of. I mean, Ginger made some good points. You really feel the strength of a spell when you're depending on it that much."

"And it does work," Ginger put in. "Remember, there's only a pinch of cinnamon in that whole batch. I know it's faint, but without the spell, you wouldn't be able to find it at all."

Professor Honeycomb nodded, but there was far more than a pinch of doubt in her expression. She leaned towards the third plate of scones. "What about the garlic? Did you follow the same exper—"

Six inches from the plate, she seemed to encounter some invisible barrier and jumped backwards, holding her nose. Mac looked like he wanted to hide behind his partner.

"Nope," Ginger said, cheerfully answering Professor Honeycomb's unfinished question. "Opposite experiment with the garlic. We only recited the spell once and then kept adding in pinches until our gut said it was right."

"I'm afraid your gut was misinformed." Professor Honeycomb's eyes were watering. Choosing the smallest of the savory scones, she held it at arm's length and gave the faintest possible sniff. "The garlic is overwhelming. Oppressive. Offensively uneatable."

Ginger nodded. "That's what we thought."

Professor Honeycomb returned the odious scone to the platter and hastily wiped off her fingers on her apron. She snatched one of the plain scones, then held it to her face and breathed in.

"There. That's better. Cleanse the palate." She looked at Ginger and Mac, her blue eyes suddenly stern. "If you were aware of the experiment's failure, why did you turn it in?"

Ginger somehow managed to shrug politely. "Because now we know. Our guts are that much more attuned. Flavor is about gut, right?" She waited for a nod of assent from Professor Honeycomb, then continued, "And baking is about creation, which requires risk. I'd rather take the risks now, at the beginning of term, and then grow from there."

Professor Honeycomb studied her for a moment, then turned to Mac. "Aspiring Baker Fondant? What do you think?"

"I think . . ." Mac's fingers toyed nervously with his apron strings, twisting them into impossible knots. "I think it was worth a try. We're here to learn. Mistakes . . . help. With learning."

After another long moment, Professor Honeycomb nodded again. "Mistakes are necessary, so long as you do indeed learn from them. I will expect to see evidence of today's lessons in next week's exam."

Mac nodded vigorously, while Ginger only smiled.

"Very well. That's it for Flavor." Professor Honeycomb turned to Professor Genoise. "Basil?"

The Presentation headmaster was already inspecting the five plates of sugar cookies. "Very interesting indeed," he said slowly. "The red, the blue, and the yellow are vibrant. The best in the class, I'd say. But the other two colors . . ."

"Those were mine," Ginger said. "Mac did the red, blue, and yellow. I handled green and purple."

"Ah." Professor Genoise took out his monocle, peering more closely at the two plates in question. "Am I to take it you approached this assignment with a similarly . . . innovative spirit as the one you brought to Flavor?"

Lyra craned her neck to get a closer look at the cookies. She bit back a gasp. "Green" and "purple" were not the terms she would use to describe the frosting on those platters. "Muddy" was a better word. Perhaps even "puke."

"I was thinking about color theory," Ginger explained. "Yellow and blue make green. Red and blue make purple. I wanted to see if the individual color charms could be combined in the same way."

"I see." Professor Genoise leaned down so close that his monocle was practically buried in frosting. "So you recited the yellow and blue charms instead of the green?"

"In addition to the green. And for the purple, I recited the purple charm once, then did a few rounds of red and blue."

Professor Genoise straightened, carefully polishing his monocle before placing it back in his pocket. "And what did you learn?"

"That color charms don't work the same as color theory," Ginger replied. "But I'm glad I tried. It was a fascinating process."

"Indeed." Professor Genoise grasped the lapels of his elegant frock coat and drew himself up to his full height, as if about to deliver a political speech. "Once again, Aspiring Baker Crumble, you have proven yourself worthy of the word I used to describe your style at the beginning of the year: daring. While I admire creativity even more than the next fellow, there is a time and a place for such excessive levels of . . . innovation. That place is not the classroom. In the future, I request that you focus on the given assignment and perform your experiments on your own time. If you waste any more of my or Aspiring Baker Fondant's time with such endeavors, there shall be consequences."

Turning to Mac, the professor gave a cordial bow. "Excellent work, Aspiring Baker Fondant. Master Brûlée himself would be pleased with the shades you have achieved. Dismissed."

This last word was addressed to Ginger as well. The Presentation headmaster's tone was perpetually kind but as hard and unyielding as a burned sourdough crust. There was nothing Ginger and Mac could do but scurry back to their seats.

Ginger was unusually quiet the rest of the morning. She didn't raise her hand once in Flavor and barely said a word during lunch. Texture and Presentation were the same.

It wasn't until halfway through dinner that the long-brewing response to Professor Genoise's evaluation finally burst forth.

"I just can't believe it," Ginger spat, staring at her untouched bowl of spicy shrimp stir-fry. "Or I couldn't, if I hadn't been there to witness it. 'There is a time and a place for innovation, and it's not the classroom'? Then where is it? If we can't try new things in school, where are we supposed to try them? How are we supposed to learn?"

"Like Professor Genoise said," Mac replied dolefully. "On your own time."

Ginger laughed. "Right. Because we have so much of that."

"It is possible," Lyra said, keeping her eyes on her plate. "Cardamom does a lot of experimenting, but it's all on the weekends. He fits it around his classwork."

Boysen coughed. Lyra shot him a look, but he suddenly became very engrossed in adding extra hot sauce to his bowl.

"That misses the point," Ginger protested. "We shouldn't have to 'fit in' our learning around our classwork. The classroom should be a place where creativity *thrives*. This stick-to-the-script attitude is warping the academy's true purpose."

"You didn't think so last term," Lyra pointed out. "At least, not to the point where you changed the assignments. That was Aniseed's thing."

Ginger rolled her eyes at the mention of her former roommate. "Aniseed thought the rules were beneath her. I have no trouble with rules. First term was all about learning those rules, which made total sense to me. Lay the foundation, right?" She stabbed moodily at a piece of red pepper. "I just expected second term to shift focus. Especially with all these projects . . . Isn't it time to start exploring outside the rules? Give us a little freedom? Then, third term, we could bring it all together. Rules plus experimentation."

"You have high ideals, Crumble." Boysen smiled sadly. "Maybe you should start your own academy someday."

Ginger brought a bite of shrimp halfway to her mouth, gave up, and plunked her fork back down in the bowl, then crossed her arms. "I just might."

"But for now," Lyra said, in her best imitation of Hyacinth's tension-smoothing tone, "could we all just be grateful to be at this academy? And . . . y'know, follow the rules so we can *stay* at this academy? Together?"

For a moment, Ginger just gazed at the steam wafting from the basket of flatbread in the table's center. Then she sighed. "Sure. For you, Lyra. And for all the Whisk Whizzes. Speaking of . . ." Turning to Mac, she gave him a wry smile. "Sorry for adding stress to your life, Macaron. I'll try to be a better partner from now on."

"No worries," Mac said amiably, scraping the last bits of sticky rice from his bowl. "It was the first weekend. We're all still finding our rhythm. As teams, I mean."

Lyra felt Boysen's eyes on her, but she focused on arranging a neat combination of shrimp, rice, and red pepper on her fork. Once this perfect bite was thoroughly chewed and swallowed, she dabbed her mouth with a napkin and stood.

"I need to stop by the kitchen," she said brightly. "Haven't seen Chef much this term. I'll see you all in Whisk later!"

Without waiting for an answer, Lyra made her way swiftly across the dining hall, narrowly avoiding a collision with a platter of individual trifles headed to the second-year table. She pushed open the kitchen door just in time to see Chef Flax come in from the greenhouse staggering under the weight of a massive pumpkin.

"Chef!" she called, darting across the kitchen. "Let me help."

Together, they deposited the giant gourd on the counter, where Bumble immediately began scoring it with a sharp knife in preparation for slicing.

"Thank you, Lyra," Chef Flax panted, sitting on a stool and leaning heavily on the counter. "Sprinkle has rather outdone herself this year with the winter squashes."

Lyra regarded the pumpkin with suitable awe. "What'll you make with it? Pies?"

"Not this week." After producing a purple handkerchief from his apron pocket, Chef wiped his forehead. "Soup, I think. At least until our egg supply is back in order."

"Eggs?" Lyra froze. "Is something wrong with Queen Penelope?"

Chef Flax chuckled, but Lyra noticed his eyes lacked some of their usual jollity. "She's a bit under the weather. Nothing too serious. She works hard and gets run down every once in a while. We're trying to give her some time to rest. Makes menu planning more of an adventure. Right, Bumble?"

The sous chef chattered something shortly in squirrel language.

"Oh, stop whining." Chef Flax flicked the flying squirrel gently with his handkerchief. "It's good to challenge ourselves every once in a while. The old bird will be back in tip-top shape soon."

Bumble chattered a longer phrase as he used his knife to point emphatically at a large tray on the counter. The tray was covered with a tightly wrapped tea towel, but Lyra could still smell the fragrant mixture of ginger, cloves, and cinnamon wafting from it in aromatic waves.

"Right. Best get a move on." Chef Flax mopped his brow once again before pushing to his feet. "Bumble's special gingersnap cookies always help Queen Penelope feel better. Baked with Sprinkle's spices, of course."

Bumble chattered animatedly to Lyra, and Chef Flax nodded. "Sprinkle's magic does make the spices more salutary. It's like she infuses them all with extra medicinal . . . oomph."

"Can I help?" Lyra asked as the chef hoisted the tray.

He smiled. "Thank you, m'dear, but I'd best make this visit solo. Queen Penelope doesn't like to be disturbed when she's feeling poorly. I'll give her your warmest regards, though."

"Please do," Lyra said gratefully. "And if there's anything more I can do to help, let me know."

The head chef paused, balancing the tray easily in one hand. "Music might help. If you want to bring your guitar some night this week, we could give it a try."

Lyra felt her stomach clenching but managed to keep her expression neutral. "I can try. The evenings are pretty busy, but . . . we'll see."

"Yes, second term is a bit of a slog. Chin up!" Giving her an encouraging smile, Chef Flax turned towards the door leading to the kitchen's direct rooftop access.

Suddenly, Lyra remembered why she had come to the kitchen in the first place. "Sorry about last night, Chef," she called after him. "I really will try to bring my guitar soon."

He paused long enough to assure her that all was well, then continued up the stairs with his tray of salutary sweets.

Lyra hesitated, not sure where to go next. She still had time before the Whisk Whiz Review. Maybe Ginger was back in Zester and needed to vent some more . . .

Sighing, Lyra turned to the door. She wasn't really in the mood for a Ginger rant, but wasn't that what roommates were for?

Before she had taken one step, though, the door from the dining hall swung open. There stood the Flavor King himself, looking as blue as the berries he had baked into such delicious scones the previous Saturday.

"Hi," Boysen said. "Can we talk?"

CHAPTER FORTY

Tangle with The Meringue . . .

It took Lyra a few moments of silence to realize that Boysen was genuinely waiting for an answer.

"Of course," Lyra said. "Though, maybe we should go somewhere else. Don't want to bother Bumble."

The flying squirrel chattered something in an amiable tone, then leaped across the room and vanished through the greenhouse door.

"He needs more nutmeg," Boysen interpreted. "But I think he's really just making an excuse to visit Sprinkle."

Lyra stared at him. "You speak squirrel now?"

"Just a few phrases. I'm trying to learn the Flavor terms. Nutmeg, salt . . . cinnamon . . ." He trailed off, his eyes scanning the room as if searching for inspiration amidst the various baking implements.

"You'll have to teach me sometime," Lyra said, eager to avoid any prolonged silences. "During our Saturday sessions, maybe."

His gaze snapped back to her. "Our Saturday sessions? You still want to work with me?"

"Of course," she repeated. After a day to cool off and get her thoughts in order, Lyra was glad for the chance to clear the air. "I just . . . want to lay down some ground rules, if that's okay."

He nodded fervently. "That's what I wanted to talk about. I'm sorry for pulling that trick. Really, *really* sorry."

"It's okay," Lyra said.

"No, it's not." Boysen's hands fidgeted, apparently at a loss for what they should do without some kind of dough in front of him. "I just wanted you to see how it could work. How amazing those songs are. I wanted you to know . . ." He sighed, his shoulders slumping. "It doesn't matter. Whatever I wanted, it was a low, lousy thing to do, and I'm sorry. I won't do anything like it again. I promise."

"Apology accepted," Lyra assured him. "And thanks. For the promise."

"Least I could do." Boysen suddenly gave his arms a vigorous shake, as though trying to rid them of some unpleasantly clinging odor. "Salts, that's better. Let's not fight again. Deal? It's been hanging over my head all day. I thought for sure you were going to ditch me and go solo like Caramelle."

"Not a chance." Lyra shuddered. "I don't want to end up like Caramelle. She's going to hurt herself one of these days."

Boysen arched one eyebrow. "Really? I mean, I'm glad you still want to be my partner and all, but Caramelle seems to be handling the work well. She looked fine in class, anyway."

"She did not look okay last night. Trust me."

Boysen's eyebrow rose higher. "You spotted The Meringue? In the wild?"

"She came looking for Cardamom, to do the preservation spells." Lyra felt heat spreading across her cheeks and fought to keep her voice cool. "He—we lost track of time, over dinner. That's why he was so late with his dorm rounds."

Boysen nodded stiffly, pressing his lips together as if afraid of what might come out.

"But it's not just that I don't want to work alone," Lyra rushed on. "I want to work with *you*. We make a good team, remember?"

Slowly, Boysen's face relaxed into a smile. It was a far cry from one of his signature grins, but Lyra still felt a corner of her heart suddenly relax, like a stubborn air bubble had finally popped.

"We do indeed," he replied. "The professors have spoken." Stepping back, he bowed with a sweeping gesture, indicating the door. "Shall we prove them right once again, starting with a Whisk review in the company of other well-paired Whizzes?"

Lyra gave an exaggerated version of her Any Weather Bards post-show curtsy. "Lead on, Flavor King."

Boysen laughed at that, the sound popping a few more of Lyra's internal air bubbles.

"That reminds me." He pushed through the door, then held it open for her. "I've been rethinking some of the family crests we designed. Is an owl really appropriate for Crumble?"

"Hmm, you're right. Maybe something more aggressive," Lyra agreed. "To show her . . . fierce dedication to creativity. How do you feel about porcupines?"

Chatting easily, they made their way across the dining hall and back to the dorms for another cheerful night of studying.

After resolving the tension with Boysen, Lyra thought the worst of the week must surely be over.

Then came Wednesday.

Second-term Texture lab days were a whole new level of grueling. Professor

Puff had announced the first week that it was time to investigate the discipline's more technical side. She would no longer be providing the spells with the equations always completed. That meant working out the pace and number of repetitions for each spell as homework so all of class time could be devoted to practice.

The other Whisk Whizzes were a huge help Tuesday night, but Lyra still felt herself floundering, like she'd been tossed into a deep bowl of cake batter without knowing how to swim. She even caught herself regretting the loss of Caramelle as a roommate. If anyone could have sorted through the page of equations with stylish ease, it was The Meringue.

This regret was short-lived, of course. Lyra only had to remember the look in Caramelle's eyes from Monday morning's exam to rejoice once again at being free of Pestle. Whatever mix was stewing under those perfect auburn curls, something was very off.

Lyra's gut was clear on this point. No superconductor required.

At least the Texture class was working on a familiar spell: Madame Brioche's Kneading Chant. The first years had used this charm to make several loaves of enriched bread during the first term, though always at the beginner level. This week's assignment of spicy cheese bread called for the intermediate level, and of course, Professor Puff was not providing any of the mathematical preparation.

Lyra had worked herself into such a tizzy by the start of lab day that it came as a true shock when Wednesday morning passed so smoothly. The silence of the classroom felt peaceful as she combined flour, sugar, salt, and yeast in a large bowl, then added butter, eggs, an egg yolk, and water heated to a precise temperature. The first round of kneading and proofing flew by. Before Lyra knew it, the dough was ready to be prepped for its second rise.

This ease was partly due to the song she had written for Madame Brioche's chant during one of the first term Whisk Whiz Review sessions. It was a catchy tune, easily adaptable to the spell's new difficulty level, and it refused to leave Lyra's brain. Despite her best efforts to focus solely on mental recitation, the tune kept weaving itself around the words, drawing her hands into the appropriate kneading rhythm.

She couldn't even keep the song out of her head as she rolled out the dough into a rectangle. It hummed incessantly through her thoughts as she covered the rectangle with a sprinkled mix of cheddar and spicy red pepper flakes. It persisted through the sequence of rolling the dough into a log, shaping the log into a coil, and brushing the coil with an egg-white glaze. The song shifted to provide the appropriate soundtrack for every stage of the process, culminating in a solid accompaniment for Lyra's final recitation of the spell just before the second proof.

Lyra wanted to be annoyed with herself. Wasn't she supposed to be breaking this music habit? How would anyone take her seriously as a baker if she couldn't get through a single Texture spell without breaking into song? What would

Professor Puff say if she knew Lyra was mentally singing Madame Brioche's carefully crafted words?

What would *Cardamom* say?

Though these questions intruded upon Lyra's peace throughout the morning, they never seemed able to break through the song's relentless tide. Besides, the results spoke for themselves. It was hard to listen to the nagging doubts when the bread's first and second rises went so perfectly. It became even harder when Lyra pulled the finished loaf out of the oven, light and springy and fragrant. By the time Professor Puff cut into the bread and announced it "an admirable first effort," the questions were little more than a faint whisper, completely overshadowed by the song's triumphant chorus.

It's not like I'm doing it on purpose, Lyra reasoned as she started on her second loaf. *The music is just there, inside me. If it helps, it helps. Doesn't mean that I'm depending on it or cheating . . .*

Shaking her head, she focused on separating another egg, setting aside the white for glazing, and adding the yolk to the dough. Lab day was not the time to sink into an internal debate or try to resolve yet another existential crisis.

Lab day was for one thing and one thing only: repetition.

Closing her eyes, Lyra dug her hands into the new batch of dough and began kneading, the determined melody starting up again to coincide perfectly with the first words of Madame Brioche's chant.

On the whole, the first years were in high spirits when they broke for lunch. Everyone's morning had passed about as pleasantly as Lyra's. They were all on track to meet Professor Puff's goal of four full loaves by the end of lab day. Best of all, Caramelle continued the habit she had begun at the beginning of second term: bringing her lunch and staying in the classroom while the others adjourned to the dining hall.

Lyra wasn't sure where Caramelle found time to prepare her own meals, but she wasn't about to complain. A Meringue-free table was definitely preferable to the alternative. She couldn't even bring herself to feel bad when they returned to the classroom, all laughing together at Mac's latest Fortescue the Foppish Fox stories, to find Caramelle sitting hunched over her workstation in the front row.

She prefers to be alone, Lyra told herself stoutly. *She never appreciated the Whizzes anyway.*

Still giggling over Mac's imitation of Fortescue's "pocket square" monologue, Lyra pulled her bowl of dough from the proofing drawer and turned it out on the counter.

That was when her good mood vanished.

The dough hadn't risen. It had *sunk,* shrinking into a ball less than half its original size. The structure was so tightly compacted, she couldn't imagine rolling it into a frisbee-sized disc, let alone a twelve-by-eighteen-inch rectangle.

"Oh my." Professor Puff's serene voice sounded from the end of her workstation. "Did you have trouble with the second round of Madame Brioche's spell, Aspiring Baker Treble?"

"Not at all, Professor," Lyra replied helplessly. "I did it exactly the same as the first time. At least, I think I did."

Professor Puff picked up the dough, weighing it gravely in her expert hands. "This has been over-kneaded. You must have recited the spell too many times."

"But I didn't," Lyra insisted. "I was going by the same equations I used for the first round, and that came out well."

"It is easy to lose track of repetitions," the professor said, her expression kind. "Especially as you move into the higher levels of these spells. That's why we practice: to hone our focusing abilities. You'll just get in an extra round of practice today. This may put you a bit behind, but you should still be able to get through four loaves. If not, you can finish the last one tonight as homework and bring it to me tomorrow. Yes?"

Lyra's insides felt like a collapsing cake. She knew she hadn't over-recited the spell, at least not enough to produce such a disaster. Still, Professor Puff's gray eyes were not inviting argument.

Lyra swallowed her protests. "Yes, Professor."

"Excellent." Professor Puff gave her a slight smile. "Don't be discouraged. Your first loaf this morning proved you can accomplish this spell. I am confident some more repetition will get you back on track in no time."

"Yes, don't be discouraged!" Caramelle's sweet voice rang out from the workstation ahead of Lyra's. "It takes a lot of time and training to master these principles. Years of focused study. Right, Professor?"

Professor Puff nodded approvingly. "Right, Aspiring Baker Meringue."

"And Lyra's only been baking for a year or so," Caramelle went on, smiling so graciously that Lyra fought the urge to gag. "Limited experience, no formal training . . . Honestly, it's incredible she's here at all. One might even say *unbelievable.*"

The auburn-haired girl's eyes narrowed briefly, so fast that Lyra doubted anyone else noticed. Then she turned back to her own work, bestowing another oh-so-kind smile as she went.

Lyra stared at her former roommate's back. Her head was spinning, flashing through the same images over and over, faster and faster and far too many times. She pictured Caramelle here in the classroom all through lunch, alone with Lyra's undefended proofing drawer . . .

Her mind ceased its circular whirl, tightening in on itself like a lump of over-kneaded dough.

Nope, she thought grimly, remembering the strange moment she'd shared with Caramelle at the end of Monday's exam. *Nope . . . definitely not done dealing with The Meringue.*

CHAPTER FORTY-ONE

Prove It

The rest of the second term passed in a mostly happy blur for Lyra. The Monday morning exams made sure each week began with a shot of adrenaline. Lab days were grueling but always left her with a sense of fulfillment. And then there were Whisk Whiz Reviews on Fridays to look forward to, followed by weekends full of baking with Boysen. The rhythm of academy life became so comfortably familiar that Lyra found herself wondering how she had ever felt at home anywhere else.

Then, of course, there was Cardamom.

It was hard to tell which Lyra looked forward to more: the weekly tutoring sessions or the Sunday night experiments. Wednesday and Thursday nights in the Presentation lab certainly had the most direct impact on Lyra's educational growth. Mainly, this impact took the form of a gradual elimination of singing in her Presentation work. Practicing spells with Cardamom standing right next to her filled Lyra's mind with an awed silence, pushing her customary mental soundtrack to the background. After several weeks of these tutoring sessions, she barely remembered any of the Presentation songs she had taught the Whisk Whizzes the previous term.

Lyra took this as a definite sign that she was making progress towards becoming a serious baker. Better still, she was confident that she would soon be able to apply this new sense of discipline to Texture and Flavor also. Thanks to Cardamom's tutoring, she would no longer be dependent on music to succeed in magical baking. Then even Caramelle would have to take her seriously.

Yes, the weekly tutoring sessions were effective. But the Sunday night experiments had their own special glow. Even though Lyra didn't get to participate directly, Cardamom assured her that her listening ear and attentive gaze were profoundly helpful.

She had no desire to object or complain. Not only was it an inspiring privilege to witness Cardamom's passion for innovation, Lyra had the additional pleasure of knowing The Meringue was furious about all of it. Realizing just how much Caramelle would love to be in her shoes made every delicious moment all the sweeter for Lyra.

The pleasant rhythm of these days did have some hiccups, of course.

Queen Penelope struggled to get back to normal, and her slow recovery cast a pall on the academy kitchens. Chef Flax, Bumble, and Sprinkle ran themselves ragged. They devised as many egg-free dishes as possible so the royal fowl could focus on providing for the students' classwork needs. They whipped up a veritable mountain of extra sweet treats for the queen with Sprinkle's salutary spices. On the few occasions when Lyra was able to stop by the kitchen for a lightning-quick visit, she either found her friends dashing out to tend to Queen Penelope or dashing back in to work on the next meal for the dining hall.

They were always so apologetic at not being able to receive her properly that Lyra felt ashamed. After all, she wasn't providing any help to them or to Queen Penelope. She still hadn't managed to bring her guitar for the long-promised concert. It was hard enough as it was to snatch an odd few minutes after dinner or before breakfast to duck her head into the kitchen and say hello. As much as she tried to convince herself that Chef Flax understood the pressures of the academy, she couldn't stop feeling guilty.

It didn't help that the other Whisk Whizzes were all doing their part for the convalescent fowl. Ginger had taken it upon herself to experiment with egg substitutes for some of their project recipes. Boysen doubled his squirrel speech vocabulary so he could consult with Sprinkle about different flavor combinations for Queen Penelope's medicinal desserts.

Mac outdid them all. He pulled a few all-nighters in one of the main hall's practice kitchens to elaborately decorate "health cakes" for the royal chicken's enjoyment and consumption. When his classmates objected, questioning whether this was truly the best use of his time, Mac revealed a hitherto buried streak of stubborn determination.

"Beauty has healing properties," he insisted, eyes flashing fiercely behind his glasses. "Making something prettier increases the health benefits. It's not just for the physical senses, you know. It's for the *soul.*"

When Chef Flax confirmed this assertion and even reported that the gorgeous cakes did indeed produce a noticeable improvement in Queen Penelope, the Whisk Whizzes surrendered. Lyra still didn't think it was wise of Mac to sacrifice that much energy, especially as the second-term final exam drew ever closer, but she kept her doubts to herself.

She tried to be more vocal with her roommate. Ginger was still pushing back against academy authority at every turn. True to her promise to Mac, Ginger curbed her innovative tendencies during their weekly projects, but lab days were a minefield of experimental disasters. Looking back over the term, Lyra couldn't list a single Thursday when Ginger didn't return to Zester muttering about Professor Genoise's "soul-crushing dictatorial tendencies."

Lyra listened sympathetically and made several cups of comforting chamomile tea, but she also felt it her duty as a roommate to speak hard truths. Whenever Ginger paused for breath between anti-establishment rants, Lyra tried to remind her that school was temporary. If they could all just put their heads down and get through the term, there would be time enough for revolutionary experimentation in the years ahead. Ginger just shook her head, took a large gulp of tea, and launched into another diatribe about Professor Genoise's monocle.

As the term drew to a close, Lyra's concern for her roommate was nearly equal to her worries about Queen Penelope. The fate of both, along with Lyra's guilt at not being able to help either, were twin clouds on the otherwise hopeful horizon of the second term.

Then, of course, there was Boysen.

The Flavor King kept his face resolutely blank whenever Lyra mentioned Cardamom, and he was careful to avoid even the appearance of any pressure about the use of music in baking. With all his efforts, though, Lyra could tell he was bothered. The air around him would occasionally start vibrating at a particularly tense frequency, disrupting his usual serene tempo and jangling uncomfortably with Lyra's nerves.

Lyra tried to ignore these moments, but this became difficult as the term progressed. Not only did the discordant frequencies start popping up more often, but they also lasted longer. By the time Lyra arrived in the Flavor classroom for the final Monday morning of second term, her inner rhythm was still slightly off following a full weekend of nonstop on-edge vibration from the Flavor King.

"Welcome, Aspiring Bakers!"

Professor Honeycomb's cheerful greeting smoothed some of Lyra's choppy thoughts, but the churning returned full force with the Flavor headmistress's next words.

"Before we begin this morning's project evaluation, we have another important event to discuss: the second term final."

Every single first year inhaled in sharp unison. Lyra found herself wondering if their collective anxiety could actually flash freeze the air in the classroom.

"As you know, this is the last week of second term," Professor Puff continued, impervious to the students' emotions.

Professor Genoise, too, seemed oblivious to any change in the room's atmosphere. "Therefore, it is time to announce the nature of this term's final exam, which will take place this Saturday morning in the exam hall. For this exam, we are asking you to revisit a familiar recipe."

"A very familiar recipe." Professor Honeycomb's blue eyes twinkled. As if revealing a tray of delectable desserts, she spread her arms wide and announced, "You get to make your final entrance exam cakes again!"

The students drew in another sharp breath in unison. Lyra now began to wonder if the academy had ever lost an entire group of first years to mass hyperventilation.

Professor Genoise took out his monocle and polished it on his sleeve as he amiably took up the thread. "Of course, as with the first-term exam, there are additional requirements. You must choose two spells for each baking principle. No more, no less. For Presentation, one of these spells must be Master Brûlée's Coloring Charm, used for any and all colors you choose to include in your cake."

"No specifications for Texture spells," Professor Puff said, almost kindly. "You are aware of your own strengths and weaknesses. I am confident you will choose wisely."

"And for Flavor, I ask only that one of your spells be Madame Hazelnut's Deepening Spell. The other is up to you." Professor Honeycomb beamed at the class. "Any questions?"

Ginger raised her hand. "Do you want any additional flavors, like you asked us to implement in the first-term exam?"

Professor Honeycomb's smile brightened. "Excellent question, Aspiring Baker Crumble. Please do keep the flavors you added for the first-term exam but no further additions."

"As we have discussed often this term," Professor Genoise added, "too many new elements can rather muddy the waters, Aspiring Baker Crumble." He gave Ginger an almost pleading smile.

"Thank you, Professor," Ginger replied, eyes wide with innocence. "No further questions."

Her voice was sweet, but Lyra knew her roommate too well to miss the steely glint in Ginger's eye. It bore an ominous resemblance to Mac's fervent defense of all-night "health cake" decoration.

Lyra's heart sank. If Ginger tried anything crazy . . .

Despite Ginger's assurance later that she would behave for the exam, Lyra's worries persisted. She tried to drive them away by immersing herself in exam prep for the rest of the week, but to no avail. It was all too easy to picture Ginger sacrificing the rest of her academy experience just to make a point.

By Thursday evening, concern was still so heavy on Lyra's heart that Cardamom noticed at the end of their tutoring session. She gave him a brief summary of her roommate worries in response to his courteous inquiry.

"Is that all?" he asked, one eyebrow raised delicately in surprise. "Lyra, you don't have time to worry about other people. No one at the academy does, but especially not you. The exam is your priority. That's enough."

"I know." She nodded wearily. "Practice, and repetition, and focus—"

He waved an elegant hand to cut her off. "Yes, yes. All that. But you also need to take some time to prepare for winning. What are you going to say to Professor Genoise when he awards you the Stellar Enchantment Pin?"

She stared at him. "You-you really think I'm going to win?"

"Yes, Lyra. I really do."

His dark eyes caught and held hers. Even if she'd wanted to, she literally could not look away.

"Remember what we said at the beginning of term?" he went on. "It's not enough to be the best. These sessions have been about making you *better* than the best. You're something special, Lyra. And on Saturday, you're going to prove it."

She nodded, as incapable of speech as of movement.

He smiled. "Let's plan on a special celebration over the break, just you and me. I can take you to dinner. We'll toast your victory and make plans for the third term. Yes?"

She nodded again. Cinnamon and honey swirled around her, the aroma so strong that she almost thought she could see it. Was it possible to drown in scent?

If so, she thought dreamily as he walked her back to the dorm, *what a way to go.*

Still floating, she said good night, then practically twirled across the first-floor common area.

"All ready for the exam, I see?"

Lyra froze. Gripping the door handle of Zester, she turned slowly to face Caramelle.

The Meringue was leaning out of Pestle's open door, her eyes sparking with anger. Had she been waiting there, listening for the sounds of Lyra's return from tutoring? Was she really getting that desperate?

Lyra shook her head. She was not about to let Caramelle steal any of this Cardamom-inspired happy haze.

"Yes," she replied coolly. "As ready as I'll ever be."

Caramelle stepped through the door, looking Lyra up and down. Her voice was a perfectly obnoxious blend of syrup and scorn.

"Enjoyed your extra time with Cardamom? Soaked up all those unfair advantages like a good little sponge?"

"There's nothing 'unfair' about it," Lyra shot back. "I'm not the one who had to sabotage her own roommate to guarantee a win."

Caramelle went rigid with fury. "I'm not the one who has to depend on secret musical powers to get ahead. Got all your illegal songs composed for Saturday morning?"

"No, actually." Lyra forced her own posture a little straighter. "I don't need those anymore. Cardamom helped me. I'm going to beat you fair and square."

"Is that so?" Caramelle tried to laugh, but it came out as a strained wheeze. "You're going to *beat* me?"

Lyra fought to keep the bubbling pot of rage in her stomach from seeping into her voice. "That's right. I'm winning the Stellar Enchantment Pin this term. No music. No tricks." She leveled one last glare at the auburn-haired girl. "I'm going to beat you, Caramelle, and I don't have to cheat to do it."

Without waiting to see her reaction, Lyra turned the door handle and swept into Zester. The sound of Pestle's door slamming seconds later sent the pot of rage boiling over into a wave of mean gladness.

This time, Lyra promised herself. *This time it will be The Meringue who winds up with egg on her face.*

CHAPTER FORTY-TWO

The Soufflé Sisters' Cooperation Chant

Aspiring Bakers, to your stations!"

Professor Genoise could have saved his breath. The five first years had been standing at their respective counters in the exam hall, ready and waiting, for a solid ten minutes. Still, the Presentation headmaster was never one to miss out on a grand moment.

What was it Boysen said before the welcome feast? Lyra found herself musing. *Wouldn't be the Royal Academy of Magical Baking without a bit of ceremony.*

As if to confirm her thoughts, all three professors raised their silver magic baking wands in a solemn salute.

"You have two hours to complete your second-term final exam cake," Professor Puff announced. "As always, you are forbidden from conferring with your fellow bakers or from making any noise whatsoever."

Professor Honeycomb's smile was as wide as ever, but her voice sounded strangely formal in the large, mostly empty room. "We wish you the very best, Aspiring Bakers. The exam begins . . . now!"

The three professors touched their silver baking spoons together, and a soft magical chime sounded through the exam hall. Five workstations erupted into five concentrated whirlpools of silent activity.

Lyra was glad to be moving at last. The temperature-controlled space felt colder than usual, and she had been shivering as she waited for the exam to begin. Perhaps it was the weather. She had risen early after a restless, anxious night to a sky heavy with dark thunderclouds. The exam hall's large windows gave the first years a perfect view of this brewing storm, and Lyra couldn't help feeling it was all rather ominous.

She shook her head and busied herself with measuring butter into her mixing bowl.

It's just nerves, she told herself firmly. *The chill, the sky; it's all normal exam-time jitters. Focus on the magic. Focus on the baking.*

At least "focusing on the magic" was even more pleasant than usual. Thanks to her tutoring sessions this week, almost every spell she was using for her exam cake now had some association with Cardamom. He had devoted both of their evenings together to exam practice, coaching her through multiple rounds of repetition on each element of the recipe. She could almost smell the cinnamon and honey in the air as his voice echoed through her memory.

You're something special, Lyra . . .

Another shiver ran down Lyra's spine, this time of excitement.

She *was* something special. And it was time to prove it.

Texture came first. Adding sugar to the butter in the mixing bowl, Lyra launched determinedly into Master Chiffon's Aeration Charm at the intermediate level. Since she was also trying not to sing in her head, she dared not attempt the spell's advanced version.

It turned out that the professors' constant harping on repetition was well-founded. Lyra had practiced this spell so many times over the past two terms, and especially during the last few days, that she was now able to get through it consistently without musical assistance. She didn't feel as confident as she had while singing through the first-term exam, and she didn't enjoy it nearly as much, but she successfully maintained the correct pace for each varying stage of the charm.

It worked. After the twenty-seventh recitation, a wave of blue light surged out of her hands and sank into the cake batter.

Breathing a sigh of relief, she turned to the second magical Texture component. Lyra felt a bit more secure about Madame Pavlova's Spell of Fluffening. She had used it in her final entrance exam cake, so the tempo was even more deeply embedded in her muscles than Master Chiffon's charm.

Unfortunately, the tune she had written so long ago was also engrained more irrevocably in her memory. It was almost impossible to ignore.

Lyra gave her head another emphatic shake. Then she began gently ladling batter into three prepared cake tins, pausing between each spoonful to recite Madame Pavlova's short spell. The song was blaring through her mind, oblivious to the fact that it was both unwelcome and unhelpful, but she pressed on.

Thankfully, Madame Pavlova had been a kindly soul, and her spells were the most forgiving examples of Texture magic available to young bakers. The Spell of Fluffening took effect quickly and played quite nicely with Master Chiffon's aerating magic. When another, even more vibrant wave of blue light encompassed each tin of batter, Lyra felt safe that the cakes would be both light and exquisitely moist.

She allowed herself a quick internal melody as she put them in the oven. No spell-music, of course. Just a short run of "The Joy Song" chorus to celebrate the fact that second-term Texture work was officially behind her.

Now she could turn her attention to Flavor. Madame Hazelnut's Deepening Spell was an old friend at this point. Lyra felt the knot of tension between her shoulders loosen slightly as she whipped cream to stiff peaks. Moving with confident care, she added sugar, followed by the first round of vanilla and boysenberry. Then, barely closing her mouth in time to catch an escaping hum, she mentally recited the short spell . . . and listened.

Professor Honeycomb had emphasized Madame Hazelnut's Deepening Spell throughout the second term. The first years had used it at least once in every weekly project. That meant Lyra was now familiar with the distinctive sound of several different flavors once they reached the perfect level for a particular dish. None were quite so loud as garlic, nor as overbearing as cinnamon, but each was unmistakably distinct.

This was the one component of this week's practice sessions that had no association with Cardamom. He had left her basically on her own for Madame Hazelnut's spell, trusting her instincts to listen correctly. She had failed to mention that the flavors never spoke to her like they did to every other baker she knew. They *sang*.

It doesn't matter, she told herself firmly. *You're not singing the spell. You can listen. You can't control how the message arrives.*

Holding her hands over the bowl of frosting, Lyra listened for the duet of vanilla and boysenberry. Her face twisted into a grimace of concentration.

Too much boysenberry. It's not supposed to be that loud.

It was a problem Lyra had run into frequently over the week of practicing. Vanilla was such a gentle flavor. Its song was pervasive but easily buried by higher or more complicated melodies.

She added a whole teaspoon of vanilla and recited the spell again. After a few moments of listening, she nodded.

Better. Now a pinch more boysenberry, for brightness.

That was the other side of the problem Lyra had set for herself by choosing these two flavors. Vanilla in large quantities could drag down the whole dish into a dark, cloyingly sweet tune. A sharp counterpoint like boysenberry was a perfect solution, but only if one got the balance right . . .

After a few more rounds of adding a pinch more of one and another dash of the other, Lyra was satisfied. Both flavors were singing at an appropriate volume in her mind. The boysenberry provided a clear descant above the vanilla's rich melody line that lifted without overpowering. Best of all, green sparkles had surged out of her fingers and were dancing above the bowl, revealing Flavor magic was at work in the frosting.

Perfect, she thought. Then she took a deep breath, setting her mouth into a grim line. *Time for The Soufflé Sisters' Cooperation Chant.*

Though this was arguably the simplest of the magical components Lyra had chosen for the exam, it was also the one she was the least confident about. Perhaps it was the spell's notoriety that made her nervous. The Soufflé Sisters were famous in the lore of magical baking.

According to legend, though Professor Honeycomb swore it was historical fact, Mesdames Rose and Honey Soufflé were two famous sister bakers whose taste buds refused to agree. When one demanded more salt, the other called adamantly for another cup of sugar. Though both Flavor masters, their instincts seemed to exist in a constant state of direct opposition. Their mutual baking ventures always ended in disaster.

Until they wrote the Cooperation Chant.

Since the start of second term, Lyra had heard a few conflicting stories about how the spell actually came about. Professor Honeycomb had insisted the two sisters simply put their heads together and devised a clever resolution to their lifelong battle: a cooperation spell born out of cooperation.

Later, in the privacy of the Whisk Whiz Review, Ginger had rolled her eyes and shared the version she'd learned from her dad. Honey Soufflé was a conniving, ambitious brat, who set out to sabotage her much more talented sister, but when her poorly executed curse backfired, Rose stepped in to alter the spell and save the day. The result was the Cooperation Chant: half curse, half recovery.

Boysen's account was Lyra's favorite. He reminded the other Whizzes that sibling squabbles were perfectly normal, especially when two sisters loved and respected each other as much as Honey and Rose did. Mr. and Mrs. Berry had always told their boys that the Soufflé Sisters, like the Berry brothers, sometimes had to let off a little steam at each other. And when two talented bakers carried their friendly feud into the kitchen, it made sense that the churn of magic would produce a genius spell. Nothing more natural in the world.

However it came into being, the Cooperation Chant *was* genius. It seemed to carve out complementary bits in the edge of each flavor, forcing them to fit together like puzzle pieces. The chant worked best when all flavors present were operating at their fullest capacity, so it was necessary to pair it with something like Madame Hazelnut's Deepening Spell for maximum impact.

But when it worked . . .

Lyra paused over the frosting, remembering a particularly exquisite custard Boysen had made during one of their weekend sessions. She'd been bewailing Professor Honeycomb's assignment, insisting that cherry and lavender did not and would not go together. Boysen just smiled, performed this Cooperation Chant a few times . . . and proved her deliciously wrong.

With a sigh, Lyra pulled herself back to the present moment. Of course, the Flavor King had mastered the Soufflé Sisters' spell. He had years of experience in both baking and sibling drama to inform him. But whenever Lyra tried to follow, her will always fell short of the spell's minimum requirement.

That was the problem with the Soufflé Sisters' Cooperation Chant. You had to *mean* it.

Lyra narrowed her eyes.

Well, Mesdames Honey and Rose . . . I really do mean it.

Staring at the bowl, Lyra let her world contract to the awareness of those two flavors. She listened to boysenberry's descant. She heard how lightly and deftly it floated over vanilla's melody. Then, focusing all her will on the idea of flavor unity, she mentally recited the chant.

A pulse of vibrant green light surged out of her hands, but it faded before it could reach the frosting.

Lyra set her lips in a determined line, planted her feet a bit more firmly on the gleaming mahogany floor, and tried again. This time the pulse of light did touch the frosting, but the green was much less vivid.

Can't have faint, watery cooperation, Lyra chided herself. *That won't do.*

Closing her eyes, Lyra called upon all her senses. She imagined the feel of the silky-smooth frosting under her fingertips and the decadent smell of vanilla with just the right ripple of boysenberry running through it. She pictured the exact shade of green the light needed to be to prove the spell a total success. Her mouth watered as she dreamed about that first bite, taste buds savoring a perfect sweet-and-sharp balance. Finally, she listened internally for the song of two flavors singing as one, without either voice being lost.

It's like when Mom and Dad sing.

Her eyes flew open at the thought, and she felt one corner of her mouth turn up in a smile.

She didn't need to recreate the Soufflé Sisters' version of cooperation. The Treble version was even more harmonious.

The words of the chant sang through her mind on their own accord. Guilt at the accidental music stabbed briefly through Lyra's happiness, but it vanished the next moment as the spell took effect. Dazzling green light pulsed from her hands and enveloped the bowl, feeling like an extension of the wave of purpose surging through her will.

Still smiling, Lyra felt Boysen's gaze from the workstation behind her. She glanced back to see him staring, open-mouthed, at the green light slowly sinking into her bowl of frosting.

He raised a single eyebrow. *Nice*, his eyes seemed to say. She grinned at him, then exchanged a quick nod before turning back to her own counter.

The exam was proceeding as smoothly as she could wish. Texture was done. Flavor was done. She'd only had one musical slipup, and no one could call it intentional. The cakes were ready to come out of the oven.

A sudden heavy silence fell over Lyra's mind, like a cloud of cinnamon and honey wafting across her imagination.

It was time for the Presentation component.

CHAPTER FORTY-THREE

Shiny Silence

Lyra felt strangely still on the inside as she put the cakes in the cooling drawer and whipped up a shiny vanilla glaze. The inner silence persisted while she coated a few dozen boysenberries with the glaze and set them aside. Even when she scooped out some frosting into two smaller bowls for coloring, her mind stayed unusually quiet.

It wasn't a jittery kind of silence. That was what made it so odd. She had no doubt regarding her abilities in this section of the exam. It was just strange to be brimming with such confidence without any desire to burst into song.

I guess I'm really starting to think like a baker.

Because she *was* a baker. Not a bard pretending to be a baker, but a true practitioner of baking magic. What was it Cardamom had said? Better than best?

Yes. *Better* than best.

The inner quiet was odd but pleasant. It provided a soothing background while Lyra held her hand over one of the bowls and recited Master Brûlée's Coloring Charm for red. A flare of purple Presentation magic burst from her fingertips and sunk into the uncolored frosting, turning it a pale crimson.

No distracting melodies. No musical training wheels to prop her up. Just the spell, working like it was supposed to.

Lyra smiled grimly and started again.

Working with Cardamom, she had discovered it took four repetitions of the red charm to achieve the desired shade. She moved through them deftly and set the bowl aside, then steeled herself for the difficulties of pink.

When Lyra had designed her entrance exam cake all those months ago, she had no idea of the problems she was creating for her future self. Red and pink roses seemed straightforward enough. Red was the most basic of Master Brûlée's Coloring Charms. Shouldn't pink just be a lighter version of red?

Apparently not. Cardamom had been downright offended when Lyra innocently suggested this strategy at their Wednesday night tutoring session.

"Every color has its own personality," he'd insisted, eyes flashing with indignation on behalf of pastels everywhere. "Master Brûlée understood that. He identified twelve different hues of pink and wrote a charm for each of them."

That had kicked off the laborious process of choosing the right shade of pink to fit Lyra's vision. After a long debate, dusky rose was agreed upon as the most suitable candidate. Only then did Lyra discover that Master Brûlée had shown great restraint in crafting the five basic color charms she knew so well.

The dusky rose charm was a doozy.

It wasn't a matter of complex equations or tempo shifts like Texture was. Master Brûlée had believed that the key to more nuanced colors was *layering*. That meant reciting the spell in a continuous round, over and over and over, until the exact shade bloomed before your eyes. If one paused even for an instant or stumbled over the words mentally, then the charm fizzled out and had to be started again from the beginning.

Lyra found this intensity of sustained concentration surprisingly troublesome. It was somehow worse than the proofing spell for Texture that took half an hour to recite. Even with Cardamom beside her for inspiration and solidarity, by the end of Wednesday's session, she hadn't been able to get further than a half-hearted blush color. She had returned to Zester that night in a state of near panic.

Thankfully, all three professors had devoted the entire week's class time to exam prep. After a full day of practice in Thursday's Presentation lab, again with Cardamom's constant supervision, Lyra felt sufficiently pleased with her dusky rose frosting performance.

It would have been easier without the melody her brain had instantly composed for the new color charm. The tune erupted in her mind whenever she started thinking about dusky rose. Exam time was no exception. As soon as Lyra began Master Brûlée's charm, the song arrived, shattering the oh-so-professional inner silence she had been enjoying. It kept singing at the edge of every thought, offering its assistance and insight regarding the quirks of this particular hue. Lyra was hard-pressed to keep her mental recitation from relaxing into the song's cadence.

Even worse, the song perfectly expressed the essence of Lyra's brother Canto. She could clearly picture all the facets of his personality weaving around each other with every note. The layers of color produced by the charm could easily be layers of Canto, piling his tenor voice and mad cello skills on top of his family loyalty and love of painting to create a winsome whole. Complex yet comforting. Just like dusky rose . . .

Stop it, Treble!

Lyra paused for a moment to make sure she hadn't actually shouted that command out loud. Then she wiped her hands on her apron and took a deep breath, wishing fervently she had never shared those color-charm personality songs with Boysen. It had carved pathways in her mind that were challenging to reroute.

Banishing all thoughts of brothers, personality songs, and music in general, Lyra held her hands over the bowl and began the mental recitation.

It didn't go smoothly. She had to toss out a few batches and start over until the right shade of pink was achieved. Thankfully, she had made a triple batch of frosting to begin with for this very purpose. Thursday's practice sessions had taught her that lesson the hard way.

With her two colors of frosting complete, Lyra turned her focus to the last and objectively most difficult part of the exam: Master Glaze's Shine Spell.

At the advanced level.

She would have chosen this spell even if Cardamom hadn't recommended it so strongly. Master Glaze's Shine Spell was an absolute cornerstone in high-end Presentation baking. Besides, Caramelle's betrayal at the end of the first term had given a sour note to Madame Temper's Chant of Precision in Lyra's mind.

Lyra also felt the need to prove that she was capable of top-tier magic like Master Glaze's work. She needed to prove it to Professor Genoise and to Cardamom. She needed to prove it to Caramelle.

She needed to prove it to herself.

Cardamom had been working with her on this spell throughout the term, gradually coaching her through the beginner and intermediate levels. They had only started practicing the advanced level two weeks ago, but Cardamom insisted Lyra could handle it for the exam.

"Remember, it's a competition," he told her at the beginning of Wednesday night's session. "Everyone else will be doing at least the intermediate level, and you need to stand out. Just getting through isn't enough. We're not settling for anything less than that Stellar Enchantment Pin. Right?"

Lyra had nodded, tightened her scarf around her hair, and set to work.

Now, standing in the exam hall, she followed the same sequence of actions. Master Glaze's spell was unique among Presentation magic. Most charms in this discipline were applied at the end of the baking process, throwing a special sheen over the completed decoration. Others, like Madame Temper's Chant of Precision, had to be cast over the materials before any decorating occurred.

Master Glaze's Shine Spell had to be recited throughout.

It was rather like the Soufflé Sisters' Cooperation Chant, in a way. The baker had to recite the spell over and over in as many rounds as it took to fill the decorating time. It was important to maintain a consistent internal tempo.

Still, Lyra found Master Glaze's approach easier than Mesdames Honey and Rose's. The Cooperation Chant had to sink deep into the core of the flavors to merge them into a new whole that would permeate the entire dish. The charm depended on the baker's concentration and purposeful intent.

The shine spell was not so . . . profound. It was Presentation, after all. Even the most complex Presentation spells were only concerned with the final product's outer layer.

Just keep going. Lyra repeated Cardamom's instructions as she held her palette knife poised over the largest bowl of frosting. *Even if you stumble over a word, move on. Master Glaze is an expert. Let his words carry you, and you'll be fine.*

Lyra took a deep breath. Then she dipped her palette knife into the bowl as she mentally recited the first words of the shine spell.

Ice cracks, bone breaks
Cloth tears, earth shakes
Glass shatters, mountains fall
Diamond stands stronger than all.

It had taken Lyra a while to get used to Master Glaze's writing. She understood the general structure of the spell, with each verse listing a different gem to imbue the idea of shine. Still, the images felt a bit violent for a Presentation spell whose sole purpose was to make food prettier.

Fire burns, gold gleams
Sun blinds, star beams
Mirror dazzles, but on light's throne
Rubies sparkle brilliant, alone.

The meter was also a bit off. Master Glaze was no poet.

She hadn't dared voice these ideas to Cardamom, of course. Master Glaze was one of his personal heroes.

When Professor Genoise first introduced this spell to the class, he had invited his assistant to speak. Cardamom had waxed so eloquently about Master Glaze's "inimitable genius" that Ginger wasn't able to contain an audible snigger. Lyra shot her roommate a withering look and promised herself she would always show Cardamom—and Master Glaze—the proper respect.

Now, watching purple light stream effortlessly from her hands, Lyra had to admit both gentlemen knew what they were about.

The shine spell was dazzlingly effective. The magic tingled against her fingers as she spread the first coat of white frosting on each tier, then disappeared into the cakes with a bright purple shimmer. The stream of light grew even brighter with the second coat, then practically danced as she stacked the tiers and began piping red and pink roses.

Lyra entered into the "amethyst" verse with a smile. Master Glaze may have been deficient as a poet, but his Presentation mastery was undeniable.

True, the process was laborious. The carefully maintained silence in Lyra's mind was heavier than song. The words of Master Glaze's spell dragged on and on in a monotonous litany of jewel descriptions. Every second seemed to take twice as long to pass. She didn't remember the arrangement of glazed boysenberries being quite so dreadfully tedious in the first-term final exam.

Lyra was actually relieved when Professor Genoise's voice rang out imperiously across the hall.

"Time's up, Aspiring Bakers!"

Wiping sticky hands on her thoroughly smudged apron, Lyra stepped back to survey her work. The frosting colors gleamed vibrantly, vivid red and dusky rose standing out against the smooth white base. Her piping skills had improved over the past two terms. The red ribbon around the top and bottom of each tier was so straight and even, it looked like she'd used a tracer. Clusters of tiny dusky-rose flowers dotted the ribbon at exact intervals. The clump of pink and red roses atop the cake was a true crowning glory, complete with shiny glazed boysenberry gems.

The last ripples of purple magic were still swirling around the cake. As Lyra watched, the light sank into each tier, starting with the bottom and ending at the crown of roses. Yet, though the purple sparkles vanished, they left a shimmering radiance in their wake: the unmistakable glow of a successful Presentation spell.

Lyra's shoulders slumped in relief and exhaustion. She had never, ever been this tired. Even if she hadn't been working hard all term to guard her brain against music, she couldn't possibly have found the strength to sing.

The professors were already making their rounds. Lyra simply sat on her stool, too weary even to pay attention. She only managed to straighten up and smile when they made their final stop at her counter. Still, though she focused with all her remaining energy, she couldn't read anything from their expressions as they judged her cake. They looked, sniffed, tasted, and looked again with faces unusually guarded. At the end, they simply gave her a bow in perfect unison before returning to the teacher's platform.

Through her haze, Lyra was dimly aware of her heart beating strangely fast.

"First of all, congratulations," Professor Honeycomb began, her voice uncharacteristically solemn. "You have completed your second term at the Royal Academy of Magical Baking, and you have all accomplished something noteworthy in this final exam. Well done."

Professor Puff's gray eyes were as calm and cool as ever. "We have reached our decision about the Stellar Enchantment Pin and about who will not be joining us for the third term. But before we make those announcements and release you for your well-deserved break, we have one last educational experience for you."

She nodded at Professor Genoise, who took up the thread.

"Last term, we delayed our detailed assessments of your final exam cakes until you returned from break. This term, we want you to take the assessment home with you, to reflect upon as you prepare for whatever comes next. Ergo, we shall proceed with an immediate thorough evaluation of each student's exam cake."

Professor Genoise smiled like he was announcing an all-you-can-eat ice cream extravaganza. Turning to Lyra, he indicated the platform beside him.

"Aspiring Baker Treble, would you be so kind as to join us? Bring your exam cake, if you please. We will begin with you."

CHAPTER FORTY-FOUR

Too Right

The exam hall felt oddly dark as Lyra carried her cake to the teachers' platform. The gray clouds still piling up outside the windows were heavy and ominous. Taking the indicated place beside Professor Genoise, Lyra suppressed a shiver.

"Let us start with the high point," Professor Genoise announced. "Which is Flavor for this cake, I believe. Right, Lavender?"

Professor Honeycomb gave Lyra an encouraging smile. "That's right. Your instincts are superb, Aspiring Baker Treble. Another delicious combination for the books. And your magical skills are coming along nicely also. I was particularly struck by your use of the Soufflé Sisters' Cooperation Chant. Beautifully accomplished."

Something was wrong. Professor Honeycomb's voice was never this subdued. Her blue eyes weren't sparkling nearly as much as they should be, at least if she were truly excited about Lyra's cake. And hadn't Professor Genoise said that Flavor was the *high* point?

Lyra felt that shiver she had suppressed take root in the pit of her stomach.

"I can say the same about your Texture magic." Professor Puff spoke as evenly as she always did, but Lyra thought she detected a hint of sadness in the Texturist's stern features. "You have labored quite diligently this term, Aspiring Baker Treble. This cake demonstrates your competence in both Master Chiffon's Aeration Charm and Madame Pavlova's Spell of Fluffening. Especially the latter. Thank you for your hard work."

"Hard work. Exactly the words I would choose." Peering through his monocle at Lyra's cake, Professor Genoise shook his head. "Alas, in baking, the final result ought not to *feel* like hard work. We put in great effort, but the consumer should never be aware of it. Our goal is to give them a moment of sweetness—easy, light, and carefree. I'm afraid this cake fails to achieve that."

The shiver spread rapidly from Lyra's stomach up to her throat. Nearly choking on it, she stammered, "Did—are the Presentation spells wrong?"

"Not at all, my dear," Professor Genoise assured her. "Quite the opposite. If anything, they are . . . too right."

She stared at him blankly. "Too right?"

"Too exact. Deliberate. Laborious." Professor Genoise waved an elegant hand over the cake. "I can feel all the strain and effort these spells cost you. Just looking at it makes me tired. And that is not how a cake is supposed to make one feel, is it?"

The shiver had taken possession of Lyra's vocal cords. All she could do was shake her head.

"This is a very correct cake," Professor Genoise went on. "Neither Master Brûlée nor Master Glaze could find any fault with your work. But Presentation, remember, is all about *style*. Your personal style has always been remarkably uplifting. 'Joyful' is the word I gave you first term, and you have earned it again and again." He gave the cake another long look through his monocle, then sighed. "I see little joy in this cake, Aspiring Baker Treble. Only effort. I believe my colleagues agree?"

Professor Puff and Professor Honeycomb nodded in silent confirmation, the latter rushing to add, "Except the Cooperation Chant. I felt a spark of something there."

"Madame Pavolova's Spell of Fluffening was a bright moment," Professor Puff commented. "A 'spark,' if you will."

"Indeed," Professor Genoise said. "And I caught a spark in the dusky-rose charm. But it was a spark only, and quickly snuffed out."

"We have come to expect such . . . delight from your cakes, Aspiring Baker Treble," Professor Puff said, almost apologetically.

"Delight!" Professor Honeycomb exclaimed. "Yes, that's it. I was looking forward to a truly enjoyable eating experience." She gave Lyra a kind smile. "There's nothing wrong with the cake technically, my dear. I believe we're all just a bit disappointed."

Professor Honeycomb's warmth failed to melt the icy shiver. Lyra couldn't meet the professor's eyes. She dared not glance out at the exam hall to see what looks her fellow students were giving her. Boysen's support would be just as unbearable as Caramelle's disdainful triumph.

Instead, Lyra just stared at her "too right" cake as the shiver took full possession of her mind, freezing her inside this one horrible moment. Echoes pinged around her brain, bouncing off the icy walls.

Just looking at it makes me tired.

I see little joy in this cake.

I believe we're all just a bit disappointed.

And then, out of nowhere, Cardamom's voice from Thursday night, vibrant with confidence: *You're something special, Lyra. And on Saturday, you're going to prove it.*

The ice in her mind cracked, melted, and threatened to come pouring out of her eyes. She cast one mute, pleading glance at Professor Honeycomb.

Thankfully, the Flavor headmistress took the hint.

"You have much to ponder over the coming break, Aspiring Baker Treble." Professor Honeycomb looked at each of her colleagues, nodded, and went on with a tone of finality, "Thank you for your work this term and in today's exam. The cake is quite a technical achievement. You may return to your workstation now."

Lyra wasn't sure if it was Ginger or Boysen who started clapping. Whoever it was, she wished they hadn't. The applause seemed to overwhelm all her senses at once as she stumbled blindly back to her seat. It roared in her already buzzing ears. Her hands and feet felt numb. Even her eyes were drowning in the noise, unless the gathering storm outside had suddenly grown much darker . . .

Only when she was back at her counter, perched on her stool, did she feel somewhat stable again. She clenched her hands tightly in her lap and stared at the platform, willing the professors to move quickly through the four remaining students.

Just throw me out, she begged silently. *Just tell me I'm not coming back and let me fall apart in peace.*

"We will continue in a similar vein," Professor Genoise announced. "Aspiring Baker Meringue, would you bring your cake and join us?"

Lyra's brain felt like a pile of melting slush, but she still managed a tiny flicker of surprise. "Similar vein"? What was *that* supposed to mean?

Then she caught a glimpse of Caramelle, and her flicker of surprise shifted into a wave of alarm.

The Meringue looked terrible.

Not messy, of course. Her hair and clothes were as fiercely perfect as ever. But the dark circles under her eyes . . . When had they grown so big? And when had she gotten so thin?

Lyra tried to think. She had just spoken to Caramelle the night before. But had she really *looked* at her? Honestly, Lyra couldn't remember the last time she had truly *seen* her former roommate, at least through the lens of anything like concern.

Not that Caramelle would have accepted concern, of course. The Meringue had been surrounding herself with a wall of determination and spite and Self-Presentation spells all term. Rather than trying to get through, Lyra had thrown up a few walls of her own.

But the walls were coming down. The only aura surrounding Caramelle now was that of exhaustion—someone who had pushed themselves several miles beyond some sacred limit and was ready to drop. Standing on the platform beside the professors, she looked ten times worse than Lyra felt.

"The parallels between your cake and Aspiring Baker Treble's are striking, Aspiring Baker Meringue," Professor Genoise began. "For one thing, the two of you chose the same spells."

"Except for Texture," Professor Puff corrected. "Both students used Master Chiffon's Aeration Charm, but Aspiring Baker Treble at the intermediate level, while Aspiring Baker Meringue performed the advanced version. And for her second magical component, Meringue selected Madame Dacquoise's Superior Sponge Spell. This is most impressive. Academy Texture curriculum does not cover that spell until third year."

Caramelle's voice was as stiff and brittle as her egg-white namesake. "The academy encourages us to push ourselves. I wanted to stand out."

"You certainly did," Professor Puff said gravely. "Both Texture spells were completed successfully. I believe my colleagues would say the same of the other two disciplines' magical components?"

The Flavor and Presentation professors nodded their confirmation.

Professor Puff went on, "But this is where the parallel with Aspiring Baker Treble continues. This cake is technically perfect, or as close as any baker could hope to achieve, let alone a first-year academy student. But . . ."

"It is not enjoyable," Professor Honeycomb said sadly. "The flavors are deep and balanced, but not of their own accord. They were forced. It's like they are terrified of being anything less than perfect."

Professor Genoise nodded again. "Terrified. That's the word. Presentation magic always reflects the personality of the baker, as you know, Aspiring Baker Meringue. Your style has always been virtuosic. You set the bar incredibly high for yourself and for all your fellow students. But I fear you have aimed too high. This cake's story is not virtuosic excellence. It is a tale of setting impossible goals, exhausting oneself trying to reach them, and the devouring fear of falling short."

"The academy does encourage students to push themselves," Professor Puff said with unusual tenderness. "But not at the sacrifice of one's health. As you and Aspiring Baker Treble have shown today, such weariness does manifest detrimentally in a baker's work. You still have much to be proud of. The cake *is* technically perfect. You also have much to learn. I encourage you, Meringue, to ponder these lessons over break."

Her tone was gentle, but it also invited no argument. Caramelle gave the slightest of nods. Then she returned to her seat, taking her "technically perfect" cake with her. She ignored the round of applause that Mac began, even when the professors joined in enthusiastically.

Before Lyra could even begin to sort through the sluggish array of emotions swirling through her mind, Professor Genoise was speaking again.

"Aspiring Baker Crumble, please join us."

Ginger marched to the platform, placed her honeycomb cake on the counter, and stepped back. Lyra could feel the defiance radiating out of her from several feet away.

Looking at the cake, Lyra's heart began sinking towards her stomach. The design was as intricate as she remembered, but the execution . . . Was the frosting supposed to be running together like that? Was the whole cake actually *melting*?

"Aspiring Baker Crumble," Professor Honeycomb began. "We are all, I confess, a bit confused about the spells you chose. Could you walk us through them, please?"

"Happy to." Ginger smiled, and Lyra's heart sank even further, plummeting towards her toes. "For Flavor, I used Madame Hazelnut's Deepening Spell, as instructed. I also used a variation of the Soufflé Sisters' Cooperation Chant."

"Variation?" Professor Honeycomb echoed.

"Yes. I wanted to focus on contrast rather than cooperation. I reversed the chant, encouraging each flavor to be as distinct as possible."

Professor Honeycomb opened her mouth, closed it, and then nodded at Ginger to continue.

"For Texture, I selected Master Chiffon's Aeration Charm at the intermediate level, followed by Madame Brioche's Proofing Chant."

Professor Puff's eyebrows rose. "The proofing chant is for bread, Aspiring Baker Crumble."

"And this cake is meant to have a bread-like consistency," Ginger countered. "I modified the equations to fit a cake recipe. Master Chiffon's charm provides plenty of airiness, so I wanted to balance that with a little density."

Professor Puff's eyebrows were still raised. Her lips pressed together in a thin line. But, like Professor Honeycomb, she did not speak. She merely nodded, and Ginger continued.

"I used Master Brûlée's Coloring Charm for Presentation, of course. For the second spell, I invented one of my own."

"So I see." Professor Genoise peered at the slowly disintegrating cake. "May I inquire as to the purpose of this new spell?"

"I wanted to create a sense of reality," Ginger explained. "It's essentially an illusion cake. Before you cut into it, didn't it look and feel and smell like an actual honeycomb?"

Professor Genoise sighed. "It did. I was quite enchanted. But the moment the knife touched it"—he closed his eyes and turned away, waving in the soggy cake's general direction—"this happened."

"I used a preservation spell for inspiration," Ginger said cheerfully. "The effect doesn't last long, I'm afraid. But it's worth it."

"Sadly, I must disagree with you there, Aspiring Baker Crumble." Professor

Genoise did look genuinely sorrowful. Even his carefully manicured beard seemed to be drooping. "Your potential is truly astounding. But raw talent alone cannot sustain a baker. To succeed in this grueling profession, one requires—"

"Discipline," Professor Puff supplied. "The ability to set aside one's personal preferences and stay the course. As we have all told you repeatedly over this term, Aspiring Baker Crumble, there is indeed a time and place for your innovative tendencies. That place might be the Royal Academy, but the time is *not* during your first year. You have to lay the foundation before you can build on it."

Ginger's voice was steady, and even respectful. "Doesn't the success of the building prove the foundation is solid enough already?"

"But the building is not a success, my dear." Professor Honeycomb's sparkling blue eyes were swimming with tears. "The flavors are a mess. They're both screaming so loudly over each other that I can't tell what either is supposed to be saying. This isn't a cake, Crumble. It's a war."

"Same with Texture," Professor Puff said bluntly. "The proofing spell is simply not meant for cake. I can tell you did some admirable work with the equations, but the result is neither cake nor bread. It's some sort of stodgy hybrid."

"And the Presentation spell . . ." Professor Genoise sighed, apparently searching for words.

Ginger saved him the trouble.

"It's a disaster cake. I aimed too high and failed spectacularly."

"I wouldn't say 'failed,'" Professor Genoise replied.

Professor Puff nodded. "No, indeed. You demonstrated your proficiency with one spell for each baking principle."

"So we know you *could* have produced something truly marvelous." Professor Honeycomb's voice was shaking slightly. "If you had not deviated so wildly with the other three spells."

Ginger, somehow, appeared much calmer than the professors. She gave a brisk nod. "Understood. Thank you." Then, to Lyra's utter bewilderment, she said, "I'm guessing you don't want me to come back next term?"

A moment of silence flashed through the hall, coinciding with a sudden streak of lightning in the sky outside.

Professor Genoise cleared his throat.

"No, Aspiring Baker Crumble. We do not."

CHAPTER FORTY-FIVE

It's Just Baking

Lyra's insides felt like a blender set to puree as she watched Ginger return to her workstation. Emotions tumbled around, bumping up against each other and refusing to mix cleanly. Lyra could barely even name them all.

She was devastated about Ginger leaving. She was equally annoyed with Ginger for refusing to follow the professors' instructions. Then she felt guilty for being annoyed and angry at herself for not trying harder to talk some sense into her roommate.

The swirling only intensified as the professors called Mac up to the platform. Lyra struggled to pay attention. She was dimly aware of Professor Honeycomb praising Mac's Flavor progress and urging him to be a little bolder with the coffee. She caught a few phrases of calmly effusive affirmation from Professor Puff. She didn't need to hear Professor Genoise's gushing to know Mac's Presentation style was as majestic as ever. The cake was shining brightly enough to push back the darkness of the gathering storm outside.

Their only critique, as far as Lyra could understand through the emotional haze, was that he seemed a little distracted. Each spell had been missing that extra degree of heightened focus that marked the most professional high-end bakers. Otherwise, though, all three professors pronounced the cake "a triumph."

Poor Mac, Lyra thought dully, watching him bow and carry his triumphal cake back to his counter. *This should be a great moment. But no one can focus. Not even him.*

His distractedness was obviously an ongoing reality. Mac's eyes kept darting around from Caramelle to Lyra to Ginger, full of sorrowful concern. True, they lingered longest on, and returned most often to, Caramelle, but Lyra knew he cared about all of them. He was probably also thinking about Queen Penelope. He'd done more for the royal chicken than the rest of them put together.

Lyra sighed. If it was possible for a cake to be "too right," then it made sense for Macaron Fondant to be "too good." They didn't deserve him. Lyra sure didn't, anyway.

And speaking of friends Lyra didn't deserve . . .

Boysen's evaluation was as beautiful and uplifting as his cake. The professors had clearly wanted to end the day on a high note. Professor Genoise was especially impressed by the vibrant colors Boysen had been able to achieve, saying repeatedly that Master Brûlée himself would be jealous of the vivid blue and even richer yellow. Professor Puff's placid exterior warmed by several degrees as she insisted on shaking Boysen's hand three separate times.

Professor Honeycomb couldn't say anything. She actually broke down weeping when Professor Puff asked her about Boysen's use of Flavor magic. But they were obviously tears of joy, which was definitely better than any words she might have employed.

Lyra's heart began to lift slowly as she watched. It was always difficult to be sad for long around Boysen, especially when he was in full baker mode. It was like watching Sprinkle tend the greenhouse or hearing the Any Weather Bards sing together. Whenever he was completely immersed in baking, Boysen took off soaring and swept everyone in the vicinity along with him.

I belong here, he seemed to be saying. *And so do you. Let's relax and stay a while.*

Lyra knew she wasn't the only one being caught up in the Berry spell. She could feel her fellow first years sitting up and leaning forward, tension easing ever so slightly from their shoulders. Even the air in the room brightened noticeably, though the clouds were still getting heavier outside.

By the time Professor Genoise awarded Boysen the Stellar Enchantment Pin, everyone was able to join in a round of applause. Ginger's cheers were actually the loudest and most enthusiastic. This surprised Lyra, though perhaps not as much as Caramelle's politely fervent clapping.

Then, at last, the second-term final exam was over.

Lyra tried to make a beeline for Ginger, but Professor Genoise's voice rose imperiously over the bustle.

"Aspiring Baker Crumble! A word, if you please?"

Ginger caught Lyra's eye and nodded. Lyra understood the silent message. They would see each other back at Zester later.

Lyra looked around for Mac, but he was already gone. So was Caramelle. Lyra could only imagine what The Meringue must be feeling . . . not that Lyra cared. Caramelle wouldn't want comfort, even if Lyra had any to give.

Besides, her next priority was Boysen.

She waited until he managed to extricate himself from Professor Honeycomb's tearful affirmations, then fell into step beside him as he hurried towards the door.

"Congratulations, Flavor King."

He was redder than the frosting ribbon on Lyra's cake, but he was also smiling. "Thanks. I didn't realize it would go *that* well."

"You need to start putting a warning label on your creations," Lyra teased. "Is Honeycomb still crying?"

Boysen glanced back over his shoulder and quickened his pace. Once they were safely out of the exam hall, he sighed. "Afraid so. I don't think it's necessarily just about my cake, though. She kept going on about my mom, and my brothers, and legacy . . ."

"*And* your cake," Lyra insisted. "You can't wriggle out of it. That cake is a work of genius. I can't wait to try it."

"Thanks," he said again. Then he stopped and pulled her aside off the stone walkway. "Seriously, thank you. I couldn't have made that cake without you."

Lyra tried to laugh. "But you did, silly. For the final entrance exam and for the first-term final."

"I couldn't have made *that* cake." Boysen took off his chef's hat and stared at the shiny new pin Professor Genoise had attached. "A Stellar Enchantment–worthy cake. That was all because of working with you this term."

"Stop it." Lyra shook her head. "You don't have to lie to make me feel better. I'll be fine. Just enjoy your win, okay?"

"It's the songs," Boysen said, his voice rising. "The songs you wrote for the color charms, and the deepening spell, and all the Texture magic. The songs you heard from each flavor. Whenever I bake, they're in my head. The whole time."

The emotional blender inside Lyra kicked into instant high gear. "You . . . you used music? In the exam?"

"No. That's not . . ." Boysen clenched his fists, apparently unaware that he was still holding his pristine chef's hat. "I didn't cheat, if that's what you mean. I still don't think using the songs *is* cheating, but whatever. I didn't use them. Not consciously. But they're just . . . there, okay? They're in my head. When I bake, I hear them. And when I hear them, I think of you. And that makes me happy, so whatever I'm baking is automatically better. That's all."

Lyra couldn't say anything. The blender was still going, but it seemed to be sucking all the sound from her mind, leaving her defenseless against Boysen's words. They echoed through her suddenly silent brain like thunder.

At the same moment, actual thunder boomed overhead, and the heavy clouds released their first drops of rain.

"The songs help, Lyra," Boysen said softly. "They helped me. So . . . thank you."

Then he ran towards the dorms, leaving her rooted to the ground in the gathering storm.

Another clap of thunder shook Lyra from her reverie. Realizing she was close to the main hall, she darted inside to get out of the rain. Her feet kept moving automatically. Before she knew it, she was back at the Presentation classroom where she had spent so much of her time this term.

Lyra drifted over to her usual workstation. Perching on the stool, she stared out at the storm through the large windows. The roiling clouds were a fitting reflection of her swirling insides. But while the thunder and rain were operating at high volume, her emotional blender was still deafeningly quiet.

She wasn't sure how long she'd been sitting there when a noise at the door made her turn. There, striding purposefully into the classroom, was Cardamom Coulis III.

"Cardamom!" she exclaimed. "Looking for me?"

He froze, then shook his head and kept moving. "No, actually. I left some of my notes here yesterday. Want to have them with me over break."

Without looking at her, he crossed to the teacher's workstation and pulled open a drawer.

"Have you heard?" she asked, watching him rifle through parchment.

"Yes. Professor Genoise just told me." Again, he paused, shook his head, and continued searching through the drawer's contents. "I don't understand it."

"Me neither," Lyra confessed. "It doesn't make any sense."

Cardamom didn't reply. He still hadn't looked at her. He pulled a stack of papers from the drawer, rolled them up, and tucked them neatly into his apron pocket. Then he closed the drawer and started for the door.

"Maybe we can figure it out when we get together over break?" Lyra called, raising her voice over the storm. "Make a plan for next term?"

Finally, he turned to look at her, one eyebrow delicately raised. "Over break?"

"F-for dinner," she stammered. "You said—"

"That was meant to be a victory celebration." His normally rich voice sounded flat and hard. "There isn't really anything to celebrate, is there?"

"I . . . No. I guess not."

"And I don't think we should continue the tutoring sessions," Cardamom went on. "This term was an experiment, of sorts. It didn't work. Best not to waste any more time on it. Especially since I have to prepare for graduation."

Lyra couldn't speak. She couldn't even nod.

He gave her a subdued version of his signature dazzling smile. "Have a good vacation, Lyra."

With that, he was gone, his clipped footsteps echoing down the empty hallway.

Lyra sat on her stool, waiting for the emotional blender in her chest to start making sounds. Surely, if ever there was an occasion for raw noise, this was it.

. . . Nothing.

The strange silence that had descended upon her insides during the exam persisted. It was oppressive. Lyra felt like she was smothering.

Her feet started moving automatically again. They carried her from the Presentation classroom, down the many flights of stairs, and out of the main hall.

The pouring rain made them break into a run. Soon, she was pushing through the front door of the dorm building and across the foyer into the first-floor common area.

"Roomie!" Ginger was coming out of Zester. She greeted Lyra with a wide grin. "I was wondering where you'd gone. I'm meeting Mac at Queen Penelope's. I think Boysen's there too. Care to join us?"

Lyra stared at her. "You're . . . fine?"

"Finer than confectioner's sugar," Ginger affirmed. "How are you? It was a rough day for the girls, all round."

"I'm . . . That's . . . How are you fine?" Lyra asked, a little desperately. "You got cut from the academy."

Ginger shrugged. "Sure, it's disappointing. I would have loved another term. But the academy and I aren't a good fit. Best to know that now."

"What about innovation?" Lyra demanded. "Isn't the academy supposed to be 'an incubator for creativity'? Aren't you mad at Professor Genoise?"

"Oh, he's all right." Ginger chuckled. "More than all right. He's a good sort. I think we finally understand each other."

Lyra just looked at her blankly.

"We had a nice talk," Ginger went on. "After the exam. He really is impressed with my potential. Said he sometimes wished the academy rules weren't so strict so we *could* have more room to explore. But tradition is a tricky thing. Sometimes you have to choose between stability and freedom. The academy chose stability a long time ago. I can understand that."

"But—"

"And he wants to keep teaching me." Ginger's smile widened. "I won't be an academy student anymore, but I can come on the weekends for private lessons. He wants to work with me on some of my new spell ideas. Maybe even get Chef Flax involved. So you don't have to miss me too much! I can probably come to Whisk Whiz Recreation on Fridays, if the group doesn't mind."

"If the group doesn't mind?" Lyra jabbed Ginger's shoulder. "You're *part* of the group. We want you here whenever you can be here." Suddenly, she threw her arms around her friend. "Sharps and flats, I'm going to miss you."

Ginger returned the hug, burying her face in Lyra's shoulder. "Same."

They stood there silently for a moment. Then Ginger stepped back, wiping her eyes.

"Salts!" she exclaimed. "I promised myself I wasn't going to be one of *those* bakers. Don't tell the boys, please? Mac has already cried enough for both of us. I'd prefer not to set him off again."

"Deal." Lyra smiled through her own tears. "I'm just . . . glad you're okay. I don't understand it, but I'm glad."

"It's just baking, after all." Ginger looked around the room where they had spent so many hours studying, and practicing, and laughing, and practicing some more. "I love it, but it's not all I love."

"It's just food," Lyra said slowly, Boysen's words from first term pealing through her mind like a magical chime calling for the end of class. "We're just making food for people to eat."

Ginger nodded. "Exactly. And I'm going to keep doing it, here and home and everywhere I can." She took off her apron, rolled it up, and tossed it into a corner. "But for now, I'm going to do the eating bit. Mac has made a gorgeous tray of goodies to share with Queen Penelope, to celebrate end of term. You coming?"

Lyra heard something rising up at the back of her mind. It started softly, then got louder at a gentle pace, gradually pushing back the day's heavy silence.

It was a sound. A sweet sound, unassuming and steady and with just a pinch of the unexpected and new.

If she listened carefully, it almost sounded like the beginning of a song.

"Absolutely, I'm coming." Lyra smiled. "But not just to eat. Let me get my guitar. I think Queen Penelope would enjoy a concert."

CHAPTER FORTY-SIX

Serious About Joy

Thank you all for coming. We're so glad you could join us for another *Berry* wonderful evening, halfway through your vacation. And now, I would like to propose a toast." Mr. Berry stood from his seat at the head of the table. Drawing himself up to his tall, lanky height, he raised a glass of sparkling cider. "To the Whisk Whizzes!"

Mrs. Berry, Boysen, Lyra, Mac, and Ginger followed suit. "To the Whisk Whizzes!"

"The brave three who are left," Ginger added after everyone had taken a large sip of cider and sat down. "That makes sense. The baking world is pretty fixated on the number three."

Lyra elbowed her in the side. "There are four of us left. You're still a Whiz, even if you're not there for every review."

"She's right, Crumble," Boysen said, passing a basket of rolls to Mac. "The Whizzes are a lifetime membership. No getting out of it, I'm afraid."

"That means there are *five* Whizzes left." Mac stared at the roll in his hand, eyes faraway behind his glasses. "Technically, Caramelle is still a Whiz."

Ginger snorted. "Technically, Caramelle is still insufferable."

"I'm worried about her," Mac insisted.

Boysen put a hand on his roommate's shoulder. "So are we, Macaron. Honest. Even Crumble is, deep down."

He glanced at Ginger, and she shrugged. "Sure. The Meringue looked rough at the exam."

"We all had a rough day." Lyra sighed. Then she smiled at Mr. and Mrs. Berry. "Except Boysen, of course. You must be very proud of him."

Mrs. Berry returned her smile warmly. "We are. We're proud of all of you, in fact."

"That's right." Mr. Berry's voice was softer than his wife's, but it still managed to fill the room. Lyra thought it was the sort of voice that would always make everyone stop and listen. "Second term is a difficult time. I didn't make it."

Boysen grinned. "You didn't need to, Dad. You'd already gotten all you wanted out of the academy, right?"

Mr. Berry placed a hand over his wife's. "Sure did."

"Me too!" Ginger said cheerfully. "Well, not the same. No eternal, undying love or anything like that. But I do feel like I got everything the academy could give me."

"Including a tutor, apparently!" Mrs. Berry gave Ginger a silent round of applause. "I've never heard of Professor Genoise taking extra students. That's as impressive as a Stellar Enchantment Pin. Maybe even more so."

"Thanks, Mom," Boysen said dryly.

Mrs. Berry swatted her napkin in her son's direction. "You know what I mean."

"The Whisk Whizzes are certainly on a roll so far this year," Mr. Berry said, passing a large bowl of roasted potatoes to Boysen. "What are all of you looking forward to about third term? Any personal goals?"

"The goals were basically set for us," Boysen replied, "after the second-term exam. The professors gave each of us 'lessons' to ponder over break." After helping himself to potatoes, he tried to pass the bowl to his roommate. "Right, Mac?"

Mac didn't answer. He was staring at the pile of brussels sprouts on his plate as if wondering how they got there.

Boysen ladled some roasted potatoes onto Mac's plate, banging the spoon around the bowl as he did so. "I said, '*Right, Mac?*'"

Mac jumped. "What? Yes. I'm sorry. What?"

Lyra laughed. "We're talking about the lessons we're all supposed to be learning over break. What did the professors say about you, Mac?"

"Oh . . ." Mac thought for a moment, then smiled. "They said I was a little . . . distracted."

"Imagine that." Boysen stretched his long arms across the table, handing the bowl of potatoes to Lyra. "What about you, Treble?"

Lyra focused on adding potatoes to the careful arrangement of brussels sprouts and sausages already on her plate. "I'm not sure. I mean, I remember what they said, but I don't know what to do about it."

"You just have to recover your joy." Ginger poured gravy all over her plate, then helpfully did the same to Lyra's. "Simple."

"Simple?" Lyra repeated.

"Sure. Just stop worrying about doing everything so right all the time." Setting the gravy bowl down firmly, Ginger grinned. "Stop being like Caramelle, basically."

"Not helping," Boysen observed.

"Boysen told us about your exam," Mr. Berry said gently. "A 'too right' cake . . . I can see how that kind of feedback would be confusing."

Mrs. Berry patted Lyra's hand. "Maybe you were just tired, my dear. You'll have the spice back in your step after break."

"I'm not sure," Lyra said again. She fiddled with her knife and fork, half-heartedly digging through the gravy to assemble a bite of sausage and potato. "I really thought I was making progress. Becoming a serious baker."

Ginger poked her finger into Lyra's shoulder. "See? That. *That.* A 'serious' baker? What does that even mean?"

"Someone other bakers will take seriously," Lyra shot back.

"But that will look different from baker to baker," Mr. Berry said calmly.

Ginger nodded. "Exactly. Think about the professors. They're all 'serious' bakers. They respect each other. But they all have very different styles."

"'Style' is a key word," Boysen agreed. "What term did Professor Genoise give your style, Treble?"

"Joyful," Mac supplied. His eyes still looked faraway behind his glasses, but Lyra suspected that had more to do with Mrs. Berry's exquisite gravy than with any absent auburn-haired perfectionists. "Lyra's style is joyful."

"So that's what you should focus on." Boysen pointed his fork dramatically across the table, like he was pronouncing sentence on Lyra's gravy-soaked plate. "You, Lyra Treble, need to get serious about *joy.*"

"But how?" Lyra asked, unable to keep a pinch of desperation out of her voice. "How do I bake joyfully? How am I supposed to learn how to do that on top of all the other things we're expected to learn?"

"I know the academy can be a bit of a pressure cooker," Mrs. Berry said sympathetically. "Not the most conducive environment for joy. But I don't think you need to worry about learning this. You already know it. You just need to remember it."

"You said Professor Genoise assigned you that style term, yes?" Mr. Berry broke in. "He called your baking joyful?"

Lyra nodded.

"Then you were already baking joyfully when you came into the academy." Mr. Berry held up his well-buttered roll as if flourishing a magic silver baking spoon. "So focus on that. Try to remember what baking was like before you got in."

"But I can't do that," Lyra protested. "I can't bake like I did before I got into the academy."

Mr. Berry chuckled around a bite of bread. "Whyever not?"

Lyra could feel Boysen's eyes on her from across the table. She put down her knife and fork, took a deep breath, and summoned her courage.

"Before the academy . . . I sang."

"Of course you did, dear." Mrs. Berry beamed. "You're from a family of bards."

"No. I mean, yes, but . . ." Lyra glanced at Boysen. He gave her the tiniest nod, and she went on, "I mean, I sang while baking. I made up tunes for all the spells, and I sang them. Out loud."

Mr. and Mrs. Berry just looked at her expectantly.

Lyra struggled to clarify. "I didn't just make up songs to help me learn the spells. I *sang the spells.* While I performed them. That's how I used baking magic."

She waited. Mr. and Mrs. Berry glanced at each other, shrugged, and looked back at her.

"So I can't just go back to baking like I did before the academy," she explained. "I can't sing the spells. That's not allowed."

"Whyever not?" Mr. Berry repeated while his wife sharply inquired, "Who said?"

Lyra looked back and forth between them. "Professor Puff said so. She didn't even want me to *think* the songs while using the spells."

Mr. and Mrs. Berry sighed simultaneously.

"Oh, Praline Puff." Mrs. Berry shook her head fondly. "If ever there was a born Texturist . . ."

"That's just it," Mr. Berry said. Suddenly noticing the half-eaten roll in his hand, he stuffed it in his mouth and somehow managed to speak around it coherently. "Texture is all about rules. Praline Puff let those rules sink way too deep into her soul."

Mrs. Berry placed a hand over his mouth. "Don't talk while eating, dearest. You're setting a bad example for the children."

"We're not children," Boysen said automatically.

Mrs. Berry shot him a warning look even more effective than the napkin swatting she'd employed earlier. Then she smiled at Lyra.

"We shouldn't be too hard on Praline. Texture is the trickiest baking principle, in my opinion. It absolutely depends upon structure. When your work requires that much rigidity, you can't be blamed for a little extra strictness in your instruction."

Lyra's heart was beating strangely fast. That song she had started to hear when she spoke to Ginger on the day of the second-term final was spinning into life again and growing in volume by the second.

"So . . . you're saying it's okay? To sing the spells?"

"Definitely okay," Mrs. Berry confirmed cheerfully. "And definitely worth a try."

Mr. Berry swallowed noisily, prompting Mrs. Berry to remove her hand from his mouth. He gave Lyra a grin that reminded her forcibly of both Boysen and Razz.

"We were saying earlier that every baker has different styles. Praline Puff may not like the idea of a student trying something outside her box of rules, but I think I can say confidently that the other two professors will. They'd at least be open to it."

"Really?" Lyra realized her hands were shaking and moved them under the table, clenching them tightly together. "Even Professor Genoise?"

"What have I been telling you?" Ginger had been focusing on her plateful of food, but she paused with a laden fork halfway to her mouth long enough to glare at Lyra. "Professor Genoise is very open to experimentation."

"Not within the academy curriculum," Lyra countered. "That's what he told you, right? Stability over freedom?"

"There's nothing unstable about your songs." Boysen picked up his roll as if to throw it at Lyra, then caught his mother's eye and began buttering it instead. "You're not writing new spells or trying to rewrite old ones like Crumble here. You're just finding a new way to do the spells that already exist."

"A *joyful* way," Mac added. He looked at her, his gaze suddenly sharp and focused. "I miss your songs, Lyra. They helped me learn and all, but really, I just felt happy whenever I thought of them. They even made Texture fun."

Boysen raised his butter knife into the air, waving it around like a torch, and shouted, "Fun!"

"And that was just when we were thinking about them or using them as learning tools," Mac went on, ignoring his roommate's victory dance. "I can only imagine what a difference it would make to *sing* them."

Lyra gazed around the table. She saw nothing but eager smiling faces staring back at her.

"Maybe . . ." She forced her hands to unclench and picked up her knife and fork, determined not to let any of this delicious meal go to waste. "I'll check with the other professors when we get back. Just to be sure if it's okay that I . . . sing in class."

The cheer that went up sent her internal song into a double-time round.

The music was still playing in her head when she left the Berry household later that evening. It provided a fitting soundtrack as she danced all the way home, reaching another crescendo when she burst through the front door of the Treble brownstone. She skipped up the stairs and knocked on her younger brother's door.

"Rondo!" she called. "Grab your mandolin and your lucky songwriting pen. I've got some melodies to workshop with you!"

A week later, Lyra returned to Zester. The room seemed awfully big without Ginger there, but Lyra tried to keep her spirits up as she unpacked from vacation. She would see her old roommate soon. Ginger planned to visit every weekend.

Besides, it was hard to feel gloomy about class starting the next day. Lyra had spent the second half of break going over all her baking-magic songs with the

Trebles, expanding and enhancing the rough melodies she had thrown together on her own. Her entire family had contributed something. Most of the credit went to Rondo, the budding songwriting prodigy, but every member of the Any Weather Bards was represented somewhere.

And working on the songs with them hadn't just enriched the music. For the first time, Lyra felt like her family understood what she was trying to do. The melodies had given the Trebles an entry point into Lyra's new baking world. They had always been behind her, all the way, but now they were *with* her. She could feel their support carrying her into this final, crucial term.

Humming the new tune Rondo had invented for Madame Brioche's Proofing Chant, Lyra twirled into the bathroom to arrange her towels in preparation for the next morning.

Then a truly horrendous *BANG* sounded from beyond Pestle's closed door, followed by a high, trembling wail.

CHAPTER FORTY-SEVEN

THE SWEETEST SONG

Lyra was through the door and into her old room in an instant, but she froze at the sight that awaited her.

"Caramelle?"

The auburn-haired girl was standing in the kitchen. Cream, egg, and flour were splattered all over the walls. Purple sparks smoldered over every available surface: the telltale signs of a Presentation spell gone horribly wrong.

Lyra's eyes, though, were fixed on Caramelle's hands.

They were three sizes too large. Their consistency had also undergone some kind of transformation. Each finger looked shiny, airy, and fragile. Rather like over-whipped meringue.

Caramelle stared at Lyra, eyes wide as she held up her bizarre new appendages.

"I . . . I messed up." Her voice was still stuck in that high, wailing register, as if it had also been whipped to an unnatural degree. "Oh, Lyra . . . Will you help me?"

Some instinct deep within Lyra took over. Crossing the room, she wrapped one arm gently around Caramelle's shoulders and guided her out of the kitchen. Only once they were both settled on the couch and a fire was blazing in the magical fire pit did Lyra speak.

"What happened?"

Caramelle gazed at the fire without seeing it. "I-I was trying to get in some extra practice. To be ready for third term. That . . . that *stupid* spell . . ."

"Which one?" Lyra glanced over at the harsh purple light still shimmering over the kitchen like a demented heat wave. "One of those Madame Dacquoise terrors?"

"No." Caramelle's too-large fingers trembled, as if trying to clench into fists. "Master Glaze."

"Master Glaze?" Lyra echoed. "The shine spell?"

Caramelle nodded, her jaw rigid with the strain of pressing her lips together.

"But . . . but you know that one," Lyra said. "You mastered the advanced level ages ago."

"Not enough," Caramelle said savagely. "Not enough to do well in the exam. Not enough for 'virtuosic excellence.'"

"Caramelle—"

"'A tale of setting impossible goals,'" Caramelle went on, her voice rising shrilly as she quoted Professor Genoise, "'exhausting oneself trying to reach them, and the devouring fear of falling short.'"

Lyra waited until the last shuddering echoes of those words had sunk back into her former roommate's shaking shoulders. Then, as quietly as possible, she asked, "How many times? Did you recite it, I mean?"

Caramelle's shoulders went still, then shrugged. "I don't know. I lost count."

"Oh, Caramelle . . ."

"I couldn't get it right!" the other girl shrieked, her flour-streaked auburn curls falling around her face. "It wasn't right. I have to keep doing it until it's right!"

"But Presentation spells are volatile. Unpredictable. You should never—"

"I know." Caramelle shook her head, forcing herself back into a desperate sort of calm. "Believe me, I know. I still had to try."

Lyra resisted the urge to poke the shiny meringue-esque fingers lying limp in Caramelle's lap. "Did you, though? Really?"

"Yes. But that doesn't matter now. What matters is *this*." Caramelle lifted her hands and presented them to Lyra. "Can you help?"

Lyra suddenly had to bite back a laugh. It wasn't like Caramelle was in any real danger, after all. Presentation spells were tricky, but they could always be reversed. And the large shiny hands *were* ridiculous enough to be comical. They reminded Lyra forcibly of the circus clowns who sometimes partnered with Thespy's theater troupe.

But there was nothing comical about the terror in Caramelle's eyes.

Averting her gaze from the humorous appendages, Lyra tried to sound confident. "Of course I can help. Do you know how to reverse it?"

"I think so. It's a pretty high-level Presentation spell. But there are some complicated hand gestures, and . . ." Caramelle shook her over-whipped fingers. "I can't manage that."

"Right." Lyra squeezed the other girl's shoulder. "A high-level Presentation spell . . . You need Professor Genoise, then. Come on. I'll go with you."

She started to stand them both up, but Caramelle pulled away and recoiled into a corner of the couch.

"I can't go to Professor Genoise!" she hissed. "They'll send me home!"

Lyra raised her eyebrows. "You think they'd punish you for something like this?"

"They wouldn't call it punishment. 'For my own good.' They warned me not to strain myself."

"Maybe some time at home would be good for you," Lyra said slowly. "I mean, just a few days, so you can head into third term strong, and—"

"Absolutely not. My parents . . ." Caramelle shuddered, curling into herself further. "It was bad enough not winning the second-term Stellar Enchantment Pin. If I get sent home before third term even starts . . . I might not have a home to go back to."

Lyra didn't know what to say. She just sat down on the couch and placed her hand on Caramelle's. The other girl's shiny fingers even *felt* remarkably like meringues, but Lyra no longer had any desire to laugh.

"No professors, then," she promised. "What about Cardamom?"

Caramelle shook her head firmly. "I don't want him to see me like this. And he'd just tell Professor Genoise anyway." Her eyes searched Lyra's face. "Could you do it?"

"The reversal spell?" Lyra raised her eyebrows. "I'm nowhere near that level in Presentation. I'd just make everything worse."

"But you could ask Cardamom to teach you," Caramelle said bitterly. "You could go see him right now. I'm sure he'd be thrilled. Isn't Sunday your date night?"

Lyra dropped her eyes. "Not anymore."

A few moments of silence followed. Lyra had been so pleasantly focused on baking-magic songs over the past week that she'd managed to avoid thinking about the third-year Presentation Apprentice Baker. Now, though, the sting of their last conversation returned with a prickly vengeance.

To Lyra's surprise, Caramelle didn't pry. She just waited silently until Lyra was able to continue.

Eventually, Lyra took a deep breath. "No more date nights. They were never really that, anyway. And no more tutoring sessions. He was . . . really disappointed when I didn't win the Stellar Enchantment Pin. Like I wasted his time, I guess."

"Salts, Lyra."

Lyra had been staring at the fire, but the softness in Caramelle's voice drew her attention back to the other girl.

"It's okay," Lyra assured her. "I mean, it's not, but it will be. I just can't go ask him to teach me some high-level Presentation spell right now. I don't think he'd be happy to see me at all."

Caramelle's eyes narrowed. Somehow, though, Lyra could tell the simmering fury there was not directed at her.

"What . . . a . . . *cad*," Caramelle muttered, her eyes narrowing even further. "What a stodgy, overcooked custard."

Lyra smiled in spite of herself. "Do you mean Cardamom?"

"Of course." Caramelle shook her disheveled auburn curls briskly. "He's a flashy, spoiled lump of overspun sugar. Who needs him? Certainly not us."

"That's right," Lyra agreed, suddenly struck by inspiration. "We don't need him or Professor Genoise. There's a budding Presentation expert right here on this floor. One with a truly 'majestic' flair." Rising again, she held out her hand to Caramelle. "Let's go see Mac."

Caramelle still didn't move. "I-I've been pretty horrid to him," she said, a tremble returning to her voice. "To all of you, really. Are you sure he'd want to help?"

Lyra smiled. "I am absolutely sure that Macaron Fondant would do absolutely anything for you."

"Why?" Caramelle covered her face with her large shiny fingers. "Why should any of you care about me anymore?"

"Love's a mystery." Lyra sighed. "Both the friend kind and . . . the other kind. Don't try to understand it. Just accept. We love you, may the salts preserve us all. And we're going to help you."

Taking both Caramelle's giant hands in her own, Lyra carefully pulled them away from the other girl's face and then used them to pull her off the couch.

"Ready to get back to normal?"

Caramelle gave her a watery smile, then looked down at her own hands with distaste. "Yes, *please.*"

As Lyra had suspected, Mac's eagerness to help Caramelle was matched only by his concern. He insisted on first making her as comfortable as possible. Once she was settled on the couch in Whisk, he proceeded to bustle around, arranging pillows and increasing the magical firelight and fetching hot chocolate like a bespectacled mother hen.

"I'm glad I did all that research over the break," he said, plumping one more cushion and placing it gingerly under Caramelle's monstrous fingers. "Professor Genoise loaned me a book on counterspells. He said my 'distraction' issue is especially dangerous in Presentation, and he wanted me to be prepared. Just in case."

He darted over to the half-unpacked bag lying on his bed and pulled out a large leatherbound book. Returning to the couch with it, he sat beside Caramelle and began flipping through the pages.

"Master Glaze's Shine Spell, you said?" Mac asked.

Caramelle nodded.

"And you don't remember how many times you recited it?"

"Afraid not. I did it so many times over break too. It's all a blur." She smiled shakily. "Maybe I should have been researching counterspells, like you. Would have been a much better use of my time."

"You practiced that spell all through break?" Boysen asked incredulously. He shook his head as he handed Lyra a mug of hot chocolate. "I can't imagine that. Master Glaze is a bit much for me, even in small doses."

"It wasn't my choice." Caramelle sighed. "Well . . . No, that's not true. I probably would have been practicing anyway, even without my parents."

Boysen's voice rose higher. "Your parents *made* you practice this spell?"

"Not just this spell. My whole exam cake. Over and over, every day." Caramelle stared down at her over-whipped hands. "Not winning the pin meant something must be very wrong. They wanted to be sure I fixed it before third term."

"Sweet and savory," Boysen muttered.

Caramelle shrugged. "Like I said, I probably would have been doing it anyway. I wasn't satisfied with that exam either. I wanted to get it right."

"But the professors told you how to get it right," Lyra pointed out. "They said you were working yourself too hard. You needed to *relax*."

Caramelle's laugh was brittle. "That word does not exist in my family's vocabulary. Sometimes . . ." She sighed again, her voice sinking to a low whisper. "Sometimes I wish I weren't a Meringue."

"I can understand that," Lyra said sympathetically. Catching Boysen's eye, she remembered one of their conversations from first term. "What would you want to do instead? If you didn't have to be a baker?"

"Oh, I'd still want to be a baker," Caramelle replied. "No matter who my family was. I love baking. At least . . . I used to."

"You still do," Boysen assured her. "No one who has seen you work or tasted your creations could think otherwise. You just . . . got a little distracted." Grinning, he clapped Mac on the shoulder. "Like Fondant here."

"I've got it!" Mac exclaimed, oblivious to the hand on his shoulder. He spread the book flat on his lap and held out his hands over Caramelle's. "Okay, nobody talk. I need to concentrate."

He took a deep breath, then began waving his hands in a slow, intricate pattern.

Lyra hardly dared to breathe. Boysen, too, was absolutely still beside her. Even the fire seemed to be watching Mac perform the counterspell.

Mac's pace never wavered. His hands moved with deliberate confidence, clearly an outward expression of the words being recited silently in his mind.

Seconds crawled by. Then minutes. Finally, just when Lyra was being to wonder if they would have to get Professor Genoise after all, a shimmer of faint purple light appeared around Mac's fingertips. It shone there for a few more seconds, the color faint but unmistakable.

Mac didn't stop. Lyra wasn't even sure he had blinked since beginning the spell.

Slowly, moving at the same measured tempo as Mac's hands, the shimmer began to spread. It drifted down from his hands towards Caramelle's and set-tled on her shiny fingers like violet snow. Lyra expected the light to sink *into* Caramelle's hands, but it just hovered over her skin, shimmering and glowing.

Caramelle gasped. The shimmer over her hands was deepening in color, as if leeching purple from beneath her skin. And as the light covering her fingers became more vivid, the fingers themselves began to shrink, slowly but surely returning to their usual size.

Still Mac didn't stop. Lyra and Boysen didn't breathe. The only sound in the room was the crackling of the magical fire as the counterspell's glow brightened over Caramelle's hands.

Only when the light was so purple that Lyra couldn't see Caramelle's fingers through it anymore did Mac's hands pause in midair. He waited. His lips moved as if counting. Lyra found herself counting as the seconds ticked on.

One . . . two . . . three . . .

When she hit twelve, the sphere of purple light vanished, popping out of existence without a sound or even a flash.

Mac looked down at Caramelle's perfectly normal fingers. "Was . . . Is that okay?"

Caramelle's gaze drifted up from her hands to his face. She stared at him for a moment.

Then she threw her arms around him.

"Okay?" she echoed, laughing through her tears. "That was *brilliant!*"

Boysen let them have their moment. Then he pulled them both up and joined the hug, bringing Lyra in with one long arm.

"You bet it was brilliant!" he crowed. "Congratulations, everyone. This is going down in the Whisk Whiz history books. Three cheers for Macaron Fondant!"

They unleashed a cacophony of noise that was equal parts joy and relief. Even Caramelle joined in, hooting and squealing with distinctly un-Meringue-ish abandon. The cheering went on and on for several minutes, raucous and undignified and horribly out of tune.

It was the sweetest song Lyra had ever heard.

CHAPTER FORTY-EIGHT

SWEET AND SAVORY

Bolstered by her fellow Whizzes, Lyra brought the baking music issue up in their very first class on Monday morning after break, with all three professors present. She simply told them about her songs and requested permission to use them in class over the coming term.

Professor Honeycomb, as predicted, took no convincing. Before Lyra had even finished her explanation, the Flavor headmistress's gray curls were bobbing up and down as she nodded in fervent agreement.

"I still have dreams about that first cake you made for your final entrance exam." Professor Honeycomb sighed. "Anything that can help you create something like that is fine by me."

Professor Genoise was open to the idea, though he did request a demonstration before giving his final answer. Thankfully, the Whizzes had predicted this too, so Lyra had come prepared.

At a wink and a nod from Boysen, she produced one of the many frosted sugar cookies they had all made together in Whisk the night before.

"This is just plain white frosting, as you can see." She held the cookie up in front of the professors. "Now let's make it green."

In honor of Ginger, she thought.

Then Lyra took a deep breath and sang Master Brûlée's Coloring Charm for green.

This was a tune she had worked on extensively with her family over the break. In fact, the coloring charms as a whole were her brother Canto's favorite of all Lyra's baking songs.

"It's not just the colors," he had told her at dinner on the last day of her vacation. "I can tell you were thinking about *people.* Each song really is a distinct personality. I want to spend time with your friends. They literally sound incredible."

Smiling at the memory, Lyra completed the tune's final run, which included a surprise key change at the end for extra Crumble-flair. Then she handed the newly colorful cookie to Professor Genoise for inspection.

He stared at the vivid green frosting in open-mouthed wonder. It took him a few seconds to remember he was holding his monocle and a full minute of peering at the cookie through the monocle to gather his thoughts.

Finally, he raised his eyes to Lyra.

"And . . . you wrote songs for *all* the coloring charms?" he asked.

She nodded cheerfully. "All the main ones. I made a start on some of the more complicated shades over break. The pink and red varieties are done, and I'm making headway in the blue-green family. Orange is next."

Professor Genoise nodded weakly. He handed the cookie back to Lyra with a care that bordered on reverence.

"Consider me both impressed and intrigued, Aspiring Baker Treble. I look forward to witnessing the impact of your . . . explorations in the term ahead."

Lyra gave him a bow of thanks. Then, with another deep breath, she turned to Professor Puff. The Texture headmistress was already gazing at Lyra, her gray eyes kind but inscrutable.

"I have been impressed with your growth in my class this year, Aspiring Baker Treble," the professor said quietly. "But I do confess I noticed something . . . missing in the second term. Your exam cake, as we have already discussed at length, left much to be desired. Am I to understand that it was your effort to omit music from your baking that led to this deficiency?"

"I think so, Professor," Lyra replied.

Professor Puff held her gaze another few moments, then gave the tiniest perceptible nod.

"Very well. I permit you to employ any songs you have written for Texture spells in my classroom—"

"Hurrah!" Boysen called.

Professor Puff held up a hand, then continued, "On a trial basis only. This is quite a leap for the academy, rather like the inclusion of a new spell in our curriculum. I deem it unwise to proceed further without proper testing. I believe my colleagues would agree?"

The Flavor and Presentation professors nodded meekly.

"Apologies, Praline." Professor Honeycomb looked rather sheepish. "I got a little carried away."

"As did I," Professor Genoise said gravely. Then he clapped both his colleagues on the shoulder. "But that is why there are three of us! Constant balance, and all that. Even when two of us lose our way in a recipe, we have a third to bring us back in line."

Lyra looked from him to Professor Honeycomb to Professor Puff. "So . . . is that a no? Or a yes?"

"A yes for now," Professor Puff assured her. "We all need the chance to observe this new technique in action and chart its effects for analysis." She raised her eyebrows at the other two professors. "Shall we say three weeks?"

"Just right," Professor Genoise agreed.

Professor Honeycomb beamed. "Perfect. Really gives time for the flavors to simmer!"

Professor Puff bowed to them, then turned back to Lyra.

"We are entering into a three-week trial period, Aspiring Baker Treble, starting now. At the end of those three weeks, we will evaluate our results and issue a final decision. You may sing the spells in any of our classes over the next three weeks, so long as it does not become a distraction or hindrance to the other students."

"No worries there!" Boysen called out cheerfully. "The songs are a help to all of us."

Professor Puff silenced him with a look before turning back to Lyra. "Understood, Aspiring Baker Treble?"

That same chorus of delight that had started at the Berry household was rising in Lyra's mind again. She tried to keep the melody from spilling over into her voice, but it still sounded a bit like singing as she said, "Absolutely, Professor. And thank you."

The song just kept rising. It carried Lyra back to her seat, enhanced by an encouraging smile from Caramelle. It sustained her through the rest of that morning's "tribunal," then through to the first full class of third term: Flavor.

Professor Honeycomb was so excited, she couldn't keep still. She bounced lightly on her toes as she addressed the class.

"I was already looking forward to this term. Not only will we deepen our knowledge of existing spells, but we have some significant new magic to acquaint ourselves with. And now, with Treble's music to look forward to . . ." She clapped her hands, her blue eyes sparkling with undiluted joy. "Oh, it's going to be a wonderful term!"

Lyra just smiled quietly. The chorus of delight had faded into the background, but it was still there, ready to serve as baking-magic music inspiration at the first available opportunity.

"Wonderful, and just plain *full*," Professor Honeycomb went on. "There's not a moment to lose. Today—the next few weeks, rather—we are focusing on one particular spell. The oldest spell in the Flavor discipline, and quite possibly in all of baking. Anyone know which spell that is or care to guess?"

Caramelle and Boysen answered at the same time. "The Sweet and Savory Spell."

"Correct!" Professor Honeycomb clapped again. "What can you tell me about this historic piece of magic?"

Caramelle opened her mouth, then caught Boysen's eye and closed it.

"Go on, Meringue," he said amiably. "You'll say it better."

Caramelle gave him a grateful smile. Drawing herself up to her full Meringue posture, she folded her hands primly in her lap and spoke as if reading from a textbook.

"The Sweet and Savory Spell is supremely foundational to baking, particularly in the discipline of Flavor. It is foundational not only in terms of subject matter, but in age. This spell is so old that we do not know who created it. That is why it is not labeled with its inventor's name, as is the practice for all other baking charms. It is known only as 'The Sweet and Savory Spell.'"

"Sweet and Savory?" Lyra repeated. "I thought that was just a phrase you use in the baking world. Like how my family says 'sharps and flats.'"

Professor Honeycomb chuckled. "That's how popular this spell is. Not only can no one remember who invented it, but it's also passed into our vernacular as an idiom in its own right. Do go on, Aspiring Baker Meringue. What does this spell do?"

"There are two primary use cases," Caramelle said. "When the spell was first created, we believe it was used quite directly to make something *more* sweet or *more* savory. Bakers had no other way to deepen flavors. The Sweet and Savory Spell paved the way for Madame Hazelnut's work."

"Exactly!" Professor Honeycomb smiled broadly at Caramelle. "Madame Hazelnut was the first to differentiate amongst all the various flavors. Before her time, bakers focused only on sweet versus savory. You're on a roll, Meringue. Care to tell us about the other use case?"

Caramelle looked happier than Lyra had ever seen her in Flavor class. Thinking back to the events of the night before, Lyra felt her own heart glowing.

Professor Honeycomb may not know it, she thought, watching Caramelle bask in the glow of the Flavor master's approval, *but Caramelle needs this. It's just the pinch of confidence that will help her get back on track for this term.*

"Certainly, Professor," Caramelle was saying. "Once Madame Hazelnut's Deepening Spell came along, bakers didn't have to depend on The Sweet and Savory Spell to impact flavors so directly. That was when the second use case began to take over. Bakers began implementing the spell as a balancing agent: to bring out a hint of sweetness in savory dishes, or to add savory complexity to meals that would otherwise be too sweet."

"My mom uses it in Bolognese sauce," Boysen offered. "She says it counteracts the tomato's acidity without having to add sugar."

Professor Honeycomb nodded. "Yes, that is an excellent use of the spell. All tomato-based dishes, actually, can benefit. Thank you, Aspiring Baker Meringue!"

The professor led the class in a round of applause for Caramelle. Then her gaze swept over the first years, suddenly shrewd. "Now, I imagine some of you are wondering why I waited until the end of the year to teach such a foundational spell. Yes?"

Lyra didn't have to glance at Caramelle to know the auburn-haired girl was nodding discreetly.

"Some may call it a matter of preference," the professor said. "But every Flavor master I've spoken to agrees with me. The Sweet and Savory Spell is the most difficult in the Flavor catalogue."

"Really?" Mac was so taken aback, he forgot his usual conscientious habit of raising his hand. "More difficult than the Soufflé Sisters?"

"Much." Professor Honeycomb turned to Boysen. "What did your parents tell you about this spell, Aspiring Baker Berry?"

Boysen grinned. "They agree with you. It's such an old spell that it's . . . rough. More dependent on the baker's will and concentration. *Very* easy to mess up."

"Indeed." Returning to her workstation, Professor Honeycomb pulled a bowl of dough from the fridge and set it on the counter. "This spell does not distinguish amongst the varying levels of Flavor. That is up to the baker. Our magical baking ancestors must have had highly developed instincts. Most Flavor experts find it necessary to train their own instincts first before applying them to this spell. This has been the guiding principle of our curriculum over the past two terms."

The professor waved her hand, and a piece of chalk rose into the air behind her. As she spoke, it moved rapidly across the chalkboard, writing the topics of conversation in her cheerful, flowing script.

"First term, we cover Flavor Identification Training. You learn to recognize each flavor on its own, without depending on any magical assistance. Second term, we move on to Madame Hazelnut's Deepening Spell. This trains you to amplify all the various flavors and hones your instincts to work with them magically. As you can all attest, each flavor responds to magic a little differently."

All four first years nodded ruefully.

"And now, with that solid foundation of instinct and deepening magic to sustain us, we can venture into this storied spell: Sweet and Savory."

The chalk wrote both these words on the chalkboard, underlining each with a flourishing twirl.

"Gather round, Aspiring Bakers." Professor Honeycomb beckoned to them, and they rose from their seats, moving towards the front of the room. "Let us travel together into the past and see what this particular piece of magic means for our future."

CHAPTER FORTY-NINE

The Song of Caramel (and Gravy)

Professor Honeycomb's blue eyes sparkled with enthusiasm as the first years assembled around her workstation.

"First, apply your instincts to this bit of dough. What flavors do you detect?" she asked.

The four students held out their hands over the bowl and closed their eyes.

"Plain?" Mac ventured.

Lyra and Caramelle nodded in agreement. Then, as one, the three of them turned to Boysen.

"Butter," he mused, half to himself. "Unsalted butter, room temperature. Fast-acting yeast. Mostly whole-wheat flour, with a small blend of oats and barley. And just a pinch of salt."

He flushed as his classmates applauded, but he managed a good-natured bow.

"Top marks, Berry. Yes." Professor Honeycomb joined the applause, then lifted her hands for quiet. "As a reward, you can be the first to try the spell. Let's add a touch of sweetness, shall we?"

"Wait a second." Lyra raised her hand. "What are the words of the spell?"

Professor Honeycomb pointed dramatically to the board. The chalk rose into the air again and drew a large circle around each of the underlined words.

Lyra looked from her to the board and back again. "That's . . . that's it?"

"That's it," Professor Honeycomb confirmed. "If you want to make something sweet, the word is 'sweet.' If you want to deepen the savoriness, the word is 'savory.'"

"How many times?" Lyra asked. "Pace? Volume?"

Professor Honeycomb shrugged. "That's where the instincts kick in. Every recipe is a wee bit different. The baker has to judge in the moment."

"I was never brave enough to try it." Caramelle sighed. "Too many factors outside my control. Give me a complicated Texture equation any day."

Lyra found herself privately agreeing with Caramelle, not that she had the heart to tell Professor Honeycomb.

"Piffle!" the Flavor professor said cheerily. "Have a little faith in yourself, Meringue. Berry, show us how it's done."

Boysen shook out his hands before placing them over the dough. "What level of sweetness, Professor?"

"Let's aim for a quarter cup of sugar," Professor Honeycomb said.

Boysen nodded and closed his eyes.

Lyra was staring at his hands, waiting for the green light of Flavor magic to emerge from his fingertips. Then a flicker from the bowl caught her eye, and she gasped.

The dough itself had turned green.

The change lasted only a few seconds, but it was unmistakable. Bright Flavor magic had erupted from within the dough. For a moment, Lyra was gazing at a lump of pale green light that sparkled like a peridot gem. Then the color faded, leaving ordinary dough in its place.

Boysen staggered backwards. Catching himself on the counter, he opened his eyes and let out a rueful chuckle.

"Salts! That packs a punch, doesn't it?" he said.

"It does, when done correctly." Professor Honeycomb beamed at him. "Let's test it, shall we?"

She held out her own hands over the bowl, and the first years joined her.

"Well?" she prompted after a few seconds. "What do your instincts say?"

Mac's eyes were wide behind his glasses. "That's . . . sweet. *Very* sweet."

"Almost too sweet." Lyra drew her hand back with a shudder. "Cloying, even."

"Salts," Boysen said again, his face twisted in disgust. "I thought I was being careful."

"You were," Professor Honeycomb assured him. "It's easy to overshoot, especially at the beginning. An admirable first attempt!"

Boysen shook his head. "If you say so."

"I do." Professor Honeycomb's voice grew stern. "Don't make me tell you the tales of when I first tried this spell. I don't think Professor Saffron ever recovered her taste for custard. Aspiring Baker Treble, care to give it a try?"

Lyra swallowed hard. "Sure, Professor."

She stretched out her hand, but Professor Honeycomb grabbed it with a radiant smile.

"I think this is a perfect opportunity to test out some baking music, don't you? A little singing might smooth our way over this initial hurdle."

"S-sure," Lyra stammered. "If you think it will help, I—"

"It will," Boysen said firmly. "Please, Treble."

Mac and Caramelle nodded vigorously, their eyes filled with silent pleading as they gazed at Lyra.

"Okay." Lyra took a deep breath. "Okay. It's just those two words, right?"

"One," Professor Honeycomb corrected. "Whichever direction you're trying to nudge the flavor."

"Okay," Lyra repeated. She looked at Boysen. "So, you just . . . *thought* that one word? 'Sweet'?"

"That's right," he replied. "It's like the Soufflé Sisters. You have to feel for the flavor you're going for, and then you have to *mean* it."

Lyra nodded. "And we're going for savory . . . What's the most savory flavor you can think of? What comes to mind when you think 'savory'?"

"Chef Flax's mushroom gravy," Boysen said immediately. "The kind he always serves with beef Wellington."

"Beef and gravy! That's perfect." Lyra thanked him with a smile. "And I already know that song. Beef Wellington and mushroom gravy have quite a duet. Hear it once, you don't forget it."

Resisting the urge to close her eyes, Lyra stretched out her hand over the bowl. "Let's try that tune with our one special magic word."

"And mean it," Boysen reminded her.

She grinned. "Trust me. With this tune, I can't help but *mean* it."

Then she sang a deep, slow melody, stretching out the three-syllable word over several measures. Lyra had loved the song of beef from the first time she heard it, when practicing Flavor Identification Training with her fellow Whizzes at dinner one night. It was a reassuring tune, steady and dependable without being stodgy or boring—as comforting as warm stew on a cold, stressful winter evening.

And when paired with the rich, earthy tones of mushroom gravy . . .

Lyra felt her soul relaxing. She sank down into the song, knowing it could hold her weight as she relished each poignant note.

Ha! I'm savoring *it!* she thought with an internal giggle that somehow wrapped itself perfectly into the melody.

She was enjoying the music so much, she forgot to watch for the magic's effect on the dough. It took the collective gasp of her classmates to draw her attention back to the bowl. Sure enough, the lump of dough was now a vibrant green, as deep and opaque as the sweet spell had been pale and sparkling.

"Rock salts and spices!" Professor Honeycomb murmured, eyes fixed on the green dough. "That . . . is . . ."

"Savory!" Boysen exclaimed, clapping a hand on Lyra's shoulder triumphantly. "Test it, Professor. Did it work?"

The first years joined Professor Honeycomb in stretching their hands over the bowl. Then they all jumped backwards, wrinkling their faces.

"It worked, all right." Professor Honeycomb's eyes were watering, but she looked happier than a kid encountering chocolate for the first time. "Too well. Even more 'too well' than your first attempt, Berry."

"I-I'm sorry," Lyra stammered. "I didn't think—"

The Flavor master held up a hand to cut off Lyra's apologies. "None of that, my dear. As I just said to Berry, it's perfectly normal to overdo it on this spell at first. For any baker with true Flavor instincts, that is. If you couldn't muster up the *oomph* this spell requires, that might be cause for concern, but this . . ." Professor Honeycomb gazed fondly at the dough, which was still deep green. The light was fading even more slowly than it had with Boysen's first attempt. "You have nothing to worry about."

"This just gives us a chance to practice the sweet song," Boysen pointed out. "Right? Try to swing it back the other direction?"

When Professor Honeycomb nodded her approval of this plan, Lyra took another deep breath.

"Right. Same principle. What is the sweetest flavor you can think of?"

"Caramel," Mac said automatically. Then he flushed, took off his glasses, and started cleaning them on his apron, apparently unable to meet anyone's eye.

Thankfully, Professor Honeycomb was too focused on the musical experiment to catch any double meaning.

"Spot-on, Fondant!" she crowed. "Well done. I assume you have a melody for caramel, Treble?"

Lyra dutifully ignored the flustered Mac, the equally flustered Meringue, and the thoroughly amused Boysen gathered around her. She just smiled at the professor and launched into the song of caramel, spreading the single word "sweet" over a few measures of melody.

It was just as rich as the beef tune, but in a directly opposite way. This song was as light and golden as the early spring sunshine pouring through the classroom windows. It moved quickly, tripping along through several intricate runs, switching often between major and minor intervals. Lyra thought this energy reflected the careful stirring and constant vigilance required when making caramel.

The complexity made the song as inspiring as the other was steadying. All in all, the two melodies were perfect foils for each other, like salt and sugar.

Or, more to the point, like savory and sweet.

Professor Honeycomb was already gushing by the time the pale green light pulsed out of the dough.

"Much better, Treble. Oh, what splendid progress!" The Flavor master's eyes sparkled even more brightly than the glow of the gemlike magic. "Still not quite right, of course. The original goal was to inject a hint of sweetness, yes? This round brought it back to baseline, where we were when we started."

Lyra glanced at Boysen, then back at the professor, who was bouncing again in uncontainable glee. "And that's . . . good?"

"It's fantastic!" Professor Honeycomb squealed. "To achieve such power so quickly, right from the start . . . Now it's just a matter of fine-tuning. Adjusting. Applying the spell to trickier, more subtle recipes." Professor Honeycomb snatched up the bowl and hugged it to herself with a sigh of contentment. "Oh, tomorrow's lab day is going to be *fun*."

The professor was right: Flavor lab day *was* fun. When the first years assembled in Whisk Tuesday evening, they spent the first twenty minutes of their review session sharing stories from the day and marveling at their own progress.

All four of them were now proficient in the "Sweet" and "Savory" melodies. Lyra had even brought her guitar to Whisk on Monday night to make sure they were ready for Flavor lab the following day. Her ongoing internal chorus of delight reached a peak crescendo at the sound of their four voices singing together.

Each Whiz had also made their own contribution to the magic music's application. It was Caramelle who suggested a more even, precise tempo for "Sweet" to help restrain its runaway power. Mac pointed out that volume made a difference in intensity.

As for the Flavor King . . . he grew so embarrassed by their praise during Tuesday night's review that he threatened to cut off the Whizzes' hot chocolate supply.

Lyra backed off with great difficulty. The application of music just seemed to enhance Boysen's already remarkable Flavor instincts. He knew just how to adapt the tunes for different recipes and how to coach his fellow first years.

By the end of class on Tuesday, they could all achieve the perfect shade of peridot or forest green in the basic bread dough on the first try. Boysen claimed this was solely because of Lyra's melodies, and Lyra insisted his insight was equally invaluable. Professor Honeycomb just said they were all incredible and sent them away laughing through tears of joy.

Lyra needed all of this success to bolster her confidence for the other two lab days.

Neither Professor Puff nor Professor Genoise had been as willing as Professor Honeycomb to leap into experimentation during Monday's short classes. The Presentation headmaster explained woefully that there simply wasn't time.

"I'm afraid I'll get too invested in it," he had told Lyra, shaking his head. "I tend to lose track of respectable hours when a new spell catches my fancy. I would just want to keep going, and then you'd all miss your dinner. Best to wait until Thursday, when we can begin in earnest."

Professor Puff, meanwhile, had made it clear that music was not to be employed until *after* the students learned a spell in the traditional method.

"That is the only way to measure the results," she announced at the start of Monday's Texture class. "There must be a before and an after. If we are to engage in experimentation, we shall do so properly."

Her gray gaze was like an immovable wall, inviting neither argument nor question. All the first years had simply nodded meekly. Lyra had resigned herself to at least another week of silent Texture class before she would be allowed to sing.

So when Texture lab began Wednesday morning, she was totally unprepared for Professor Puff to begin by addressing her directly.

"I hope you are feeling both focused and musical today, Aspiring Baker Treble," the Texture headmistress said. "For this first lab of third term, we are beginning the work of Madame Dacquoise. Famously difficult. I expect you to master our first spell before we break for lunch."

Professor Puff's lips turned up in a tiny smile as a spark of challenge—or mischief—flared in her usually calm eyes. "Because after lunch, I expect to hear some singing."

CHAPTER FIFTY

Butter, Sugar, Flour

Lyra really wished she didn't know so much about Madame Dacquoise. Unfortunately, that wasn't an option when you were friends with Caramelle.

The young Texturist didn't talk about Madame Dacquoise as much as she name-dropped Master Chiffon, but that was only because Caramelle viewed Madame Dacquoise with a reverence bordering on awe. Still, Lyra had heard enough during first term in Pestle to form a fairly complete picture of Madame Dacquoise in her imagination.

And the picture was terrifying.

The daughter of a baker and a mathematics professor, Madame Dacquoise had viewed Texture as one giant equation. She structured her spells accordingly. For one thing, there were no "magic words." It was the equations themselves that were recited mentally by the baker. Most of the prep work was devoted to determining the ideal *order* for those equations to be recited.

And that wasn't even the most striking difference. While all other Texture magic was organized according to recipe categories, Dacquoise spells were sorted by *individual ingredients.*

Lyra vividly remembered her reaction the first time Caramelle had explained this to her.

"Every ingredient?" she had repeated, certain she was hearing wrong. "So, for every recipe, you'd have to—"

"Do different equations for everything," Caramelle had explained, glowing with enthusiasm. "Brown sugar, white sugar, butter—salted or unsalted, that matters—and milk, and eggs, and all the different spices . . . The amount is a factor too, of course. *And* at what point in the recipe you incorporate that ingredient. So you can never just copy your sugar equations from one recipe to another. No shortcuts with Madame Dacquoise!"

Now, as Professor Puff's floating chalk outlined the first round of equations on the board, Lyra found herself longing for the simple days of Master Chiffon.

The man wrote one spell for cake, she thought glumly, watching the chalk's writing get smaller and smaller to fit everything onto the board. *It's a hard spell, but it works for every cake. This is . . . madness.*

"I know I need not explain the inimitable methods of Madame Dacquoise to Royal Academy students," Professor Puff was saying. "Not in the third term. This year, you have the unique advantage of having already witnessed Dacquoise's work in action. Aspiring Baker Meringue employed the Superior Sponge Spell for her second-term final."

Caramelle kept her head high, but Lyra noted a slight slumping in her shoulders. "Not very well," Caramelle whispered.

Professor Puff shook her head. "I had no complaints with your technical execution of the spell. It lacked only a certain . . . spirit, shall we say. But you need not fear," she went on, turning to the rest of the class. "We will not be attempting anything so advanced for many weeks yet. For today, we shall seek to master the basics using a simple spell with only three ingredients: butter, flour, and sugar."

Mac's hand flew into the air. "Shortbread?"

"Correct, Aspiring Baker Fondant." Professor Puff smiled graciously at the students. "Our old friend shortbread. Let us begin with butter, shall we?"

The rest of the morning was a blur to Lyra. She couldn't remember ever focusing so hard for so long in her entire life.

First, Professor Puff took them through the equations for Madame Dacquoise's butter spell. She spent several minutes factoring in the amount of unsalted butter required for a single batch of shortbread, then a double batch, and even a triple. Finally, she applied the equations to the spell and silently demonstrated its successful execution.

"As you can see, the magic manifests differently than other Texture spells. The blue light is so pale as to be nearly translucent." Professor Puff held up the bowl, displaying the faint shimmer still rippling over the butter. "That is the true genius of Madame Dacquoise. Once all the ingredients are combined, the various hues will layer on top of one another, resulting in a shade of blue more vibrant than you have ever seen in this classroom."

Setting down the bowl, she swept her keen eyes over the students.

"Now, who can tell me how this might compound the difficulty of a Dacquoise spell? Aspiring Baker Meringue?"

Caramelle answered immediately. "If you make a mistake, it's almost impossible to notice until it's too late."

"Exactly," Professor Puff confirmed. "With all other Texture spells, you can adjust in-process to achieve the required shade of blue. But with Madame Dacquoise, only once all the ingredients have been enchanted and combined can you discern success or failure. And with the latter . . ."

"You have to just start all over again," Boysen said slowly. "Because all the ingredients are mixed together. Even if you could tell which one was 'off,' you couldn't just take that one out and replace it."

Professor Puff nodded in approval. "Well said, Aspiring Baker Berry."

Raising her hand, she gave a single wave. The board was instantly wiped clean. All the equations the professor had worked out for butter vanished.

"Now it is your turn to try," she told the startled first years. "Once you have all completed the spell for butter, single batch, we will move on to sugar."

The next half hour was among the most grueling experiences Lyra had faced at the academy thus far. She covered several pages of parchment with notes and scribbled equations. Her first attempt at performing the spell herself produced no light at all, let alone a Dacquoise-esque translucent shimmer.

Focus, Lyra told herself sternly. *If you can't do it right, she won't let you set it to music.*

And Madame Dacquoise's spells were *meant* to be sung. Lyra could feel it in her bones. Even the numbers in the equations seemed to be calling out to her, begging her to unleash the tune locked just beneath their surface.

Music was mostly math, after all.

Smiling to herself, Lyra told the numbers to wait just a little longer. Then she shook her head, lifted her hands, and began silently reciting the equation for butter, taking care to adjust the order based on her failed first attempt.

Butter: one cup, sixteen tablespoons, 227 grams. At room temperature, seventy degrees. So, 227 divided by seventy is 3.243. Oven preheated to three hundred degrees. Three hundred minus seventy is 230. Then 227 divided by 230 is 0.987, and 3.243 minus 0.987 is . . .

It took her three more attempts to get the order right. But just as Professor Puff's calm voice reclaimed the class's attention, Lyra was rewarded by a faint, almost clear shimmer sliding from her fingers and into the bowl.

"Well done, all of you." Professor Puff gave them all a rare faint smile. "We at least have something to work with. Moving on to white sugar, then."

Flour followed white sugar, then the all-important mixing, and finally the baking and taste testing. By the time she dismissed them for lunch, all four of the first years were glassy-eyed with exhaustion.

But they had done it. Every single one of them had managed to perform Madame Dacquoise's spells over butter, white sugar, and flour. Only Caramelle's final shortbread dough was anywhere close to the right shade of blue, but Professor Puff seemed pleased all the same.

"No student I have ever taught has achieved more than a watered-down hue on the first day," the Texture headmistress assured them all. "Not without prior experience in Madame Dacquoise's methods."

Again, her eyes landed on Lyra. "I do look forward to this afternoon. It promises to be most . . . intriguing."

Conversation at the lunch table was almost nonexistent. Everyone was conserving their energy for the afternoon's ordeal. Even Caramelle, who found as much cozy joy in complicated Texture spells as most people drew from a cup of hot chocolate, was quiet.

Yet it was a peaceful quiet. Lyra kept expecting to feel anxious, but the closest she got was a hint of excitement amidst the haze of weariness.

She was about to get the chance to sing a *Texture* spell. *In class.*

That was something to look forward to, no matter what happened afterwards.

Professor Puff wasted no time when they returned from lunch. Before they could settle into their seats, she beckoned them all to join her on the front platform.

"Normally, we would move right on to practicing Madame Dacquoise's spells for a double batch of shortbread," she said as they gathered around her workstation. "But we have an experiment to perform. Therefore, we shall do another round of the single-batch spell, with the additional variable of singing. Aspiring Baker Treble, have you had a chance to devise some musical accompaniment? Even just a line, to get us started?"

Lyra nodded. "I have, Professor. I think I have music for the whole spell, actually."

"The whole spell?" Professor Puff raised a single eyebrow. "Butter, sugar, and flour?"

"Yes, Professor."

"Well, then." Professor Puff handed Lyra a bowl of butter. "Carry on, Aspiring Baker Treble."

Lyra raised her hands over the bowl. Fixing her eyes on the butter, she opened her mouth . . . and let the song come out.

That was the best way to describe it. She wasn't inventing, or composing, or forcing anything to happen. In fact, it had taken a great deal of effort to hold the music *in* through the morning's practice sessions. Letting the numbers express their own inner music felt like a release.

The effect wasn't instant. Lyra still had to make it all the way through the spell before anything happened. But something did happen. Just as the intricate, complicated melody line drew to its natural conclusion, streams of faint blue light erupted from Lyra's fingers and covered the butter with a semi-translucent radiance.

Lyra was delighted. She had known it would work, of course, but she'd been prepared to make a few attempts before achieving the desired result.

If Lyra was surprised, Professor Puff was downright gobsmacked.

"That . . . is . . . extraordinary," the Texture headmistress murmured. Her gray eyes stared at the pale blue glow, utterly transfixed. "And on the first try . . ." Without looking away from the butter, she grabbed the nearby bowl of white sugar and thrust it into Lyra's hands. "Please, do proceed, Aspiring Baker Treble."

So Lyra did. The spells for white sugar and flour proved slightly trickier than butter. The equations themselves were more complex, even breaking down individual grains of sugar and flour into exponentially compounding numbers. Even so, Lyra's song for white sugar produced a satisfactory blue shimmer on the third attempt, and her song for flour on only the second.

Professor Puff herself mixed the ingredients, folding carefully so as not to disturb the lingering magic. Lyra even thought the professor was holding her breath.

When the three layers of pale light combined to form a warm, royal-blue shimmer, Professor Puff stepped back with a quiet sigh.

"Extraordinary," she said again, so softly that she might have been talking to herself. "Not a conclusive result, of course. More experimentation is certainly needed. But for a first foray . . ." Professor Puff looked up at Lyra. "Auspicious. A most auspicious beginning, Aspiring Baker Treble."

"Thank you, Professor." Lyra felt like she was glowing, like the blue magic still tingling in her fingertips had spread to the rest of her skin.

"What about the rest of you?" Professor Puff looked at the other first years. "Have you tried Treble's Texture music in the past?"

Caramelle flushed, as if remembering every awful thing she had ever said to Lyra on the subject. "Not for a while, I'm afraid."

"Of course. You wouldn't need it, Meringue," Professor Puff said kindly.

Mac raised his hand. "I-I used some of her songs first term," he stammered. "Not in class, but just to study. The tunes helped me learn the spells."

"Same here," Boysen affirmed. "Her Presentation stuff was always more helpful, for me at least. But Texture came in handy a few times too."

Professor Puff looked around at each of them thoughtfully. "Yes . . . Yes, that makes sense . . ." Suddenly, she gave a sharp nod, snapping back into full Puff efficiency. "The experiment has only just begun. Next, we must ascertain how, if at all, this method works for a baker who does not possess Treble's particular musical abilities. Aspiring Baker Fondant can go first."

"M-me?" Mac stammered.

"You, Fondant." After pulling a parchment and pen from her apron pocket, the professor began making rapid notes. "You must all try singing the songs. One at a time, I think, to ensure accurate data. Treble, would you care to run us all through that tune for butter once more? Then Fondant can begin our individual trials."

Lyra glanced around at her classmates. Boysen grinned back at her, obviously ecstatic. Caramelle's face was a perfectly precise mixture of nerves and excitement, in exactly equal amounts.

Mac just looked terrified. But when Lyra caught his eye and smiled, he swallowed hard and gave her a tiny nod.

We can do this, she thought as hard as she could, trying to send the message to him through the silent air. *It's just baking. And music.*

Professor Puff looked up from her parchment, pen poised for more action. "Whenever you are ready, Treble."

Lyra took a deep breath.

"All right. Repeat after me . . ."

CHAPTER FIFTY-ONE

Normal Strange

The rest of the afternoon in Texture lab was as auspicious as its start.

Mac and Boysen both showed marked improvement in their Madame Dacquoise spellwork while using Lyra's musical technique. Only Caramelle's results were unchanged, though she was anxious to assure Professor Puff that this had nothing to do with the efficacy of the songs.

"I think they really are helpful," Caramelle insisted. "I can see how the music keeps you in rhythm and makes it easier to remember the words. The numbers, I mean. But I—"

Professor Puff held up a hand to silence her. "Understood, Aspiring Baker Meringue. I was not expecting the music to increase *your* skills, so highly developed as they already are. With you, I was watching for any effect in the opposite direction. I am glad to note that the music is not detrimental. So far, at least." She looked at each of them for a long moment with her keenest, shrewdest gaze. "This is a most suitable group for such experimentation. With your varying strengths and weaknesses, we have an opportunity to measure a wide range of effects over the next three weeks. Or, as seems more likely after today's events, over the entire term."

Then, to the shock of all four first years, Professor Puff *winked*.

After such success in Flavor and Texture, Lyra felt reasonably confident walking into Presentation lab on Thursday morning. If she had had any lingering anxiety, Professor Genoise's greeting would have banished it instantly.

"At last!" he sighed as the magical chime rang to mark the start of class. "My colleagues have been taunting me all week with tales of wonder and discovery. But now, at last, it is my turn!" Noticing that they had taken their seats, he began waving vigorously. "No, no! Up here, all of you. This instant. I shall wait no longer. We begin at once!"

The first years gathered around the professor's workstation, which was crowded with bowl after bowl of frosting.

Plain white frosting, just begging to be transformed into various colors.

Boysen nudged Lyra. "I wonder what spell you'll be singing today?" he whispered loudly.

"No time for your famous family wit, I'm afraid, Berry." Professor Genoise bustled in between Lyra and Boysen, actually rolling up his elegantly tailored sleeves. "Treble gave me a crumb of her work with Master Brûlée on Monday, and I have been waiting ever since for the full meal. Primary colors first and then on to the lighter shades!"

"Don't you want to do a normal round first?" Caramelle asked hesitantly. "To establish a baseline?"

"Spoken like a true Texturist." Professor Genoise smiled at Caramelle before polishing his monocle and affixing it firmly to his eye. "You do yourself and my esteemed colleague proud, Meringue, but to each their own style. I have seen plenty of 'normal' coloring charms from all of you to establish miles of baseline. Now it's time for some abnormal dazzling! Which color first?"

"Blue," Boysen suggested innocently. Then he winked at Lyra. "It's Treble's favorite."

She stuck out her tongue at him, then switched to a radiant smile when Professor Genoise looked at her. "That is true. Blue is my favorite of the primary color melodies."

"Then let's hear it." Professor Genoise pointed to the nearest bowl of white frosting. "Do your magic, Treble. Literally."

Lyra gladly obliged. She sang the familiar tune for blue, steady and straightforward with a surprising thread of richness. The wave of Presentation magic that erupted from her fingertips was definitely brighter than it had ever been before, and the resulting color had never been so vivid. It was the exact shade of Professor Puff's Texture apron and headscarf, actually—perfectly, absolutely *blue*.

The first years had all been expecting success, but even Lyra was surprised at the potency of it.

Maybe it's a cumulative effect, she thought, savoring the frosting's vibrant hue while her internal chorus of delight shifted to a higher key. *I've been singing the spells all week, so I know it works. Now I can just enjoy it.*

Professor Genoise, meanwhile, was beside himself. His eyes widened so quickly that his monocle popped out and dangled from its golden chain, forgotten.

"Never seen anything like it," he whispered. "Master Brûlée himself would . . . Oh, if only he were alive to see it!"

He selected another bowl and thrust it into Lyra's hands. "Purple next, please? That's *my* favorite."

The whole day was even better than the Flavor and Texture lab days. For one thing, Lyra wasn't making up all the songs on the spot. Master Brûlée's Coloring Charm felt just as comfortable and familiar as her old Any Weather Bards repertoire. She did have to get a little creative towards the end, when Professor Genoise insisted on venturing into some truly obscure shades, but it was fun.

"Aureolin? Celadon? I didn't even know those colors existed," she confided to the other Whizzes that night. "But I'm glad I know now. The world feels a little richer, somehow. More . . . varied."

"More dramatic?" Mac suggested.

Lyra grinned at the budding Presentation expert. "Yes. Exactly."

But an even bigger factor in Lyra's enjoyment of the day was Professor Genoise himself. His enthusiasm was even deeper than Professor Honeycomb's, though more elegantly expressed. Not content to watch the students try the different color-charm songs, he insisted on joining in, learning and singing along with gusto. He turned out to have a marvelous tenor voice.

"Every baker needs a hobby," he reminded them, laughing at their astonishment. "Mine was opera. 'Twas a wrench to give it up, honestly."

Lyra believed it. Professor Genoise was a baker to the core, but some special part of him seemed to come alive when he sang. He performed the coloring charms with deep feeling and a stage presence that would make Thespy weep for joy.

When the magical chime rang to announce the end of Thursday's lab, Professor Genoise seemed genuinely crestfallen.

"Fie on this 'three-week trial period' nonsense," he said stoutly. "This has been the most enlivening lab day I've had in years! I shall confer with the other professors, and we'll see what the morrow brings."

The Presentation headmaster was true to his word. After a full day of review in all three classes on Friday, the end-of-week debrief kicked off with a special announcement.

"It has been a most illuminating week," Professor Puff said calmly. "We have all been surprised by the impact of Aspiring Baker Treble's . . . unique contributions. None more so than I."

Professor Honeycomb patted her sedate colleague's shoulder. "Which is why we have come to a unanimous decision. We are—"

"Music at will!" Professor Genoise burst out. "If anyone feels inclined to set spells to music, they may do so. In class, for homework—with abandon!"

"With decorum," Professor Puff corrected gently. "I do agree that a single week has been sufficient for the trial period. I waive my original 'three week' request, but I stand by my original condition: students may sing spells only so long as it does not become a distraction or a hindrance."

Professor Genoise bowed gallantly. "Of course. No one likes a loud diva."

Then he gazed out at the first years, smiling fondly. "But I doubt we will have an issue with this particular group."

"No, indeed." Professor Honeycomb clapped as she gave the students her own affectionate smile. "It is going to be a third term like no other. Oh, what a week!"

"What a week," Mac sighed, accepting his mug of hot chocolate from Boysen.

They had all gathered in Whisk after dinner. Since it was Friday, this would be the first Whisk Whiz Recreation of the third term. Even Ginger was there. She was starting private lessons with Professor Genoise the following day and planned to spend the weekend with Lyra.

"You said it, Fondant." Boysen collapsed into the extra chair he'd stolen from Spatula the previous term. "Don't know what you did to Genoise, Treble, but I'm not sure he'll ever recover."

Ginger smirked. "Let's hope not. Sounds like he and the whole academy are getting just what they need."

"It's certainly not a negative change," Caramelle said slowly. She had been very quiet in the Whisk Whiz Reviews all week, as if not yet sure she had reclaimed the right of speaking. "For Professor Genoise especially. In fact, I'd say he seemed . . ."

"Relieved," Lyra finished. She gripped her mug with both hands and settled back into the couch between Ginger and Caramelle. "I thought so too. I could understand him being interested, at least, but I never expected this level of . . . fervor. It surprised me."

"Not me." Mac blew on his hot chocolate, ignoring the steam that fogged his glasses. "He's a Presentationist, after all."

Lyra looked at him curiously. "What's that got to do with it?"

"It's like the colors from yesterday," Mac replied. "You said the world felt richer now that you knew about all these different colors. Right? That's what Presentation is all about. Making things beautiful so that everyone who sees them feels richer. You've just shown Professor Genoise a whole new way to do that."

"Which is significant," Boysen mused, "for someone who cares as much about Presentation as he does."

Mac shook his head. "It's not just Presentation. I think Professor Genoise just really loves spectacle. Beautiful things, new things . . . He's dramatic, if you will."

"I will! Keen eye, Mac." Ginger drained her cup in one gulp and set the mug on the floor triumphantly. "Third term *is* off to a thumping start. Fondant over here has turned his insight meter up to 'broil.' Maybe he can get a side gig as the academy therapist."

"Or medic." Caramelle gave Mac a shy smile. "He's certainly proven to have a calm head under pressure."

Mac seemed unable to speak. He blew even harder on his hot chocolate, apparently taking refuge behind his fogged glasses.

"So how does it feel, Treble?" Boysen asked. "You're out of hiding at last. Singing the spells in front of The Puff and everybody."

Lyra took a long reflective sip of hot chocolate. "It feels . . . normal. Which is strange."

"Normal and strange?" Caramelle repeated. "How?"

"Not both at once," Lyra explained. "It's . . . strange that it feels so normal. I've been holding it all back for so long—the music, I mean. I was so sure that singing didn't belong at the academy. That it would make me feel even more out of place. Or that it was just plain *wrong*."

Caramelle sighed. "Like . . . cheating?"

Lyra shrugged a silent affirmative, and Caramelle lowered her eyes.

"I'm so sorry, Lyra," she said quietly, staring into her untouched hot chocolate. "I'm sorry I ever made you think that."

"You didn't," Lyra assured her. "I mean, you didn't help, but I was thinking it on my own, deep down."

"Despite all arguments to the contrary," Boysen said dryly.

Lyra grinned. "Yes. Sorry about that." She drained the last of her hot chocolate and handed it to him with a flourish. "As penance, I will allow you to make me more hot chocolate."

"The penance is satisfactory." Boysen bowed deeply, then collected Ginger's empty cup and took both to the kitchen.

"So the singing feels normal?" Ginger asked, wrapping her arms around a pillow. "Like you've always been meant to bake like that?"

"Always."

Ginger nodded shrewdly. "That was my hypothesis. Glad to see it confirmed."

"You sound like Professor Puff." Mac shuddered slightly, but it felt more like a habitual response than actual nerves. "I still can't believe she got on board so fast."

"The results of this week were incontrovertible," Caramelle said. "And the other two professors were keen. It was the only logical conclusion for the overall good of the academy."

Ginger laughed outright. "Thank you, Professor Meringue. No, I'm serious," she continued, when Lyra shot her a look. "Caramelle was born to Texture. I can definitely see her in The Puff's place one day."

Caramelle's eyes widened. "Me? Teach at the *Royal Academy*?"

"Absolutely," Ginger replied. "You'd be great."

"If you wanted to," Lyra hastened to add. "I mean, I know you said—I didn't think you wanted to work in a school."

Lyra vividly remembered Caramelle's scathing words about Chef Flax's job at the beginning of the year, but she was not going to repeat them in front of Ginger.

Still, Caramelle flushed, apparently remembering the same thing.

"I'm rethinking a lot of things right now," she said quietly. "Honestly, the thought of teaching here . . . That would be an honor. Quite an honor."

"And you'd be great," Ginger repeated.

Caramelle's eyes darted up to her. "You really think so?"

"I do. They'd be lucky to have you." Ginger turned to Mac. "Wouldn't you agree, Fondant?"

"Oh y-yes," Mac stammered. "Lucky. So lucky. Anyone would be great to—I mean, lucky to—you're great."

If Caramelle noticed Ginger's and Lyra's stifled giggles, she didn't show it. She just smiled sweetly at Mac.

"Thank you, Macaron. Truly. That means a lot." Then her shoulders slumped, and her gaze lowered to rest on her cup again. "Of course, I'd have to make it into the academy first. Past the first year."

Silence fell.

Lyra felt her own eyes pulled down to stare glumly at the fire. The week had been such a whirlwind of new delights, they had all managed to forget the harsh flavor waiting at the bottom of the third term bowl: only three of them could go on to second year. In a matter of weeks, one of them would be leaving.

For good.

"Enough of that," Boysen called gaily, striding in from the kitchen with refills of hot chocolate and good cheer. "We have a long term ahead of us. Got to keep up our strength. And what's the most important ingredient in a Whisk Whiz's recipe for academy survival?"

"Review?" Mac guessed.

"Close. Recreation." Boysen knelt before Ginger, regally presenting her new mug. "I hereby appoint Crumble as master of the revels. She can regale us with tales from outside the academy walls."

"Only if Mac fills us in on Fortescue," Ginger shot back.

Mac nodded demurely. "Oh, I will. He could give Professor Genoise a run for his money, believe me."

"Fortescue?" Caramelle echoed. Then her eyes lit up. "Oh, your fox! Yes, please, Macaron. I so missed hearing about him all last term."

"Sounds like we have a full program. Lots of catching up to do." Boysen caught Lyra's eye and gave her a special Lyra-only grin. "All together, Whizzes. Ready, set—"

Three voices spoke as one, with Caramelle's joining on the last syllable.

"Recreate!"

CHAPTER FIFTY-TWO

Third-Term Medley

To Lyra's unending astonishment, every new week of third term was better than the one before.

She had spent so much of the first two terms trying not to think too far ahead. Either she wouldn't make it through to third term, which would be sad, or she *would* make it, which would be incredibly stressful. To be so close to second year, knowing all along that she might still be cut . . . Lyra had been sure that third term, *if* she made it that far, would be a nightmarish slog of nerves.

She had been wrong.

She kept waiting for the nerves to kick in. It was usually the first thought that greeted her upon waking each day. *Maybe today's the day. Something will go wrong, and I'll fall down the anxiety-well, and I'll just keep falling for the rest of term.* But each night, she was humming peacefully as she went to bed in Zester, and she always fell asleep with a smile on her face.

It was hard to tell which was the biggest contributing factor to her ongoing peace of mind. Like all the notes in a song, or all the flavors in a cake, the different areas in Lyra's life were operating together in wondrous harmony.

The singing issue, of course, had been a source of immediate relief. But the chorus of delight that had sprung up in Lyra hadn't faded after the initial shine of newness wore off. Instead, it had continued rising throughout the term, adding new notes each week.

Baking with music was extraordinary.

Every class contained some form of joy. Singing the old spells injected fresh life into them, easing the tedium of repetition. Learning new spells wasn't nearly as scary as it had been. Even through the long weeks of practicing Madame Dacquoise's higher-level work in Texture, Lyra was not overcome. She just focused on how she would set each tricky charm or complicated chant to music.

It wasn't like singing the spells automatically made her the best at everything.

Even with the musical element, she couldn't touch Boysen in Flavor. Mac had quietly pulled ahead of everyone in Presentation some time during second term, and he was still getting better every day. And Caramelle . . . No amount of melodic assistance would ever bring Lyra anywhere near that level of Texture expertise.

But that wasn't the point. The point was that music helped Lyra rediscover why she had started baking in the first place. She could finally *enjoy* baking again, which in turn produced food that other people enjoyed eating.

Lyra was not the only one experiencing this rejuvenation. She began bringing her guitar to every Whisk Whiz Review, and all the first years found some benefit in her approach.

They abided by Professor Puff's condition. All four were careful to keep their own musical practice from distracting the others in class. But it soon became customary to hear at least one student softly singing through their work when passing by any first-year classroom.

Boysen swore by the efficacy of Lyra's Presentation songs, especially the coloring charms. Mac was so grateful for his growth in Texture thanks to the song for Madame Brioche's Proofing Chant that he insisted on baking Lyra a different kind of cupcake every weekend, all exquisitely decorated.

As for Caramelle, she couldn't stop gushing about Lyra's Flavor music.

"I never thought I'd get the hang of that Soufflé Sisters' Cooperation Chant," she told Lyra as they walked to Professor Honeycomb's class one day. "But the melody you wrote is so catchy. It reminds me of my favorite dance, from when I took dancing lessons . . . So I just imagine myself dancing, and then the flavors are dancing, and then they're dancing together!"

Caramelle was another of the ingredients contributing to Lyra's enjoyment of third term. Lyra hadn't realized how heavily her concern for the Texturist had been weighing on her during second term, or how much she had missed the Caramelle Experience.

Not that it was the same as first term. The two girls weren't roommates, though Lyra reserved the right to move back into Pestle if Caramelle skipped any meals or showed signs of sleeplessness. Caramelle herself was making a conscious effort to temper the zeal that had nearly driven her over the edge.

It just felt so surprisingly *right* to have Caramelle back in their lives. Lyra enjoyed her company at the first-year table in the dining hall, especially now that Ginger wasn't there to help balance out the Boysen-and-Mac duo. Caramelle's diligence and determination were as inspiring to be around as ever. Her presence in the Whisk Whiz Review was invaluable, particularly when it came to Texture homework.

Even Ginger had to admit it was a positive change.

"The Meringue's not too bad," she confessed quietly to Lyra in Zester after one Friday's Whisk Whiz Recreation. "As long as she's not being too Meringue-y."

There were some difficult days, of course. Caramelle had a lifetime of perfectionist habits and family pressure to work through. The other Whisk Whizzes learned to watch for the telltale signs of what Lyra named the Meringue Malady. If Caramelle made a few too many snappish comments, or if the air around her began vibrating at a particular frequency, her first-year colleagues would step in.

Boysen and Lyra usually let Mac handle these episodes. Caramelle never forgot Mac's help in that crucial moment when The Meringue had almost taken over, quite literally. She was often more likely to listen to a warning from him than from anyone else.

Macaron, meanwhile, proved as adept in the subject of Caramelle as he was in Presentation counterspells. Whether through a lavish new treat for the next Whisk Whiz Review or the latest tale about Fortescue the Foppish Fox, he could almost always make her smile.

As if music and Caramelle weren't enough to give Lyra a superior third-term experience, there was also the *lack* of certain persons in her weekly routine.

The third-year students did not assist in the first-year classes during third term. They were all immersed in their final thesis projects and thereby absent from most of their apprentice duties. Other than occasional glimpses in the dining hall or when they made their dorm rounds in the evening, Lyra could count on one hand the number of times she saw Razz, Hyacinth, or Cardamom.

Which was just fine by Lyra. More than fine. She missed Razz and Hyacinth, but she knew she'd be seeing them at the Berry household over break. As for the other . . . Third term was full of far too many pleasant flavors to miss that particular spice.

In fact, Lyra smiled every time she entered the Presentation classroom these days. It really was lovely to have an entire term of memories in that room untainted by the intoxicating scent of cinnamon and honey.

Last, but certainly not least, third term also contained the "kitchen friends" ingredient.

Lyra gave Chef Flax and Bumble—and Sprinkle, of course—their long-promised concert on the very first Sunday night of third term. It was hard to tell who was more delighted: the head chef, singing along in his booming tenor; the flying squirrels, dancing and occasionally joining in with their piping baritone and powerful alto voices; or Lyra herself. They all enjoyed the experience so much, she couldn't believe she had delayed two whole terms.

Chef Flax was particularly impressed by her baking music. He insisted on pulling out ingredients so he could see the song magic in action. Her melody for Madame Hazelnut's Deepening Spell in particular left Bumble speechless with joy.

"You're going to have to write that one down for me." Chef Flax chuckled. "I'll start making notes myself so I can try to implement a song or two in my own work each week. I think you might be onto something here."

The next Sunday night, she brought the other Whisk Whizzes along. Chef Flax and the squirrels were thrilled to host. They insisted on whipping up four extra batches of brownies, flavoring each for a different first year: almond for Mac, raspberry for Boysen—he thanked them for not using his actual namesake, which didn't always play nicely with chocolate—and salted caramel for Caramelle.

Lyra received a mysterious "dark-chocolate madness" batch of Bumble's own invention.

"The secret is a hint of chili powder and cayenne," Chef Flax whispered to her. "Not overpowering. Just a nice surprise that brings out even more of the chocolate flavor. He's terribly proud of it."

After one bite, Lyra agreed that the sous-chef inventor absolutely should be.

Brownies in hand, they enjoyed a singalong of baking tunes mixed in with some old Any Weather Bards favorites. The evening culminated in a visit to Queen Penelope, who finished their many uneaten brownies with gusto and clucked appreciatively at their choral performance of the "Sweet" song. When everyone said good night, it was only with the promise that this event would be a weekly tradition all through third term.

This proved incredibly motivating for the first years. They all were careful to complete their weekend homework by dinnertime on Sunday so they could spend the evening in the kitchens. Caramelle exclaimed more than once how well these nights of music and rest prepared her for the week ahead.

They all needed such preparation. The third-term workload was one ingredient that fully lived up to Lyra's apprehensions. The Monday morning exams continued for the multiple projects each professor was assigning over every weekend. But teams were a thing of the past. If second term had been about collaboration, third term was focused entirely on solo execution. Each student was expected to complete the assignments alone.

Saturdays became the longest day of the week. Boysen left the Whisk kitchen to Mac and practically moved into Spatula, the neighboring room, on the weekends. Lyra needed all of Caramelle's organizational tips to keep the long lists of spells and recipes straight in her head and to devise a realistic schedule for getting everything done in time.

But still, no one fell down the anxiety-well. No matter how intense the workload, every Friday night's Whisk Whiz Recreation included at least one element of celebratory fun. The first years always shared at least one meal together on Saturdays to make sure everyone got some nourishment. And no matter how daunting the week ahead, every Sunday night saw Lyra heading towards the kitchen with her guitar and friends in tow.

It was during one of these Sunday night concerts towards the end of term that Chef Flax summed up Lyra's feelings perfectly.

"I've seen you bake, Lyra," he said, after she led them all in a rousing rendition of Master Glaze's Shine Spell. "I said from the start you belong here. And now I've seen you sing. You seem like you belong in that world too. But never in all the time I've known you have you looked so at home as you do now, combining the two. When you turn baking into music, you seem so . . ."

"Joyful?" Boysen suggested.

Chef Flax's red face creased in a wide grin. "Yes. That's it. *Joyful.*"

His words were still singing in Lyra's ears as she fell into bed that night, fusing effortlessly with the chorus of delight that had been playing in the background of her thoughts all term.

You belong here.

Lyra believed him. What's more, for the first time, she knew everyone around her believed it too.

She, Lyra Treble, belonged at the Royal Academy of Magical Baking.

But so does Caramelle, she thought, giving brief attention to the one sour note always hovering beneath the term's bright melody. *And Boysen. And Mac. All four of us belong. But only three of us can stay.*

Lyra sighed and rolled over, burying her face in her pillow. There was no point in worrying about it now. As her mother often said, all she could do was sing each note in order, measure by measure.

Or, as Professor Honeycomb would say, "Add each ingredient in its own time, flavor by flavor."

Until they're all dancing together . . .

Smiling, Lyra drifted off to sleep, Master Glaze's Shine Spell mixing inextricably with "The Joy Song" in her head.

CHAPTER FIFTY-THREE

Stop Whining, Start Baking

"Take your seats, Aspiring Bakers," Professor Genoise called as the other two professors entered the Presentation classroom. "That's all for this week. I shall confer briefly with my colleagues, that we may then proceed with our traditional end-of-week meeting."

Boysen caught Lyra's eye and mouthed, *Tribunal.* She stifled a laugh.

Settling onto her stool, Lyra took a moment to appreciate the simple beauty of the scene. Late afternoon sunlight streamed through the windows, somehow even more magical in early summer than it had been in spring, or winter, or the autumn before that. Each season at the academy held its own beauty. Come what may, Lyra was grateful to have witnessed them all.

The beauty outside the building, of course, was far surpassed by the beauty within. Lyra's gaze drifted over each of her three companions, all perched on their stools. She let her eyes wander to the professors huddled together in whispered conference.

Idly, she stared at the notes Professor Genoise had written on the board, then his silver baking spoons gleaming on the counter, then the plate of Mac's entremets the professor had shown to the class as a demonstration of excellence in edible illusion spells.

I'm . . . content, she thought dreamily. *Right now, sitting in this room, I feel at home.*

Her thoughts drifted to the weekend ahead. Ginger was coming for Whisk Whiz Recreation that night. She had promised to bring a special treat from her parents' bakery since the term was almost over. Lyra wondered what form that night's festivities would take . . .

Professor Genoise clapped his hands briskly, then spread his arms wide.

"Congratulations on the conclusion of another week," he proclaimed, and Lyra had to stifle another laugh. Somehow, Professor Genoise found opportunities for grand ceremony in even the most mundane occasions. It was an admirable trait, especially in a Presentation master, but Lyra also found it could be amusing in certain scenarios. Such as at the end of class on a Friday, when all the first years really just wanted to get their homework assignments and escape.

Professor Genoise continued, oblivious to any hidden mirth in his audience. "But not just any week, of course. This, as you are doubtless well aware, is the penultimate week of third term, and thus of the entire year."

Professor Puff took up the thread. "One week from tomorrow, you will take your final exam. I do not need to remind you that this event holds special significance. Your performance in this exam will determine which three of you will advance to the second year."

"So the exam itself has to be special," Professor Honeycomb said. "We have designed it to showcase your individual strengths *and* challenge the weaknesses we've sought to address this year. Anyone care to guess what the nature of the exam might be?"

Boysen raised his hand. "Our old exam cakes but with assigned spells for each discipline?"

"Close, Aspiring Baker Berry." Professor Honeycomb beamed at him. "You're going to make each *other's* exam cakes!"

Four students stared blankly back at her.

"Each . . . other's?" Caramelle echoed weakly.

Professor Honeycomb directed her radiant smile at Caramelle. "That's right! The versions you made for the second-term exam, with those exact recipes and spells."

"We analyzed all of your various growth journeys over this past year," Professor Puff explained. "You each will be assigned the cake of a fellow student who excels at your weakest point."

"You all know your own exam cakes," Professor Genoise pointed out. "I'd imagine you're rather bored of them by now. This way you have the opportunity to shed those stale recipes and try something new!"

All three professors smiled at the students. Clearly, they found this plan as satisfying as one of Chef Flax's four-course dinners.

Mac raised his hand tentatively. "You . . . you mentioned our 'weakest points'?"

"Indeed, Aspiring Baker Fondant," Professor Puff replied. "For you, that is Texture. Though you have made remarkable progress this year, you still struggle with the necessary concentration and exactitude. That is why you have been assigned Aspiring Baker Meringue's exam cake."

Mac looked like he had just seen the ghost of all the recipes he'd ever failed to complete. "M-M-Meringue?" he stammered.

"Correct." Professor Puff's gray eyes gleamed with a rare hint of mischief.

"Texture is Aspiring Baker Meringue's strength. The spells she employed for her exam cake should be a healthy level of difficulty for you."

Mac opened his mouth, but no words came out. His shocked gaze turned slowly from Professor Puff to Caramelle and stayed there, as if pleading for help.

Caramelle, however, was focused on her own troubles.

"If Macaron is doing my exam cake," she said slowly, "then I'll be making . . . what?"

"You are so adept at challenging yourself, Aspiring Baker Meringue," Professor Puff said fondly. "Almost to your detriment. Your diligence certainly reached dangerous heights towards the end of second term. I believe, and my colleagues agree, that you have demonstrated admirable moderation this term. Even so . . . with you, we need not test your mastery of high-level spells."

Professor Genoise leaped in. "We had to approach your exam from the other end. For such a virtuosic baker, what could be more challenging than simplicity?"

"So you'll be making Aspiring Baker Treble's cake!" Professor Honeycomb clapped her hands as if unable to contain the secret any longer. "Just vanilla with a hint of boysenberry. Oh, you're going to do marvelously, Meringue! It will be a thrilling challenge for you. I'm sure of it."

Caramelle clearly did not share the professor's confidence, but she dared not object. She merely pressed her lips together tightly and gave a sharp, very Meringue-ish nod.

"As for Aspiring Baker Treble," Professor Genosie went on, "I confess we were momentarily at a loss. Throughout the year, you have both excelled and struggled with all three baking principles."

"I would say your most consistent weak link has been Texture," Professor Puff admitted. "But not to the same degree as Fondant. It was more important for him to take on Meringue's recipe."

"Fortunately, Aspiring Baker Berry's cake combines difficult elements from Presentation and Texture as well as Flavor." Professor Honeycomb clapped again, bouncing slightly on the tips of her toes. "So you'll be making his cake!"

Lyra froze. A sudden vision leaped up in her mind of Boysen's exam cake: a perfect cerulean sphere, carefully balanced and covered with gorgeous swirls of whipped cream clouds . . .

She tried to swallow, but a lump the size of that impossible cake seemed to have lodged in her throat.

"That means Aspiring Baker Berry will be making Aspiring Baker Fondant's cake." Professor Genoise stroked his neatly trimmed gray beard. "Which is what I would have assigned him anyway. Berry's exam cake is impressive, but he is nowhere near Fondant's level in Presentation."

Professor Honeycomb sighed. "It all worked out so perfectly. Like it was meant to be."

"You say that every year," Professor Puff observed calmly.

"Because it's true every year!" the Flavor headmistress shot back. "It's still a lovely surprise."

Professor Genoise smiled indulgently at both his colleagues, then turned to the first years. "There will be no homework this weekend and no test on Monday. We wish you to have a full week to consult with your exam cake's original creator and practice the recipes."

He spread his hands again in a grand ceremonial flourish, but Lyra no longer found it so amusing.

"We have the utmost confidence in you all, Aspiring Bakers. Go and study, that you may prove this confidence justified. Good luck!"

"This is it," Mac announced. Caramelle's recipe book was open on the counter in front of him, and he was staring at it with calm despair. "This is how I go."

They had all gathered in the first-floor common area's kitchen after dinner for Whisk Whiz Recreation, but no one felt particularly festive.

Boysen slammed Mac's notebook shut with a groan. "Not if I get there first, Fondant. And I will. Unless there's a spell to turn me into a majestic Presentation expert in seven days."

"You're one to talk," Lyra retorted. "Care to explain why the *Flavor* King chose a third-year *Presentation* spell for his exam cake?"

"I told you." Boysen shrugged helplessly. "It's the only one I knew at the time."

Lyra glared at him as she flipped through the seven pages of *Madame Patisserie's Shaping Spell: Fifth Spherical Edition.* "Well, it's a doozy."

"Trick I learned from my brother Straw. Find one really impressive Presentation spell and practice it for years until you get it right. If it's flashy enough, and if you focus on keeping your bakes tidy, people won't notice you're pretty hopeless otherwise. In Presentation, I mean." Boysen shrugged again. "Blame Straw."

Lyra continued glaring. "I do. Doesn't mean I can't blame you too."

"You'll be fine, Lyra." Caramelle sighed, holding Lyra's stack of notes listlessly in one hand. "It's me you should be worried about."

"You?" Lyra felt hysterical laughter and equally hysterical tears surging up her throat at the same time. She managed to swallow both before replying, "But my cake . . . It's all basic. Intermediate level, except for Master Glaze. You could do each and every one of those spells in your sleep. *Backwards.*"

"That's just it," Caramelle cried, her voice rising swiftly to a plaintive wail. "There's nowhere to hide. It's like Boysen was saying. If it's flashy enough, people won't notice any little defects. But your cake isn't flashy, Lyra. It's just *good.* It's so, so good. And I'm not *good.* I'm . . . *virtuosic.*" She spat the word out like it was an unwelcome grape seed. Then she turned to the counter, thumbing furiously through Lyra's papers with shaking hands.

Lyra exchanged glances with Mac and Boysen. The air around Caramelle was approaching Meringue Malady frequency levels. But before they could intervene, Ginger laughed.

"Poor Aspiring Bakers." Hopping up onto the counter, Ginger pinned the rest of Lyra's notes down with one hand, putting an end to Caramelle's rifling. "It's almost like the professors know what they're doing. It's an exam! It's supposed to be challenging, right?"

"This isn't challenging," Mac said woefully. "It's . . . it's . . ."

"Cruel," Caramelle finished.

"My, my. Sounds like Flax went a little heavy on the drama sauce in tonight's dinner." Ginger selected one of the frosted profiteroles she had brought for the group and took a bite, chewing noisily as she spoke. "Lyra, what's the name of that theater guy your family is friends with? Thespy, right? Tell him he's got four new actors to work with."

"This is serious, Crumble," Boysen said sternly.

"Of course it is. It's baking." Ginger threw a profiterole at him, cheering when he caught it. "Something all four of you are incredibly good at."

"I'm not *good*," Caramelle repeated sullenly. "I haven't had time to be *good*. I've been too busy showing off. Virtuosic . . . might as well just say 'fraud' and be done with it."

Ginger silenced her by shoving a profiterole directly into her mouth. "Spun sugar. That's what that is." Turning to the others, Ginger spread her hands and continued in her best imitation of Professor Genoise. "The Royal Academy of Magical Baking is a place of growth. And how can one grow without being challenged? All of you—yes, even you, Meringue—are *good bakers*. I am confident you can rise to this exhilarating challenge and show the world that—"

Caramelle suddenly rammed a particularly large profiterole into Ginger's mouth, returning the favor.

"Thanks, Caramelle," Lyra said. Then she sighed. "Though, Ginger is right."

"Of course I am." Ginger swallowed the pastry with remarkable ease and grinned. "You all are acting like this exam is some terrible hardship. Sure, I'm glad it's you and not me. I'm thrilled to be out of it, honestly. But you all love baking. You're all incredibly talented. So just . . . go be incredible at the thing you love. Doesn't sound so bad, does it?"

"Nope." Boysen shook his head, returning Ginger's grin. "Not so bad at all."

Caramelle took a profiterole in her hand. She seemed to be examining it closely, but her eyes had a faraway look in them.

"Stop whining," she said slowly, "and start baking."

Ginger raised both arms in silent victory.

"Stop whining. Start baking." Mac took off his glasses and wiped them on his apron before settling them firmly back on his face. "Sounds like a battle cry."

"Sounds like a song," Lyra corrected.

Ginger nodded in agreement. "A song is more like it. Not a lot of battle vibes in the Whisk Whizzes. Which is another point: you all know you're going to be helping each other this week, right? It's not like you have to struggle through these new recipes on your own."

"They're not even new," Caramelle pointed out. "We've seen each other practicing all year. Every exam."

"Heed The Meringue," Ginger proclaimed. "She speaks the truth."

Boysen rolled his shoulders and shook out his hands in a businesslike manner. "Stop whining, start baking. Great song. I can't wait to hear the theme Treble writes for it."

"Don't hold your breath, Flavor King." Lyra placed all seven pages of his globe cake's Presentation spell on the counter in front of him, one by one. "First you're going to help me come up with a tune for *this*."

"Yes, ma'am," Boysen said meekly. Then he shot Ginger an apologetic smile. "I don't think there's going to be much recreation happening tonight. Sorry, Crumble."

"Are you kidding?" Ginger settled back into her perch on the counter, sorting idly through the profiteroles. "This is way more entertaining. I should have brought popcorn."

Boysen looked at Lyra. Lyra looked at Caramelle. Caramelle looked at Mac, giving him a radiant smile.

"Stop whining?" she whispered, as if offering the first half of a secret code.

Macaron Fondant drew himself up to his full height of five feet five inches.

"Start baking," he declared solemnly.

CHAPTER FIFTY-FOUR

The Current

Lyra's parents had always told her to "keep on singing."

She once thought this advice was only applicable in certain circumstances or for certain people. Much of the past year seemed to be trying to convince her that such a musical mantra did not belong outside an exclusively musical world. "Keep on singing" worked only for the Trebles.

They were bards, after all.

But now, sitting in the exam hall of the Royal Academy of Magical Baking, Lyra could confidently say that her parents' motto had proved itself as adaptable as it was crucial.

The long-dreaded third-term exam had flown by. Lyra felt like she had been swept along on the current of a gentle, generous river, one that buoyed her up instead of dragging her under.

The current hadn't started with the exam, though. Looking back, Lyra thought she could trace its beginning to exactly one week before, when Caramelle had rounded all the first years up for a day-long group study session . . .

After a rather chaotic Recreation-turned-Review on Friday, Caramelle had sprung into action early Saturday morning. The Whisk Whizzes would *not* be attacking such an important exam haphazardly. Not on her watch.

Employing all the organizational skills that made her an admirable student of Texture, and a formidable student in general, she gathered the first years into the common area kitchen and set about making a plan for the entire week.

"First step is to get all the recipes out in the open," she said, her tone as calm and clipped as Professor Puff at her most businesslike. "Confirm all the spells needed for each. I'll go first."

Caramelle took her recipe book from Mac's willing hands and opened it on the counter. Then she laid out four pieces of parchment and wrote "Caramelle Meringue—Exam Cake" across the top of one.

"For Texture, I used Master Chiffon's Aeration Charm, advanced. And Madame Dacquoise's Superior Sponge Spell."

Mac gulped. "Um, can—"

Caramelle held up a hand to silence him, looking remarkably like the Texture headmistress herself. "Let's just make a list of everything for now. We'll address questions later, if any remain after we make a plan."

Mac nodded meekly.

"We were all required to use Madame Hazelnut for Flavor and Master Brûlée for Presentation," Caramelle continued, writing constantly on the parchment as she spoke. "My flavors are lemon, white chocolate, and caramel. Colors are white and gold. Regarding the other spell for each discipline, I employed The Soufflé Sisters' Cooperation Chant in Flavor and Master Glaze's Shine Spell, advanced, in Presentation."

"So did I," Lyra pointed out.

Caramelle nodded and wrote "Lyra Treble—Exam Cake" across the top of another parchment. "We did use all the same spells, didn't we? Except for Texture. You used Master Chiffon at the intermediate level, and . . ."

"Madame Pavlova's Spell of Fluffening," Lyra said. "Also intermediate."

Caramelle nodded again. "Colors?"

"White, red, and dusky rose."

"Dusky rose?" Caramelle repeated, raising her eyebrows.

"It was tricky to get, but it's lovely," Lyra assured her. "I taught all of you that song at the beginning of term, when Professor Genoise had me go through all the coloring charms. You'll be great after some practice."

"Right . . ." Caramelle took a deep, steadying breath and turned back to the parchment. "Flavors are vanilla and boysenberry, right?"

"That's right!" Boysen clapped a hand on Caramelle's shoulder. "All due respect to Master Glaze, but it's the berry that really makes this cake shine."

Mac groaned. "Make him stop, Caramelle."

"I'll make him work instead." Caramelle wrote Boysen's name on another piece of parchment. "Spells, flavors, and colors, Berry. Now."

"Pretty standard, except for Presentation," Boysen replied. "Madame Hazelnut and the Soufflé Sisters for Flavor. Chocolate and peanut butter with whipped cream frosting. Madame Pavlova and Master Chiffon for Texture, both advanced."

"Advanced?" Lyra echoed. She had managed to miss that detail when going over the recipe the night before.

Boysen held up a hand in an uncanny imitation of Caramelle. "Let's just make a list of everything for now, Treble."

"But—"

"Blue and white for the colors," he blazed on, "with a dash of yellow." He winked at Lyra. "For an extra shot of joy."

"And then there's that truly wicked Presentation spell," Caramelle finished, pausing her notation to give Lyra a look of sympathy. "Madame Patisserie's Shaping Spell, spherical edition."

"*Fifth* spherical edition," Boysen corrected her.

Caramelle actually stuck her tongue out at him, then turned to Mac.

"Do tell us about *your* cake, Macaron. For Boysen's sake, I hope it's fiendishly difficult."

"Pretty boring," Mac said apologetically. "Coffee genoise sponge with marzipan filling. Fondant on the top layer. Swirled coating of caramel buttercream, with some piping. Covered with a drizzled lattice of caramel and tempered chocolate."

"Ah yes, so boring." Boysen covered his face with his hands. "Kill me now."

"The spells are basic, though," Mac rushed to reassure him. "The Soufflé Sisters really do help blend all the flavors. I only did intermediate levels of Master Chiffon and Madame Pavlova for Texture. And the colors are easy. I just tried to bring out the natural richness of brown, gold, and cream."

"What about the other Presentation spell?" Boysen demanded.

"It's just Master Glaze . . ." Mac took off his glasses and became very focused on polishing them. "At the . . . um, expert level."

Boysen flopped over onto the counter and lay there like a beached whale.

"Expert," Caramelle murmured. She wrote the word with reverent awe. "Well done, Macaron."

"Don't encourage him," Boysen said, his voice muffled by the countertop.

Lyra nudged the prone Flavor King. "Stop whining."

"Start baking," answered Caramelle and Mac simultaneously, which made all four laugh.

"We have our work cut out for us," Caramelle said once they'd recovered. "But these *are* mostly familiar spells, and we have music to help as needed. Right, Lyra?"

"Absolutely," Lyra replied.

Caramelle looked over the four pieces of parchment. "I think it makes sense to start with Flavor," she mused. "We all have to use Madame Hazelnut's Deepening Spell and the Soufflé Sisters' Cooperation Chant. Why don't we review those basic songs first and then start going over the flavors for the individual cakes?"

Lyra picked up her guitar, which she had managed to grab when Caramelle had woken her up and demanded her presence in the common area kitchen. After making sure it was in tune, she strummed the first chord of Madame Hazelnut's melody.

"Ready when you are!"

* * *

Lyra grinned at the memory as she sat on her stool in the exam hall, watching the professors perform their silent judging ritual of Mac's cake. Yes, that was definitely when the current had begun. It had carried them through that whole long week of constant practice.

And it had never stopped. Her ears still rang with the hum of low singing that had filled the hall all morning. Far from being a distraction, the work of her fellow first years had provided a soothing soundtrack to her own exam efforts.

Lyra had smiled every time she heard Boysen's voice behind her steadily repeating her Master Glaze melody. She'd giggled outright when Mac burst into the tune she'd written for Madame Dacquoise's Superior Sponge Spell. Poor Mac had found it worked best when he started the song extra loud, just to give himself an extra jolt of confidence.

"It's like jumping off a cliff," he'd explained in one of their many group practice sessions the week before. "I just have to make a running leap, and then I can moderate as I fall."

Best of all were the occasional faint melodies coming from Caramelle's workstation. She had worked diligently with Lyra all week, learning the songs Lyra had devised for her vanilla-boysenberry exam cake.

Caramelle was never going to be a noisy baker. She rarely got any louder than whispering. She also didn't need any help in Texture. For Caramelle, the equations and precise rhythms in that brand of magic were their own kind of music.

But she had thanked Lyra repeatedly for the Flavor songs, and Lyra knew she was using them in the exam. All morning, whenever Lyra caught a hint of "The Soufflé Sisters' Cooperation Chant" tune or the chorus from "Madame Hazelnut's Deepening Spell," she had sighed in quiet delight.

Her classmates' voices mixed amiably with the song-spells Lyra herself was performing. The melodies all swirled together inside her head in a relaxing tide. The flow of music, without and within, was a pleasant contrast to the forced silence of the second-term final exam.

And the musical flow enhanced the magic. It was an undeniable fact.

Lyra knew the green glow of Madame Hazelnut's Deepening Spell had never been so vivid around her hands than it was that morning, when accompanied by the simple tune Rondo had helped her develop. The songs of chocolate and peanut butter had never come through so clearly, nor blended so harmoniously. It was like the Soufflé Sisters had always meant their Cooperation Chant to be sung.

The musical benefit carried over into Texture. Boysen's exam cake used Madame Pavlova's Spell of Fluffening and Master Chiffon's Aeration Charm, both at the advanced level. Madame Pavlova felt like an old friend to Lyra, but Master Chiffon . . . She still couldn't think it past the intermediate level without trembling.

Thankfully, Lyra's mother had been particularly fascinated with Master Chiffon's Aeration Charm during the break before third term. She had worked for hours with Lyra to fine-tune an appropriately intricate melody. The other first years had been using it ever since, delighting in the burst of blue sparkles it always called forth. Even Professor Puff, when witnessing this audiovisual display in Texture lab, had given a slight approving nod.

Caramelle had worked with Lyra over the past week to adapt the melody to the advanced level. When Lyra sang the last complicated trill in the exam hall that morning, she couldn't help thinking the blue sparkles looked particularly radiant. And the heightened effect lingered. Even now, when the exam was technically over, Master Chiffon's song sang on beneath Lyra's skin, making her soul feel lighter and fluffier than the three-layer cake she'd produced.

Never had Master Chiffon's work been so uplifting, in every sense of the word.

As for Presentation . . .

Lyra gazed with shining eyes at her perfectly spherical cake resting in a bank of fluffy whipped-cream clouds. Her fingers still tingled with the streams of purple Presentation magic that had carved the three layers into this clean shape before her very eyes.

It had been a rough road. Madame Patisserie's Shaping Spell was an absolute terror. Though a properly grand and dramatic Presentation spell, it required enough equations and precision to make most baking spellbooks double classify it with Texture. This hybrid difficulty made the spell especially tricky to capture in music. It had resisted all of Lyra's initial attempts, to the point that she had despaired halfway through the week.

Wednesday night had been the turning point. Boysen disappeared after Texture lab and returned just before dinner with two of Lyra's brothers. Canto and Rondo had been more than happy to work with Lyra. Together, they wrestled all seven pages of Madame Patisserie's work into a charming tune that was catchy enough to stick in even a busy baker's memory.

It was so catchy, in fact, that Boysen had complained it was still stuck in his head two full days later. Lyra sweetly reminded him that he was the one who had chosen such a diabolical spell in the first place. She then proceeded to sing it several more times in his presence, loudly, claiming to need the practice.

Lyra smirked as she stood beside her cake in the exam hall. That song was probably still blaring through Boysen's head, even now.

It was certainly rolling around in her own mind, mixing with all the other music she'd employed that morning. Madame Hazelnut's melody, Master Chiffon's song, Master Brûlée's tune for cerulean blue . . . even "The Joy Song" made an appearance, flowing effortlessly in and out of the baking magic like it belonged there. Lyra leaned into the medley, letting the mysterious third-term-exam current hold her up as she waited for the professors to finish judging.

The music is the current, she thought, watching Professor Genoise study Caramelle's cake. *It's not necessary for good baking. It's not the same for every baker. But it can help. It's carried us all through this exam.*

The three professors nodded at Caramelle, then moved swiftly to the platform, where they bent their heads together and began whispering. Lyra sat a little straighter on her stool.

Now to see where that current would lead.

CHAPTER FIFTY-FIVE

A Baker After All

The professors' whispering seemed to go on for a long time. When it ceased, they stood back and just looked at each other for several more seconds, as if still communicating in some silent language known only to baking colleagues.

Lyra glanced at the other students. Caramelle, Boysen, and Mac were all staring at the professors, leaning slightly forward on their stools. Lyra wondered if they were all having as hard a time remembering to breathe as she was.

Finally, the three professors shared one simultaneous nod, then turned to face the students.

"I said at the beginning of the first term that this would be a year of special excellence in the exalted history of the Royal Academy of Magical Baking," Professor Genoise began. "Little did I know how true those words would prove."

Professor Puff nodded. "Indeed. Today's exam is . . . unusual, but it is merely the culmination of a truly remarkable chain of events."

"Thank you, Aspiring Bakers." Professor Honeycomb seemed on the verge of tears. "You have given us quite a gift this year. It's good for old recipes like us to be shaken up a bit and forced to deal with some new ingredients. New techniques. New . . . everything."

Lyra leaned forward even further on her stool, somehow aware that the other first years were doing the same.

"Every year, we go into the third-term exam with a fair idea of what the outcome will be," Professor Puff went on. "We are always open to surprises, of course. It has happened on a few occasions. But those are the exception, not the rule."

Professor Genoise took up the thread. "We were watching closely throughout the year, each seeking to identify the student with the most aptitude for our particular discipline. The student we can imagine becoming our Apprentice Baker eventually. By the third term, as my Texture colleague said, it is usually clear. This year was no exception."

"Boysen," Professor Honeycomb said immediately.

Professor Puff nodded at Caramelle. "Aspiring Baker Meringue."

"Fondant." Professor Genoise bowed cordially in Mac's direction. "Three exceptional bakers, each suited for one particular baking discipline. In any other year, this would have been the end."

Professor Honeycomb clasped her hands in front of her, as if pleading. "But this year . . . there was Lyra."

A great stillness settled over the exam hall. The song in Lyra's head hadn't stopped, but she felt enveloped in silence, as if she and the song had been caught out of time together.

"At different moments throughout the year," Professor Puff continued, "we have each thought Lyra might overtake her classmates in our particular discipline. But that was not the case. If I were to give the Stellar Enchantment Pin today purely on the basis of Texture, it would go to Aspiring Baker Meringue."

"For Presentation, I'd give it to Fondant," Professor Genoise agreed.

Professor Honeycomb beamed. "Berry for Flavor, of course."

"Thus, our expectations for today were confirmed, in one sense." Professor Puff's gray eyes gazed coolly at each first year in turn. "Even with a different baker's recipe, our three candidates excelled in their prospective disciplines."

"Normally, the only remaining variable would be the Stellar Enchantment Pin," Professor Genoise explained. "For that is not a matter of excellence in one particular baking principle. The pin must go to the best overall cake."

"And that's where we've hit our snag," Professor Honeycomb explained. "Our delightful hiccup. Today, the best overall cake, by unanimous agreement, is Lyra's."

The stillness in the hall seemed to gasp, momentarily sucking the breath out of the room. Lyra felt weightless, like she was suspended in the air, hovering just above her stool.

Professor Puff, somehow, sounded as calm as ever. "So, you see our dilemma. We cannot award the Stellar Enchantment Pin to a student who is being cut from the academy. And yet we cannot, in good conscience, award it to anyone other than Aspiring Baker Treble. Neither can we cut one of the other students."

Professor Genoise shook his head. "Fondant still beats Treble in Presentation. Meringue is the clear Texture winner. No one can touch Berry in Flavor."

"And yet, Lyra's cake is the best." Professor Honeycomb sighed. "It's like the entrance exam cake you made all those months ago, my dear. Each of the principles, taken individually, isn't quite at the level of your classmates. But put it all together, and it's—"

"Fun." Professor Puff's gaze rested on Lyra, full of grave wonder. "As Professor Honeycomb said at your entrance exam, the most fun bite of cake I've had in years."

Boysen glanced back at Lyra just long enough to shoot her a full-flavored Berry grin.

"We have been pondering this matter all term." Professor Genoise took out his monocle and polished it thoughtfully on his sleeve. "Ever since you introduced the idea of singing the spells. It was a new ingredient. We wondered if it might be the secret behind your signature . . . flair."

"But it's not!" Professor Honeycomb was crying outright now. Dabbing at her eyes with the edge of her apron, she went on, "Not fully. I'm sure the music makes a difference, but it seems to be the *means,* not the end."

Professor Puff patted her colleague lightly on the shoulder. "True. The 'end' appears to be a new category in the evaluation of baking excellence: enjoyment."

There was a long moment of silence.

"A new . . . category?" Caramelle repeated, her voice sounding small and breathless. "You mean, a fourth principle?"

"That's right, Meringue!" Professor Genoise suddenly flung his arms wide. "A whole new principle of baking, devoted to the overall *experience* of the consumer. Enjoyment—a fourth discipline!"

Mac looked more stunned than Lyra had ever seen him. "Is—that's—this has never happened before. Right?"

"Not never," Professor Honeycomb corrected. "Just not recently."

Professor Puff nodded. "When the academy was founded, Flavor and Texture were the only recognized baking disciplines. Presentation was added much later, though still many decades ago."

"And now it is happening again." Professor Genoise seemed on the verge of breaking into song. "We stand here on the precipice of *history,* ready to leap into the great beyond!"

"I would prefer to build a bridge first," Professor Puff said dryly. "Which requires planning."

Professor Honeycomb blew her nose loudly on her apron. "Oh, we have to talk to so many people. The board, the royal family, the royal chefs—"

"Everything will have to be redesigned," Professor Genoise gushed, his eyes flashing with excitement. "The curriculum, the academy crest . . . What color best expresses *joy,* I wonder?"

"Yellow," Boysen called. Then, belatedly, he raised his hand. "So, what does that mean for us?"

"Oh! Of course, my dear ones." Professor Honeycomb beamed at the group through eyes still swimming with tears. "Lyra gets the Stellar Enchantment Pin, and we want you back next year. All of you."

Mac squeaked, nearly falling off his stool. "All of us?"

"All four of you," Professor Honeycomb confirmed. "Isn't it splendid?"

"It is unsettling." Professor Puff sighed. "But necessary. Any other course would betray the core tenets of the Royal Academy and of baking itself. This is the only logical solution."

The first years looked at each other. Lyra saw her own bewilderment reflected in their eyes, along with something else: a happiness so heavy it was almost painful. Even Caramelle's face was shining with the kind of wordless glee that could only be expressed in music . . . and baking.

Lyra's fingers itched for a lump of dough to knead. Melodies were piling up in their frantic haste to get out of her throat. She clenched her hands, willing herself to wait just a bit longer.

"Next year will be a whole new world," Professor Genoise proclaimed. "Four young Aspiring Bakers, striding forth with their three intrepid mentors beyond the edges of the baking map. Together, we shall quest through Flavor, and Texture, and Presentation, charting the mysterious paths of Enjoyment, until—"

Professor Puff silenced him with a single raised hand, then turned to the first years. "It will be a very different sort of year. Finding balance takes time and careful effort. We shall, no doubt, suffer some disasters until we find the right equations to achieve that balance. But it is with pride and the utmost confidence in your abilities that we invite you to make this journey with us." Her impassive lips curled up in a true smile. "All *four* of you."

Music exploded in Lyra's soul, all the pent-up melodies crashing into each other in a sweet cacophony of joy.

There was a song for her family and all the support they had given her, even when they didn't understand. There was a song for Ginger, the tune as frank and determined as Crumble herself. There was one for Chef Flax, bubbling with the joy he always poured into every piece of food that came from his kitchen.

There was another for Bumble, and for Sprinkle, and one for Queen Penelope. There were three songs for the three professors, and one for the Berrys, and even a medley representing the differing contributions of the third-year students.

Including Cardamom, Lyra realized, smiling ruefully to herself. *I was silly, and I have plenty of regrets, but I still learned a lot from . . . that. Whatever "that" was.*

Loudest and most vibrant of all were the songs for each of her friends in the exam hall.

There was Mac's melody, which started out quiet but broke into a harmonic structure more complex and dramatic than most songs in the Any Weather Bards repertoire. Mac was truly born to Presentation. His passion for beauty and elegance rivaled that of Professor Genoise.

But it was a passion rooted in purpose. Mac knew beauty was good for the soul. He loved making things beautiful not for the show of it, but because he understood how much people needed beautiful things.

That was why he would always be a better Presentationist than Cardamom.

There was a song for Caramelle, expressing every nuanced facet of the auburn-haired girl. The steady rhythm reflected her diligence and precision. The complicated melodic runs were a tribute to her incredible skills, especially—but not exclusively—in Texture.

Yet, there was something more to the tune, an indefinable quality that made it stick deep in Lyra's soul. Caramelle was more than a Texture expert. She was more than an exemplary student with an unreplicable work ethic. She was more than a Meringue. She was Caramelle, more than the sum of her parts. A truly fantastic baker—and maybe, if given the chance, she could become an even better friend.

Then there was a song for Boysen. The rhythm was even steadier than Caramelle's, while the harmonic complexity was even more surprising than Mac's. Boysen's song was relentlessly adaptable. No matter what key you sang it in, or what mood, or what crowd, it would be fun. There was always a new note to delight the heart and soothe the mind.

It's just . . . great, Lyra thought, sharing a grin with the Flavor King in question. *He's great. Always, always great. How is he so great? He's just . . .*

"What say you, Aspiring Bakers?" Professor Genoise's voice pierced through the jumble of music in Lyra's head. "Will you venture forth with us into the unknown?"

The four first years shared one more look. By silent agreement, it was Mac who spoke. He rose from his stool, eyes bright behind his glasses.

"Sweet and *savory*, yes!"

The cheering and laughter that followed merged into Lyra's ongoing chaos of internal joy. The melodies for all these wonderful people blared loudly alongside a song of celebration for the year they had shared and one full of hope for the year ahead.

Lyra let them all play at once in her head, smiling as the music swallowed her whole. She had plenty of time to sort through it.

Two more years at the academy. Two whole years to explore these songs and discover new ones. Two years to identify the various Flavor tunings, and to perfect the melodic Texture equations, and to polish the beauty of the Presentation harmonies. Two years to savor the unique Enjoyment they contained and to share it with the world.

Each one deserved to be sung. And Lyra Treble was going to keep on singing.

She was a baker, after all.

About the Author

Anne Crews is the author of the Royal Academy of Magical Baking series, originally released on Royal Road. Crews loves writing, baking, and combining the two with clever wordplay. When not penning tales of cozy sweetness, she can be found pursuing her other two life ambitions: crafting a well-seasoned baking pun and perfecting her chocolate chip cookie recipe.

JOIN THE FELLOWSHIP

follow us on our socials

 podiumentertainment.com

 @podiumentertainment

 /podiumentertainment

 @podium_ent

 @podiumentertainment